Reunion

Book 3 of the Rift Runners Trilogy

JJ FALLON

snapping turtle
snappingturtlebooks.com

First published in Australia in 2012
by HarperCollins Publishers

This edition published in 2013
by Snapping Turtle Books

Jennifer Fallon Media Ltd.
PO Box 638, Rangiora, Canterbury, 7440
New Zealand

Cover design by David Tonkin, Snapping Turtle Books
Cover Images: shutterstock.com

ISBN-13: 978-0473254162
ISBN-10: 0473254166

PROLOGUE

Pete wasn't expecting his home reality to be so... white. He'd imagined any number of scenes when they finally found this realm: the rolling green hills of Ireland were what he'd been expecting, but not necessarily the Ireland he knew. Perhaps a world where faerie roamed free and the air sang with magic, like it did in the reality they'd just come from - an odd reality where the rulers of Ireland were feudal Japanese lords answerable to a couple of precocious ten-year-old girls who seemed more Scandinavian than Oriental.

He wasn't expecting snow and ice, as far as the eye could see. "Where are we, exactly?"

Logan shrugged, looking about in bewilderment. Pete turned to the young man who'd brought them here. He was dressed in a loose cotton *yabagin*, the marrow-freezing cold not touching him through the magical shield of warmth he had, in fact, woven around the three of them.

Ren's expression was grim as he studied the

barren snowscape. "I think it's Hawaii."

"That's a glacier over there."

"Clearly they're not having problems with global warming, then," Logan quipped, flashing his brother a quick grin. "There's magic here, though. I can feel it."

"It's fading," Ren said.

"What do you mean?"

"Magic needs living things to sustain it. This world is dead."

"We don't know that for certain."

"This is the fourth stone circle we've tried, Logan. They've all been the same. No sun, no life, just snow and ice." "Maybe there are other, warmer places ..."

"We're virtually standing on the Equator. Where do you suppose it's going to be any warmer?"

"What did this?" Pete asked. He directed the question at Ren and it wasn't rhetorical. This was the world from which Delphine had stolen Pete and his twin brother as babies. She had planned to use them as breeding stock for the *Matrarchaí*, while ensuring they were ignorant of their heritage. She thought they would never learn that they were powerful sorcerers in their own right, because they were Undivided. They only lacked the magical tattoo on their palms which would make them capable of sharing their magic with other human sorcerers, as well as wielding it themselves.

Then Ren and Darragh had happened along, and nobody's life had been the same since. Especially now that Ren had all of Delphine's memories, so he had the answers the others wanted. Ren had shared some of her surface memories through the *Comhroinn*, but the really meaty stuff that Pete and Logan were interested in was hoarded almost jealously by Ren. He claimed Delphine's memories were too hard to sort out, therefore too hard to isolate and reveal in the *Comhroinn*, the Druid magic mind sharing that was more art than magic.

Pete knew that some things Ren learned from his *Comhroinn* with Delphine were near the surface and so could be easily accessed and shared. Other things were hidden, requiring Ren to delve far deeper. His reluctance to do so annoyed Pete, who believed the answers to all their questions were hidden in Ren's mind. It was selfish of Ren to deny them answers, just because the memories were unwanted and he was afraid of a little bit of a headache.

"Hey, did you hear me?"

Ren was staring off into space. There was a blank look on his face suggesting he was either bored, or lost in the memories he'd accessed to bring them to this place.

"Kavanaugh?" Logan looked at Ren with concern. When Ren didn't answer he turned to Pete. "Is he usually this annoying?"

"Yes," Pete said. He stepped up to Ren and snapped his fingers in front of the young man's face. "Hey! Wizard boy! Snap out of it!"

Ren blinked and fixed his gaze on Pete. "You should be dead."

"Yeah, pity about that. Now why don't you -"

"You should both be dead," Ren said, casting his eyes over Logan as if Pete hadn't spoken. "I cannot permit you to live, knowing what you are. You were never meant to gain this self-knowledge."

"Ren?" Pete said.

"I don't think that's Ren any longer," Logan said, as the air about them suddenly chilled. Ren - or whoever it was - had dropped the warming shield.

"Delphine?" Pete's breath frosted as he asked the question, afraid he already knew the answer. This was what Ren had feared. He wasn't skilled enough to hold back the memories he carried. Pete shivered, and not entirely because of the cold.

"I was prepared to let you live ordinary lives," Ren said, although it was clear the words were not his. This was Delphine, just before she died. Before Ren killed her. The Delphine who was able to justify the murder of two men she had raised as her own sons. "But you just couldn't help poking your nose in where it wasn't needed, could you? I told you I was safe. You should have left it at that."

With the preternatural instincts of identical twins, Pete knew that if he could distract Ren long enough, Logan would be able to get around behind him. Pete didn't know what it would take to shake Delphine loose from Ren's mind, but he was pretty sure that neither he nor Logan understood their newfound magical abilities enough to counter someone as powerful as Ren - souped up as he was with Delphine's centuries of knowledge about how to use that power.

"Who'd have thought some mundane little terrorist attack that had nothing to do with the *Matrarchaí* would interfere with your plans to rule the world?"

Ren raised his hand and Pete started to choke, as

if his windpipe was being crushed by an invisible hand. "How dare you mock me? After all I've done for you. And for your information, the *Matrarchaí* has much bigger plans than just ruling one world."

Pete couldn't breathe. He collapsed to his knees, wondering where Logan was. He didn't have much time, he knew, before the memories of Delphine that were possessing Ren crushed the very life out of him.

"Ren..." he gasped with his last breath, appealing to the young man who owned this power crushing the life from him. Surely Ren could fight back? He wouldn't have surrendered willingly...

And Logan... where was Logan?

In answer to his question, he saw his brother fly past him and land heavily against the bole of a dead, snow-covered palm tree. Pete couldn't tell if he was unconscious or dead. He just knew there'd be no help coming from that direction.

If he was going to survive this, he needed to get Ren back. But he was already starting to black out. Desperately, he groped around on the snow-covered ground until his hands closed over the closest thing he had to a weapon. The rock he found was rough and cold. Pete scooped it up and smashed it down onto Ren's foot, the only part of him he could still focus on.

Ren cried out in pain and the pressure eased on Pete's throat. He staggered to his feet and lurched at Ren, driving his fist into his solar plexus with the full weight of his body behind him. They crashed to the ground. Pete landed on top on Ren and raised the rock, ready to crush Ren's skull if that's what it was going to take to shake Delphine loose from his mind.

"No! Pete! It's me!"

Pete hesitated, the rock still raised above his head. He sat astride Ren, who was staring up at him with genuine fear. The arrogance of Delphine was gone.

"How do I know it's you?"

"Delphine wouldn't be talking to you. She'd go back to killing you."

Cautiously, Pete lowered the rock. "Are you sure she's gone?"

Ren nodded.

"What happened?" "I did what you asked, Pete. I tried to access her memories. Next thing I know, I was Delphine. Are you going to let me up?"

"Maybe." Pete glanced across the snow-covered stone circle to where Logan lay, relieved see him groaning as he pushed himself up onto his hands and knees. He turned back to Ren. "Can you stop her doing that again?"

Ren shrugged. "I think so. Darragh knew how to do it. I'd have to lock down her memories, though, and everything she knows will get locked down with it."

"Small price to pay if it means you're not going to go postal on us without warning."

Logan staggered over to them, studying his brother - sitting astride Ren and still clutching the rock - with a puzzled expression. "Is that Ren?"

"For the moment," Pete assured his brother and then turned back to Ren. "Do it."

"Now?"

"You ever want to leave this realm?" Ren nodded and closed his eyes. Pete could feel him drawing from the faded magic of this world and then, after a few moments, he opened his eyes. "It's done."

"How can we be sure?" Logan asked.

"Because as soon as we get back to the ninja reality, we're going to hand him over to Trása and she can make sure it's done."

"Do you trust Trása to do that?"

"I trust her to want her boyfriend to stay alive," Pete said, climbing to his feet, "because if he goes Delphine on us again, we're going to have to kill him." He reached down and offered Ren his hand. "You okay with that?"

Ren nodded as Pete pulled him to his feet. "You're not staying here, then? This realm is your home."

"What's to stay for?" Logan asked, looking around. "Besides," Pete said, "Delphine said the *Matrarchaí* has much bigger plans than ruling the world. I think we need to find out what she meant by that."

PART ONE

CHAPTER 1

The would-be bank robber entered the bank, stopping to look up at the security camera long enough for his image to be captured clearly. He wanted no mistake made about his identity. It was important the authorities knew who he was, important there be no question of his guilt.

The wickedly sharp boning knife he'd stolen from a hardware store yesterday remained concealed by the long sleeve of his jacket, the hilt firmly in his grasp. The guard on the entrance - a young man in his thirties with a paunch and a neatly trimmed ginger beard - barely glanced at him as he walked through the door, assuming, like everybody else, he was just another customer.

A flicker of doubt made the robber pause for a moment, although to the casual observer he probably appeared to be deciding nothing more important than where he needed to go in order to take care of his banking business.

Is there another way?

Is this really what it has come to?

He had other options. He could return home, back to his own realm. He had a magic-infused talisman tucked in the pocket of his jacket that would allow him to scry out someone in his own reality and arrange for them to open a rift.

But he hadn't taken that option in more than three years.

What would he tell the *Tuatha Dé Danann* Brethren?

No, this is the better way.

Unfortunately, to be convicted of a crime serious enough to be sent to Portlaoise, a simple bank robbery would not be enough. There must be violence involved, although he balked at the idea of a cold-blooded killing just to serve his own ends, no matter how noble he believed those ends to be. He'd realized some time ago it would serve his purposes to maim a few people. There was no need for unnecessary death.

There was another quirk of this realm that he had often puzzled over - the bizarre concept of a war on terror. The phrase made no sense to him, but he soon figured out that while it was absurd to declare war on an idea or a feeling, the notion would serve his purpose well. When they arrested him for robbing the bank, he intended to inform the Gardaí that he was raising funds for Al Qaeda.

He only had the barest notion of what an Al Qaeda was, but it seemed to occupy the minds of many politicians and much of the news media in this realm, and - so he'd gathered from watching television - it was an insidious enough force that he would be roundly condemned for supporting it and, almost certainly, sent to prison if he was in any way associated with it.

But first, he had to rob this bank, something else he'd been researching on television.

He glanced around again, but nobody spared him as much as a glance. The people here were all intent on their own business. The tellers were busy serving their customers. The guard by the front door seemed to be counting the minutes until his lunch break. Near the counter a mother waited in line with a fussy toddler who was in no mood to wait for anything, and many of the bank's customers were glaring at the woman as if their silent disapproval would somehow spur her to greater efforts in controlling her unruly two-year-old. Others were ignoring the loud child, talking into cell phones or doing inexplicable things with their thumbs on the small devices. But one man did more than glare. As the robber studied the layout of the bank, the annoyed man lowered his cell phone, turned to the mother of the toddler and asked loudly, "Can't you keep that brat under control?"

The woman looked mortified. She gathered her child to her, but the youngster ignored her attempts to quiet him, squirming and crying even more loudly. With an angry glare, the man resumed his call, while others just looked away, embarrassed for the woman and her child.

The bank robber owned no cell phone nor saw the need for one. There was nobody in this realm he wanted to call.

Glancing over his shoulder, he noticed another guard had joined the first one by the door - it was lunchtime and for a short while there would be two guards on duty. This was what he needed. Two men were more likely than one to take him on once he declared his intention to rob the bank, and hopefully they would feel there was safety in numbers and be less inclined to shoot him. That was the theory, at any rate. If he was wrong and they shot him... well, at least he would die while trying to protect those he was sworn to safeguard.

A warrior could ask for no better end than that.

He moved his arm, easing the eight-inch long boning knife from his sleeve. He focused on the mother and her toddler. He'd been hoping there would be a small child in the bank, gambling on the guards being even less inclined to shoot if they risked hurting a child. Not that there was much risk to any innocent bystander. He intended to surrender the moment he was called upon to do so.

He shook the knife down a little further and turned it so he had a sound grip on the yellow plastic hilt - a color he had chosen deliberately for high visibility. Let there be no mistaking that he was armed.

For a long moment, although he was standing in the middle of a busy bank at lunchtime holding a wicked-looking boning knife, nobody registered it. It was one of the guards on the door who noticed him first and alerted the second guard. He didn't even get time to call out his prepared speech: *Everybody put your hands up!* which seemed to be the traditional announcement of an armed robbery in this realm.

The two guards didn't call out to him either. They signaled to one another and split up, walking carefully toward him, loosening the clips on their holstered weapons as they approached from either side, making it difficult to keep both of them in his line of sight.

"Whoa there, big fella," the red-bearded guard said softly as he approached. "Whatcha got in mind, lad, that needs a carving knife?"

The bank robber frowned as his head swiveled between the approaching guards. This wouldn't do at all. If they arrested him before he had a chance to announce his intentions, he'd be charged with little more than a misdemeanor. He'd not get anywhere near Portlaoise Prison. Given he was carrying a weapon in a bank, he would no doubt get some jail time, but it would probably be in some other less secure prison and, far from being able to help those he was charged to protect, he would be incapable of doing anything at all to assist them.

The warrior from another reality had only a few seconds to make his decision. There was a scream from somewhere behind him as a bank patron noticed the knife and realized the security guards were closing in on a robber in an effort to disarm him.

"No need for a fuss," the bearded guard crooned. He still hadn't drawn his weapon, obviously convinced he could talk down this knife-wielding patron who had yet to do anything more threatening than produce a kitchen implement.

"I intend to rob this bank," he announced loudly, deciding it was important to establish that at the outset. He raised the knife, holding it out so everyone could see it. "I will kill anybody who tries to stop me."

"Not on my watch, sunshine," the guard replied, just as they did in the movies. *Is that something they train bank guards to say, or just something this one has been itching to utter if the opportunity ever arose?* There was no time to worry about it, though, because the young man was removing his gun from the holster at his waist. He raised the weapon, aiming it squarely at his chest. "Now be a good lad. Put the knife down and place your hands on your head. Slowly."

There were more screams behind him as the rest of the bank's patrons realized what was happening and a strident alarm began to sound, triggered by one of the tellers, probably. People began dropping to the floor. The noise was deafening and distracting and he'd lost sight of the other guard, but he couldn't risk taking his eyes off the younger one who was doing all the talking in order to find out how close the other guard was.

The 'not on my watch' comment had alarmed him. The young man no doubt watched far too much television, a trap he'd fallen into himself since arriving in this realm. He was reluctant to give him an opportunity to act out any other fantasies he might be harboring, but still, this had to be a convincing robbery.

"I want all the cash here!" he shouted, mostly to be heard over the alarm. In the distance, he could hear sirens, as the Gardaí sped to the aid of the two security guards, who had no doubt come to work this morning assuming this day would be as uneventful as any other. "Have someone load the money into two bags and nobody will be hurt!"

"Only one getting hurt today is you, matey. Drop the knife."

He knew the smart thing to do was comply with the order, but he wasn't convinced he'd done enough. There had been no violence. Nothing but a shouted demand and a lot of noise. He glanced around. The other guard was close behind, certainly close enough to shoot and not miss if he chose. The mother with the toddler was squatting on the floor, behind a stand of brochures offering excellent mortgage rates and interest-free transfers on credit card balances, holding her child close. There were others peeking around the bank's stately marble columns, taking pictures of him with their cell phones.

The man who had spoken so harshly to the mother about her noisy child was paying no attention to the whole affair, talking on his cell phone as if nothing was awry.

That offended him. *How dare you play down the severity of my crime by ignoring it?*

The man's arrogance decided him. There was no escape, but there had been no blood, either. He needed to hurt someone, and this fool standing in the middle of an armed robbery talking on his cell phone as if the events around him were unimportant, seemed as good a candidate as any.

The robber hurled the knife before anyone could stop him. There were more screams and a deafening noise as he was slammed in the chest and knocked to the ground.

Damn, he thought as he fell. *That wasn't supposed to happen.*

As he collapsed to the floor and the world exploded in chaos around him, he reached up to feel his life force leaking from his chest ... but his hand came away dry.

Amazed, he realized there was no blood seeping from an open wound. The bullet hadn't missed; it had hit the iron triskalion pendant he had stowed in his jacket pocket, the magical talisman he had brought with him to contact home.

He could feel that it was bent and twisted out of shape. Likely the mundane lead from this world had leeched the last remaining magic from the pendant - and with it, any chance he had of connecting with his own realm. He could barely breathe and his chest would be black and blue within a day, he knew, but as the guards and the newly arrived Gardaí swarmed over him, shouting so excitedly he could barely make out their words, he smiled.

The talisman had done its job. It had protected him. He'd been shot trying to rob a bank. He'd wounded an innocent bystander, but he certainly hadn't hit anything vital if the man's outraged howling was any gauge of his condition. And he'd survived in one piece.

Soon, he would be where he was meant to be.

Soon he could resume his role as protector of the Undivided.

All he had to do then was wait for rescue to come for them and he could go home.

CHAPTER 2

Trása stepped through the rift into a thunderstorm. The forecourt of the *hommaru* - the inner palace of the vast Edo fortress - glistened in the darkness, the rain pelting down as thunder rent the air. A few of the lesser *Youkai* who lived in and around the palace clustered near her for protection as imperial attendants hurried forward, holding a wide, oiled-silk canopy aloft by the gilded poles at each corner to keep the rain off their honored guest.

As the rift's lightning faded, mundane lightning from the storm bathed the forecourt in bright light, followed a few seconds later by another crash of thunder. Several of the pixies who had followed her through the rift giggled at the noise. Toyoda Mulrayn, the ginger-bearded *Leipreachán* who fancied himself a ninja, let out an involuntary squawk of fright. It made his little black shinobi shozoko, which hid all his flesh except for his hands and a small slit around the eyes, and his *tabi* boots with their slit between his ungainly big toe and the second toe - making it easier for climbing ropes and scaling walls, apparently - all the more ridiculous.

The welcoming committee was small. Understandable, Trása supposed, given the inclement weather. Under another oiled canopy on the edge of the *rifuto* stones stood Wakiko, the blonde and very Nordic mother of the Empresses, whose betrayal of the *Matrarchaí* had saved the girls from the Lady Delphine and her plans to eliminate all the Faerie from this reality more than three years ago.

Wakiko - her real name was Ingrid - hadn't changed much in the years since Delphine had died by Ren's hand. She was still dressing like a geisha and still wore that perpetually worried expression that Trása figured would not go away anytime soon, given her twin daughters, the Empresses, had just turned thirteen.

"Welcome to Edo Palace, Trása," Wakiko said with a very Japanese bow, and a weary smile that spoke volumes about the strain of the upcoming birthday celebrations.

Another clap of thunder rent the air before Trása could return the greeting but there was no lightning accompanying the sound, which struck her as odd. She stepped forward, trusting Toyoda and the pixies to stay close. They'd been very brave to follow her here into what had, until a few years ago, been ruled the *Konketsu*, who'd spent years trying to eliminate their kind. It wasn't often the lesser *Youkai* left *Tír Na nÓg* and they were still wary of the *Konketsu*. It was three years since Delphine was killed and the *Matrarchaí* banished from this realm, but it was still proving difficult to convince them the days of pogroms and purges were done and that the Empresses had ordered the *Konketsu* to protect the Faerie rather than exterminate them.

"I'm honored to be invited," Trása said, glancing around. "Not every day the empresses turn thirteen."

Wakiko must have guessed who she was looking for. "He's here," she said, in English, a language only five people in this reality understood, "along with the other two. They ..." she stopped for a moment as the ground shook with another clap of nearby thunder. With a sigh she added, "That would be them."

"What are they doing?"

"Being boys," Wakiko said. Then she turned her attention to Toyoda and the pixies, bowed to them with the same gravity and respect she had shown Trása, and spoke in the odd mixture of Japanese and Gaelic that was the language of much of this realm. "You and your cousins are most welcome to Edo, Sā Mulrayn."

The little *Leipreachán* seemed to grow a couple of inches taller, so chuffed was he to be greeted with such formality. "Thank ye, *Ojōsama*," he said, with a bow not nearly so elegant or deep as Wakiko's.

Trása smiled in amusement. He was so thrilled to be greeted like an equal he seemed to have overlooked the fact that, despite his ninja disguise, Wakiko knew exactly who it was under the hood of his shinobi shozoko.

The ground shook again with another shudder of thunder. Wakiko shook her head, spared the drenched imperial attendants holding the canopies over them a sympathetic glance, and beckoned Trása forward. "Let's talk as we walk."

Trása stepped under Wakiko's canopy and the two of them began walking toward the palace proper, trusting the attendants to keep up and keep them dry. The *Leipreachán* and the pixies were clustered together under the other canopy bringing up the rear, giggling at the quaint notion of avoiding the rain. They were elemental creatures, and the desire to avoid the elements was a uniquely mammalian concept they found quite strange.

"Exactly what are they doing?" Trása asked, falling back into the English that afforded them such effective privacy.

"Ren claims he's trying to master *ori mahou* so he can risk accessing Delphine's memories again someday," Wakiko explained. "Personally, I think he's just looking for an excuse to blow things up."

That sounds a very male thing to do, Trása thought. *More importantly, a very Rónán thing to do.*

"Pete and Logan are here already?"

Wakiko nodded. "They arrived a few days ago."

"Are they encouraging Rónán to access Delphine's memories?" She remembered how adamant they'd been after finally visiting their home realm that Rónán never go near their foster-mother's memories again, although she didn't know *why* they were so determined to stop Ren mining such a rich vein of intelligence. It was something they all needed to get over, because Darragh was still trapped and only Delphine's memories held the key to finding him and bringing him home.

23

"I doubt it. I believe they're trying to convince Renkavana that with a mastery of *ori mahou* he might be able to discover the true purpose of the *Matrarchaí* without the need to delve into such murky waters," she said.

Trása stopped. She stared at Wakiko, catching the imperial attendants unawares. They took several steps forward and then hurried back to cover her, which not only exposed the mother of the Empresses to the rain but made them collide with the canopy bearers following behind with Toyoda and the pixies.

She ignored the almost comical fuss going on around her as the attendants endeavored to sort themselves out, her gaze fixed on Wakiko. "That's ridiculous. Delphine's memories are the only way back to the realm where Renkavana's brother is trapped. Why is he not doing everything he can to unlock them safely?" It just didn't make sense.

Admittedly, she hadn't seen Rónán since he'd announced he was coming here to Edo with Pete and Logan Doherty to master the secret of the folding magic they used in this realm. But when she had seen him last he was determined to find his brother, Darragh, and bring him home. What hadn't made sense to Trása then, and still didn't now, was why he was making a fuss about mastering *ori mahou* to open a rift. She knew he'd shared the *Comhroinn* with Delphine as she died and that he had Delphine's knowledge in his head if only he was willing to access it. His refusal to do so was the reason Trása hadn't seen him for over two years. That Logan and Pete Doherty were so determined to keep him from ever accessing those memories was the reason she was angry with them, too.

Trása wanted Rónán to do everything possible to find Darragh and get him out of the magic-less realm where he was stranded. Since coming back from Pete and Logan's dead world, he had refused to even try.

When she realized that, far from searching Delphine's memories, he was deliberately locking them away, she was furious. She couldn't believe he would be so selfish. Darragh was out there somewhere and only Rónán knew where... and he was going to do nothing, egged on by two interlopers who should just mind their own business. *I should have let Delphine murder you*, she'd told them, when she found out it was Pete and Logan who had made Rónán lock away Delphine's knowledge.

They parted on such angry terms, she wasn't sure what reaction she was going to get when she saw the Doherty brothers again.

Another thunderous concussion shook the ground. Trása wondered briefly if it might be safer to just turn around and go back to *Tír Na nÓg*.

"Renkavana will be glad to see you, Trása," Wakiko said, as if she could tell what she was thinking.

"I'm not so sure about that."

Wakiko slipped her arm through Trása's and they resumed walking. "He'll be glad, Trása. He's in pain and you're one of the few people in this entire reality who understands the reason. He needs your friendship, Trása. And your love."

She shook her head, wondering how Wakiko could be so pragmatic, and yet so irrationally romantic and sentimental at the same time. "That's not the impression I got the last time we spoke, Wakiko."

"Don't let him push you away," she urged, as the ground shook with another explosion. Then Wakiko smiled at her. "And if you could persuade him and his friends not to destroy my palace while he battles his internal demons, I would be very grateful."

CHAPTER 3

It took Pete Doherty less than a minute to fold the shape he needed from the square of washi paper, beating both his brother Logan, and Ren Kavanaugh, despite the amount of shōchū he'd consumed. He infused the tiny paper grenade with magic and tossed it into the moat. The ground shook as the water exploded in a staggering plume that rose a good thirty feet into the air, drenching the guards on the walls overlooking the moat that surrounded the inner hommaru of Edo Palace.

Laughing, he scooped up the flask of shōchū he was sharing with his equally inebriated companions and raised it in salute. "I rule!"

"You pissed off the guards on the wall," Logan pointed out, laughing, as he completed his own grenade and tossed it into the moat. It landed much closer, and when it exploded this time it doused them with water, rather than the guards, which sent the three of them into more gales of drunken laughter.

Even Ren was laughing, something Pete was sure the alcohol was responsible for. Between the rain and the water grenades they were launching the paper Ren was working with was sodden and it began to crumble under his fumble-fingered attempt to fold it into the required shape. After a few more unsuccessful attempts he scrunched the paper into a ball and tossed it onto the ground.

"Fuck that," Ren said, turning unsteadily to face the water, the rain running in rivulets down his face. "I'll give you a splash." He threw his arm out as if he was tossing an invisible grenade and the water exploded, driving a pillar of water fifty feet into the air. It crashed down around them and over the wall guards and the small crowd watching their antics from the other side of the moat on Daikan-cho Street, soaking everyone within reach to the skin.

Pete and Logan stared at Ren in stunned surprise. Ren wasn't supposed to be able to do that without *ori mahou*. Had Pete been less inebriated, the implications of that single drunken act might have resonated more clearly with him, might even have set off warning bells in his head, but they were wasted and having a high old time blowing up the moat, so he didn't think to question it.

The silence lasted on for a few seconds and then they all burst out laughing again.

"How did you do that?" Logan asked.

"Ninja magic," Ren said, grinning.

Pete wasn't sure Ren was joking. He'd heard rumours since he been here in this strange reality where everything was mixed up and weird - up to and including his own identity - about the art of kuji-in, the ninja hand magic. Toyoda had tried to explain it to him once. Something about the thumb being the source of power and the fingers representing the elements of earth, water, fire and wind. Not unlike the Loch Ness monster, plenty of people claimed to know about it, although nobody could say they'd ever seen it in action.

"You mean that hand waving and finger pointing crap?"

Ren nodded.

Logan doubled over in hysterics. "He gave it the finger!" That sent them into another spasm of drunken, side-splitting laughter. Pete staggered so close to the edge of the drawbridge, he almost fell in the moat. He circled his arms wildly to recover his balance and spun around. It was then he noticed the northern, tall studded gate to the hommaru enceinte - the innermost continuous line of Edo Palace's, seemingly endless, fortifications - had opened behind them and a lone figure was walking out onto the drawbridge.

"Trása!" Logan cried when he spied their visitor and realized who it was. He held up the flask he was holding. "You tried this shōchū shit? It's like rice-flavored whiskey mixed with jet fuel."

Trása stopped when she reached the edge of the drawbridge. Like the rest of them, she was soaked to the skin; the thin shift she wore clung to her in all the places likely to get a man into trouble. Pete wasn't sure if she was wet because she'd been caught in Ren's explosion, or if she'd walked here through the thunderstorm. Either way, she didn't look pleased to see any of them. The lightning and the rain made her expression hard to read, but she sure wasn't acting like she'd come here to join in the fun.

"Hi, Logan," Trása said in a toneless voice that said more about her disapproval of their entertainment than if she'd stormed out here yelling and screaming at them. Her footsteps barely made a sound as she walked onto the puddled drawbridge known locally as Kitahanebashi-mo.

"Pete." She treated him to a single word and cursory nod by way of greeting.

Ren remained facing the water, making no attempt to even acknowledge Trása's presence.

"Sure I can't interest you in some shōchū?" Logan persisted, his inebriation making him oblivious to Trása's mood. "It's made from barley and sweet potatoes and rice and chestnuts and a good dollop of crude oil, I suspect. Tastes like a blacksmith's armpit, but it's good for a laugh."

"I'm sure it is," Trása agreed without so much as cracking a smile. "Some other time, perhaps. Right now, Wakiko would greatly appreciate it if you would stop terrifying the locals by trying to destroy the inner moat."

"We were just having a bit of fun, Trása," Pete felt compelled to point out. "We started out skipping stones. It kind of escalated from there."

"Haven't you got something better to do with your time?"

"Apparently not," Logan said. He took another swig, but the bottle was empty. He turned it upside down and shook it, but there wasn't a drop left. With a frown, he tossed the bottle into the moat and fixed his unsteady gaze on Trása. "You see, it turns out we're going to live forever. Well. Maybe not forever, but much longer than we ever thought. Comes from being Faerie, you see." He staggered forward and put his hands on Trása's shoulders. "So time, my little Faerie Queen, time is the one thing we have plenty of to waste."

"That's not the fault of anybody here in Edo," Trása reminded them. "So it's hardly fair that you're indulging your boredom by making things explode."

That got a reaction from Ren. For the first time since arriving here in the Imperial Palace, Pete wished he'd refused the endless hospitality the Empresses afforded those considered responsible for saving this realm from the *Matrarchaí*. It wasn't as if they even deserved the title of saviors. He and his brother had been hogtied and unconscious for most of it.

Ren turned to face Trása. He no longer seemed even a little bit inebriated, Pete thought, a little envious of how quickly he had sobered up. "I was under the impression we'd established some time ago that you don't get to dictate what I do with my time."

Logan looked as if he wanted to offer his opinion, but Pete grabbed him by the arm and pulled him out of the way. Drunk as he was, he knew this confrontation had little to do with him and his brother, and probably not a lot to do with their magical concussion grenades. It had everything to do with the falling out between Ren and Trása over his refusal to access Delphine's memories. As he and his brother were in no small way responsible for

Ren's position on that, he thought it wise they not do anything to remind Trása of the fact.

"I'm not dictating anything to anybody," Trása said, showing no hint of backing down. "I'm merely passing on a request from our hostess. You're here for Teagan and Isleen's birthday celebrations ... all of you," she reminded them, glaring at Pete and Logan. "The only thing you're achieving at the moment is reminding those Imperial Court members of the *Konketsu* who fondly look back on the days when they were allowed to hunt the Faerie for sport, why that was so much fun."

She has a point, Pete thought. He wasn't sure if telling Ren that, was such good idea.

Perhaps there was a way to gracefully extricate themselves from this potentially awkward scene. At the very least, a way to have them back down without losing face. *Christ, how long have I been here that I care about losing face?*

He took a step forward, steadying himself by hanging onto Logan. "If Wakiko has requested we refrain from blowing up her moat," he announced, deliberately enunciating his words, which he suspected just made him sound drunker, "then it behooves us to heed our hostess's wishes and refrain from any further ... you know ... exploding stuff."

"Jesus, Pete," Logan chuckled, "how pissed do you have to be to drop the word 'behooves' into normal conversation?"

Trása must have been thinking along similar lines. She glanced at him with the faintest of smiles. "Behooves?"

He shrugged. "I'm feeling poetic."

"Well, I'm feeling cold," Trása said, wisely taking the opportunity Pete offered her to back down without seeming to lose the argument; perhaps a sign of how much she'd matured these past three years. She turned her back on Ren and smiled at him and Logan, the first sign of her thawing toward them since they'd returned from the dead realm that had once been their home. "Let's go back to the palace. I don't know about you, but I'm soaked to the skin and Wakiko promised me my own fiefdom if I could get you lot to stop blowing up things."

"Far be it from us to rob you of a fiefdom!" Logan cried, throwing his arms wide, which made them both stagger. "You coming, Ren? Trása's getting a fiefdom."

Ren didn't answer. He was staring at Trása with a dark look, his earlier good mood a distant memory.

"Logan, why don't you go with Trása? We'll tidy up here and be along presently."

Trása gave Pete a thankful smile, took Logan by the arm and began to guide him back toward the gate, no mean feat the way Logan was weaving about.

Ren watched them leave and then turned to Pete. "You don't need to watch over me, Pete."

He shook his head, which was a stupid thing to do, because it just made everything spin. "Yeah ... actually, maybe I do."

"Trása and I have a difference of opinion, that's all. It doesn't require adult supervision."

"A difference of opinion?" Pete rubbed his temples, wishing the Faerie ability to heal one's own wounds extended to sobering up in a hurry. "Is that what you're calling it? Jesus, I could cut the air between you two with a knife."

"You wanna fix it? Fine. Why don't I unlock Delphine's memories like Trása wants me to and see what happens?" Ren thrust his hands into the pockets of his trousers and began to walk back across the drawbridge to the gate.

Pete hurried after him, grabbing him by the arm to turn and face him. "That's not what I meant."

"It's why Trása is mad at me."

"And you're mad at her because you think she doesn't understand why you won't do it. I get that. But you need to take a deep breath, sunshine. It's everybody's business when you're pissed off about something, Ren."

"That's ridiculous."

"Is it?" Pete asked, as another bolt of lightning lit the sky in the distance. The storm was moving away, the thunder muted by the distance, but he hardly noticed. He had something to say and the alcohol had driven away his natural caution. "You've got a head full of other people's memories, no small percentage of which belong to that psychotic bitch, Delphine, and you're on such a huge guilt trip about leaving your brother behind, you should be paying excess baggage. You just about blew that moat clean into the middle of next week with a wave of your arm just now. No *ori mahou*, no spells, you just willed it to happen. And that was for a bit of light entertainment. We don't need you going postal on us again, Ren. Not with that sort of power at your command."

It occurred to Pete just after he finished his rather impressive, if somewhat verbose, analysis that if Ren really was pissed off with the world, it might not be a good idea to be the one who pointed it out to him so bluntly.

"She thinks I've abandoned them," Ren said, surprising Pete with his openness. Maybe he just needed someone to call him out.

"Darragh?"

Ren nodded. "And Hayley. And Sorcha. Even old Jack O'Righin."

"It's not your fault, Ren. We've been searching for some way back to that damn reality for three years. I had a life there once remember? So did Logan. If we could have found a way back, we'd have done it long before now. Do you want me to explain that to Trása?"

"She'll just tell you that I need to unlock Delphine's memories. We tried that once ... didn't go so well, did it?" Ren sighed, as if he was weary with the discussion. "Look, I know what she's mad about, and it's more than Delphine's memories. I could go home to the realm I come from. There's enough gampi paper here to fold the rift. And because it's my origin reality, I can always find it."

"Then why don't you?"

"That's what I can't explain to Trása." He did not elaborate or offer the reason, Pete noted, for why he was refusing to do it. "Why doesn't she just open a rift and go back herself, if it's that important to her."

"Trása's cursed, remember? If she steps into our home reality, she'll turn back into a barn owl."

"You two coming?" Logan called from the gate. "We're coming," Pete called back, and then turned to Ren. "Sort it out, Ren," he advised. "Do something about it or let it go, but don't keep chewing your on own liver about it."

Ren nodded, but whether he was planning to accept Pete's advice it was hard to say and they didn't get a chance to discuss it further because at that moment a loud crack rent the air; a sound that Pete hadn't heard for three years.

"Jesus Christ, that was a gunshot!"

Ren looked at him in confusion. Over by the gate, Logan and Trása had stopped, looking bewildered. They were probably the only other people in this reality who recognized the sound.

Another shot rang out, but there was no way of telling where it was coming from.

"There are no guns in this reality," Pete said.

"Then it's coming from a rift," Ren said. He blinked out of existence before Pete could respond.

A shout went up from the wall above as Pete broke into a run. Someone was yelling for reinforcements. Several more shots rang out. He caught up with Logan and Trása and quickly outdistanced them, running for the *rifuto* stones.

The Imperial Palace was under attack.

By someone with automatic weapons.

CHAPTER 4

The shooting was a rearguard action, Ren realized, almost as soon as he waned into the forecourt of the hommaru where the *rifuto* stones were located. There was nobody coming through with guns blazing. Whoever it was had probably come through a rift somewhere else in this reality, sneaked into the palace by mundane means, and were now using the palace *rifuto* stones to escape.

There were several bodies lying on the ground in front of the lightning-filled stone circle. Imperial Guards, by the look of them, come to investigate who had opened the rift, with no idea their bamboo armor wouldn't stop a bullet.

Ren had arrived in the forecourt behind the tall pillars that flanked the entrance to the outer hall of the Imperial donjon. He flattened himself against the nearest pillar as another shot rang out, this one so close a chip of granite grazed his cheek when the bullet struck the column and ricocheted.

Whoever was escaping was determined not to be followed. Ren closed his eyes for a moment, wondering if he had enough control in waning from one location to another to get closer to the rift without being shot. He wasn't confident. When he'd left Pete on the drawbridge, he'd intended to wane into the forecourt right next to the *rifuto* stones. Whether it was his own lack of finesse, or the alcohol, he'd appeared nowhere near the stones. Instead, he was around four hundred yards away on the steps of the *donjon*.

If he was going to get to the rift, he was going to have to do it the hard way - by running across the forecourt through a hail of bullets.

Or maybe not. He'd just blown the moat to kingdom-come with a wave of his arm. What would happen if he tried the same with an open rift? Would it destroy the *rifuto* stones? Close the rift? Tear a hole in the space-time continuum and bring on the end of all life in the universe? Ren was banking on the latter being a remote possibility.

The invaders were escaping to another reality, a magic-less one at that, he figured, as a staccato burst of gunfire mowed down a dozen more Imperial Guards advancing on the intruders: there were no automatic weapons in a world full of magic. But, at the same time, whoever had invaded this realm had access to magic or they'd not be able to open a rift.

The *Matrarchaí*.

Ren forced the thought away. Although he'd assured Logan and Pete they were inaccessible, in truth he kept Delphine's memories at bay only by sheer force of will.

If he merely tried to forget the omnipresent burden he carried the opposite effect occurred and he found that the walls he'd built in his mind to contain her memories bulged inward under the pressure, trying to escape and overwhelm him.

Why now? Why can't you just stay away from this realm and leave us alone?

He risked another glance around the column, but all he could make out clearly was the lightning-streaked rift, the edges of which were almost too bright to look upon, with a dark hollow of nothingness in the center. From this distance, he couldn't tell where the rift originated, but if it was the *Matrarchaí*, it probably opened into a high-rise building somewhere...

Ren cut the thought off. Knowledge like that came with a brutal price.

He took a deep breath and closed his eyes, drawing power to him. He touched his thumbs to his index fingers, closing the circle. There was a reason he didn't need to work the folding spells of this realm any longer. He'd come to the Imperial Palace to learn how use *ori mahou* and stumbled instead over the lost secrets of the kuji-in.

Rin for strength of mind and body, he reminded himself, aware he couldn't control anything if he wasn't calm. His explosion at the moat had proved that. He'd been aiming for something much less spectacular.

Hei to focus psychic power in order to mask one's presence. If he was going to do this, it would be useful not to get shot.

Toh to balance the solid and liquid states of the body. Ren still hadn't worked out what that even meant, let alone how to harness the power of it.

Sha to heal oneself or another - an ability he'd inherited from his *sídhe* ancestors, fortunately, because it was one less thing he needed to master.

Kai for complete control over the body's functions, to slow the heart rate, endure extreme heat and cold. Ren hadn't come close to figuring this one out, or even finding a reason why he might need to.

Jin to focus the mind's telepathic powers. Retsu to harness one's telekinetic powers. Both useful skills he owned anyway, but kuji-in had enabled him to gain some mastery over them.

Zai, as best Ren could tell, was meant to bring harmony by merging with the universe. Whatever that meant.

And, of course, *Zen* which was supposed to bring enlightenment and understanding, and was the one skill he suspected he may never master.

It took only a few seconds to calm his breathing and run through the list in his mind. He felt magic coursing through him, gathered it to him, ready to unleash it on whoever had dared invade his realm.

Ren stepped out from behind the pillar.

Time seemed to slow down. Out of the corner of his eye he saw Pete, Logan and Trása just reaching the forecourt, diving for cover behind the large ornamental pots housing the carefully manicured cherry trees whose blooms were just beginning to fade, when the spray of bullets was directed their way.

In front of him lay a score of unmoving bodies and they continued to fall as the Imperial Guard officers shouted at their troops to advance, either not understanding or not caring what the hail of bullets might do to their men.

Ren raised his arm and opened his fingers.

By the light of the rift he could make out several figures, although he was too far away to identify them. Two of the figures - he couldn't even tell if they were male or female - were positioned either side of the open rift, down on one knee firing the automatic weapons that were doing so much damage to a defending force armed with nothing more than swords and grim determination. The lightning from the rift and the incessant rain served to plunge the rest of the forecourt into darkness.

Only a split second before Ren let loose his power, through the shouts and the gunfire and the rain hitting the metal *kabuto* of the Imperial Guardsmen, he heard a child scream.

There was no chance to pull back. As he unleashed all the force he could marshal and hurled it toward the rift and the gunmen defending it, from the darkness emerged two other figures, each one carrying a struggling child in their arms.

Ren had no time to react. He'd sent his devastating magical warhead on its way before he realized these interlopers had a very specific purpose.

He should have known the *Matrarchaí* would not let Delphine's death go unpunished.

He should have known they would come for Teagan and Isleen.

And he *would* have known, if he'd allowed Delphine's memories to do something other than fester at the back of his mind, while he blocked out everything she knew for fear of what truly knowing her might do to him.

It must have been only seconds, although it felt like a lifetime, as Ren waited for his magic to hit the rift, powerless to do anything to stop it, or to stop the men carrying the screaming twin Empresses toward some unknown alternate reality that the imminent explosion would destroy any chance of finding.

He opened his mouth to scream a warning, but it was lost in the melee as the ground shook and the rift disappeared in a spectacular cascade of bright light that seared his retinas and left him temporarily blinded. Anybody still standing in the forecourt was knocked off their feet. The sound of the explosion rumbled over him, so deep, so loud, that he felt, rather than heard the rift collapse.

The sound moved on, rumbling over the rest of the palace and left them in a momentary lull of shock and stunned silence.

Ren picked himself up, unable to remember when exactly he had fallen.

He looked across the courtyard as the white lights faded from his eyes. The rift was gone, and from here it looked as if much of the stone circle had disintegrated with it. He stumbled forward as the remaining guards began to climb to their feet. At the sound of someone groaning, he glanced over at the forecourt gate to find Logan, Pete and Trása climbing to their feet, apparently unharmed.

And then, in the stunned silence, he heard a whimper.

Ren staggered into a run, suddenly filled with hope. Perhaps the explosion had thrown Teagan and Isleen back into this realm. Perhaps it had closed before they could be taken through. Perhaps it had only seemed like they were already into the rift when it collapsed. It was raining, after all, and dark, and hard to tell...

He could hear the others running close behind him, although whether it was because they believed he might have seen or heard something, or they'd heard the whimper for themselves, Ren didn't know.

"Teagan!" he called. "Isleen!"

He reached the remains of the stone circle and cast about in the darkness, uncaring of the rain. There were several bodies scattered about, dressed in ordinary linen yukata that would have made it seem as if they belonged here - right up until they pulled out the machine guns and opened fire.

The rain kept pelting down, making it hard to see, and even harder to hear.

Then Trása called out, "Over here!"

She was squatting over the body of a large man with a shaved head and distinctly Asian features - probably the reason he'd been chosen for this foray into enemy territory. She grunted with the effort of pushing him out of the way. By the time Ren and the others got to her, she was dragging one of the empresses clear and helping her to her feet.

Miraculously, she seemed unharmed. The man's bulk must have protected her from the explosion.

Dishevelled and terrified, the little girl clung to Trása and looked about in a panic. "Teagan!" she demanded. "Where is my sister, Teagan? She was right in front of me. Where is she?"

Nobody answered her.

Nobody wanted to be the one to tell the little empress that her sister had been taken by the *Matrarchaí* and that with the *rifuto* stones destroyed, there was almost no chance of getting her back.

CHAPTER 5

It amazed Trása to see a man disembowel himself and not utter a sound. She couldn't imagine how anybody could do that. Couldn't imagine, for that matter, how a man could disembowel himself in the first place, let alone do it with silent dignity and honor.

But they could and they did. As she stood with Rónán and Pete and Logan Doherty, staring down over the forecourt from the balcony of the throne room watching the commanders of the Imperial Guard commit *harakiri*, she realized that despite living in this realm for the past three years, she didn't understand these people at all.

"How could they just walk into the palace and walk out with the Empresses?" Logan asked in a low tone that sounded as if he was trying to think about something else besides what was happening down in the rainy forecourt.

Trása doubted he expected an answer. Logan Doherty, of all people, understood the power and the reach of the *Matrarchaí*.

"Does anyone have any idea where they might have taken her?" Pete asked. He sounded like a cop, again, Trása thought. He'd certainly sobered up since last night when he, Logan and Rónán had their stupid party out by the moat. He was standing beside her, like all of them, morbidly fascinated by the ritual taking place below them.

Wakiko, as regent of the empire, was overseeing the sacrifices with a grim expression, although what she actually thought about this harsh reckoning was impossible to tell from this distance. Rónán was standing beside Trása looking out over the palace forecourt where, behind the *harakiri* ceremony, in the harsh light of the early morning servants were cleaning the blood off the paving stones, and making preparations to bury the dead after each of the three commanders offered up their lives in recompense for their failure to protect the Empresses and the empire.

"They came through a rift," Trása said with a shrug, "and there's an infinite number of realities out there, Pete. Pick one."

"Wakiko might have some idea," Logan suggested. "She belonged to the *Matrarchaí* once."

Trása shook her head. "She was never high enough up the ranks to know where any of the strongholds are. Her job was to bear children for the *Matrarchaí*."

"I don't think they'll hurt Teagan," Logan suggested. "If they'd wanted to kill the girls, they could have done that while they were still in the palace."

Below them, the last of the Imperial Guard commanders was readying to present himself to the regent. Around him were ranked the surviving members of the guard, those who hadn't been on duty, standing to attention in the drizzling rain, ignoring the rivulets of blood-tinged water pooling at their feet as their second-in-command was carried away. Trása wondered if Wakiko was expecting the lives of all of the guard, rather than just the officers.

"They could have murdered them while they were still babies in the crib," Rónán muttered darkly beside her. Trása suspected only she had heard the comment.

Pete turned to glance at him. "What was that?"

"Nothing."

The third officer now stepped forward to stand before the regent. It was hard to say who it was. He was dressed in full *samurai* armor, but Trása thought it might be Andoryū Tanabe, cousin of the *Konketsu* magician, Chishihero, who'd tried to kill both her and Rónán when they first arrived in this realm. Chishihero was long dead and Trása had never grieved her passing, but she liked Andoryū and was sorry his young life was going to end in this absurd, yet fiercely proud, ritual of taking your own life when an apology and a good look at what could be done to prevent the situation happening again seemed the more reasonable course of action.

"If we don't know where she is, how are we going to get her back?" Pete asked.

Trása turned on him, venting some of her despair at what was happening in the forecourt on the unsuspecting former cop. "Well, then... do something about it, Pete. You used to be a detective, didn't you? Get out there and... detect!"

"Hey!"

She sighed. "I'm sorry."

"We could just wait for them to come back," Rónán suggested softly, not taking his eyes off the events unfolding below.

Trása couldn't bear to look any longer. She turned her back to the window, leaned on the sill and folded her arms across her body against the chill. The brazier on the other side of the room did nothing to combat the cold here by the open window. "How can you know they'll be back?"

Pete nodded. "That's a thought. They're after a set of Empress twins, aren't they? Thanks to you, they only got away with one of them."

"I think your gratitude is a bit misplaced," Rónán said, his gaze still fixed on the gut-wrenching scene. "Thanks to my misguided heroics the *rifuto* stones are pulverized. There's no chance of even guessing where they went with Teagan."

"Actually, that's not entirely true," Trása said.

"What are you talking about?" Logan asked. He had turned away too. It seemed only Rónán and Pete had the stomach to watch three ritual suicides in a row.

"Delphine would know."

"No," Pete and Logan said, almost simultaneously.

Trása glared at them, wondering why, in their most dire hour of need, they were trying to prevent Rónán from accessing the one thing they needed to rescue Wakiko's daughter - intelligence about the enemy. She turned to Rónán. "You have all her memories. You should be able to locate every one of the *Matrarchaí* strongholds."

Delphine would have known how to get back to the world Pete and Logan came from. The same world where Rónán had been raised thinking his name was Ren Kavanaugh... all he had to do was access Delphine's memories and he could open a rift, and could have done so anytime he wanted in the past three years.

However, it wasn't just Rónán she was fighting about this. For some reason, Pete and Logan were just as determined Ren not have anything to do with Delphine's memories. "I can't understand why you're siding with Rónán. Don't you want to go home?"

"Home?" Pete asked, turning to look at her. "You think we can go *home*? We have no *home*, Trása. We belong somewhere we have no memory of. We're Undivided," he reminded them. "We're almost pure *sídhe*. We can heal with a thought. We can blow things up by folding a bit of paper. What do you think we'd go back to? The night shift? The weather report? There is no place for either of us in that world any longer."

"That's not your call," Trása said. "Rónán is the one who has the information. It's his decision whether to use what he knows or not."

"It's not that simple," Rónán said, leaning against the sill.

"Seems pretty simple to me," Trása said, turning on him. "You've always known how to find the realm where Darragh is trapped, Rónán, and you won't do it because... why? You like it here with the ninja-*Leipreachán* and your new best friends?"

Rónán was glaring at her, fists clenched by his sides. "I wish I could tell you the location of the other realm, Trása, if just to be rid of your nagging me about it, but I can't. I spend every waking moment fighting the memories that evil bitch dumped on me. I don't know what Delphine knows because if I open up to her, I don't know if I can come back. Ask Pete and Logan what happened the last time I tried."

"Trust me, Trása ... you don't want him to go there."

"Shut up, Logan," she said, fixing her gaze on Rónán. She'd shared a *Comhroinn* plenty of times, but they'd been controlled and only those memories or information the other person wanted to share had passed between them. Delphine was dying when everything she knew, everything she was, passed between her and Rónán. Trása couldn't imagine what it must be like to try and hold that at bay. She turned to him, placing herself between him and the Doherty twins. She could not bring herself to believe Rónán would have left Darragh behind for anything but the direst of reasons.

"Have you tried to sort through her memories for the location of the rifts?"

"Jesus Christ, Trása, if I could find a way back, don't you think I'd open a rift tomorrow and be gone from here?" As if to punctuate his words, a

50

tormented scream echoed across the forecourt. The argument paused for a moment. Trása's heart constricted a little for the man who had just died by his own hand to satisfy the forms of some twisted sense of honor. *Poor Andoryū. It seems he lacked the stoicism to take his own life in silence.*

Rónán broke the awkward hush that followed Andoryū's final scream, adding, "Do really you think I've not said anything because this place is such a barrel of frigging laughs?"

He pushed off the balcony and walked across the woven matting to the brazier, holding his hands out to warm them. It was an odd gesture, because he could have warmed himself with magic much more effectively.

"Could you not even *try*?" Trása asked gently. "You did it to help Logan and Pete find their realm. Can't you do the same for Darragh? For Teagan?"

The question hung between them for a long moment. When he finally answered her, his response was nothing like she expected.

"If you were offered everything you ever wanted," Rónán said, staring down at the coals in the wrought-iron brazier, "what would you do for it?"

"If it meant getting out of this lunatic asylum, whatever it took," Trása muttered.

"Really?" Rónán said, turning to look at her. He held his hand out over the brazier. "What if the cost was unthinkable, intolerable agony? What if, to get the prize, you had to plunge your hand into these coals? The pain would be unbearable. You'd probably lose a part of the limb, but that's okay, because the payoff would be amazing. All the power you ever wanted or could imagine. All the knowledge..." He stopped and looked down into the coals and added softly. "Of course, you'd be in agony and lost your hand in the process, so there'd be a piece of you missing, and the nightmares would be unendurable, but you'd have everything else you could desire." He looked up again. "Would you do it?"

"If it meant saving a little girl from being turned into monster, then yes," Trása said. "In a heartbeat."

"Then you're a braver soul than me, Trása," Rónán said, pulling his hand back from the fire.

"This isn't about you, Ren," she said in a much more conciliatory tone. "It's not even about Darragh. For all we know he could have escaped back to our home realm three years ago. This is about two little girls who don't deserve to be turned into breeding cows, at best - genocidal monsters, at worst."

Rónán nodded, his expression grim. "You think I don't know that?"

"Then do something about it," she said. "Or go down to the forecourt and throw yourself on your sword with the others right now, because trust me, even if you can convince yourself that Darragh's fine and we don't need to go anywhere, you're not going to be able to live with the fact that you abandoned a little girl to the fate awaiting her in the hands of the *Matrarchaí*."

Rónán didn't answer her. He just plunged his hands in his pockets and stalked out of the room without another word.

CHAPTER 6

Darragh had been in prison in this strange magic-depleted reality long enough to know he was a target.

Had he been a little more contrite, more willing to confess to the crimes of which he was so unjustly convicted, he might have avoided transfer to Portlaoise Prison when he turned twenty-one, and been sent to a less terrifying medium-security prison to serve the remainder of his life sentence.

Had he not gained a reputation for being troublesome.

Had he not knifed that stupid skinhead with a shank...

He should never have gotten involved with that particular fight - the fight which resulted in him being sent here to Portlaoise. It had nothing to do with him. The guards would have got there eventually and broken it up... a few heads would have been broken, but nobody would have died.

Only it wasn't a fight, as much as a massacre. Four against one wasn't even close to being a fight, certainly not a fair one. The kid he'd stepped in to assist was a Traveller named Tyson Sheedy, and - as if to highlight the foolishness of intervention - he'd not been in the least bit grateful to Darragh. Worse, it had cost Darragh the last of his remission and brought him here to Portlaoise, the most heavily guarded prison in Europe.

He'd arrived with a clutch of other prisoners: some were transfers like him, others newly sentenced. He'd suffered the indignity of admission, which included a full body search, and then spent a week in solitary confinement, while the prison authorities decided where to place him.

A week of breakfast in his cell, an hour in the morning to use the gym on his own, back to his cell for a time, then out into a yard measuring 64 paces by 18 paces, more solitary time in the tiny cell, lunch, boredom, half an hour in the poolroom before dinner and then a long night waiting for the morning to come and the same routine to be repeated.

After more than a week of pondering the question, the Warden had ordered Darragh placed in the general population. He was - in this realm, at least - no better or worse than any other man convicted of kidnapping and conspiracy to murder. There was nothing about him that warranted special consideration. Far from it. His refusal to accept responsibility for his crimes was seen as proof of his recidivist nature.

Portlaoise wasn't a stop on the way to somewhere more suitable. This was where they believed he belonged. Darragh Aquitania was a lost cause. There was no point in trying to rehabilitate someone who refused to take responsibility for his actions.

Finally, eight days after he arrived, they'd let him out into the yard on this cold, misty morning to discover his new home.

Darragh stopped and looked around, not so much at the other prisoners milling about in their own private groups, but at the oppressive razor wire circling the narrow yard. For a fleeting moment of time, he found himself almost overwhelmed by the pervasive gloom that seemed to seep from the very walls of this grim and unappealing place.

Still, it was better than solitary confinement in the Alcatraz wing - a name whose significance was known to him only because he had his brother's memories to call upon.

Rónán had no memories of ever being in prison, however; for that, Darragh needed to rely on his own sources. The information he gleaned about this place was mostly from the guards and inmates of St Patrick's Institution for Juveniles, where he'd been previously. Portlaoise - so they'd been quick to inform him when they heard about his imminent transfer - could accommodate nearly four hundred prisoners. It usually housed well below that number, he was somewhat relieved to discover, although in the end it probably made little difference to the degree of danger for Darragh.

After the first half-dozen or so, he figured, *whether it's one hundred or four hundred stir-crazy, gang-affiliated murderers, terrorists, child molesters and rapists looking for a fight doesn't really matter.*

There was a company of Irish Defence Forces' soldiers armed with assault rifles and anti-aircraft machine guns guarding the inmates, his remarkably well-informed cellmates at St Patrick's informed him, making it one of the most secure prisons in Europe. That would make getting him out somewhat problematic for Rónán - even after three years stranded in this realm, Darragh had not lost hope that any day now, his brother would appear, escape plan well in hand, and they could both return to the reality where they belonged.

Darragh did not doubt Rónán would come for him and would figure out how to get past the high walls, the razor wire, the cameras, sensors, the air exclusion zone and the acres of tank traps around the perimeter.

"Well, looky what we have here."

Darragh forced himself not to glance in the direction of the man who'd spoken, aware that appearing concerned or vulnerable was fatal in such a place. He focused on looking up, as if examining the exercise yard walls for a possible escape route and not in the least bit interested or bothered by the small group of men closing in on him.

"Face that pretty is just askin' to be messed up," another man laughed as they moved nearer.

"You can mess him up, Liam," somebody else joked, "but you won't be looking at his face!"

"You're the nut job they just transferred from St Paddy's, aren't you?"

The man who posed the question was blocking Darragh's way. There was no possible chance of avoiding him or the question. Darragh slowly and quite deliberately met the man's eyes. He was a slender, dark-haired fellow with a swastika tattooed on the left side of his neck, an intricate Celtic cross on the other side, intertwined with a four-leaf clover with the initials IRA below the cross on the other - a political conundrum he doubted the man was astute enough to appreciate. Behind Liam stood another three men, all similarly marked, all equally threatening.

Darragh knew his survival might depend on quickly acquiring membership of a prison gang, and that nothing announced which gang one belonged to louder than an illegally-acquired prison tattoo designed to inspire fear and respect in anyone who saw it. Darragh wished he'd known about that before being sent to St Patrick's three years ago and, in hindsight, perhaps a few well-chosen gang emblems tattooed somewhere obvious before he left the juvenile facility might have made life a lot safer here in Portlaoise.

Or maybe not. Being caught wearing a gang's emblem fraudulently could just as easily get you killed.

"I suppose I must be," he replied as inoffensively as possible, wondering what had happened to the guards. It wouldn't do to look around for help. That was a sign of weakness. A man who knew how to survive in this place had eyes in the back of his head.

"I hear you've a liking for them gypsy boys," Liam said, as one of the others moved around behind him, effectively blocking him in and, more importantly, blocking the guards' view of what they were doing.

What? Are they going to try to rape me out here in the middle of the yard?

"You a gyppo, too, pretty boy?"

That was a loaded question. Darragh had no ethnic ties to the Travellers. His only connection to them was foolishly stepping in to help one a couple of weeks ago in another prison. For a moment, he debated claiming he was a gyppo and proud of it. But he had not an ounce of Romany blood in him and the Travellers knew it. Even if there were gypsies here who had heard about the incident at St Patrick's and appreciated his interference on behalf of one of their number, there was a vast gulf between gratitude and returning the favor.

"No."

The man behind him was so close now that Darragh could feel his warm moist breath on his neck.

"What are you then?" the man named Liam asked, examining Darragh closely for any tattoos that might identify his allegiance. For a fleeting moment, Darragh wished he still had the triskalion tattoo of the Undivided on the palm of his hand. He could have invented his own gang.

"Fresh meat," the big man on the left announced, leering at Darragh with a broken-toothed smile.

Two large hands gripped Darragh by the shoulders as he was jerked backward, almost losing his footing. Liam moved even closer. He could feel the hard-muscled bodies of the inmates pressed against his, had nowhere to go and no way of getting out of this potentially fatal encounter. It was no secret that prisoners were stabbed, beaten or brutalized in some manner on a daily basis here. Darragh knew that if he couldn't find a way out of this in the next few moments, he would become today's statistic.

"What do you say, pretty gyppo boy?" Liam said, so close now they were sharing the same breath. "You gonna be *my* fresh meat?"

Darragh responded by bringing his knee up sharply into Liam's groin. The man dropped like a sack of wheat. Before the others had time to react, he drove his elbow backward into the solar plexus of the man holding him by the shoulders, ducking as he did so to avoid the punch thrown by the big man with the broken teeth. The punch connected with the man behind who grunted and let him go, doubled over with pain, his nose bloodied. Liam was writhing on the ground clutching his groin, swearing and screaming with pain. The broken-toothed man overbalanced with the force of his punch, but when he righted himself, he came at Darragh again, only this time, clutched in his right hand, was a short-bladed shank.

Darragh had only a split second to recognize the danger before the man was on him, holding the shank high, aiming to slash at his face or perhaps take out an eye. Still off balance himself, he stumbled backward into the arms of another prisoner. The man grabbed him and held him fast. Darragh struggled wildly to get free, but he was trapped. There was no way to avoid being slashed with the wickedly sharp sliver of metal. Everything was happening so quickly. The broken-toothed man lunged at him. Darragh fought against the man holding him, but the man had him in a crushing bear hug, trapping his arms against his body. He could see nothing but the shank coming for him, wondering if that would be the last thing he would ever see...

And then the shank went flying as another prisoner slammed into the broken-toothed man. Darragh had no idea who his rescuer was or time to thank him. He wriggled his right arm enough to grab a chunk of fleshy thing on the inside leg of the man holding him and twisted savagely. The man let go with a yell. His heart pounding, Darragh staggered clear and looked around. There were a dozen or more men surrounding him now.

Is this how it ends? I'm sorry, Rónán...

But his tormentors seemed suddenly reluctant to continue the fight as they picked themselves up, which Darragh figured meant the new spectators were a different gang to those who'd singled him out. In the background he could hear the guards running toward them to break up the fight.

The man who'd stopped the broken-toothed man from taking Darragh's eye climbed to his feet, glared at Liam's cohorts and then turned to Darragh.

He almost fainted from shock when he realized who it was who'd come to his rescue.

"Ciarán?"

Before Ciarán could answer, the guards arrived. Everyone stood back as if they were entirely innocent of anything more than standing around chatting about the weather. The shank had miraculously disappeared.

"All right, break it up," they yelled, batons in hand. "Come on ... what's going on here?"

"Donny slipped and fell, Mr Hughes," another man announced. Darragh turned to look at him and realized with shock that it was Jack O'Righin, Rónán's erstwhile friend and neighbor in this realm who was, without a doubt, back behind bars because of his involvement with Darragh and the disappearance of Hayley Boyle.

"Is that a fact?" Hughes said skeptically, as the other guards arrived to stop the fight. There must have been a dozen of them, not quite, but almost, outnumbering the prisoners gathered about. Hughes pointed to Liam, who was still writhing on the ground, tears running down his face. "What happened to that one?"

"Cramp," Jack replied with a perfectly straight face.

Hughes seemed to debate the advisability of calling Jack out in his obvious lie. He glanced at the other guards, none of whom seemed to be in the mood to provoke a confrontation. Then he nodded slowly, pointed to Darragh and asked, "This lad one of yours?"

Jack stared at Darragh thoughtfully for a moment and then nodded. "Aye. I'll keep an eye on him."

"See that you do," the guard said. "I've got plans tonight. If he gets himself killed, we'll have to stay back to fill out the paperwork. You really don't want any of us that pissed at you, O'Righin." The guard turned and found himself face to face with the man whose nose had been bloodied in the fight. "Watch where you're walking next time, bozo," Hughes said. "You keep tripping up like that you might get hurt."

Nobody said anything while the guards departed, until they were out of earshot. By then, someone had helped Liam to his feet. The man was still bent double, but the fight had gone out of him. He ignored Darragh, and looked at Jack. "Sorry, Mr O'Righin. Didn't know he was one of ours."

"That's because you're a first-class fuckwit, Liam," Jack informed him pleasantly. "Now get out of here before I decide you're pissing me off."

"Sorry, Mr O'Righin," Liam said, and he and his friends skulked away quickly without looking back, finding another place in the yard to nurse their wounds.

Darragh was astounded. Jack O'Righin was a little old man compared to these thugs, and yet he commanded their obedience as if they were schoolboys.

But that was not the biggest puzzle here. That puzzle was how Ciarán mac Connaught, Celtic warrior, Druid sorcerer and guardian of the Undivided, came to be here, in this realm, in this place...

"You okay?" Jack asked.

Darragh nodded. Other than a heart pounding so hard it felt like it might burst out of his chest, he was unharmed.

"Let's find somewhere we can talk in private, then," Ciarán said. "And I'll explain what's going on.

CHAPTER 7

An insistent knock on the door of Trása's room in the *hommaru* woke her during the night. She glanced at the incense clock as she threw back the covers and climbed off the futon. It was almost midnight. The *Youkai* who had come through the rift with her were nowhere to be found. Neither was Toyoda, her frequent *Leipreachán* companion. She wondered what mischief they were getting up to in the palace and how much she'd have to apologize for in the morning.

As she stumbled to the door, she couldn't imagine who'd be visiting at this hour and wasn't in the mood to entertain. After the events of the past day, Trása had lain awake for hours going over everything in her head, wondering if there was something she could have done. Something she *should* have done...

It had taken her hours to fall asleep. She didn't appreciate being woken again so soon.

Trása slid the door open, wishing the flimsy rice paper screen could withstand her slamming it open in order to offer an impressive demonstration of her anger.

Her visitor was Rónán. He looked haggard.

"I'm not speaking to you."

"I need your help."

"What part of *I'm not speaking to you* didn't you hear me tell you?"

Rónán cocked his head to one side, genuinely puzzled. "That is truly the most absurd question I have ever been asked."

"Really? And here I was, thinking that *'Why have you left your brother stranded in another reality all this time?'* was going to win the prize."

Rónán stared at her for a moment and then turned and walked away. Trása let out a long-suffering sigh and called, "Wait!"

He stopped and turned to look at her. Trása threw her hands up in defeat. "All right. I'll bite. What's so difficult for the great and all-powerful Renkavana that he needs my help with it?"

"Accessing Delphine's memories."

That surprised Trása. She'd thought, given the way he was talking earlier, the subject was closed and would not be allowed to be opened again for discussion. She glanced up and down the wide, rattan-matted hall, lit only by the evenly-spaced gilded lamps, to see if anybody might have overheard him, but they were alone.

Trása debated the issue for a moment. She wasn't speaking to him, after all.

"Come in, then," she said, finally. "We probably shouldn't discuss this out here."

Rónán didn't say anything, but he walked back and stepped across the threshold before stopping to look around the room. Trása wondered what he thought of the intricate woodcarvings on the furniture or the gold leaf, silk-screened walls, or the beautifully painted sliding doors. Perhaps he wasn't impressed. He'd been here for three years now and, even in the other realm where he'd been abandoned, he'd grown up amidst substantial wealth, after all. Perhaps he barely noticed the beauty of this place.

He waved his hand, lighting the lamps with magic as casually as Darragh might have done in Sí an Bhrú. Then he turned to her as she slid the door shut and said in English, "Is there anybody about who can overhear us?"

That was always a problem in a society where lacquered rice paper was considered a building material. And it explained why he was speaking a language only a few people in this reality understood.

"I don't think so. Why?"

"Because I have to ask you something difficult."

She snorted at that. "Wow, is it so hard for you to ask for help that you don't want anybody else to know about it?"

He glared at her and said nothing.

She sighed again - something she seemed to do a lot around Rónán - and moved away from the door. "I'm sorry. You truly do bring out the worst in me, Rónán. What do you want?"

"Help to go into Delphine's memories."

"You don't need my help. You put the walls up in your mind to keep the memories out. You can take them down anytime you want. Why do you need me?"

"Because I'm afraid."

Trása's anger withered in the face of his simple admission. She'd been imagining all sorts of nefarious reasons for Rónán's inaction. Fear hadn't even been on her list.

"Afraid of what?"

He shrugged and sat down on the edge of the futon, hands clasped together, his head hanging down. "Afraid I'll go mad, or do something dangerous. Afraid of what they'll do to me. Afraid they'll make me like her."

"That's absurd," she said, crossing her legs to sit in front of him on the floor. "You won't become her. You didn't become Darragh when you shared his memories, did you?"

He lifted his head to look at her in surprise. "Didn't I? You're the one who's always telling me how like Darragh I am."

"That's because you're identical twins, idiot, not because of the *Comhroinn* you shared with him."

He shook his head. Trása wasn't sure why. "I never told you what happened when we went back to Pete and Logan's true realm, did I?"

"It was a dead world. Pete said there was nothing left alive there. He didn't know why."

"I tried to find out why."

Suddenly, Trása thought she understood. "You accessed Delphine's memories?"

He shook his head. "I *became* Delphine. I tried to kill Pete and Logan. I couldn't control it, Trása.

She's dead, for God's sake and she took me over like she'd found another body to inhabit."

"That's why Pete and Logan are so insistent that you don't try again?"

"You can't blame them."

"But... Rónán, that was three years ago. You've learned so much since then."

"But what if I haven't learned enough?"

"Then Pete and Logan will probably kill you," she said, only half joking.

"I can feel her, you know... Delphine pushing against my mind... trying to break out. And I'm not an idiot, Trása. I do know what a gold mine of intelligence I've got tucked away inside my head. It's just -"

"You don't want to turn into an evil, murderous, child-stealing bitch with a lingering affection for Pete and Logan?" she finished for him.

Rónán managed a thin smile in response. "If it were only that, I'd have done this a couple of years ago."

"Then what's stopping you?" she asked, some of her frustration with him leaking into her voice. "We've been stuck here for three years, Rónán. You've been studying everything you can get your hands on. You've pretty much mastered everything this realm has to offer, including that crazy ninja kuji-in stuff. What's your problem?"

Rónán was silent for a time before he answered. When he did finally speak, what he said took Trása completely by surprise.

"I have nightmares."

"Nightmares?"

"Actually, it's only one nightmare that repeats itself over and over."

"Nightmares about what?" she asked, a little impatiently. Rónán seemed to be wallowing in a fair bit of maudlin self-pity. Trása couldn't figure out why and was in no mood to indulge him. Somewhere out there, Teagan was alone and frightened, a prisoner of the *Matrarchaí*, and she needed their help. The gods alone knew what had become of Darragh and Sorcha these past few years. Or Hayley - not that Trása really gave a fig about what happened to Hayley Boyle. But Rónán certainly didn't have time to feel sorry for himself.

"I dream about murdering babies." Trása really had no idea how to answer that. "I'm not sure whose children they are," Rónán continued, apparently content that she was listening. She didn't need to comment, "but in my dream I kill them in their cradle. I *think* they're Darragh's kids. He's in the dream, too, trying to talk me out of doing it."

"Talk you out of it?" she asked. "Not fight you or wrestle the weapon from your hands? Just calmly discuss why you shouldn't murder his babies?"

He shrugged. "In my dream, Darragh seems to know it has to be done."

"Do you think he's afraid they might be Empress twins?" She was intrigued now, in spite of herself. Besides, she was unable to imagine any other circumstance - even in his brother's imagination - where Darragh would agree to something so heinous. "Maybe you're trying to kill them in your dream so they won't become tools of the *Matrarchaí*?"

He nodded. "I realize that now, but here's the kicker. I've been having those dreams since I was twelve or thirteen. Darragh had them, too."

This was very interesting, but hardly helpful. "What does any of this have to do with why you won't access Delphine's memories, or us finding a way to rescue Teagan?"

"Since I locked away Delphine's memories, the nightmares have stopped."

Trása was silent for a moment as she let that sink in.

"You selfish prick," she said finally, disgusted at him. "You've let everyone rot here in this realm, you've left your brother stranded in another... all because you don't want your sleep disturbed. You're unbelievable!"

Rónán glared at her, clearly annoyed by her anger. He stood up, shaking his head. "I knew you wouldn't be any help."

"You got that much right."

"Well, I'm sorry I disturbed your sleep," he said, heading for the door. "I'll not burden you again with my trivial, selfish problems."

Trása didn't bother to respond. She was glad to be rid of him. *How could anybody do such a thing? How could he be so self-absorbed, so callous, so –*

She jumped to her feet, staring at him in shock, as it suddenly occurred to her exactly what he was trying to tell her. "Oh, my God, it's the Sight! You're having a *true* dream, aren't you?"

He stopped, his hand on the door latch with his back to her. "Don't worry about it, Trása. It's not your problem."

In three strides she was across the room. Grabbing him by the arm she turned him around to face her. "You're afraid if you delve into Delphine's memories you'll change something and the dream will come back. And if it's a *true* dream then it has to happen someday."

"Selfish of me to fear that, I know," he said, shaking off her grasp. "I'll be sure to be more thoughtful in the future."

"Get over it, Rónán. I was just ..." She threw her hands up. This was much bigger than she imagined and she really didn't want to fight with Rónán. Quite the opposite, in fact. He was just so... so... She sighed, yet again. "Okay, I'm sorry. I shouldn't have said you were being selfish. I didn't understand." "You meant it, though."

"Only because I wasn't thinking things through. You know me. I start yelling first, and then ask questions later. I said I was sorry."

He seemed unconvinced by her remorse.

"*Please.*"

Rónán studied her in the dim light, as if debating how much he could trust her, and then he shrugged. "Do you *really* understand, Trása? Because I do want to help Teagan, I truly do. And it's eating me up that I can't go back for Darragh, but do you really appreciate the risk?"

She nodded. "If you do anything to change the status quo, then the dream will come back and then one day you really will have to kill Darragh's children."

"It's more than that," he confessed. "You see, if that nightmare ever comes true and if I don't have the balls to do it, something even worse will happen, because if there is one thing about that dream that rings loud and clear, it's that a lot more people will die if I stay my hand."

Trása was silent for a moment as she found herself forced to reassess everything she had thought about Rónán and what fuelled his inaction these past three years.

"How can I help?" she asked in the end. Nothing else really mattered.

"Tell me how to get into Delphine's memories without going mad. Without her taking me over. And without making that dream come back."

"Maybe it's not her memories being locked away," Trása said, as it occurred to her that Rónán's fear, while legitimate, might be misplaced. "What if it was Delphine's death that caused the dreams to stop, not the *Comhroinn* or anything she might have known?"

"How does that work?"

"Well... maybe she was going to do something in the future that meant one day those children would be born and you killed her, which stopped it from happening? If that's the case, it doesn't matter what she knew, because you're not her, so you can't do the same thing in the same way and cause the problem."

Rónán frowned. "That almost makes sense. But what could she do?"

"The *Matrarchaí* are in the business of making babies, Rónán. She probably had some floozy lined up for Darragh to impregnate-"

"She did," Rónán cut in. "Brydie."

"Who is Brydie?"

"The girl the *Matrarchaí* threw at him. I have Darragh's memories too, remember. There was a girl back in Sí an Bhrú, her name was Brydie and she was sleeping with Darragh just before I arrived. Queen Álmhath introduced them at the shindig where they announced they were replacing the Undivided."

Trása pushed aside a fleeting stab of jealousy to concentrate on the more immediate issue of Rónán's dream. "That was more than three years ago, Rónán."

"I know, but..."

"But nothing ... Don't you see? That must be why the dreams have stopped. If this Brydie girl had been pregnant when you and Darragh left our realm, she'd have had the babies long ago and you'd still be dreaming of murdering them."

"So you think she never got pregnant?"

"Maybe she did. Maybe she had a baby but didn't have twins. Maybe when they were born the babies weren't what the *Matrarchaí* were after, so there's no need for you or anyone else to kill them, and nothing for you to See."

"So without Delphine around," Rónán asked, looking relieved, "to introduce me or Darragh to the right girl to complete their plans to breed more Empress twins, there're no twins for me to dream of killing? And none in the future."

Trása nodded. "There you go! Nothing to worry about. Now will you drop the walls around the information in that crazy mixed-up head of yours and find out where they've taken Teagan?"

"I might still go mad, Trása," he warned, still looking uncertain. "Don't worry about it, Rónán. Trust me, nobody will notice any difference to the way you are now."

"Cute," he said, pulling a face at her. "Do you have any useful suggestions as to how I do this without going mad? Even if nobody notices?"

She thought about it for a moment and then nodded. "We need the Pool of Tranquillity."

"Where is that? *What* is that?"

"It's a special place back in *Tír Na nÓg*," she said, thinking that was the safest place to be for such a potentially catastrophic situation. She decided not to mention it might be catastrophic to him, though... no need for worry. "Let's do this somewhere there is plenty of magic and nothing breakable. Besides, if we do it in *Tír Na nÓg* and you do lose your mind completely, there are plenty of lesser *Youkai* there to help me contain you."

"Are you trying to make me feel better or worse?"

She smiled briefly, realizing that - jokes aside - she really would be much more at ease doing this in a place where she had some measure of control.

And where Pete and Logan weren't around.

After all, Rónán was about to access all the memories of their dead foster mother after expressly promising them he wouldn't do anything of the kind. Better to do this away from the Doherty twins and before they got wind of it happening.

"How long before they can repair the *rifuto* circle, do you think, so we can get out of here?"

Rónán reached out and pulled her to him, slipping his arms around her waist and forcing her face so close to his, she could feel his warm breath on her lips.

Dear God, is he going to kiss me? Now?

As if he guessed the direction of her thoughts, he suddenly grinned at her. "I don't need a rift."

"Whoa!" she cried, as she realized what he intended. "Wait a min-"

She never got a chance to finish the sentence as Rónán's magic surged and he tightened his arms around her, and the beautiful guest suite in the Imperial Edo Palace in Chucho vanished to be replaced by the impossibly tall trees and eternal twilight of *Tír Na nÓg* on the other side of the world.

CHAPTER 8

Teagan thought it odd that she wasn't more frightened.

She didn't remember much about coming through the rift. Just waking to find someone in her room, her sister Isleen screaming, and then the oblivion of the *Brionglóid Gorm*, the magical blue powder that induced instant unconsciousness.

Sometime later, she awoke in this magic-less realm with a pounding headache in a room that seemed to float high above a sea of light.

The room she was confined to seemed both strange and familiar at the same time. The bed was deliciously comfortable, with crisp white linen and a down-filled quilt so soft and fluffy it was like being wrapped in a cloud. There was a small table and chair, and another comfortable padded chair by the window, all of unfamiliar design and covered in unfamiliar fabrics. But that was where any familiarity stopped.

There was an odd box-like instrument with glowing numbers, whose function she could not fathom, on the side table. The light in this room came from small holes in the ceiling, which came on at the flick of a switch. There was also a small room near the perpetually locked door that contained the largest and most perfect mirror Teagan had ever laid eyes on, a deep bath with hot water anytime she wanted and a waterfall that came out of the ceiling above it. There was a strange device for relieving herself that flushed away her bodily wastes with drinking water.

Her captors were kind but uncommunicative. They gave her something for the headache and having assured themselves that she was unharmed and not fretting too much, they left her alone in this room that seemed to hover above a light ocean, telling her nothing about where she was or why they had brought her here.

The glass on the huge window was smooth and flawless. It was cool against her forehead as she looked down, trying to guess how far she was above ground. It was impossible to say, but the vista that lay before her was a sight to behold. There were so many other tall buildings. Below her, many of the lights moved in orderly ribbons weaving between the static lights, while others turned red, then orange then green, over and over in an endless cycle. Teagan couldn't image what was going on down there on the ground. She only knew one thing for certain - this was not her reality.

It was, in all likelihood, the realm without magic where Renkavana and Pete and Logan Doherty came from.

Her excitement at the prospect of seeing their world compensated more than adequately - at least for the time being - for the loss of her sister.

She turned at the sound of the door opening. This time it wasn't one of her silent captors come to bring her food or water. It was an attractive and disturbingly familiar woman dressed in a grey tweed jacket and a matching skirt that stopped - shockingly - just above her knees, revealing shapely legs encased in stockings so sheer they appeared to be painted on. She was wearing shoes with high heels that tapered to a narrow point, which looked impossible to walk on, and had her dark hair pulled into a sleek chignon. Teagan was sure she'd seen her before, but she couldn't remember where.

The woman closed the door behind her and leaned on it for a moment, studying Teagan with interest.

"Do I know you?"

Her visitor pushed off the door and walked into the room. She seemed amused. "So much for the famed Japanese grace and manners I've heard so much about. Are you always so forthright?"

"Only after being kidnapped."

The woman smiled. "My, aren't you a feisty little thing?" She took a seat on the edge of the bed and crossed her legs, content to keep some distance between them.

You don't know the half of it, lady. Teagan decided it was about time to take charge of her fate.

She stepped away from the window and squared her shoulders, drawing herself up to her full height. "I am Kōgō Heika Teagan, Empress of the Universe. You should address me as Heika."

The woman smiled. "And you may call me Mother."

"You're not my mother."

"It is a title of respect, Heika, not a bid for your affection. Is there anything you need?"

"You could send me home."

"Other than that."

"Where's my sister?"

"Back in your realm."

"Is she unharmed?"

"I couldn't say," Mother said with a shrug. "Whoever exploded the rift on the other side, did it without any thought for the danger to the people in or around the rift when it collapsed. I lost quite a few good people in that explosion, either killed or trapped in your realm."

Teagan was shocked. "Someone exploded the rift? How is that possible?"

"I was rather hoping you might tell me. Even among Undivided, that sort of power is unheard of. I know it wasn't you or your sister, and as your father and uncle are long dead and there are no *Tuatha Dé Danann* in your realm any longer. So that leaves whoever it was who also killed my sister three years ago."

That was news to Teagan, and it explained why this woman looked so familiar. "Lady Delphine was your sister?"

Mother nodded. "My *eileféin* might be a better description, so if the purpose of killing Delphine was to bring her twin down with her - and the *Matrarchaí* along with her - then it was a foolish and ultimately futile plan."

So I'm definitely a prisoner of the Matrarchaí, Teagan thought, less bothered by that prospect than she thought she ought to be. And they seemed to be attributing far more planning and forethought to a three-year-old incident that was, in the end, little more than a lucky accident, although it was doubtful Delphine would have considered it lucky, given the outcome.

"I don't think Renkavana meant to kill Delphine," Teagan said, as it occurred to her that this kidnapping might be an act of vengeance, rather than a strategic move in a much bigger game, which did not augur well for her future.

But she was still alive, so they obviously had a use for her. She just had to hope it didn't involve sending her back home a finger at a time in order to force Delphine's killer to surrender.

"Is that who killed her? Ren Kavanaugh?" The woman pronounced his name with a subtle change of inflection that Teagan found quite curious. It made him sound like a completely different person.

"I thought you knew... oh, well, of course you didn't know. Nobody from the *Matrarchaí* has come through the rift since then."

"Do you know Ren well?"

"Well enough," Teagan said, realizing her knowledge of him might be leverage in whatever game the *Matrarchaí* was playing. She had something they wanted. Excellent.

And they certainly had something Teagan wanted. "I knew Delphine, too."

Mother nodded. "I know. My sister described you and Isleen to me. She said that of the two of you, Teagan was the one who showed the most promise."

Teagan stood a little straighter, preening under the unexpected praise. "Did she really?"

Mother smiled. "You seem surprised."

"Back home I'm considered the troublemaker."

"Are you?"

Teagan pondered the question for a moment. She was not prone to self-reflection, so she'd not really given the matter much thought, other than to rail against the unfairness of always being the one in trouble.

It hadn't been like that before Renkavana and Trása and Pete and Logan came along. Until then, her mother, Wakiko, had been their meek, compliant servant, not their sovereign. The world had trembled at the mention of her name before then - well, also Isleen's, but mostly hers, she liked to believe.

These days they smiled indulgently at her tantrums and treated her like a little girl. They deferred the important decisions to her mother. They sometimes didn't bother to ask Teagan's opinion at all.

Delphine had shared the *Comhroinn* with her and Isleen when they were seven years old and then locked down the secrets of their power until they were old enough to deal with the responsibility.

Teagan was thirteen now. She was old enough.

But Renkavana refused to let it happen. Worse, as he studied and learned the ways of the *ori mahou* and the kuji-in, he'd grown jealous of the Empresses' power - or so Teagan believed. He hadn't helped them discover their knowledge. He'd locked the information down even tighter, until it would take a magician of enormous power to break through the barrier.

Mother, Teagan realized, a sly smile creeping across her face, was one such magician. This was Delphine's *eileféin*. She was of the Undivided line. She could do anything Lady Delphine could do. Except, this world had no magic. Teagan couldn't feel any at all. So she probably couldn't do much of anything here.

Still, it wouldn't hurt to play along for a while and see what they had in mind for her. "I'm the one who still believes we are best aligned with the *Matrarchaí*," she said. "I'm the one who wanted the destiny Lady Delphine promised me."

Mother studied her, perhaps debating her sincerity. "And what of your sister?"

"She is weak-minded," Teagan said, the first time she'd ever dared voice such a thought out loud. It was oddly liberating to be able to articulate the unspeakable and not be held in contempt or suspicion for her views. "She's glad Renkavana locked away the information Lady Delphine shared with us."

"And you're not?"

"I want the power Lady Delphine promised."

Mother's smiled widened, but it was a knowing, satisfied sort of smile, rather than one of amusement. "Then we will have to see that you get it."

That cheered Teagan considerably, but there were still a few things she wanted cleared up. "This world has no magic," she said. "How did you open a rift from here into my realm?"

"This realm is not completely denuded," Mother assured her. "There is an Enchanted Sphere, a point where the remaining magic in a denuded realm seems to settle until it's completely obliterated - a circumstance I fear will come sooner rather than later in this realm."

"Is that why we're in a tower?"

Mother seemed amused by her question. "They call them skyscrapers here, but yes, a few floors above us is the Enchanted Sphere. The city below us is called Taipei."

The city's name meant nothing to Teagan, and she didn't really care. She had other questions that were far more important to her. "Are you going back for Isleen?"

"Did you want us to?"

Teagan didn't even have to think about it. "No."

"You won't be lonely without her?"

She shook her head. "I'm glad to be free of her."

"Aren't you worried about her fate?"

"Nothing will happen to my sister," Teagan said with complete certainty and more than a little contempt. "They are too squeamish in my realm to harm her, even knowing I am probably a prisoner of the *Matrarchaí*."

"That seems harsh, Teagan. Are you sure?"

Teagan nodded. "I'm sure."

Mother rose to her feet. "Is there anything else we can get you?" Apparently this interview was over.

"I want you to unlock Lady Delphine's memories in my mind."

Mother nodded. "All in good time, cherie. First, you have to do something for me."

"What do you want?"

"Everything you know about the man who killed my sister," Mother said in a quiet voice that chilled Teagan to her core. "When I come back you can tell me what you know, and if you're a really good girl I might even let you help me avenge her someday."

CHAPTER 9

There was no special ceremony or spell involved in accessing the memories Ren had acquired when he inadvertently killed Delphine of the *Matrarchaí*. He'd been holding her memories back by sheer force of will. All he had to do, in theory, was let go and open his mind.

Easier said than done.

Although it irked Ren to admit it, Trása was right. If he was going to do this, then it had to be here, where he had some hope of drawing on the rich magic of this place to soothe his pain. He needed a balm for his scorched and tormented soul.

It *was* good to be back in this reality's version of *Tír Na nÓg*, his estrangement from Trása having kept him away these past few years.

And it was only here that Trása might have some hope of restraining him, if opening himself to Delphine's memories overwhelmed him again. He was afraid Delphine's desire to eradicate all *Youkai* from this realm might overtake him before he could wrestle it back from the forefront of his mind.

But he was reluctant to tell Trása how right she was... she took far too much delight in being right. Not that he had the opportunity, because the moment they appeared in *Tír Na nÓg* they were swamped by scores of lesser *Youkai* clamoring for her attention.

The lesser *Youkai* - those pixies, sprites, *Leipreachán*, brownies and scores of other elementals left behind after the purges - had gone into hiding when the *Tuatha Dé Danann* and their cousins had been driven from this realm. Until he and Trása appeared - quite by accident - they'd cowered in the dark and shadowy places, waiting for someone to save them from the *Matrarchaí*.

It was impossible to convince the lesser *Youkai* that Trása was here for any other reason than to restore the greater *Youkai* to this reality. Ren was almost bowled over by the swarm of excited pixies, beside themselves at the prospect of company, as soon as they waned into *Tír Na nÓg*.

"You know, you really should explain to these guys that you're not the messiah," he said, as he tried to push the swarm away.

"I tell them all the time," Trása said as she stepped out of his embrace and almost vanished in a cloud of chattering faerie creatures. "All right," she cried, "enough already! I can't breathe!"

"They be pests, the lot of them," a grumpy voice behind them announced. "Be off with ye!"

The swarm of elementals drew back a little as Ren turned to find the *Leipreachán*, Toyoda

Mulrayn, standing behind them, glaring at the lesser *Youkai* with disapproval. He managed to disentangle himself and smiled down at the little man, interested to note that he still wore his tiny - and quite absurd - ninja outfit.

"Hey, Toyoda," Ren said. "I thought you were back in Chucho?"

"Hey, yeself," Toyoda grumbled. "I be feeling ye waning back here. Ye make a lot magical noise when ye wane, did ye know that?"

"Actually, I didn't."

"Well, ye be able to wane like a *sídhe*, but ye be very clumsy at it. Does it be true about the attack on the palace? The *Matrarchaí* be back?"

At his question the swarm of Faerie creatures vanished with a squeal of fright.

Ren glanced around, shaking his head in amazement. "There's a way to clear a room in a hurry."

"Do it be true?" Toyoda demanded. "Do the *Matrarchaí* be back?"

"It was them who raided the Imperial Palace," Trása confirmed. "They took Teagan."

Toyoda frowned. "Then what ye be doin' here? Why ye not be going after her?"

"Rónán needs to access Delphine's memories to find out where they took her," Trása explained.

The *Leipreachán* nodded. "And ye've brought him back here to do it. That be a wise thing."

"I'm so glad you approve," Ren said, knowing his sarcasm would be lost on Toyoda. The *Leipreachán* glared at him for a moment longer and then vanished. Ren shook his head at the fickle nature of the *Leipreachán* and turned to Trása. "Shall we get on with it?"

Trása shook her head. "Not here. We need to go to the pool."

"The Pool of Tranquillity, right?"

"Come with me," she said. "I'll show you."

The Pool of Tranquillity turned out to be exactly that: a pool of clear, still water nestled in the forest, but some distance from the main area of trees where the creatures of this enchanted place resided. A small waterfall trickled into the pool on the other side, down a pile of mossy rocks some thirty feet away, and a faint wisp of steam was rising from the water.

"It's a hot spring," Ren said in surprise, wishing he'd known where to find this place sooner. It looked delightful.

"It's not really. The heat doesn't come from underground," Trása told him, as she began to undress. "It comes from magic."

That information didn't really register. He was too distracted by the fact that Trása was undressing. "What are you doing?"

"I'm coming in with you. The magic in that pool is intense. It can drain your mind so completely you forget why you're there," she said, with her shirt pulled half over her head. She took it off, exposing two quite perfect breasts, tossed it on the ground and put her hands on her hips. "Oh my God, Rónán, you're blushing."

"I am not," he lied, even as he felt his face burning. "It's the heat from the pool. Why are we doing this in water?"

"Not just any water," she said, stepping out of her skirt and undergarments without a glimmer of embarrassment. "The water in the Pool of Tranquillity is so magical it will make your head spin."

Ren truly didn't understand her logic. "Wouldn't it make more sense to limit the magic I can use while I access the memories of a woman with magical power who is bent on destroying the Faerie?"

Trása shook her head. "That's not the problem. You're not going to turn into Delphine again, Rónán," she said, sounding a little impatient. "Sharing someone's memories in the *Comhroinn* doesn't give you their moral code or their opinions, although you might understand them better."

"It didn't feel like that the last time."

"That's because you weren't ready for it. This time it will be better. You know more. You have better control..."

"But ... I can hear the 'but' in there."

She shrugged. "The problem is that you've built a barrier out of solid rock in your head against Delphine - not unlike the rest of your head, I suspect. Anyway, there are only two ways to break a mental wall like that down: bust through it with the equivalent of a magical sledgehammer and break something in the process - like your mind, for instance. Or you can let it dissolve gently, so you can digest the memories a bit at a time and not go insane, or let her take you over."

Ren really wasn't sure exactly when his world had turned on its ear to such an extent that Trása was now the sensible one. And she was making sense, even standing there without a stitch of clothing.

God, she is so perfect...

"Hey! Eyes up here," she said, snapping her fingers in front of his face.

"Sorry, I was just thinking -"

"Sure you were. Get your gear off. Unless you're planning to do this fully clothed."

Ren had to resist turning his back to her as he started taking his shirt off. It proved unnecessary, in any case, as by the time his clothes were lying on the ground beside the pool, Trása had dived in. He followed her as soon as he was naked, hoping Trása would assume it meant he was eager to get this done and not that he was seeking the illusion of privacy the clear warm water offered.

Trása smiled as he surfaced next to her, his skin tingling from the magical water. She was right. The Pool of Tranquillity was so suffused with magic it made him dizzy.

And more than a little relaxed. It was if the magical water had instantly robbed him of any cares, or any inhibitions. The water tasted sweet on his lips, the temperature as soothing as a deliciously warm bath. Although he could see the bottom of the pool, his feet couldn't touch it.

Trása swam up to him. "Feels amazing, doesn't it?"

Ren nodded, pushing his wet hair back out of his eyes as he trod water to stay afloat. "This place is insane."

Trása smiled. "I can't believe you're supposed to be almost pure *Tuatha Dé Danann*."

"Why not?"

"You're such a tightly-wound prude for one thing."

Any other time he might have objected to her accusation. But not here. Not in this magical pool of bliss. He just smiled. "So... I'm a tightly-wound prude," he said, rolling onto his back to stare up at the twilight sky. He had no notion of the time in the real world and didn't care a jot about it, either. "Then you're a shameless hussy."

"Nobody says hussy, anymore," she said with a soft laugh. "Why did you go away?"

"You weren't speaking to me."

"Don't you ever want to kiss me?"

That is a very good question, Ren thought, not in the least bit alarmed by it while immersed in this strange and delightful pool. He rolled over to face her. She was so beautiful. "You belong to Darragh."

Out of this mellow haven, Trása might have slapped him for suggesting she belonged to anyone. But here, where extremes of emotion were leached away by the magical waters of the Pool of Tranquillity, she seemed merely amused by the idea. "Darragh hates me."

Ren smiled at that. "As the keeper of my brother's memories, I can assure you that is not the case."

"He didn't stick up for me when they sent me away."

"He was overruled by Amergin. Your father."

"He slept with Brydie."

"That doesn't mean he hates you, Trása, just that..."

"I wasn't there?" There was no anger or hurt in her question. It sounded like idle curiosity.

Ren shrugged. "I suppose."

"So why don't you kiss me now?"

"We came here to do something."

"What?"

"I'm not sure," Ren said, realizing he'd forgotten the reason. Maybe it was the water. Maybe it was Trása being so close. So naked...

"Delphine," Trása said as she swam so near that Ren could feel the heat of her body even through the warm waters of the pool. "It had something to do with Delphine."

Ren kissed her then, sliding his arms around her, pulling her slick, firm body against his, losing himself in the bliss of her soft mouth and the taste of the sweet, magical water. If there was a reason he was here, it must be this, he thought. It was too perfect, too delicious for it not to be fated.

Trása broke the kiss and pushed him away with a look of regret. "Delphine's memories, remember?"

She was right. It wounded him a little to realize he'd been so lost in their embrace he couldn't remember his own name, and yet she'd been able to recall why they were here.

"Delphine," he said, a little vaguely. "Who is she, again?"

Trása smiled, splashing him to wake him out of his torpor. "She's the evil *Matrarchaí* bitch whose memories you're too scared to look into."

"Oh," he said, wiping the water from his eyes, "that Delphine. Do we have to do it now?" *Kiss me again.*

"After you've done what you came here to do," she promised, which made Ren realize he must have said it out loud. "Now close your eyes."

"Why?"

"You need to concentrate."

"Will it hurt?"

"Not much."

Ren nodded. He remembered now. *Teagan's been kidnapped. Darragh is missing. Delphine knows the way home.*

He closed his eyes, felt Trása swim up behind him. Ren leaned back into her arms, the warm magical water lapping at his chin. *I can do this.* He *had* to do this. Lives depended on it.

The magical water had all but dissolved his fears. He took a deep breath and turned his attention inward.

Rin for strength of mind and body.

Hei to focus psychic power.

Toh to balance the solid and liquid states...

Ren couldn't be bothered remembering the rest. He surrendered to the magic instead and for the first time in three years, since he'd tried to kill Logan and Pete on a snowbound beach in Hawaii, he faced the walls he'd built around Delphine's knowledge in his mind and let them come gently tumbling down.

CHAPTER 10

Brydie could no longer recall how long she had been trapped in her amethyst prison. There was nothing to mark the days, here inside this enchanted jewel. She couldn't count the hours until her next meal, because she was never hungry. She couldn't etch the wall with a tally of the days because the walls were hard, smooth, crystalline and impervious to any mark, even had she owned a tool with which to scrape or write on them.

Besides, what was there to tally? Her days blurred into one another. She wanted nothing. Needed nothing.

And the solitude was driving her insane.

Brydie couldn't remember the last time she had spoken to a living, breathing being. Not even a magical one.

At first, when he'd trapped her inside this jewel in order to coerce a confession from her about what Darragh of the Undivided was up to, the djinni, Jamaspa, had visited her often and dogged her with questions she couldn't answer. She longed for those days now, for all that Jamaspa was a poor conversationalist. Brydie ached to speak to someone other than herself. But she hadn't seen Jamaspa for so long, she reasoned he'd either forgotten about her, or lost track of her completely.

The latter was probably more likely. Anwen's plan to hide the jewel in plain sight by setting it into her bridal necklace had succeeded beyond the girl's wildest dreams. Jamaspa couldn't find the jewel, which meant he couldn't release Brydie from the spell that trapped her inside it. Ever.

She was entombed here, like a lost princess in an elaborate bard's tale, waiting for a handsome prince to rescue her.

Brydie didn't care if he was handsome. Any prince would do. He didn't even have to be a prince. The village idiot would suffice. Anyone with a pulse would be fine, if it meant escaping her facetted cell and breathing real air again.

But there were no princes on their way to save her.

No help. No rescue. No hope.

A movement in the room outside her jeweled prison caught her eye, breaking her maudlin train of thought. Someone was in Anwen's room, she realized.

She pressed her face against the cool crystal and tried to make out who dared sneak into the room of the Queen of the Celts' daughter-in-law in the dead of night. Brydie couldn't image how the intruder had sneaked past the many guards in Temair or how they'd managed to open the creaking door to

Anwen's chamber without waking half the residents of the keep.

The figure moved smoothly and silently, heading for the bed. Brydie wanted to cry out, to warn Anwen someone was in her chamber, although why she felt the need to alert her, she wasn't sure. Brydie owed Anwen no favors, didn't like her, knew she was a traitor to the Celts, and a spy for a society of evil *Matrarchaí* from another realm who were bent on manipulating the bloodlines of the Undivided in this realm for their own nefarious purposes.

And yet she pounded uselessly on the jeweled walls of her prison to warn the sleeping young woman that danger approached.

The figure stepped closer. Brydie couldn't make out his features but it was definitely a man. He was dressed in black from head to foot. His flesh was completely hidden by his black clothing, except for a small slit around the eyes and his hands. Although he clung stealthily to the shadows, he couldn't avoid the sliver of moonlight coming from the high window beside the bed. He stepped carefully and noiselessly. Brydie watched him with growing trepidation, unable to fathom why his boots apparently had a slit in between the big toe and the second toe. Before she could puzzle out the reason for anything so odd, the figure reached the side of the bed where Anwen's bridal necklace - and Brydie's jeweled cell set within it - lay discarded on the side table beside the long-cooled lamp.

It was then that Brydie realized the black-clad figure wasn't here to do Anwen harm. He was here for her, or rather Anwen's valuable necklace.

Who had the gall to commit such a crime?

Brydie wished she could make out something more than this black-clad shadow who moved as if he was a part of the night. He barely glanced at Anwen, other than to assure himself she was still asleep. A hand reached out for the necklace and even the thin moonlight vanished, albeit briefly, as the thief scooped the necklace off the table, then held it up to the light.

The movement knocked Brydie off her feet. She scrambled up in time to see the tip of a blade heading for her. She ducked and then realized the thief wasn't trying to harm her. He was trying to lever the amethyst out of the setting.

This robber, whoever he was, had no interest in the heavy gold setting or the other gems surrounding her amethyst. He was after her jewel only.

"Are you my handsome prince?" she asked, knowing he couldn't hear her. "Are you come to save me? Or are you just an opportunist with an eye for pretty baubles?"

The thief carried on as if she hadn't spoken. *He can't hear me. He doesn't even know I'm stuck in here.*

Or does he?

Brydie felt a surge of unreasonable hope. Perhaps this thief wasn't a thief at all, but an envoy sent by Jamaspa to rescue her. Perhaps he was taking the jewel and planning to deliver her to the djinni, the only creature in this realm or any other who could save her.

She might be only moments away from rescue.

"Please be stealing my jewel because Jamaspa sent you," she begged, as he levered the stone out of the setting. He discarded the rest of the necklace, throwing her off her feet again as he plunged her into the thick, warm darkness of the pocket nearest his heart.

Brydie landed on her backside and decided to stay on the floor, figuring there wasn't much point in doing anything else until they reached wherever it was the thief was taking her.

In the background, like the faintest hint of a drum tattoo in the far distance, she could hear the steady beating of his heart. It was hypnotic and made her want to sleep.

I might as well take a nap, she reasoned, yawning inelegantly. While ever she was in his pocket, she would be enveloped by a darkness so intense she couldn't make out her own fingers in front of her face, and the thief - whoever he was - needed to escape Temair and return to Jamaspa before she could be rescued.

That might take days. It was certainly going to take a few hours, she figured. Brydie smiled in the darkness and lay down, cradling her head on her arms. She closed her eyes, intrigued that there was no difference in the darkness between her eyes being open and closed, so complete was the absence of light.

Wake me up when it's time to be rescued, she told the thief silently. *I'll be here. Waiting.*

Brydie had become very good at waiting. And with luck, it wouldn't be much longer now before she was free.

CHAPTER 11

Trása woke to discover Rónán missing. She rubbed her eyes and sat up. They'd fallen asleep on the soft grassy lip of the pool, Rónán cradled in her arms. And now he was gone.

"He be gone through the *rifuto* stones."

She looked across the pool to discover Toyoda perched on the mossy rocks by the waterfall watching over her while she slept - a sweet but entirely unnecessary precaution. Nobody could harm her here in *Tír Na nÓg*. "How long ago?"

"A while," the *Leipreachán* said, which was about as specific as a *Leipreachán* could get.

"Did he say where he was going?"

Toyoda shook his head. "If I be taking a guess, I be saying he was headed to another realm."

She shook her head. "That's not possible. Even if he knew where to go, he'd need gampi paper to fold the *ori mahou*, and then he'd have to know where to..." Her words trailed off as it occurred to her that if Rónán knew where to find gampi paper - which the *Konketsu* used here to open rifts - then with Delphine's memories now available to him, he probably knew exactly where to go.

Had he gone to rescue Teagan on his own?

"Did Rónán say anything before he left?"

"No."

Trása bit her lip, trying to wonder what it meant that he'd just up and disappeared like that. He'd seemed fine before they fell asleep. He had a headache, he claimed, and he was struggling with the memories he'd unleashed from Delphine, but the Pool of Tranquillity had done its job. When they'd finally pulled themselves out of the water and collapsed on the grass, he'd seemed fine. Better than fine. He'd been wonderful. They'd made love by the water for a good part of the night, in the way only a *beansídhe* could make love, full of passion and wild abandon. Afterwards, he'd held her close, assured her he was fine, that he could handle the memories and then fallen into a deep, restful sleep.

Rónán said he'd start sorting through Delphine's memories as soon as he woke.

It won't be long, he'd promised her, as he held her in his arms, *and we can bring Teagan home.*

"Trása!"

The harsh call rang out across *Tír Na nÓg*. Toyoda blinked out of existence along with the other lesser *Youkai* who'd been watching over her while she slept.

Trása closed her eyes for a moment as she realized things were about to get even more complicated.

Pete and Logan had arrived. From the tone of Pete's call, she knew they were not going to be happy with the news that not only had Rónán finally delved into their foster mother's memories, but she'd mislaid him and all the information he now had.

Trása climbed to her feet and began to get dressed. The Doherty twins had found her very quickly, so she was certain one of her *Youkai* "friends' had told them where she was.

"Trása, where the hell..." Pete demanded, slipping a little on the steep path as he and Logan approached the pool. His brother was right behind him. "Whoa! Put some clothes on!"

"I am putting some clothes on," she pointed out, as she pulled her shirt down over her head. Once she was decent, she turned to face the brothers, frowning. "And would you mind not yelling. You'll frighten the *Youkai*."

"Where is Ren?"

"I don't know."

"You two vanished out of Edo nearly a month ago," Logan said. "Have you been here all this time?" Trása didn't think they'd been here that long and, normally, the time dilation effects of *Tír Na nÓg* did not affect her and Rónán - or Pete and Logan either, given they were almost wholly Faerie. But they had been in the Pool of Tranquillity, after all, where the magic was so concentrated they might easily have lost years had they not managed to drag themselves out of the water.

"It didn't seem like..." she decided it wasn't worth explaining. "What are you doing here?"

"Looking for you two," Pete said, clearly annoyed. "Dammit, don't you realize what's been going on? Wakiko is beside herself. The whole Empire is in an uproar. To make matters worse, the *Konketsu* are trying to worm their way back into favor by blaming us for Teagan's kidnapping."

"So you can imagine how it looked," Logan added, "when the two of you vanished into thin air."

Trása hadn't really thought about what might happen in the palace after they left. And she hadn't really left by choice. Rónán had whisked her out of there without warning.

"I'm sorry," she said, crossing her arms. "I didn't mean to cause more trouble. But Rónán had to come back here to unlock Delphine's memories."

"You couldn't take five seconds to leave a note?" Pete asked, sounding quite disgusted with them. "How the hell did you get back here to *Tír Na nÓg*, anyway? With the stone circle shattered you... oh, of course. He did that waning thing, didn't he?"

"He didn't give me five seconds, Pete."

"Did he do it?" Logan asked. "Did he manage to unlock Delphine's memories?"

She nodded. "Yes."

"Shit," Logan said, looking at his brother.

Pete frowned. "How did he seem? Afterwards."

"He seemed fine."

"So where is he then?" Pete demanded. "The *Youkai* are claiming he's not here."

"I told you before, I don't know where he is. Has it really been a month since we left Chucho?"

"And a few days," Pete said. "Is Isleen okay?" If she was still alive and unharmed, it meant the *Matrarchaí* had not hurt Teagan.

"She's fretting for her sister, but other than that, she seems fine. Where did Ren go?"

"I told you already, I don't know."

"It doesn't matter anyway," Rónán said, suddenly appearing behind Logan, "because I'm back."

The Doherty twins turned on Rónán angrily, giving Trása time to wonder why he was dressed in black from head to toe like a ninja.

Where has he been - and more importantly - what has he been up to that requires him to dress like that?

And how long had he been gone? Down here by the pool, Trása had lost any sense of time. Perhaps they hadn't made love and fallen asleep entwined in each other's arms last night, but days, maybe weeks ago.

Rónán held up his hand to halt Pete and Logan's barrage of angry questions. "I don't know where Teagan is," he said, "or how to get back to our realm."

Funny how the three men insisted on calling the reality where they had been raised "ours," when none of them really belonged there.

"Why don't we *try* first," Pete suggested, "before we write off the idea completely."

"I did try," Rónán said, as he pushed back his hood and began to unlace the fastenings at the top of his *shinobi shozoko*. "That's where I've been. The rift Delphine brought you through in the Sears Tower is no longer there."

"There must have been other rifts in our realm," Logan said. "We know the *Matrarchaí* had at least two stone circles, just in the US alone."

Ren nodded in agreement. "They have quite a few. There's one in Dubai, another in Taiwan ... trouble is, Delphine never used them. She knew about them, but she wasn't responsible for setting them up and she doesn't have any memory of coming through them that I can find."

"It's early days yet," Pete said. "If you just keep looking..."

"The information simply isn't there, Pete," Rónán said, shaking his head. "The only other circle in our reality that Delphine knew how to access is one she was arranging to be built, but it's not there yet."

"When will it be there?"

"In another seven years or so."

"Are you kidding me?" Pete exclaimed. "Seven fucking years!"

"Teagan will be a grown-up by then," Trása said, watching Rónán closely. She was trying to work out what was different about him. Having access to Delphine's memories was bound to have an impact on him. What that impact might be, remained to be seen.

Logan seemed to take the news better than his brother. "Were you able to get to any other realities?"

Rónán nodded. "Quite a few. A lot of them the *Matrarchaí* have already cleansed of the Faerie, but there are plenty more realities they scheduled for intervention that we can get to. I didn't want to waste the gampi paper by visiting too many."

There's something he's not telling us, Trása decided, as she watched Rónán explaining things to Pete and Logan. *He's too calm, too controlled. Where has he really been?*

"Can you get back to our realm?" she asked.

Trása wouldn't have noticed the hesitation had she not been looking for it

"No luck with that, either, I'm afraid. Delphine never visited your realm."

He's lying. Trása was certain of it. Her realm was his realm, too. He didn't need Delphine's memories to find it.

"Then we're stuck here," Logan said, throwing his hands up.

Pete shook his head. "No, we're not. Ren said he could open rifts to other realms the *Matrarchaí* have marked. He can show us how to get there, and maybe we can capture someone from the *Matrarchaí* who knows another way back our to reality. I say we start doing a bit of rift running of our own. Let's take this fight to the *Matrarchaí*."

"What about Teagan?" Ren asked.

"She's probably lost to us," Pete said, "unless they send her back."

"Is that likely?"

Pete looked at him closely. Perhaps he sensed Rónán was lying, too. "You tell me, Ren. You're the one with the head full of intelligence taken from a *Matrarchaí* general. Speaking of which, why don't you share the *Comhroinn* with us now, so Logan and I can start searching these new realities?"

Rónán nodded and smiled, and Trása just knew he was stalling. "Sure," he said. "Give me some time to get my head sorted and I'll share whatever you want to know."

He had to say that. Even if Teagan's life had not been in danger, Pete and Logan would still not accept excuses from Ren for not sharing knowledge of their origins and the reason they had been raised by the *Matrarchaí* in complete ignorance of who or what they were.

Rónán turned to head back up the path.

"What's with the outfit, by the way?" Pete called after him. "You planning a new career as a ninja."

Ren glanced over his shoulder with a smile that didn't reach his eyes. "I know it's ridiculous, but I wasn't sure what I'd find when I opened rifts to those other realities, so I thought it best to wear something dark. You know what this place is like ... it was the only thing I could find to wear that wasn't embroidered to death and colored like a circus tent."

It sounded plausible. It might have even been the truth. But Trása knew he'd been up to something and the reason for it eluded her. She would find out, she promised herself.

Because if she didn't - if Rónán was telling the truth about not being able to get back to the other realm until the new stone circle was built - Darragh and Sorcha would be stranded in that other reality for another seven years.

PART TWO

CHAPTER 12

Trása wasn't sure what woke her. She lingered for a moment in that limbo between sleep and consciousness, trying to remember simple things like where she was, what time it might be and who was holding her in his embrace while she slept.

The first answer came easily. She was in *Tír Na nÓg* in this strange alternate reality that had become her home these last ten years. The magic tingling against her skin gave that away. In light of that revelation, the second question was meaningless. Time was different here in *Tír Na nÓg*. Who knew what time it was out in the real world?

The second answer brought a smile to her face. The warm body holding her was Rónán.

He'd come to *Tír Na nÓg* last night, after returning from a reality he refused to name. As usual, he wouldn't tell her about the realm he'd been visiting and Trása had learned not to press him for details. Rónán carried a burden she couldn't comprehend and even though she'd begged him, time and again, to share the *Comhroinn* so she could understand, he always refused.

She turned to study his sleeping face in the soft twilight of her bower cave. His dark hair was longer than it had been when they first met, his chin shadowed by a three-day growth, his face relaxed and at peace - something she rarely saw when he was awake. Just beneath his ear was that tiny, wretched cut that never seemed to heal and there were lines on his brow now, even while he slept, that could not be attributed to age. Although Rónán was almost pure Faerie and would never age like a normal man, the lines came from the burden he carried, the terrible knowledge he owned, not the passage of years.

And, she suspected, his inability to do anything meaningful about his lost twin.

He would wake soon, she guessed. He'd smile, get up and shave, and joke around with the lesser *Youkai*. But the smile would never reach his eyes and the jokes weren't all that funny, although the lesser *Youkai* weren't sophisticated enough to appreciate that.

Trása smiled to herself, knowing there was one burden she would soon be able to take from him.

Something tickled Trása's cheek and she realized what had woken her. She batted away the irritation, a little annoyed Echo had woken her so early and was undoubtedly going to disturb Rónán if she tried to ignore her.

"The boys are back. The boys are back. The boys are back." The pixie's high-pitched buzz hummed around Trása's ear as the little *Youkai* hovered above her head, wings flapping like a hummingbird. If she didn't move or at least acknowledge she was awake, Trása knew from long experience that Echo would start nipping at her ear.

"All right, I heard you. They're back," she whispered, turning her head to look at the pixie as a surge of excitement welled up inside her. If Pete and Logan were back, her laborious and secretive plan to finally bring Darragh home might be about to bear fruit.

"Hurry up. Hurry up," the pixie buzzed impatiently. Echo was naked except for a strip of brightly colored ribbon around her neck and some shiny silver string tied around her wrists that looked suspiciously like bits of Christmas tinsel. As there was no Christmas in this reality, and certainly nothing like Christmas decorations, she guessed Pete or Logan had brought it back for her on one of their runs. It also accounted for the pixie knowing they were back from their latest rift running expedition.

Taking great care not to disturb Rónán, she carefully wiggled from his embrace and stepped out of the bower cave and onto the wide branch outside her home. *Tír Na nÓg* was laid out before her, no longer sad and empty. It was filled with *Youkai* now, although few were the original inhabitants of this realm. Most of them, like her little pixie, Echo, were refugees from other realities where the *Matrarchaí* were making their presence felt.

"Better put come clothes on. Better put some clothes on," the pixie sang, buzzing around her ear to be certain she'd heard. The pixie's annoying habit of repeating everything at least twice had earned her the name Echo. Trása forgot who first called her that. She thought it might have Isleen. Whoever it was, the name had stuck and now everyone called her Echo.

"Boys will blush. Boys will blush."

Trása smiled at that. Pete and Logan, even though they had spent the last decade among the *sídhe* folk of this realm and countless others, still suffered traces of the inhibitions their upbringing had ingrained in them. Echo was right. If she didn't put some clothes on before she greeted Pete and Logan on their return, they wouldn't know where to look.

Trása returned to the bower cave and grabbed her clothes, including her boots, and took them outside onto the ledge so as not to disturb Rónán while she dressed. Not only did she not want to alert him to her plans until everything was in place, he'd looked exhausted when he came to her last night. She figured he needed all the sleep he could get, and here in *Tír Na nÓg* was the only place he ever slept soundly.

"Nika's home, too. Nika's home, too," Echo chanted as Trása got dressed.

The news gave Trása pause. She hadn't even realized the Merlin had gone with Pete and Logan on a mission that was supposed to be secret. Not that the news bothered her unduly. If anything, she probably should have thought of it herself. Trása didn't doubt Nika would be looking out for her interests. The Merlin was ridiculously loyal to the *Tuatha Dé Danann* half-*beansídhe* she considered responsible for her rescue. "Was she rift running with Pete and Logan or does she just happen to have arrived home at the same time?"

"Running with them, running with them," Echo told her, darting about Trása's head, probably because she liked the way it made the tinsel around her tiny wrists glitter. "Brought you a present. Brought you a -"

Echo gasped and suddenly blinked out of existence.

Trása sighed. The present, she guessed, was meant to be a secret. "You didn't tell me which *rifuto* they came through," she called, but knew it was useless. Echo was probably miles away by now, fretting that "the boys" - her collective name for Pete and Logan - might be mad at her for ruining their surprise.

Trása made her way down the organic wooden stairs that encircled the massive trunk of her tree home, trying to work out the most logical place for Pete and Logan to have entered this realm. She had impressed upon them the importance of keeping their mission a secret from Rónán so they were unlikely to have emerged at the stone circle near Nara in Chucho, in this reality's version of Japan, where Rónán normally resided. They would not be expecting to find him here.

She didn't think the others knew about her and Rónán. They certainly didn't live together or do anything else normal couples might do. Since he'd unlocked Delphine's memories seven years ago and discovered how long they had to wait until they could return to the realm where they'd left Darragh, they'd lived in different hemispheres, and even when they were together, Rónán was not one for public displays of affection. Trása wondered about that sometimes, figuring it was nothing to do with the burden of responsibility he carried, and everything to do with being raised by a woman who thrived on making a spectacle of herself.

"An Bhantiarna, a word, if I may?"

Trása stopped, as one of the refugee *Tuatha Dé Danann* Pete and Logan had rescued from another reality about four years ago stepped in front of her, blocking her way. She silently braced herself and forced a smile, wondering how much noise he would make if she pushed him off the stairs. He wouldn't die. They weren't so far up the branches it would kill him if he fell. Besides, he was pure *sídhe*. And even if it hurt when he hit the forest floor, he could heal himself.

It's nice to dream sometimes.

"I'm sorry, Stiofán, I'm in kind of a hurry. Can we talk later?"

"You are here and I am ready to speak. Why should it not be now?"

Because you're an insufferable pain in the backside and Nika should have let the Matrarchaí slaughter you, so I wouldn't have to put up with your self-important pomposity. That's what Trása really wanted to say to this tall, handsome Faerie. She knew his type well. In his own reality he'd been a *sídhe* of high standing and had the ear of his queen. Here he was safe from the *Matrarchaí*, but a nobody. The work they were doing, the battle to save as many *sídhe* as they could from the *Matrarchaí* in this reality and countless others, was a job only the mongrel *sídhe* like her could fight. Stiofán couldn't step out of a magical realm without dying and it was in the magic-depleted realms where the *Matrarchaí* had their strongholds. When it came down to it, though, Trása knew this swaggering, displaced *Tuatha Dé Danann* lord wasn't upset that he couldn't join the fight; he was just having trouble coping with the notion that he owed his life to a bunch of mongrel *sídhe*.

She sighed. "You have one minute."

Stiofán sniffed. "I do not know what a minute is, but I will assume it is all the time I need to state my case regarding my accommodation."

"What's wrong with your accommodation?"

"It's intolerable."

"Why is it intolerable?" she asked, the temptation to shove him off the stairs something she found herself having to consciously control.

"I sleep only a short distance off the ground."

"And that makes your accommodation intolerable, how exactly?"

"A *sídhe* of my stature should be much further up. The higher branches are filled with *Leipreachán*, pixies and sprites. It is beyond comprehension how you can allow the normal order of things to be so perverted, you would honor lesser *sídhe* over those of the *Tuatha Dé Danann*."

Trása couldn't stop herself from smiling, although she did manage to control the urge to laugh out loud. "Really? That's your problem, Stiofán? You think we're perverted because you don't have the penthouse suite?"

The *sídhe* glared at her, not understanding her words, although he understood her tone. Sarcasm was the same in any language.

The *sídhe* drew himself up and looked down his long, aquiline nose at her. "This unacceptable state of affairs would not be tolerated in a realm where there was a proper *Tuatha Dé Danann* queen, rather than a mongrel pretender."

Trása took a deep breath. *Sticks and stones may break my bones, but names will never hurt me.* Logan had taught her that a few years ago. He claimed it was the only way to cope with living in the public eye and not go mad listening to everyone else's opinion on how you were living your life. He'd gone so far as to make her memorize the tiny refrain and promise to repeat it over and over - or at least until the urge to throttle the name-caller receded - whenever she found herself in a situation such as this.

It had taken a while for her to accept his way of thinking, but she was grateful for it because she was in too much of a hurry to let anything this pompous windbag said, get to her.

"Feel free to find another realm where the social order is more to your liking," she suggested. "Now get out of my way, Stiofán, or I'll arrange to have some of my honored lesser *sídhe* evict your sorry ass out of *Tír Na nÓg* and you can go live in the mundane world. You never know, those filthy humans out there struggling to get by might be a little more sympathetic to your need for a room with a view."

Stiofán had probably never been spoken to so harshly, and if he decided to retaliate with magic Trása wasn't powerful enough to stop him. In her own realm, she had been cursed by Marcroy Tarth and was doomed - in that reality at least - to spend her days as a barn owl. It was the reason she could never return and was relying on the others to do what needed to be done for her. Stiofán was more than capable of doing the same to her here, or worse.

But he wasn't as sure of himself as Marcroy. And perhaps he sensed Rónán was back. He might be brave enough to insult Trása to her face. He wasn't going to challenge one of the Undivided.

He hesitated, and then stood aside to let her pass.

Trása did not spare the *Tuatha Dé Danann* lord another thought as she headed down the tree-trunk stairs, hoping "the boys" had come through the rift near the entrance to *Tír Na nÓg*. If they hadn't, she was going to have to get undressed, pack up her clothes and boots, change into a bird large enough to carry them, and fly to wherever they had emerged with a surprise for her.

CHAPTER 13

Although he had no magical powers in this reality, Darragh had developed almost preternatural senses over the past ten years. Without them, he would have died long ago. They were tingling now as he ate his meal in the dining hall of Portlaoise Prison, his arm circling his plate to protect it from any of the other inmates with mischief in mind.

Darragh looked up and surreptitiously surveyed the hall. There was nothing untoward happening that he could see. The line at the servery was moving at a steady pace. The guards on duty seemed relaxed. Those prisoners already served their meals were eating with their heads down, their eyes fixed on their plates. They ate like men consuming food to survive, not to savor it.

But something was up. He could feel it on some unconscious level, in that part of himself that had allowed him to survive in one of the toughest and most secure prisons in Europe.

He risked a glance sideways. Beside him sat a big, ginger-haired brute named Gerald Madden. Gerald was serving a life sentence for murdering his girlfriend in a fit of pique and wasn't having any luck with the Parole Board because he kept insisting she made him do it.

Beside Gerald sat Fergus Gilligan who was serving time for yet another series of burglaries. Fergus seemed inordinately proud of his occupation as a thief, bragging often about his exploits - probably a ploy designed to uncover snitches seeking to do deals with the prison guards in order to have their own sentences reduced. He wasn't a very good thief, Darragh surmised, given he was serving his fifth stretch behind bars, but he'd learned not to point such things out, particularly to lunatics like Fergus, who had earned this particular stretch in maximum security because, during his last job, the unfortunate owner had arrived home mid-burglary and Fergus had beaten him senseless with a tire iron before making his getaway covered in his victim's blood.

That was the victim's fault, too, Darragh was quite certain.

Among the many things he'd learned was that prisons were full of men who were only incarcerated because their victims had either selfishly reported their crimes to the police, or - as in Fergus's case - had the temerity to bleed over the man beating them with a tire iron, thus creating a bountiful trail of DNA evidence.

Beside Fergus sat Darragh's cellmate and the only man in this place he truly trusted. The only other living being in this reality who belonged in the same realm Darragh longed to return to. Ciarán mac Connacht.

Ciarán was serving time now for killing another prisoner. He'd only got eight years for the bank robbery and with remissions they were ready to let him out much sooner than he'd anticipated. Killing a convicted and unrepentant child molester had been Ciarán's rather heavy-handed - albeit very effective - solution to the problem of being released on parole three years ago for good behavior. Now the warrior had a life sentence and was guaranteed a place next to Darragh where he believed he belonged.

Like Darragh, Ciaran's weary blue eyes were constantly surveying the hall. His reason was more practical than Darragh's vaguely unsettled feeling. Ciarán was here fulfilling his oath to protect Darragh of the Undivided.

Although he was touched by the warrior's devotion, the fool had committed an armed robbery, and now a murder, to get himself placed next to his charge. There were days when Darragh found himself catching a glimpse of Ciarán across the way and recalling his shock when his protector and mentor had taken him aside the day he was released into the general prison population seven years ago and announced that Marcroy Tarth had sent him here to guard Darragh, because he and his brother were supposed to be the savior of all *sídhe*-kind.

He had watched over Darragh every day since then, assuring him that Rónán would come for them soon.

Darragh had been tempted to point out that Ciarán would have been far better served staying on the outside and making contact with him by more mundane means... say, coming to see him during visiting hours. On the outside he might have been able to do something useful to orchestrate Darragh's escape, either through the legal channels of this world, or more deceitful means.

It was great having a bodyguard, but Darragh was more than capable of taking care of himself; he had Jack O'Righin's protection to call on when he needed assistance, and really didn't need the big surly warrior hovering nearby, every moment of the day, watching for an attack that never eventuated.

But Darragh said nothing, accepting Ciarán's guardianship with grace and resignation. Ciarán was a noble warrior and a powerful sorcerer, but despite having the ability to cross realities he was ill-equipped for this magic-less, complex world.

The old man might think he was protecting Darragh, but in truth, Darragh felt more like it was up to him to protect Ciarán.

Across the aisle, at the table on Darragh's right sat the few dark-haired, dark-eyed Travellers in Portlaoise. He got on well enough with them and, for some reason, they accepted Ciarán almost as one of their own, but they tended to keep to themselves as a rule, probably because they all appeared to be related to each other somehow. Beyond the Travellers were a couple of the local drug gangs whose members stuck together, despite the best efforts of the prison officers to keep them apart. External feuds and affiliations did not stop when people were sent to jail and protecting inmates from each other probably consumed more of the prison's resources than protecting society at large from those incarcerated here.

On the far side of the hall, as far away from him as they could get, were Dominic O'Hara's gang. The man himself was holding court in the center of his table, probably still running his drug empire from inside the prison. His gang kept away from the Republicans. Jack had made it clear after Darragh arrived that this young man was under the protection of the Republican gang and no attempts to make him pay for the crimes of his missing twin brother would be tolerated - a message reinforced by the constant presence of Gerald and Fergus.

Between that and Ciarán's threatening, if somewhat redundant, presence Darragh was well shielded from the less desirable nocturnal shenanigans that inevitably resulted when far too many unprincipled men were incarcerated together.

The rest of the dining hall was filled with inmates who sat in their own gangs and watched out for anybody who might be marked for some kind of trouble or retribution.

All seemed well. But there was something not right and Darragh couldn't figure out what it was.

"Is something wrong?" Ciarán must have noticed his unease.

"I'm not sure."

"What's the matter with ya, then?"

Darragh glanced at Gerald who was staring at him with a puzzled look. Being far from the brightest man in the room, Gerald often looked puzzled, but he seemed concerned, which was unusual. Darragh didn't know if that was because like Ciarán, he was feeling the oddness too, or if he could sense Darragh's disquiet. "Nothing's the matter. Why?"

"You're not eating."

"The food is shit."

"Aye," Gerald agreed with a nod. "Can I have it?"

Darragh was only half listening. Across the hall he spied one of the guards looking about the dining hall. The man stopped looking when he spied Darragh and began to walk purposefully across the linoleum toward their table.

"Didn't ya hear me?" Gerald asked. "If ya not eatin' ya lunch, can I have it?"

"Be my guest," Darragh said, sliding his plate with its rubbery roast lamb and gelatinous mashed potatoes across the table to the big man just as the guard stopped beside the table. He looked up at the guard and smiled politely. "Good afternoon, Officer Connors."

"Sorry to interrupt your dining experience here in Chez Portlaoise, lads," the guard told them, "but young Darragh here has a visitor."

"Who?" Ciarán demanded, jumping to his feet. "None of your business, Mac," the officer informed him. "Now sit down."

Ciarán did as he was ordered, although reluctantly. Disobeying a direct order would see him sent to solitary for a spell, and he wouldn't risk being separated from the young man he was here to protect.

"I really have a visitor?" Darragh asked, once he was satisfied Ciarán didn't need settling down.

"Aye, your lawyer's here."

For a moment, Darragh didn't know what to say. He literally couldn't remember the last time he had spoken to a lawyer. He certainly didn't have one on retainer.

Darragh stood up. "It'll be okay," he promised Ciarán and then he turned to the prison officer. "Take me to him."

"It's a her, actually," Connors said. "Come on."

The lawyer was a woman Darragh had never seen before. She was tall, blonde, thin, severe and all business. She wore a grey suit and spoke perfect English, but she clearly wasn't Irish by birth. As Darragh took his seat in the glass-fronted booth, she sat down on the other side and picked up the telephone that enabled them to speak through the bulletproof glass.

"My name is Eunice Ravenel," she said, saving Darragh from having to ask. "I represent Kiva Kavanaugh and the family of Hayley Boyle."

Darragh didn't answer for a moment. The flood of his brother's memories that her words released, needed time to wash over him. Time for them to settle into some semblance of order.

"What can I do for you, Ms Ravenel?" he asked, while the memories flashed through his mind like little snippets of lightning. Eunice Ravenel bailing him - or rather his brother, Rónán - out of jail... Kerry Boyle making him hot chocolate... Kiva having a tantrum because she looked fat on the

Oprah Show... Patrick Boyle teaching him to ride a bike... Hayley and Neil playing hide and seek in the grounds of Kiva's house...

"It's been ten years since Hayley disappeared," Eunice reminded him, her clipped English making the sentence sound like an accusation.

"I'm aware of that." *More than you will ever know.*

What's stopping you coming for us, Rónán? I came for you.

"Hayley's parents, Patrick and Kerry Boyle, and her brother, Neil, would like to move on with their lives."

"I'm sure they would."

"In order to do that," the lawyer told him, "they have decided to petition the courts to have Hayley declared legally dead."

Darragh was silent for a moment. He'd been in this reality long enough to appreciate the complexity of its legal system, and he was quite sure such a thing would not be achieved without considerable effort. He was also quite sure Eunice Ravenel had not come here to Portlaoise Prison to tell him this news as a mere courtesy.

When he didn't respond to her statement, she frowned. "You could make this traumatic process considerably easier for them."

"I wish none of the Boyle family any ill," Darragh assured her. "My brother was exceedingly fond of them." It was true. Rónán's memories of the Boyles were good ones. "How can I help?"

"You can confess to murdering Hayley and tell me where her body is."

Ah! That could be a problem.

Darragh wanted to help. He really did. But helping didn't extend to confessing to a murder he didn't commit. Particularly as the victim of this non-existent murder was not only alive and well, but probably being feted as an honored guest in the reality where Darragh and Rónán came from.

"I can't do that."

Eunice didn't seem surprised. "Can't, or won't?"

"Both," Darragh said. "I did not kill Hayley and was never party to any plan to bring her to harm, therefore I would have to commit perjury to claim I have any knowledge of her fate. Furthermore, as she is - to the best of my knowledge - alive and well, it would be even more irresponsible of me to distress her family further by lying to them and declaring her dead."

"Where is she, then?" Eunice asked. "And so help me, I will come through this glass and throttle you, young man, if you give me that rubbish about her being sent to an alternate reality to have her sight healed."

Darragh sighed and pushed himself to his feet. "Then we're done, Miss Ravenel, because I have no other explanation I can offer you."

He replaced the phone in the cradle and turned to the door, waving to Officer Connors through the small observation window to let him know he was ready to return to his lunch. There was nothing more he could say to Eunice Ravenel and he was done trying to explain anything to these people.

Rónán will come for me one day, and then you'll see I've been right all along.

But until that day, he would have to suffer the accusatory looks of people like Eunice Ravenel and the far too real consequences of their ignorance of even the mere existence of other realms.

As the door opened, he turned back and glanced at Eunice. She was still sitting there, clutching the phone, glaring at him.

What did she think my response would be?

"That was quick," Connors remarked, as Darragh compliantly turned to face the wall and put his hands behind his back so the officer could cuff him.

"She wanted something I couldn't give her," Darragh explained.

Connors chuckled as he clicked the cuffs closed, and turned Darragh around to face him. "She's a woman, lad. What did you expect? They all want something you can't give 'em. I've been married three times. Trust me, I know."

"If she comes back, I don't want to see her," he said.

"Why don't you want to see your lawyer?"

"She's not my lawyer. She represents my alleged victim's family."

"Awkward."

"You have no idea."

"What did she want?"

"She's trying to have the girl they think I kidnapped declared dead."

Connors' jovial mood faded a little. "Which, of course, you can't do, because like every other poor bugger in here, you were framed, right?"

"No, I wasn't framed," Darragh said patiently. "Framed implies someone deliberately set me up, which was not the case at all, Officer Connors. It's just that there's been a misunderstanding caused by this world's ignorance of the true nature of the cosmos. I'm innocent and one day they'll come for me and you'll see I was right."

"Oh, well then," Connors said, giving Darragh a shove in the direction of the door, "I'll be sure to alert the media."

It was hard to tell if Connors was being sarcastic. He had a reputation as one of the guards you could count on to acquire things for you, if the price was right and he decided you were worth the risk.

"Do you think they'll care?"

"About as much as I do, lad," the officer told him. He shoved Darragh forward. "Get a move on."

Darragh did as he was ordered. There was nothing to be gained doing anything else.

But Eunice Ravenel's visit awakened his urge to return home. He was a patient man, but it was ten years since Rónán and Trása stepped through the rift.

What could possibly stop Rónán coming for me? Don't leave it too much longer, brother.

Perhaps it was time to contact Rónán again, to ask him what the hold-up was. In a strange way he had been in contact with Rónán through these years. There was a cut behind his ear - a tiny, insignificant nick - that healed and reappeared every couple of weeks. It was Rónán, cutting himself with an airgead *sídhe* blade, to let him know he hadn't forgotten about him.

Perhaps it was time to do more than take comfort from a small wound behind his ear. He had a way to communicate with his brother, after all, although it was no easy thing to achieve in a maximum security prison. Even Ciarán didn't know about that.

"If I wanted something special, Officer Connors," he asked, glancing over his shoulder, "what would it cost me?"

"I've no idea what you're talking about."

"Humour me, then," Darragh said, accustomed to how this game was played. "If I wanted to get hold of something small. Something not even illegal ... what would it cost."

"That depends," Connors said behind him, as they walked down the long empty corridor.

"On what?"

"On what you wanted. And assuming there was any guard in here willing to risk his job and the possibility of joining you as an inmate to get it for you."

"Let's just assume for a minute that there is. What would it cost me?"

"What do you want?"

"An electric shaver. A Remington Microscreen, cordless, rechargeable shaver to be exact."

Connors was silent for a moment and then he laughed. "Something like that would take more money than you've got, my lad."

Darragh sighed. He didn't blame Connors for being careful, and it was a moot point anyway. He had nothing with which to buy off Connors, or any other guard, assuming he could find out who were the few who could be bribed, and nothing to purchase an electric razor with, either.

Perhaps an opportunity would present itself. Maybe he should do what some of the inmates in here were fond of doing and start writing to some lonely, gullible spinster on the outside, looking for a penpal. Fergus had several and they often sent him presents, not all of which were confiscated as contraband.

If he grew desperate enough, he might ask Eunice Ravenel back and offer to do a trade with her, he supposed. That would be a last resort. He didn't want to give the Boyles false hope.

No, he needed to find another way.

Somehow, one way or another, Darragh needed to get his hands on a sliver of titanium.

It didn't need to be much. Just enough to cut his skin and let Rónán know - in whatever reality he was hiding - that it was time to bring his brother and their guardian home.

CHAPTER 14

As it turned out, Trása didn't have to go far at all. By the time she'd reached the forest floor, Pete and Logan had entered *Tír Na nÓg* and were coming to her.

The reporter and the cop who had been brought to this realm bound and unconscious by the woman they believed was their mother were, in many ways, unrecognizable. In other ways, they hadn't changed at all.

They looked the same. Like Rónán, although they hadn't known it growing up in a world almost devoid of magic, they were mostly *sídhe*, despite looking human. Neither had aged like ordinary men. In the realm where they had been raised, they should have been approaching middle age, yet neither Pete nor Logan looked a day older than when Delphine, Tiffany and Chishihero had carried them into this realm through the rift Delphine had opened at the very top of the Sears Tower in Chicago.

As Trása watched them approach carrying a large sack between them, it occurred to her that Delphine must have been planning for these twins to have "accidents" at some time in their early thirties in order to avoid awkward questions about why they weren't aging as they should. Maybe she'd planned to murder them once they'd fathered children for her with one of the *Matrarchaí*'s many protégés who she controlled under the guise of running a modeling agency. Poor Logan. He would have been first. After Delphine confirmed Trephina was pregnant, his days had probably been numbered.

Good thing then, Trása mused, *that Rónán destroyed the heartless bitch before she had a chance to act on that part of her nefarious plan.*

That the late and unlamented Delphine had a nefarious plan went without saying. The exact details of the plan, however, were something only Rónán knew for certain, although Trása wondered sometimes if Rónán had shared everything with Pete and Logan, or just given them an edited version. It was likely - Trása figured - that the only reason Delphine brought Logan and his brother to this reality was to kill them without any questions being asked in the realm where she had raised them. In the other reality, Logan, at least, had been quite well known and might be missed when he disappeared, particularly as his twin was a cop and would have left no stone unturned in his quest to find his brother if anything happened to him.

Even now, although he shared her bed, Trása still wondered if Rónán didn't trust the Doherty boys more than her. Trouble is, wondering about that led down a path she didn't want to go. She didn't know if Rónán loved her. She wasn't sure if she loved him or if he was just a convenient stand-in for his brother, Darragh, whom Trása had loved for as long as she could remember. She wasn't even sure if her love for Darragh was real anymore, or just a fond memory that had never been tarnished by reality.

She had a plan to find out though, one way or another. Rónán just didn't know about it yet.

In spite of whatever loyalty the Doherty boys felt toward Rónán, right at this moment Pete and Logan had come to visit her and the burlap sack they carried between them - sealed closed with a magical spell Trása could sense from several feet away - was wiggling and jiggling and protesting loudly at the indignity of its predicament.

Trása smiled as Logan and Pete stopped before her and lowered the sack to the ground.

"Echo said Nika was with you."

"She's still at the circle," Pete explained. "Taking care of a... complication."

That sounded a little ominous, but as Logan and Pete had left the Merlin to deal with the "complication" on her own, Trása figured it couldn't be too important.

She looked down at the wiggling sack and smiled. "Rumour has it you've brought me a present."

"Rumour has a big mouth," Logan said, glancing about, probably for the loose-lipped pixie who'd spoiled the surprise.

"She's right, though," Pete added. Dressed in the garb of a Celtic warrior from her own reality, he might not have visibly aged these past ten years, but he was unrecognizable from the man Delphine had brought through the rift. Anybody who had known him in the reality where he had lived and worked for the first twenty-seven years of his life would barely recognize him now.

Trása felt the surge of magic as Pete released the spell, and with his brother's help, unceremoniously dumped its occupant on the leafy ground at Trása's feet.

Trása took a step back and waited for the creature to take stock of his surroundings. The *Leipreachán* looked around suspiciously, taking in the many curious *sídhe* gathered on the edge of the clearing to see what all the fuss was, the magical trees, the eternal glimmering twilight of *Tír Na nÓg*, and then his eyes fixed on Trása. He stared at her for a long moment.

"Well then," he said after a time, his wrinkled face drawn into a thunderous scowl, "that be explainin' how these two brigands be knowing me true name."

"Hello, Plunkett."

The *Leipreachán* drew himself up to his full height and glanced around, glowering at the crowd, and then rested his eyes on Trása once more. "Ye found a way to break ye uncle's curse, I see."

Actually, Trása hadn't found a way to break the curse that doomed her to life as a barn owl, courtesy of Marcroy. Flying headlong through a rift into a world without magic had broken it, and this world, although drenched in magic, was not the realm where the curse held sway. She had no doubt that if she tried to return to her world, she would immediately revert to avian form. Rónán had the power to break the curse and with the combined memories of Darragh and Delphine, had the knowledge, as well.

But Rónán had pointedly refused to do anything to break the curse. He didn't want Trása, or anybody else for that matter, returning to his native realm, and he figured - quite rightly - that the curse would prevent her from doing so.

He hadn't counted on her ingenuity, however. Or the fact that she might eventually co-opt Pete and Logan to her cause.

"I've managed quite a bit since I saw you last, Plunkett. And how is dear Uncle Marcroy?" Trása needed to know that urgently. She was reasonably certain she could talk Rónán into forgiving her for breaking her promise not to return to their own reality. She was much less confident of her ability to predict Marcroy's likely reaction to the news that his errant niece was alive and well, free of his curse and living it up in another realm with one half of the Undivided whom he thought he'd disposed of.

Plunkett shrugged. "How should I be knowing? He don't be confiding in the likes of me." The *Leipreachán* glanced around again and nodded approvingly. "Seems like ye've carved yeself a handy wee niche in this realm, by the look of things. Ye uncle be very interested to learn ye whereabouts, I suspect."

"I'll speak to Marcroy when I'm good and ready," Trása informed him, a little amazed that, even after ten years, the idea that Marcroy might come after her could still spark a small sliver of fear in her belly.

Maybe Rónán was right. Maybe I should just leave well enough alone.

Pity that was no longer an option.

She looked up at Pete and Logan. "Did Abbán give you any trouble?"

Logan sighed. "That would be the complication Pete spoke of."

Trása cursed under her breath. "Tell me he didn't ..."

"Oh, yes," Pete assured her, "he did."

Rónán is going to kill me.

Trása forced a smile. It wouldn't do to let the fact that Rónán knew nothing of their expedition slip now. "Well, we'll just have to deal with him." She turned her attention back to Plunkett. "Would you like to meet your *eiléféin*, Plunkett?"

The *Leipreachán* gasped. "Ye canna be introducing me to me own self! It be a grievous flauntin' of the rules!"

"The rules are different here," Logan explained, amused by the *Leipreachán*'s alarm. He glanced at Trása, adding. "Are you sure you want to let this guy and the knee-high ninja swap notes?"

She nodded and glanced up at the canopy of trees. Rónán had been sound asleep in her bower when she left him, but he might wake anytime and decide to come looking for her. She didn't want him finding out that Plunkett was here until she'd gleaned some useful intelligence from the *Leipreachán*. If she could produce proof that Darragh had found his way home, or that Hayley was cured and safely back home, perhaps he'd be willing to finally break the curse that kept her here and she'd able to go home, too.

If not... if Darragh was still stranded in Rónán's magic-less realm... well then, it was time to bring him home.

Trása didn't seriously believe Darragh had managed to get home, because he would have tried to contact Rónán and they'd have been reunited long before now. If he was anywhere there was magic, Darragh could easily have scried Rónán out and let him know he was safe.

Darragh's long silence meant only one thing. He was still in the reality with no magic, where they'd left him, and it was up to them to get him back.

That time was soon approaching. Seven years, Rónán had said after Teagan was taken. That's how long it would take the *Matrarchaí* to construct another stone circle in the Enchanted Sphere of that magic-less world.

There would soon be a way into that realm that Rónán had knowledge of, thanks to Delphine's memories.

And it was likely to drive him and anyone who stepped through the rift with him, straight into the arms of the *Matrarchaí* who had commissioned the stone circle, something Rónán never seemed to consider and refused to discuss whenever she tried to bring it up.

But now, thanks to her brilliant plan, there was another way into that realm. A safer way. It was such a good plan that Pete, Logan and the normally hyper-cautious Nika had agreed to it.

Now, she only had to break it to Rónán...

Perhaps then, when he smiled, it would reach his eyes for a change.

"The *Leipreachán* will be fine," she told Logan, pushing aside the niggling doubt that, far from earning Rónán's gratitude, he was likely to be furious with her. She had more immediate problems to deal with. "My cousin, Abbán, on the other hand, I'm not so sure about. Will you do the honors?"

"Sure. I'll introduce them," Logan said. "Do you know where Toyoda is?"

"Not offhand. But I'm sure if you call him, he'll be here in flash. After all," she added, looking pointedly at Plunkett O'Bannon, "you know his real name."

The *Leipreachán* muttered darkly and crossed his arms over his waistcoat, not well pleased.

Pete pointed back down the path. "Nika's waiting with him at the circle. We'd better get there before she decides to take matters into her own hands."

"Don't let them get into any trouble," Trása ordered Logan, as she hurried after Pete down the leaf-strewn path, wondering what had possessed her to think she could arrange to kidnap a *Leipreachán* from another realm without causing problems, or that she could rely on her cousin, the merman Abbán, to do anything but make trouble.

CHAPTER 15

Pete Doherty sometimes felt the need to pinch himself just to be sure he was still conscious and the last decade of his life hadn't been one spectacularly complicated and fantastic dream from which he could not wake.

He was having one of those moments now as he escorted Trása back to the stone circle just outside *Tír Na nÓg*, so she could do something about the merman they'd brought back from another reality.

The merman in question was Trása's cousin. Somehow, whether by fair means or foul, Trása had scried Abbán out and convinced him to open a rift to his reality to allow Pete, Logan and Nika through and then to open it again to allow them to return to this reality with a kidnapped *Leipreachán*.

Such an event was such an absurdly long way from the life he'd once known, it didn't seem possible it could be real. Sometimes, he felt as if the real dream had been the first twenty-seven years of his life, and this life he had now - where he and his twin brother, Logan, could wield magic and cross realities at will - was the only life he had ever known.

Other times he wondered if, perhaps, he was just going mad.

For now, though, the bit where he was mostly Faerie and able to move from one reality to another was winning.

Trása had organized this particular cross-reality excursion, claiming she was doing it on Ren's behalf, although Pete was beginning to doubt that. She'd been very cagey about them discussing the trip with him. Pete gathered, given the fuss Abbán had made when he realized Trása wasn't coming through the rift, that she'd made some sort of promise to turn herself over to Marcroy, to get her cousin - all the *Tuatha Dé Danann* seemed to be cousins of one sort or another - to open the rift in the first place. The honor and kudos the merman could claim by handing her over to Marcroy was apparently sufficient enticement to get Abbán to open a rift.

Foolish merman. Anybody with even a passing acquaintance with Trása should have known the chances of her voluntarily stepping into the reality where she was cursed to spend her life as a barn owl were vanishingly small. Abbán had fallen for it, however, and became quite vocal when he realized he'd been duped.

At that point, Nika, their refugee Merlin from yet another realm depopulated by the *Matrarchaí*, had become concerned about the noise Abbán was making, so - without any thought as to the consequences - she'd wrapped him in a magical cocoon and shoved him through the rift after Logan and Pete and then closed the rift behind them.

"Did anybody see you in the other realm?" Trása asked as they hurried along the leaf-strewn path toward the entrance to *Tír Na nÓg*.

He shook his head. "We did exactly as you asked. In and out as quickly as possible. Some of the lesser *sídhe* may have seen us, but I doubt they'd know who we were or what we were up to."

Trása frowned. "But you bought Abbán back with you."

Pete didn't appreciate the accusation in her tone. "Hey, *you* were the one who got Abbán involved, O Great and Omnipotent Acting Faerie Queen. Logan's suggestion, if you recall, was that if you wanted to go back to your own reality so badly, you should just ask Ren to lift the curse on you."

Trása shook her head. "That would have ruined the surprise."

"Yeah ... about that. Ren doesn't know a damned thing about this little expedition, does he?"

All hint of reprimand vanished as Trása flashed him a smile that was as blinding as it was forced. "You have a wild imagination, Pete. It's a hangover from being a cop. You think everybody is up to no good."

"That doesn't mean you *aren't* up to no good," he pointed out... quite reasonably, he thought.

Trása didn't answer him and because they'd reached the entrance to *Tír Na nÓg* it was easy enough for her to avoid the subject. As they stepped through the veil into the mundane world outside, Pete could feel not only the temperature dropping, but the magic draining from the air and he wanted to weep for the loss of it. This whole reality was seeped in magic, but it was never as concentrated, or as heady, as it was in *Tír Na nÓg*.

The stone circle was only few minutes from the entrance, located at the very top of the cliff known in other realities as the Giant's Staircase. The stones were similar to those they had stepped through in Trása and Ren's reality, except these were covered in Japanese symbols, rather than the Celtic designs of the other reality.

The top of the cliff had a windswept, flat area on which the circle sat overlooking the Giant's Staircase. Nika was sitting on one of the low stones, her back to the ocean, watching over a young man who stood naked and scowling in the center of the circle, his arms pressed to his sides, held there by the invisible bonds the Merlin had wrapped around him. Pete smiled at Nika's ingenuity and made a mental note to be careful he never did anything that might tempt her to try the same trick on him.

Trása's *mara-warra* cousin, Abbán, wasn't quite as tall as Trása. Although his upper body was muscular and well-tanned - only the gills running in line with his ribs marking him as different - his legs were spindly and pale, a sure sign, Pete now knew, that he spent as little time as possible on land. As soon as they let Abbán back into the water, his fishtail would return and he would once again be the magnificent specimen of mermanity - if there were such a word - he fancied himself to be.

But that wasn't going to happen while he was threatening to run straight to Marcroy Tarth and tell him where Trása and one half of the missing Undivided had been hiding all these years.

The Merlin rose to her feet as they approached, bowing low to Trása with a respect that Pete found hard to credit. Nika was a powerful woman, both physically and magically and in Pete's eyes, quite the most beautiful creature he'd ever met. Another of the countless refugees they'd gathered here over the past seven years, Nika's reality had been devastated by the *Matrarchaí* just before she'd inherited her position from the previous Merlin who had died trying to fight them off. Alone, exhausted and helpless, Nika had been fighting a last-ditch battle against the *Matrarchaí* to save what Faerie she could when they'd stumbled into her world.

Perhaps it was because she'd seen Trása first, that day, or because here in this reality, Trása had - by default - become Queen of the Faerie, Nika had sworn her allegiance to the mongrel half-*beansídhe* and had been Trása's most ardent supporter ever since, even when it meant disagreeing with her lover.

They'd been too late to save Nika's realm from the *Matrarchaí*, but she was one of their first refugees. They'd saved her and the scores of *sídhe* she was defending and brought them back here to this world full of enchanted trees where the magic was strong. Her gratitude toward Trása for rescuing her people was perhaps only outmatched by her love for Pete, who still couldn't quite figure out what she saw in him.

The *Matrarchaí*'s plans in this realm, at least, had - for the time being - been foiled.

At least, Pete hoped they'd been foiled. They all watched Isleen like a hawk when they were around her, looking for some hint she was about to turn nasty. Ren claimed he'd locked away the *Comhroinn* Delphine had performed on the girls when they were children and they could never become the monsters she had planned for, but Pete wasn't so sure. If the *Matrarchaí* had Teagan, it was certain they had now unlocked Delphine's memories in her. Although nobody ever said it out loud, he knew everyone but Isleen thought the same as him - Teagan had probably turned into the psychopathic Faerie-killer the *Matrarchaí* had bred her and her sister to be.

Pete might be mostly *sídhe* and able to wield magic, but he also had a Masters Degree in Criminal Psychology and he knew what the *Matrarchaí* were breeding better than most.

But that was a problem for another time. Right now, they had a very pissed off merman to deal with.

"I see you brought us a guest, Nika," Trása said, stopping just outside the stone circle to study their captive.

Abbán made some muffled noises but could not produce any intelligible sounds as Nika had covered his mouth with her magical bonds as well as his limbs and torso.

"A guest would not be so rude, my lady," Nika said as she bowed to Trása, her thick red braid almost touching the ground she bent so low. "Are you really a cousin to this creature?"

"So the story goes," Trása replied. "Release his mouth. I want to talk to him."

"You can talk to him, my lady," Nika said, tossing the braid over her shoulder, out of the way. "I haven't covered his ears."

Trása smiled. "Please, Nika, if you wouldn't mind."

Nika muttered something under her breath - in her reality all magic wielded by humans was via hand gestures and incantation - and Pete felt her unravel the magical bonds covering the merman's mouth.

Once he was free, Abbán didn't immediately launch into a diatribe. If anything, he seemed to be speechless. His eyes were fixed on Trása and full of suspicion.

Trása stepped into the circle, eyeing her cousin up and down for a moment, and then smiled. "Well, I'll bet this isn't how you planned on things turning out."

"You said you wanted to make amends." The merman was wide-eyed with anger. Pete feared he was about to burst something. "You told me you were ready to come home."

"I've been ready to come home for years," Trása agreed airily. "Not my fault if you thought I meant today."

"When Marcroy finds out you've broken through his curse -"

"He'll be very angry with me," Trása said. "Yes, I know that. What's he going to say to you, I wonder, Abbán, when he learns you opened an unauthroized rift so foreign rift runners could step into his realm and kidnap a merman and one of his *Leipreachán*?"

"You claimed Marcroy would reward me for aiding you! That I'd be a hero when I took you back to him in chains."

"I don't doubt it," Trása agreed. She glanced at Pete who got the feeling she was enjoying this immensely. "And just how are you planning to do that?"

"I know where you are now, Trása. I can come back to this realm anytime I want. I have Marcroy's jewel."

"Actually, merman, you don't," Nika announced, holding up a pigeon egg-sized ruby for them to see. "I have it."

Trása's eyes widened and Pete realized this was the prize.

In this reality, the *Youkai* and the humans who could wield magic opened rifts using *ori mahou* - folding magic. The flaw with this method was that not only was the paper exceedingly rare, it was a single-use item, as it was destroyed in the process of opening the rift. Pete had heard many tales of the jewels used in Trása and Ren's reality, but never seen one before. Curious to see the ruby, he held out his hand and Nika smiled and dropped it into his palm for his inspection. The gem was still warm and he could feel the magic pulsing inside it. On closer inspection, he noticed the center of the jewel was etched with a symbol that presumably was some magical rune written in the script of the *Tuatha Dé Danann*.

He closed his hand over it for a moment, and realized this jewel was his gateway home.

All this time, they'd had a different plan - search every reality they could find in the hope of capturing an agent of the *Matrarchaí* and forcing the location from them. The backup plan was to wait until the new stone circle commissioned by the *Matrarchaí* was functioning and return through there, a plan that had seemed the only logical choice.

Until now. Until Trása decided to change the rules.

This was the jewel Marcroy had used to open the first rift to their world so he could toss the infant Rónán through. This jewel - or at least the magic contained within it - knew the location of the reality where he'd been raised. The reality where he and his brother had worked in jobs they loved and had careers and nice apartments.

A reality where he was a nobody, really. Not like here.

It took Pete a moment to realize a return to that world was in his grasp. He met Nika's eye for a moment. It occurred to him that he might have to consider carefully whether or not he wanted to reach for it.

In the center of the *rifuto*, Abbán gamely tried to struggle against his bonds, but he was held fast, and Trása seemed to be getting a lot of satisfaction from the merman's predicament. Pete supposed, given they were related, there was some history between them; perhaps Trása was thrilled by his humiliation because she finally had the upper hand.

But gloating over this merman was an indulgence they really didn't have time for.

"What are we going to do with him, my lady?" Nika asked, before Pete had a chance to voice the same question.

"I can think of any number of things," Trása said, with a little too much relish.

"Pick *one*," Pete said.

"Well, we can't send him home," Trása mused, staring at the merman for a moment before turning to Pete and Nika. "He'll run straight to Marcroy if we do."

"Perhaps something you should have considered before you called him up on the puddle phone and asked him to open a rift back to Marcroy's realm," Pete suggested, pocketing the jewel for safekeeping.

Trása glanced over her shoulder and with anything but regal poise, pulled a face at him. Then she turned back to her cousin and pondered the problem for a moment before announcing her solution. "We'll release him into the ocean here," she said. She turned to them again. "I mean, without a jewel he can't go home, can he? And by the time he's figured out how the *Youkai* in this reality use folding magic, it won't matter. At least, not in time to do us any damage."

Pete rolled his eye at her naivety. "You think wielding magic is the only harm this guy can do?"

Trása threw her hands up impatiently. "Well, what am I supposed to do with him? We don't exactly have a *sídhe* jail to lock him in."

"I'll tell you what you do with him. You talk to Ren and get him to wipe this guy's memory and then send him home with some story about how he lost the jewel in a bog. That way he's not our problem, the jewel remains here, we can come and go as we please to your realm and, through that, to my home realm as well, and we won't have to sleep with one eye open for fear of some crazy, pissed-off merman trying to slit our throats in the middle of the night."

"I fear Pete speaks truly, my lady."

Trása shook her head with determination. "No. Rónán is not to know about this until I'm ready to tell him."

"As you wish," Nika replied with a small bow.

Pete wasn't nearly so willing to comply with Trása's every whim. "And your mer-cousin stays here, champing at the bit? This place drips magic, Trása. You don't think the moment your back is turned he isn't going to dial up your reality on the puddle phone and tell Marcroy where he is? And even if he doesn't know precisely where he is, just exactly how long are you going to be able to keep the fact that you have Marcroy's jewel a secret from Ren? Assuming, of course, Ren doesn't spot the *Leipreachán* you had us kidnap, and let loose in *Tír Na nÓg*, as soon as he gets back from wherever he is."

Trása chewed her bottom lip for a moment, something she did quite unconsciously when she was feeling pressured. Pete was certain she didn't know she did it and he chose not to mention it, because he found it a useful gauge of her mood. The Faerie refugees in this realm were - for the most part - absurdly loyal to their adopted queen, particularly the lesser *sídhe* who considered her akin to a goddess. It wasn't a good idea to do anything they might think would be upsetting to their precious

Trása. The lesser *sídhe* had limited power compared to Pete, Logan, Trása and even Nika - and none at all compared to Ren - but they were like a swarm of angry wasps when they were annoyed. Had they been standing in *Tír Na nÓg* having this discussion and not just outside it, he probably wouldn't have spoken nearly so bluntly, either.

Before she could respond, however, the hairs on Pete's forearms stood on end and the air about them began to tingle.

"Get back! Someone's opening a rift," he called urgently, although he had no need to tell the others. They could feel the magic building just as well as he could. He grabbed Trása by the arm and pulled her clear of the stone circle as Nika shoved Abbán magically, and none too gently, away from the circle.

The merman landed on the rocks outside the circle with a thud and a loud, indignant cry as the circle stones arced with lightning. "Expecting visitors?" Pete asked Trása as he caught her to stop her tripping.

Trása regained her balance and turned to watch the rift opening inside the circle, her expression concerned. "You don't suppose Marcroy figured out how to follow you back here, do you?"

He shook his head. "The lightning is white. This is coming from someone belonging to this reality. Whoever is opening the rift is using *ori mahou*."

And wasting precious washi paper doing it, Pete thought, wondering who - of the limited number of people, human and Faerie, in this realm with the ability to fold a rift-opening spell - would chance an unauthroized rift for anything other than the direst need.

Magic was plentiful in this realm, but rifts took more than just magic. They needed a talisman: some tangible focus for the rift, hence the stone circles in every reality and objects like Marcroy Tarth's precious engraved ruby. Nika's reality had used human bones marked with Celtic runes, and she still carried her talisman - a grotesque, mummified baby's foot tattooed with woad - tied to a leather thong around her neck, which he insisted she remove when they were in bed.

Here, magicians used folding magic, but not the ordinary kind that used *kozo* trees for wielding spells using origami. A dimensional rift needed a spell folded with washi paper and there were so few washi trees left in this reality, the paper was more precious than Faerie Lord sweat - something Pete was convinced was impossibly rare because he'd never met a *Tuatha Dé Danann* among Trása's refugees prepared to do even a lick of honest hard work.

The rift opened to reveal a picture perfect courtyard, a cloudless blue sky and a garden complete with cherry blossoms and quaint, upturned eaves on the corner of the slate-tiled roofs. Standing on the other side, waiting for the rift to stabilize, was a blond, middle-aged woman dressed in a gorgeous kimono. Beside her was a much younger man. Pete took a deep breath to brace himself. Wakiko wouldn't be coming here unannounced - and, significantly, without Isleen - to do anything other than deliver bad news.

A few moments later they stepped through the rift. With his right hand, the young man crushed the small hexagon he'd folded from washi paper and the rift flickered out of existence behind him.

"What's happened?" Pete asked, stepping forward before anybody could start in on the elaborate greeting ceremonies of which these people were so fond.

"It's Isleen," Wakiko said, her eyes red-rimmed from crying, Pete noticed, now he was close enough to see.

"Is she all right?" Nika demanded, a little impatiently. Wakiko glanced over her shoulder at Nika and shook her head, her eyes welling up with fresh tears as she turned back to face Trása and Pete. "She's broken through the *Comhroinn*," the young woman said.

Pete looked to Trása for an explanation. She had gone quite pale.

"How bad is it?" Trása asked.

"Bad," her mother Wakiko said. "She remembers it all."

"Everything?" Trása gasped.

Wakiko nodded. "Everything Delphine imprinted her with. All the dreadful secrets Renkavana locked away in her mind to protect her. She remembers them all."

Pete swore under his breath before asking, "Where is she now?"

Wakiko shrugged helplessly. "I don't know. She opened a rift and left, claiming she was going to look for Teagan and her true family."

"Her true family?" Nika asked. "Are you not her mother?"

"She means the *Matrarchaí*," Pete explained, afraid to even guess how much trouble this turn of events was about to unleash. "Jesus Christ, she knows everything there is to know about us and this reality and now she's gone looking for the *Matrarchaí*."

CHAPTER 16

After years of having no visitors at all, Darragh received two in as many days. The day after Eunice Ravenel came to see him the Gardaí psychologist, Dr Annad Semaj, came to visit.

The doctor had aged somewhat since Darragh saw him last. His temples were grey and there were a few more lines on his face. Seeing him after so many years drove home to Darragh how long he'd been here in this reality. Annad Semaj's face was a billboard advertising how abandoned Darragh was starting to feel.

He took his seat in the glass cubicle and picked up the telephone handset. Dr Semaj did the same on the other side of the glass.

"Hello, Darragh."

"Doctor."

"You're looking well." Darragh spared the doctor a wry smile. "It's all the fresh air, good food and exercise I get in here."

Annad smiled. "Well, you *are* looking well. You've hardly changed at all."

"To look at perhaps," he agreed with a shrug. "I am not so sure I remain mentally unaffected by this lengthy incarceration."

"Did you want to talk about it?"

Darragh shook his head. *What would be the point? Nobody here but Ciarán believes what I have to tell them.* "I'm fine, thank you. But you must have something you wish to discuss with me or you'd not have made the journey here."

Annad nodded and shifted in his seat. "I heard Hayley's family are going to have her declared legally dead."

"I know. I received a visit from the family's lawyer yesterday. She wants me to confess to the crime."

"Are you going to?" Annad asked the question like he knew what the answer would be, but he felt the need to ask it anyway.

"Of course not. I didn't kill her."

"Do you think Ren killed her?"

"No."

"She's not been seen or heard of in ten years."

"Because she's not here," Darragh reminded the psychologist. "She's in another-"

"Reality," Annad finished for him with a resigned smile. "Still sticking with that? I'm impressed by your recall, lad. Thought you might have forgotten about that story by now."

"There is a very wise judge I like watching on television," Darragh explained. "She says that if one tells the truth, one doesn't need a good memory."

"Fair comment," Annad agreed, "but do you realize what declaring Hayley dead would mean to you, Darragh?"

Darragh glanced around with a shrug. "I am incarcerated in a maximum security prison for allegedly kidnapping Hayley and for conspiring to murder Warren Maher. This country does not condone capital punishment. What more can be done to me in this realm that has not already been done?"

"If Hayley is declared dead, they can go ahead and charge you with her murder," Annad explained. "That's another mandatory life sentence and the judge can rule your sentences be served consecutively, rather than concurrently, if you're found guilty and still showing no sign of remorse. You could be in here until you're fifty, lad."

Darragh shook his head, refusing to believe it. "Rónán will come for me."

"You've been saying that for ten years, Darragh," the psychologist reminded him gently. "Don't you think it's time to consider the possibility your twin brother might not be coming from another reality to magically whisk you away from this one?"

"No."

"I see." Annad studied him closely for a moment in silence, cradling the handset loosely. "How are you coping in here?"

"Well enough."

"Do you have many visitors?"

"One a day, lately."

"And your cellmate? Does he give you any trouble?"

"Not since I dislocated his shoulder when he tried to make me his girlfriend."

It was true. Before Ciarán had been assigned to his cell, he'd had some trouble, but he'd taken care of it and nobody had bothered him much since then. If he tried to explain that his current cellmate was from his own realm and was also waiting to be rescued, he'd just bring Ciarán unwanted attention.

A brief smile flicked over Annad's face. "You've learned to look after yourself in here, then?"

"I knew how to look after myself before I got here," Darragh reminded him with a shrug. "It has been necessary to show a few of my fellow inmates that I am not interested in their... activities, but the message gets through after a few... effective demonstrations."

"Ah. Well, that explains what you're still doing here in Portlaoise and why they haven't remitted any part of your sentence for good behavior."

That option, Darragh knew, was one he had forfeited years ago. But it had been worth it. "I have learned, doctor, that in prison, as in great literature, it is much more effective to show than tell."

"I don't see any tattoos," Annad remarked, looking at Darragh's hands and the open neck of his prison-issue shirt. "Does that mean you're not still affiliated with any of the prison gangs?"

That was a harder question to answer. Darragh had been able to avoid the hard-core gangs because of his connection to Jack, but his position here wasn't so cut and dried as to whether or not he belonged to a gang. "I have ... friends, I suppose you could call them," he conceded, "who look out for me when I need someone to watch my back."

"Do you have legal representation? You'll need it if the Gardaí lay any further charges relating to Hayley's disappearance."

Darragh shook his head. "I don't, but I'm sure there are plenty of inmates who could recommend a good lawyer." He smiled. "Lawyers and their comparative worth are something of an obsession in here."

Annad Semaj smiled, but it didn't touch his eyes. He seemed sad. "Well, it's a relief to see you're surviving so well. You certainly look none the worse for your experience."

"Good genes," Darragh said. The comment reminded him he had been here far too long. When he arrived in this world, he had no idea what genes or DNA were.

"Can I get you anything?"

Darragh didn't hesitate. "I'd like an electric razor, actually."

Annad seemed surprised. "Really? Are you allowed an electric razor?"

"They're certainly preferable to the alternative."

The psychologist nodded. "Yes, I suppose they are, in this place."

"Will you get it for me?"

"I don't see why not," Annad said, after thinking it over for a moment.

Darragh had to force himself to hide his relief. "I have a particular model in mind, if that's okay?"

"Really. You've researched this? Which particular razor do you want?"

"A Remington Titanium 700. I'm not that hung up on the brand, but I really want the titanium."

Annad Semaj studied him curiously for a moment longer and then nodded. "I'll see what I can do."

"Thank you, doctor." There was an awkward silence as Darragh waited for Annad to say something else.

"Um ... if you don't get many visitors, would you like me to come back next week?"

"If you want."

"Good. Well, I'll see what I can do about a razor for you and I'll see you in a few days then." Annad replaced the handset and rose to his feet, watching Darragh closely.

Darragh smiled at him through the glass and turned to knock on the door to let the guard know he was finished. As he turned back, he saw the doctor tap the glass and point to the handset again. He picked it up at the same time as the psychologist.

"I'm curious," Annad said into the telephone, his eyes fixed on Darragh to gauge, no doubt, the reaction to his question. "Why does it have to be titanium?"

"How else am I supposed to contact my brother?"

Darragh watched Annad Semaj smile uncertainly as he replaced the handset. Behind Darragh the door opened. Annad watched as the guard led him out into the hall, his expression one of puzzlement and concern.

Darragh smiled to himself, certain Annad would do as he asked, if only to discover what insane plan he had in mind and how he intended to contact an alternate reality from his prison cell with nothing more than an electric razor.

CHAPTER 17

Trása's clever if somewhat devious plan to surprise Rónán by rescuing Darragh and bringing him home disintegrated like the crumpled piece of washi paper in Daibbido's hand. There was no chance, now, of interrogating Plunkett before Rónán woke and no chance of getting rid of Abbán by tossing him back into the sea before Rónán realized he was here.

The news that Isleen had broken through the magical bonds Rónán had placed on her mind to prevent her ever learning what the *Matrarchaí* had in store for her future was bad enough. That she had gone looking for Teagan made everything else pale into insignificance. In light of this, plus the gift of Marcroy's jewel, perhaps it would be enough to make Rónán forgive her for ignoring his rule about contacting anybody in her reality. With Marcroy's jewel maybe they could find Isleen; maybe they could return to their home realm. Darragh was probably waiting for them...

He wasn't though, Trása knew that for certain. She'd tried time and again to contact Darragh by scrying him out - or using the puddle phone, as everyone from Rónán, Logan and Pete's reality insisted on calling it - but she couldn't locate him. That meant he was either in a realm without magic, or he was dead.

He clearly wasn't dead. Even across realities, if one Undivided twin died, the other would follow within a day or so, and Rónán was alive and well, so there was no chance Darragh was dead.

That meant he was trapped somewhere her scrying couldn't reach him, and most likely, that meant a realm without magic.

Logically, he was still trapped in the reality where Rónán had grown up.

Trása knew Rónán had figured that out, too, but was reluctant to do anything about retrieving his twin. He had his reasons, she knew that, but Darragh had spent his every waking moment searching for Rónán when their situations were reversed. Rónán had found a way to be okay with doing nothing.

Whenever Trása pressed him on the subject he wouldn't say whether his nightmares had returned. All he would say were things like "all in good time", or claim Darragh would be living it up in the other realm pretending he was Ren Kavanaugh, settled into the lap of luxury with Kiva: wintering in St Tropez, summering in Spain and doing the red carpet awards circuit in London, Hollywood and Cannes.

They'd find out soon enough, she supposed. She hadn't been able to save Darragh directly, but with

Marcroy's jewel they could finally return to the realm where Darragh and Sorcha were stranded.

With Marcroy's jewel, they could finally bring them home.

But the news Wakiko brought meant that Darragh's return was no longer a high priority. *He's been gone ten years*, she could almost hear Rónán saying. *A little longer won't make much difference.*

She wanted to weep with frustration. They were so close...

"How did she break through the spell?" Trása asked, pushing aside her disappointment to deal with the matter at hand. "Rónán said it would take someone with the same sort of power as him to unravel the memories."

"Isn't that the point, though?" Pete asked beside her. "Potentially, Isleen and Teagan are as powerful as Ren. That's why Delphine blocked their powers until they were old enough to deal with them in the first place, and why Ren reinforced the block after she died."

"Teagan was always the impatient and curious one," Wakiko added, as if that somehow mitigated the disaster. "With her gone, I never thought to worry about -"

"We knew Isleen was looking for a way to break through the bonds," Daibbido said. He was a Tanabe so, on principle, Trása distrusted him, but he'd done nothing so far that she could fault and he'd been Wakiko's right-hand man since the harakiri suicides seven years ago, which had been prompted by Teagan's abduction. "I believe she asked Renkavana outright if he would release the bonds only a couple of months ago. I would have said something had I realized she'd find a way to undo them on her own."

"Would you?" Trása asked. "I thought the Tanabe would be thrilled by the prospect of the *Matrarchaí* returning to this world and elevating your family back to where you think you belong."

"I am the personal aide of the Imperial Regent, Ojōsama," he reminded her. "How much higher do you think I can climb?"

"It's not Daibbido's fault," Rónán said, making Trása jump with fright. She hadn't realized he was behind her.

She thought he was still sound asleep in the bower back in *Tír Na nÓg*.

It was very rude of him to just appear out of thin air like that. Not to mention just plain showing off.

"Renkavana," Wakiko cried and ran to him, throwing herself into his arms with a sob. "Isleen's gone! What are we going to do?"

"Let's start by not falling to pieces," Rónán said, gently but firmly pushing Wakiko away. Trása was surprised by her outburst. She was usually much more in control, particularly in front of Daibbido.

Rónán was dressed in nothing more than loose cotton gi trousers, his chest bare despite the chilly winds here on the cliff top outside *Tír Na nÓg*. Before Trása could offer any sort of explanation about why they were here or what else might be going on, Rónán turned to Pete. "What's with the pissed-off looking merman?"

Pete hesitated and glanced at Trása. Rónán turned to her for an explanation. He seemed angry, but she would have bet money his rage was directed at himself and his failure to protect Isleen. He'd been just as hard on himself after the *Matrarchaí* took Teagan. "Trása?"

She took a deep breath before she answered. "This is Abbán. My cousin."

"You mean your cousin's *eileféin*, don't you? Because Abbán is back in your home realm."

"No," Pete said, "she means this is her real cousin."

Rónán was silent for a moment. Trása wished she could tell what he was thinking. "You've been back to our home realm," he said after an uncomfortably long silence. There was an accusation in his tone that gave Trása chills.

"No, she has not," Nika said, always ready to defend her adopted queen. "The Lady Trása promised she would not go back. My queen would not break her word." Trása was normally quite chuffed by Nika's stubborn insistence she was a queen, but this was not the time to be throwing around titles she didn't have any right to. "My queen sent us. That is to say, me, Pete and Logan."

Trása wanted to slap her for being so forthcoming.

"Typical Faerie, you see. Can't break a promise but she can always find a loophole."

"Shut up, Pete." Rónán wasn't amused. "So the *Leipreachán* who woke me up complaining he'd been kidnapped from his own realm and dragged here against his will is the real Plunkett and not his *eileféin* from another realm?"

Trása nodded. *Do something Rónán, so I can tell what you're thinking. Yell, scream, rant ... just do something.*

But Rónán did nothing that gave away his opinion, which was a thousand times worse. "I see. Who opened the rift on this side?"

"Abbán opened it from the other side," Pete told him. "Trása scried him out on the puddle phone a few weeks ago."

"How did he open it?"

"With this," Pete said, handing the large ruby to him. "Apparently, it's Marcroy's very own stone."

Ren studied the gem for a moment in the palm of his hand and then closed his hand over it. "You do realize this means we finally have a way back into our world," Pete pointed out. "That jewel is the same one they used to open the rift into our realm."

"Through Ren's realm, though," Logan reminded him. "Will it even work from here?"

Rónán didn't answer Logan's question. Perhaps he didn't know the answer. "So, what we have," Rónán said instead, looking pointedly at Trása, "is a pissed-off *Tuatha Dé Danann* prince looking to retrieve his priceless, stolen rift-opening gem, in addition to an aggrieved *Leipreachán* storming around *Tír Na nÓg*. Oh, did I mention the angry merman, on top of a mischief-making Empress twin going rogue?" Rónán fixed his gaze on Trása with such intensity she wished the ground would open up and swallow her whole. "Anything else I should know about? Any other grand plans you've got underway while I was sleeping?"

"I'm sorry, Rónán. But you said yourself it would be seven years before we could get back into that realm. And it has been..." Her voice faltered under his withering stare. "I was just trying to help."

"Don't ever turn on me, then," he said. "I'm not sure I'd survive it."

Trása couldn't tell if he was joking.

"Does Marcroy know you have his jewel?" Rónán asked, turning to Abbán.

The merman nodded his head, his eyes wide. It occurred to her that in her realm they would have assumed Darragh and Rónán were long gone.

Shit, Trása thought. *Abbán wasn't supposed to know they're still alive. Maybe Rónán is right. Maybe I should have just left well enough alone.*

"How long before you're supposed to return the jewel?"

"You're... alive!" Abbán finally blurted out, looking completed flabbergasted. Not surprising, Trása supposed. It was unheard of for the Undivided to survive the transfer of power to their heirs. Everyone probably though Rónán and Darragh long dead. For that matter, he might not even realize this was Rónán, and not Darragh.

"Clearly," Rónán agreed, a little impatiently. "How long before Marcroy expects you to give it back?"

"I don't know... he had me open a rift to send the human girl home, but he never said when he wanted me to give it back. How are you still alive?"

"Magic," Rónán said. "What human girl?"

Abbán shrugged. "I don't know. Some human girl he found a while back. She's not of our realm.

Marcroy tired of her, I suppose, and so he sent her home."

"Marcroy finds human girls amusing," Trása explained, acutely aware of Marcroy's carelessly cruel fascination with innocent young women too foolish to realize he was not the enchanting Faerie Prince they thought he was. "Particularly if they're young and naive."

"He had this one in *Tír Na nÓg* for quite a while," Abbán added, nodding in agreement. "She didn't realize how long she'd been there, I suppose. I only met her the once when I took her to the stone circle to open the rift. Pretty little thing she was. But boring. Kept going on about how the magic in our realm cured her blindness."

Trása felt Rónán tense beside her. "What was her name?"

"Who? The human girl? I don't know. Why would I care? She was Marcroy's pet, not mine. How can you be alive, *Leath tiarna*? The new Undivided have been in power long enough to become men."

Rónán didn't answer him. Instead, he turned to Trása and said in a flat, emotionless tone. "All this time, it was Marcroy who had Hayley."

"You don't know that..." Pete began, but before he could finish his sentence, Ren waned himself away from the stone circle, vanishing before their very eyes without another word, taking Marcroy's precious rift-opening jewel with him and leaving Trása to deal with the problem of Abbán and with no indication of what they were supposed to do about the missing Empress Isleen.

CHAPTER 18

"Why didn't you tell this police doctor who came to visit, about me?" Ciarán asked Darragh after he'd finished telling him the details of his latest visit with the Gardaí psychologist, Annad Semaj. "I could reassure him you are not insane. And that I am also from another realm. Perhaps then the authorities here will realize their mistake, let us out of this dreadful place and we can return home."

That was three days ago and, with this morning's mail, a parcel had arrived - already opened by the guards to check for contraband. A shiny new Remington Titanium 700.

It was after lights out and the only illumination in the cell came from the corridor outside. Ciarán and Darragh spoke in whispers and in their own language, to avoid disturbing their neighbors as much as to keep their discussion private. The prison was silent, but for the distant sound of doors clanging shut as the guards did their nightly rounds, and the soft but persistent sobs coming from one of the cells a few doors down. Darragh didn't know who was crying, but tears were not an uncommon nighttime sound in this place. Although whoever it was would deny it in the cold light of day, even the toughest men, in the darkest hours of the night, could be crushed under the weight of the demeaning and soul-destroying environment of hopelessness that pervaded this place.

Darragh could only hear Ciarán, not see him. The warrior lay on the bunk below pondering the arrival of the doctor's gift and the implications for Darragh if what he said were true about another charge of murder being laid against him once Hayley Boyle was legally declared dead.

Darragh smiled in the darkness at Ciarán's optimistic suggestion that he introduce his cellmate to the psychiatrist and explain who he was. "If I tell them my cellmate is also from another reality and is willing to swear to it, they will just think I talked you into believing my delusion and we'll both wind up in a psych ward pumped full of psychotropic medication."

"I would like to show these people how wrong they are," the older man grumbled.

"Wouldn't we all." Darragh lay on his bunk, folding his hands behind his head. The ceiling was close enough to touch if he reached up, and if he leaned out of his bunk he could touch the wall on the other side of his cell. "And to that end, I've decided to contact Rónán."

His announcement was met by a stony silence.

"Did you hear me?"

In the dim light, Ciarán's face suddenly appeared beside Darragh's top bunk. It was astonishing how quietly a big man like him could move. "What do you mean, you're going to contact Rónán?"

"I'm going to send him a message," Darragh explained softly. "Ask him what's taking so long. I asked Dr Semaj to bring me some titanium, because that's the only metal in this magic depleted realm that seems to have the same properties as airgead *sídhe*."

"You can contact Rónán? With titanium?"

"There is a way, yes." Ciarán's eyes were intense, even in the dim light coming from the hall outside.

"All this time. All this time we've been trapped in here you've had a way to contact the other half of the Undivided, and you've done nothing?"

Ah, Darragh thought, that's not the reaction I was hoping for.

"But ... but, why?" Ciarán seemed lost for words.

"Because like you, old friend, I believe that if Rónán was able to return to this realm to help us, he would have."

Ciarán was disgusted. "I cannot believe you have had the means to call for help anytime these past ten years and not availed yourself of it before now. Why, Darragh? Do you like it here?"

I should have known he wouldn't understand.

Darragh sighed. "Getting a message to Rónán is neither simple, easily acquired, nor a particularly effective method of communication and it's liable to have me back in that psych ward I mentioned, if they notice what I'm doing. I learned my lesson last time. I'm not fond of tranquillizers, straightjackets, large doses of antidepressants or padded cells."

"Then do it," Ciarán hissed, not understanding the references to tranquillizers and padded cells. "Do it now. Call your brother and demand he come for us. Do you realize how long we've been here?"

"I've been incarcerated longer than you, Ciarán, " he reminded him. "Of course I realize."

"Well, I don't know about you, but I am sick of kowtowing to these ignorant prison guards and sleeping with one eye open. Call your brother. Get us out of here."

"I'm not exactly enjoying my stay in this realm, either, you know," Darragh reminded him, a little offended by Ciarán's suggestion that he had not contacted Rónán because he was comfortable here. "Getting a message to Rónán is no guarantee of help. And there are consequences to trying, with no assurance that Rónán is any better placed to get us out of here than the last time we communicated."

"How long ago was that?"

Darragh didn't answer for a moment. Ciarán knew nothing about his time in Saint Patrick's Institution for Juveniles prior to Portlaoise. When Ciarán had arrived full of his wild tale about being sent by Marcroy Tarth to find him and Rónán because if they had survived the *Lughnasadh* transfer of power that somehow made them the saviors of the *Tuatha Dé Danann*, they'd not spent much time discussing what Darragh had gone through as an inmate in St Patrick's.

Ciaran had committed armed robbery and murder to get here. He was so proud of his efforts to secure himself a place alongside Darragh, where he might fulfill his oath to protect the Undivided, he'd not questioned whether or not his arrival was timely. Darragh had not had the heart to explain that in some ways, the juvenile facility was far worse than this place; at least here the threats were physically real and you could usually see them coming. The well-meaning counselors at St Patrick's had listened sympathetically to his tales about the alternate reality he came from and assumed - just like Annad Semaj - that he was delusional. He was diagnosed at different times as having schizophrenia, bipolar disorder, schizo-affective disorder and post-traumatic stress disorder, sometimes all of them at once.

They'd counseled him and medicated him with lithium and when he'd attempted to contact Rónán, by putting the sharpened titanium bicycle spoke he'd stolen from the metalwork shop to use, they'd decided he was self-harming and had doped him so heavily with various neuroleptic medications that for a time Darragh found it difficult to remember who he was.

In the end, he stopped trying to carve messages into his skin to his brother across realities and let them think they'd cured him. It was easier that way. But he'd stayed in touch with Rónán. There were no messages exchanged - although once Dr Semaj came good on his promise to provide Darragh with an electric razor with a titanium sheath that situation could change.

But that spot just behind his ear where a tiny cut healed and then reappeared a day or so later and had done for years... that was Rónán. That was his brother's way of letting him know he hadn't been forgotten.

Darragh moved his hand and touched the spot just to reassure himself it was still there. It was almost healed again, the tiny scab ready to drop off.

"I haven't communicated with Rónán since before I came here," he lied.

"Why didn't you mention this before?"

"Your current reaction to the news should tell you that, Ciarán," Darragh replied, a little impatiently.

"So why now?" Ciarán asked. "Why are you willing to risk these consequences today and not yesterday, or last year, or five years ago?"

"Because they're probably going to charge me with Hayley Boyle's murder."

"Why does that matter?" Ciarán asked, echoing the same question Darragh had put to Annad Semaj. "They have no capital punishment here. What difference does it make?"

"I'll have to appear in court."

"So?" Ciarán said, still not understanding what had changed.

"I'll be moved. I'll have to appear in court in the city to answer the murder charge."

Ciarán was silent for a moment and then he nodded. "You'll be out of this prison with its high security and perimeter guarded by machine guns. You could be freed in transit, or from the courthouse cells. That's a good plan. What about me?"

"What about you?"

"Another trial will get you moved, Darragh, but I will still be here rotting away."

Darragh hadn't thought of that. He considered the problem in silence for a few seconds and then the solution came to him. He smiled. "I'll tell them you were my accomplice. That way you'll have to stand trial with me."

The big warrior thought on that for a moment and then smiled. "That's actually a good idea."

"It wounds me that you sound so surprised, Ciarán."

"I will be astonished if it works, lad. Even more amazed if your brother comes for us."

The statement surprised Darragh. He had thought the warrior was just as full of faith in their eventual rescue by Rónán as he was. "If you doubt my brother so much, old friend, why are you here?"

The older man shrugged in the darkness. "It was join you or go back to our realm and admit to Marcroy Tarth that I had failed. You were less likely to kill me."

Darragh smiled. "Go back to bed, Ciarán. Get some sleep."

"In this place? Fat chance." Nonetheless, the older man climbed back on his bunk and before long the tiny cell was filled with his deep, even breathing that was not quite a snore, but loud enough to be heard in the top bunk.

Darragh smiled at the sound, surprised at how comforting it was, eternally grateful that the distant sobs of despair, still audible down the hall, belonged to somebody else. He waited a while longer, listening to the heartbreaking sobs, to make certain Ciarán was deeply asleep.

When the older man's gentle snores had settled into a slower, steadier rhythm, Darragh reached under his pillow for the thin sliver of titanium sheathing from the electric razor Dr Semaj had delivered earlier today. He tested the edge with his thumb and winced as the sharp edge drew a tiny bead of blood.

It was sharp enough to do the trick but a trickier question remained.

Where to place his message?

Anywhere visible was likely to see him back in the psych ward.

Darragh settled on his abdomen after running through all the places on his body he could reach and be able to stand the pain. Anywhere normally covered by clothing would do, but at least on his abdomen he would be able to see what he was writing.

He sat up and listened for a time - not to Ciarán's snores or the sobs down the hall, but for some betraying sound that might warn him in a guard was coming.

There was nothing.

The next patrol was not due for about forty minutes, he guessed.

Darragh took a deep breath and lifted his t-shirt, wondering what he should say. There was, after all, a great deal to be said.

In the end, he settled on something quite simple. Long discussions could take place later. Face to face.

For now, he just needed to let Rónán know he was still expecting his help.

Biting his bottom lip to prevent himself from crying out from the pain, Darragh began to carefully, methodically, carve the words of his plea to his twin brother in his own flesh with the thin, sharpened sliver of titanium.

It was three small words: *get me out*.

CHAPTER 19

There was ruined lighthouse atop a windy cliff some hours away from the entrance to *Tír Na nÓg*. It was isolated, barren and had obviously been abandoned for centuries. Ren had stumbled across it in his travels years ago and he went there now, as he often did when he wanted to be alone to sort out his thoughts.

When he arrived, blinking into existence only seconds after he had left Trása and the others outside the entrance to *Tír Na nÓg*, it was raining. He shivered and realized he was still wearing nothing more than the gi trousers he'd pulled on when Plunkett woke him in the tree bower in *Tír Na nÓg*, complaining about his abduction. Almost without thinking, Ren wrapped a bubble of warm air around himself to keep hypothermia at bay, which served to isolate him even more and not just from the blustery squall battering the old ruin. Once he was warm and sheltered, he glanced around to make sure he was alone - although who else would brave this inhospitable spot he couldn't imagine - and then sat himself down on one of the huge, moss-encrusted, fallen masonry blocks that had once been a part of the main tower and fished a small black velvet bag from his trouser pocket.

Ren shook the large gem it contained into the palm of his hand and examined it for a moment. It was unchanged from the last time he had studied it.

"A lot's happened since the last time we spoke," he informed the jewel. He didn't know if the young woman trapped in the jewel's depth's could hear him or not, but it gave him some comfort to imagine she could. "I found another set of Empress twins, right where Delphine's memories said they would be. And there they were, driving another lot of Faerie through a rift into a realm that would kill them."

He stopped, not sure if he wanted to go on, but he knew he had to. This chance to confess was cathartic.

Ren was not particularly religious. His foster mother, Kiva, had worked her way through any number of religions while he was growing up, never sticking with one long enough for it to really affect her adopted son. But being Irish, Kiva was nominally a Roman Catholic despite her flirtation with other religions. As a child, Ren had been baptized at least three times that he could recall: once by a priest, once by a Native American shaman and once by a man claiming he came from another planet.

Kiva had never forced Ren to believe anything in particular, but as the best schools in Dublin were inevitably run by the church, he'd absorbed a religious education - almost by default - that included most of the rituals of Catholicism, including confession.

As a child, Ren had found the idea of a confessional rather unsettling and had avoided it as much as he could, in large part because he lacked any sins worthy of confessing, which had - perversely - made him feel quite guilty. But now, now that he knew so much more of the larger universe, now that he could perform his own miracles and knew for a fact that the God of the Judaeo-Christian pantheon was just one god among many, now he craved that cleansing absolution the confessional had promised him as a child.

When he thought about it, he figured it was because he finally had sins worth confessing, even though intellectually he considered the concept of sin so subjective that he scoffed at the very notion of it.

After all, one man's sins were another man's heroic deeds.

But Ren needed to confide in someone or go mad, and the young woman trapped in this pigeon egg-sized amethyst was as good a confessor as any. Better, probably, because without one of the Djinn she would never be released and could never betray anything Ren told her... even assuming she could hear a word of what he was saying in the first place.

"I had to kill them," he told the stone, in a matter-of-fact tone. It wasn't the first time he'd confessed to killing Empress or Emperor twins and he was quite certain it would not be the last. But, somehow, by confiding in the young woman who inhabited the stone, it eased his burden. And his guilt. "Killed one of them, at any rate. I guess the other one will be dead by now." He stopped for a moment and closed his eyes, recalling the cold, unrelenting look on the young woman's face as he'd appeared in her chamber. She hadn't screamed. She'd barely even blinked before hurling a magical bolt of lightning at him, as if she had confronted assassins before and knew exactly what to do about them.

"It was self-defense," he was able to assure Brydie. "She attacked me first. Does that get me off the hook?"

As usual, the stone offered no response.

"Do you think I'm a monster?" he asked the jewel. "If I can kill and feel no remorse, doesn't that make me some sort of psychopathic fiend?" He smiled thinly. "Do they even have psychopathic fiends where you come from? Have you any idea what I'm talking about? Can you even hear me?"

He glanced up. The rain was falling harder, the wind driving it almost horizontally across the ruin, although he felt nothing wrapped in his magical cocoon. It was almost midday, he guessed, but the cloud cover was so thick, it obscured the sun and made it seem much later.

"I figure it's because of all the Faerie blood I have," he surmised, still puzzled that he wasn't more guilt-ridden over the number of these dangerous twins he'd disposed of in the past few years. "I'm more *sídhe* than human, so I can kill humans and not bat an eyelid. I wonder what would happen if I tried to kill a Faerie?"

He didn't really mean it. He sighed and continued with his confession. "I got the location of another reality where they're about to unleash another set of Emperor twins. Boys, which makes a change. They're itching to get into it, according to the memories of Alean - she's the twin I killed yesterday. You know how I know that? She was pissed at the idea that there were some other little psychos about to come online that might outdo her and her sister in the Let's See How Many Faerie We Can Kill In One Go stakes. That's what her mind was full of - jealousy and anger." He shook his head as he remembered being almost overwhelmed by her emotional state. "Stupid bitch. I'm glad I killed her. And her stupid, fucking sister, too."

Ren realized he meant it. He was glad he'd killed Alean and her sister. Their realities, and many other realities besides, were better off without them.

"And now Isleen's going to turn into one of them."

Learning that Isleen had broken through the magical bond placed on her mind to prevent her learning the secrets of the *Matrarchaí* that Delphine had shared with her and her sister stung, but he wasn't as surprised by the news as the others were. Since he'd first met the twins when they were ten years old, Teagan had always been the troublesome twin, Isleen the quiet, thoughtful one. Teagan would have railed against the restrictions had she still been here.

Isleen had said nothing while quietly working to undo them. She'd always been the curious one; the one who wanted to know what was so terrible about the memories Delphine had left for her. And she'd picked away at the bonds holding them in place like a beggar picking at a loose thread in a blanket.

Had Teagan and Isleen been in contact, the same way Ren had kept in touch with Darragh? It only took a small, unnoticeable nick, which meant nothing to anyone other than the twins who could manifest each other's wounds and feel each other's pain.

There was no way of knowing. The only thing of which he was certain was that this wasn't going to end well for anybody.

"She's got Delphine's information, and she went rift running as soon as she unlocked the knowledge, probably looking for the rest of the *Matrarchaí*. Or at least where they're holed up. Doubt she'll have much luck with that. The intelligence she has from Delphine is more than a decade old, so I don't know what Isleen thinks she's going to achieve taking off like that. Unless she found a way to contact Teagan..."

He sighed. "Guess I should have pointed that out to Wakiko before I waned out of there. Might have helped her worry a little less to realize Isleen will probably be back as soon as it occurs to her that no matter what Delphine told her about the *Matrarchaí*, I know more."

Ren turned the jewel over in his hand wondering, as he always did when he confided in her, if Brydie was trapped in place or able to move about inside the gem. He also wondered if he should be more worried about Isleen.

The Undivided twins of this world were powerful sorcerers in their own right, with all the raw material to become as heartless and dangerous as the twins Ren had just killed. But Teagan and Isleen's life had taken a different path to Alean and her sister. They'd had the memories of their *Matrarchaí* mentor blocked when they were still young enough not to be corrupted by them and, until Teagan was abducted, a determined mother to raise them with some kind of moral compass. More importantly, they'd been brought up in a world where there was someone more powerful than they were and who would brook no thought of eradicating the Faerie.

Wakiko still refused to consider it, but Ren, Trása, Pete and Logan had pretty much reconciled themselves to the idea that Teagan, by now, had thrown her lot in with the *Matrarchaí*. What else could she have done?

But Isleen's betrayal wounded Ren. He'd trusted her. Since Ren disposed of Delphine, Wakiko had dedicated herself to ensuring her daughters' destiny took a different path than Delphine intended for them, an effort she redoubled when the *Matrarchaí* took one of her daughters from her. She'd made their world a refuge for *Youkai*, and had taught her remaining daughter to welcome the refugees rather than turn them away. Backed by four part-*sídhe* sorcerers from other realities, she had organized the *Konketsu* to gather as many refugee *Youkai* to their realm as possible. The magicians of this reality, who had once devoted their lives to preserving their own magical bloodlines by eliminating any *sídhe* competition for their magic, had finally turned their efforts to saving the *Youkai* . It had been a struggle, at first, but once they learned their own power came from diluted *Youkai* blood, and that if they continued to eradicate the *Youkai*, the *Konketsu* would soon die out themselves, they'd been very pragmatic about the whole thing.

It was easy to fall into the trap of thinking the changed attitude in this reality regarding *sídhe* was all his or Trása's doing, or was the result of things Pete or Logan Doherty had done since learning about their true origins. In fact, the *Konketsu* had identified their thinning bloodlines long before Ren and his friends appeared. Preserving those bloodlines had been the intention of the Ikushima when they first met Ren and Aoi tried to seduce him into fathering a magically-gifted child with her.

Fortunately, the Ikushima clan had gone back to doing what they did best - making fireworks. Now they were the official suppliers to the Imperial Court, and their fortunes had taken a significant turn for the better.

Thinking of the Ikushima made Ren realize he hadn't seen Aoi for quite a while. He should make time to pay the family a visit. Kazusa would be a grown-up by now.

Pity it was going to be a while before he had time to make social calls.

"Of course, that's not my only problem right now," he told his unseen confidante, as he realized he was stalling. "I have to decide what to do about Hayley."

Ren had thought the problem of Hayley far in his past. He assumed someone in Trása's reality would have realized she didn't belong and sent her back through the rift, preferably with her sight healed, long before now. It never occurred to him she might still be in the other reality, and it certainly never occurred to him that Marcroy Tarth would have been holding her all this time.

He should have gone back for her, he supposed. It would not be the first time he'd sneaked into the reality where he was born, despite banning Trása from making contact with anybody there. He'd done it, the first time, the morning after his first visit to the Pool of Tranquillity when he'd finally dared delve into Delphine's memories and stumbled across a scene that still haunted him.

In Delphine's memory she'd been standing in the sacred grove near Sí an Bhrú. Ren recognized it from Darragh's memories.

Anwen, the daughter-in-law of Álmhath, the queen of the Celts, was explaining how she had convinced the queen to steal a child from Darragh before the transfer of power to the Undivided heirs killed him and his brother.

"We need the bloodline preserved, my lady, you said so yourself," Anwen had explained to Delphine. *"It wasn't hard to convince Álmhath to send a suitable vessel to Darragh's bed so his seed might be collected. Any children spawned from such a union would be raised by herself, ensuring their loyalty to her rather than the Treaty of* Tír Na nÓg. *"*

Far from being pleased by this news, Delphine had been annoyed by it. *"If only it were that simple."*

"I didn't feel explaining the flaw in her logic would achieve anything, my lady, given her

184

ambition coincided enough with our needs to achieve the same outcome."

She'd smiled sourly at that. *"Well, you have to give her kudos for trying, I suppose. It's a grand idea, but not one likely to succeed if the union results in offspring tied to the Tuatha by blood."*

"I didn't have the heart to tell her how little chance her plan has of succeeding," Anwen said.

"It's not an impossible ambition though," Delphine conceded. *"There are realms where nobody has heard of the Undivided. Preserving the bloodlines in realms devoid of magic is much less problematic there. Believe me, I know. Who did you assign the task?"*

"Brydie Ni'Seanan," Anwen had said. *"Mogue Ni'Farrell's daughter."*

The mention of her name had caused a flood of Darragh's memories to overtake Delphine, which felt a little like having two people screaming at him at the same time, one in each ear and both with something different to stay. He'd fought down Darragh's lustful reminiscences and dragged Delphine's memory back. From the discussion that followed the announcement of her name, Ren gathered the *Matrarchaí* suffered from defections more often than they'd like. Brydie's mother, like Wakiko, had rebelled at being nothing more than a human incubator in the *Matrarchaí*'s grand plan.

"The girl in question was the right bloodline and had few other prospects at court," Anwen had explained to Delphine in her memories. *"She was destined to be someone's mistress, not a wife. The men who come to Álmhath's court looking for a*

woman to bear their children and housekeep their estates, don't want a wife they know every other man in their kingdom will be lusting after. I did her a favor, my lady, not a disservice. Darragh of the Undivided was healthy, virile and not unattractive. One day, she'll thank me for the opportunity."

That statement had made Ren smile. Darragh would like to hear about that one.

But then came the real kicker and the reason Ren had risked visiting a realm where his safety was best assured if everyone kept believing he was dead.

"Perhaps," Delphine had agreed, with some reluctance. *"Where is she now?"*

Anwen untied the ostentatious, gem-encrusted necklace she was wearing and handed it to Delphine. *"She's in here."*

Delphine had accepted the necklace on the palm of her hand and stared at it for a long moment. *"Did you...?"*

Anwen shook her head. *"I've not the power to do anything of the kind, Lady Delphine. That's why I was chosen to come to this court, if you recall. Had I any magical ability to speak of, the Druids or the Undivided may have recognized it in me, and I would have been discovered as soon as I arrived."*

"Then who did this?"

"I'm guessing it was one of the Djinn," Anwen said.

Delphine looked up from the gems. *"What interest would they have in this girl? More to the point, what are the Djinn doing, sneaking around Sí an Bhrú?"*

"I don't know, Lady Delphine. I just know that, in this realm, the only species of sídhe *who use inanimate objects to trap unwary humans are the Djinn. And as you no doubt can tell, she is trapped in the jewel."*

Delphine wasn't in any great hurry to release the stone and studied the necklace with interest. *"Do they know you have her?"*

"I don't know, my lady. I suspect not."

"Then for the time being, she is safe. It is almost impossible to release someone trapped by a djinni without the help of the Djinn. If this girl succeeded in her task and managed to conceive, then we will have need of her. Until we can find a safe way to release her and the precious burden she may well be carrying, she is better off where she is."

"And in the meantime?"

"In the meantime, the transfer will take place on Lughnasadh *as scheduled, Darragh and Rónán will die and we will be rid of one more potential threat to our plans."* Delphine handed the necklace back to Anwen. *"If Brydie conceived a child - or better yet, twins - then you did well to preserve the line. I wish we were having as much success in other realms."*

That was the reason, he'd known immediately, why the nightmares had stopped. Trása was right. It wasn't taking Delphine's memories that had stopped the dreams of him murdering Darragh's children. It was some nameless djinni who, for no reason Ren could fathom, decided to trap Brydie in suspended animation.

She was pregnant and the jewel prevented the pregnancy from progressing. If she ever got out, then Ren's worst fears would come true.

He felt bad for Brydie. The innocent young woman the *Matrarchaí* had thrown at Darragh in the hope of getting a child from him was trapped in this jewel through no fault of her own. The *Matrarchaí* wanted her kept safe because she might well be the mother of Darragh's children.

And it was that frightening possibility that had caused Ren to risk visiting Darragh's realm and steal the gem from Anwen.

He didn't do it to save Brydie, however. He intended to ensure she stayed trapped in the jewel forever.

And to be certain she never brought the babies he was destined to kill to term, he never let the jewel out of his sight. If Brydie was carrying Darragh's children and she remained in the jewel, Ren would never have to live out that terrible scene burned so indelibly into his brain.

Ren had informed Brydie of this unfortunate truth as soon as he'd returned to this realm, feeling he owed her some explanation for her continued imprisonment. He hadn't told her about the dreams, of course, but had warned her to to expect to be released anytime soon. It was one of the reasons he spoke to her as often as he did. It assuaged his guilt a little to acknowledge her presence, even if he did nothing to restore her.

He could not tell her the reason. There was no way he could think of to explain that he still remembered a dream which had haunted him most of his life, and he had become more and more certain as he got older that it was not his own children, in the dream, he was killing, but his brother's children.

And had he realized Hayley was still there when he stole Brydie's jewel, he could have sought her out on the same trip and maybe brought her here to this world seven years ago. Or would he have done so?

There other were things he'd taken from Delphine's mind that made a public return to his own realm to find Hayley somewhat problematic, even if he didn't factor in the simple fact that everybody thought he was dead and he had a lot more to do before he was ready to reveal that that was not the case.

With the exception of Ciarán, there was nobody in the other reality he could completely trust not to reveal that he and Darragh still lived. But he'd not been able to contact the old warrior since arriving in this realm.

If the puddle phone was working, Ciarán wasn't picking up.

Damn you, Hayley.

Ren tried to recall the burning need he'd had to be the one who saved Hayley when he was younger. He wasn't nearly so foolish, passionate, or absurdly heroic these days. That reckless desire had caused a catastrophic chain if events that had led him here to this place, and this moment, with the blood of a dozen or more people on his hands.

Perhaps she was okay. Abbán had sent her back to her own realm. She'd been gone a long time and it was unlikely anybody would believe her when she tried to explain where she'd been, but Kerry and Patrick would be thrilled to have their daughter home. Even Neil would probably be glad to see his sister again.

There's nothing I can do about it, anyway, he reminded himself. *She's home now. Back in my world...*

Strange how I haven't stepped foot in that reality in ten years and I still think of it as mine.

Ren reached into his pocket and retrieved the other jewel he carried today - the ruby Trása's cousin Abbán had used to open the rift from their reality to this one. That was not what made it special, though. Ren had the ability to come and go as he pleased to this realm. This jewel had opened a rift to the reality where Darragh was stranded and could do it again.

For the first time in a decade, Ren had the means to bring his brother home, quite literally, in the palm of his hand.

But if he did that, as soon as he found him Darragh would expect to share the *Comhroinn* with his brother. That meant giving away the presence of Brydie and the amethyst and the certainty that Darragh would insist on asking a djinni to release her, and then they'd know if she was pregnant, and Ren's nightmare would come true...

"I'd like to help," he said after a time, studying the multifaceted gem. "I'd like to get Darragh. But I can't. Not now. Not with this crisis with Isleen. Trása can't understand why I'm not moving heaven and earth to find my brother and bring him home. God knows, Logan and Pete want to go back and get some answers from the *Matrarchaí*, even though I've shared a lot of Delphine's memories that I've been able to make sense of." Ren hadn't shared all of her memories, partly because he couldn't access them either. Knowing what Delphine knew was only useful if something triggered the memory. He'd had the same problem with Darragh's memories when he tried to figure out how Darragh had managed to teleport himself out of danger when he first arrived in this realm and the Tanabe tried to kill him. He'd searched Darragh's memories to no avail, until Trása told him the skill was called waning and he had to have something to search for. That, more than anything, drove his need to share the *Comhroinn* with other Empress twins as they died - not for information, so much as context for the memories already filling his head.

"The more I learn, the more it seems our reality is the key. It's where the *Matrarchaí* are headquartered. And now Trása's gone and messed everything up trying to be helpful. Marcroy is going to miss Abbán soon and wonder where his ruby is, so I guess I'm not going to be able to put off dealing with him for much longer, either."

He sighed heavily at that thought. There were consequences attached to confronting Marcroy Tarth.

"There're things I know that Marcroy doesn't... or rather, things Delphine knew."

He took a deep breath and closed his eyes for a moment.

"How do you think Darragh's going to take the news that -" Ren doubled over, his thought cut short by a searing pain slicing across his abdomen.

He fell to his knees on the wet stony ground. The pain shot through him in white bolts of agony. It felt as if he were being stabbed and his hand came away bloody when he tried to feel his abdomen for the source of the pain.

Darragh. It was the only explanation.

Darragh was trying to contact him and he was doing it with the equivalent of *airgead sídhe* in the other realm. Titanium. Darragh had done this years ago, when they were first separated and naive enough to believe they would be reunited any day now.

Ren had communicated with Darragh the same way, reminding him of the accident Ren had had as a child by carving the word "bike" into his forearm. He knew Darragh would see it and then dredge it from Ren's memories - shared during the *Comhroinn* - and make the connection between the titanium bike spoke that had injured Ren, and the matching wound he'd manifested in another reality years before, the only time the psychic link between them had worked the other way.

For a time, after that, they'd kept in touch, but then Darragh had asked Ren to stop. He'd sent him one last message: *no more.* Since then, they'd stayed in touch with nothing more than the tiny nick behind the ear that Ren reopened every few days, just to let his brother know he hadn't been forgotten.

Things must have changed dramatically for Darragh for him to reach out like this. When Ren peeled away the bloodied fabric of his gi pants and read what Darragh had hacked into his own flesh, he knew his previous rationaizations were moot.

It didn't matter any longer whether this was the right time. It didn't matter about Hayley. It didn't matter about Isleen and Teagan. It didn't matter that the nightmares might return. It didn't matter that they might one day come true.

None of it mattered.

It was time to bring his brother home.

PART THREE

CHAPTER 20

The *Tuatha Dé Danann*, although long-lived, were not particularly forward thinking. It was hard sometimes, Marcroy reflected, to remember how they owed the Druids a debt of honor and wondered - as he often did - if the treaty they had sworn almost two thousand years ago had been worth the long-term cost.

As this evening's ceremony drew to a close in the sacred grove outside Temair, Marcroy wished more of his ilk possessed the ability to see into the future. The gift of Sight sadly seemed to belong almost exclusively to human practitioners of magic and a few of the Brethren he would likely never meet. *Tuatha Dé Danann* seers were almost unheard of.

Had there been one around at the time the treaty was worked out between human and *sídhe*, Marcroy was convinced it would never have been agreed upon. *But, then again, perhaps it still would have.* The *Tuatha Dé Danann* possessed the ability to cross into other realities where similar treaties had been forged and there had been no warning, in those realities, of the trouble to come. In fact, Marcroy had got the very idea for the treaty after hearing how successfully it had worked in other realms. Pity he didn't get to see any of those other realms a millennia or so after the fact. He may not have been so quick to embrace the notion of sharing *sídhe* magic with humans to fight off a common foe.

"The reason humans think the *Tuatha Dé Danann* are so arrogant," a small voice whispered in his ear, "is because you always look so bored when presiding over their ceremonies."

Jamaspa. Marcroy hadn't seen or heard from the djinni in years. His sudden appearance - if that's what the faint wisp of blue smoke hovering beside his ear could be called - could only mean trouble.

Marcroy couldn't answer him, either. Queen Álmhath was staring at him, waiting for his response to her spring offering. He was here to accept this gift on behalf of Orlagh, the queen of the *Tuatha Dé Danann*. Fortunately, the ceremony was almost done. Soon he could leave this mundane world and return to the peace and serenity of *Tír Na nÓg*.

"I thank thee on behalf of Orlagh and all the *Tuatha Dé Danann*," he said, annoyed he was required to appear grateful. Back before the Treaty of *Tír Na nÓg*, although the gifts were the same, there had never been a need to say thank you. Supplicants didn't expect thanks from their betters. Thanks were something reserved for equals and Marcroy considered humans to be woefully short of being his equal.

The queen bowed and turned to face her people, gathered among the trees, throwing her arms wide to welcome them to the celebrations. As they let out a cheer, Marcroy took the wicker basket laden with food none of his kind would ever eat and turned away, at the same time catching sight of Álmhath's son, Torcán and his wife, Anwen. Torcán seemed to be itching for the party to begin. Anwen, however, was watching Marcroy with eyes that were both cold and suspicious.

"She is not what she seems, that one," the djinni whispered in his ear. "You should be careful of the queen's daughter-in-law."

"Is that why you came?" Marcroy asked as he turned his back on the humans. "To warn me about some chit of a girl."

"Not at all," Jamaspa said, his voice tickling Marcroy's ear and sending ominous shivers down his spine. "I came to fetch you."

"For what?"

"For the Brethren," Jamaspa said. "They want to see you."

Marcroy Tarth was a prince among the *Tuatha Dé Danann*. He had the ear of Orlagh, queen of the *Tuatha Dé Danann*. He was her envoy to the mundane world. Lesser *sídhe* quivered with terror at his approach. Humans spoke his name in whispers for fear of invoking his wrath.

And yet, when confronted with the Brethren, he felt as puny as a small child.

Even though they had sent the irritating and smug Jamaspa to fetch him, Marcroy couldn't imagine refusing the invitation, even if it meant his doom.

When he met with the Brethren, however, he was not taken to some fabulous palace hidden among the clouds, or a shining temple atop a high mountain. Jamaspa brought him to a jungle so humid and teeming with every imaginable creature, both magical and mundane, that for the first time in his long existence, Marcroy felt a little lost.

The Hag was waiting for him, seated on a decaying log, her wrinkled skin so weathered and brown that he wondered if she counted her age in years or millennia, assuming she bothered to keep count at all. A thick, silent mist began to close in around them as he approached. Lit from some indefinable source, the fog tendrils gave the Hag an air of mystery and power that was not undeserved.

"My lady," Marcroy said with the deepest respect, bowing as he approached her in the clearing across a thick layer of warm rotting detritus that smelled earthy and rank.

The ragged old woman looked up at him with ancient, watery eyes, almost as if she was surprised to see him, even though he was answering her summons. "You came."

"I live to do thine bidding, my lady," he said formally. "How may I aid thee?"

The Hag closed her eyes and said nothing for such a long time that Marcroy feared she had fallen asleep.

He waited in silence for her to move, to say something. He did not dare so much as twitch in case it displeased her. The mist grew steadily thicker until it blocked out every sound from the jungle, enveloping them in a white cone of silence and fear.

Finally, the Hag opened her pale eyes and fixed her gaze on her visitor.

"I am cursed with the Sight," she said. Her voice was rasping and dry, as if autumn leaves rustled through her throat. "As if that is not bad enough, my Sight is filled with images of you and your cursed mongrel progeny."

Marcroy was shocked by the accusation. He had no half-blood get. He was very careful about that sort of thing, although if there was some mistaken belief among the Brethren that such abominations existed... well, it explained the summons, at least.

He smiled with all the charm he could muster. "I can assure you, my lady, if that is what disturbs thee, I will make certain your visions never see the light of day. You need not fear. I will make no mongrel child to sully the proud line of Tarth."

His charm made no impression on her. She glared at him. "Too late for hollow promises, lad."

Marcroy couldn't ever remember anybody daring to call him "lad". He squared his shoulders and raised his chin proudly. Nobody, not even the Hag, spoke that way about the *Tuatha Dé Danann.* "Forgive me, my lady, but I am a prince of the *Tuatha Dé Danann.* How could you not trust my word?"

"Because the damage is already done, fool. And it's your progeny's progeny that keeps me - and my brethren - awake at nights."

"You are mistaken, my lady," Marcroy said, before he could stop himself.

The Hag snorted at him. "You are the mistaken one, Tarth. Your lust... your mistake... spawned RónánDarragh."

The accusation took Marcroy by surprise. He shook his head, refusing to believe it. "That cannot be."

"Their mother was a Druidess," the Hag reminded him, "impregnated during a *Lá an Dreoilín* festival. Too much wine and not enough sense. It is the cause of most ills that beset most realms."

Marcroy shook his head. It couldn't possibly be true. And even if it were true, what difference did it make? Rónán and Darragh were long dead.

There had been many *Lá an Dreoilín* festivals in Marcroy's long life, but no pregnancies, he was certain of that. If he occasionally weakened and allowed himself to dabble in a little bit of harmless fun, Marcroy made a point of taking any human lovers he fancied to *Tír Na nÓg* where he could magically ensure no half-breed child would be spawned by his indulgences. He made a point of never...

... well there was that one time, he supposed, *but that was years ago and she was masked ... and surely nothing had come of it. I mean, what Druidess would conceive a child sired by a prince of*

the Tuatha Dé Danann *and not shout it from the rooftops?*

"You lay with a *Matrarchaí* spy," the Hag said, answering his unspoken question. "Ready, willing and able to harvest your precious *Tuatha Dé Danann* seed. Sybille of Aquitania was her name. Did you ever bother to check if she actually *came* from Aquitania? In this realm or any other?"

"Why would I need to check on such a thing?" Marcroy asked, wondering if the masked seductress he vaguely recalled laying with in that *Lá an Dreoilín* festival so long ago really was a *Matrarchaí* spy. "As I recall, Sybille was an opinionated troublemaker. Some time after Rónán was removed from this realm she disappeared in mysterious circumstances which some tried to blame on us."

"Her disappearance was not so mysterious," the Hag scoffed. "Once you separated her boys, she had no further need to remain in this realm. She went back to doing what she does best - finding ways to force Partition."

Marcroy shook his head again, still not believing the *Matrarchaí* had the power or the knowledge to do such a thing. He glanced around. The fog seemed even closer. Would he get out of here alive if his answers displeased the Hag?

He dragged his attention back the Hag's words.

Who would be so foolish as to try to force Partition?

Marcroy knew the Hag wasn't talking about the human Partitionist movement who simply wanted to destroy the Treaty of *Tír Na nÓg*, and return to lives without magic or the need for it. The Hag spoke of true Partition. The ability to reset the universe. The implosion of realities to leave only a single realm - a feat that even the *Tuatha Dé Danann* considered too dangerous to attempt.

"Do you understand what the *Matrarchaí* are trying to do, Marcroy Tarth?"

"Other than cause trouble for trouble's sake?"

"They are attempting to splinter realities," the Hag warned. "They're trying to free themselves of us."

"Why not let them?" Marcroy asked, before he could stop himself. He usually cared nothing for what the *Matrarchaí* might be plotting, but he had been summoned before the Brethren to answer for something he knew nothing about and he couldn't believe those annoying human women had the power or the knowledge to do what the Hag was suggesting. Perhaps it was time to start paying attention. "Even if the *Matrarchaí* managed to achieve true Partition, of what matter is it to us? Of what use is such a realm?"

"Do you not appreciate what it means to sunder reality?"

Marcroy's first instinct was to respond that of course he knew what it meant, but the Hag's obvious irritation prompted caution. "Perhaps you should explain it to me, my lady."

"It means one reality."

"Yes..."

"That's it. One reality. If the *Matrarchaí* are successful, every other reality will cease to exist."

Marcroy stared at the Hag for a moment, not sure if he'd heard her correctly. "Excuse me?"

"You heard me."

"That's not possible."

"So you say."

"But..."

The Hag shifted on her log as if she'd been sitting in the same position for too long. "It is possible. Worse than that, it's becoming likely."

"I don't see how... Why have the Brethren not warned us this could happen?"

"Because we never believed it could," the Hag said, with a sigh that seemed to ooze regret. "The circumstances seemed so unlikely... a world almost completely denuded of magic populated by an organized group that could maintain its focus long enough to produce Undivided so powerful they make even the Brethren seem less than pixies... Undivided, with polluted human blood, linked so closely they think as one... we found it hard to imagine such a circumstance, even without it staring us in the face."

Marcroy had seen evidence of the *Matrarchaí*'s unrelenting focus for himself: the wanton genocide of the *sídhe* races was pursued so relentlessly, whole realities had been denuded of their presence. But he never imagined for a moment that they posed a threat on the scale of the one the Hag was describing.

"I don't understand," he admitted, something Marcroy was not wont to admit lightly. "The *Matrarchaí* have been trying to drive our people from their realities for centuries. They haven't been trying to create new worlds, they've been trying to eradicate the *sídhe* races."

"They are experimenting," the Hag said. "They want to find out how few true Faerie they need to maintain a partitioned world. Make no mistake, Marcroy Tarth, their plan is the obliteration of us all."

Marcroy didn't want to appear to doubt the Hag, but what she was suggesting was unthinkable. "And the *Matrarchaí* want this realm, I suppose?"

She snorted, and fixed her rheumy eyes on him, full of contempt and derision. "I suspect they don't care about this realm, one way or another. This realm is only of use to them in so far as it has spawned the instruments of our destruction. The realm they are focused on is almost denuded of magic. Soon it will be beyond any hope of redemption."

"What is the use of such a world?"

"You cannot fill a cup that is already full, Marcroy Tarth. They have chosen their world wisely. Its very lack of magic makes it a syphon for all the realms connected to it. Why do you think they have tried to empty so many realms of Faerie? Each of those realms full of magic with none of our kind to defend it will be sucked dry when Partition happens. The magic will flood into the *Matrarchaí* realm and it will become so powerful it will not need any other realities to sustain it."

Marcroy struggled to comprehend the scope or the audacity of such a plan. "You have seen this, my lady?"

"I have seen them try," she said, "and I have seen them succeed."

"Then what is the point of fighting them?"

"Because I have also seen them fail. You are a part of that vision, Marcroy Tarth, much as it pains us to admit it. The Brethren need you."

Marcroy was silent for a moment, not sure he wanted the responsibility. But in the end, he had no choice. He was *Tuatha Dé Danann*. He would defend his own kind. "How can I be of service, my lady?"

"I'm not sure you can," the Hag snorted. "Each time you help, things seem to get worse."

Marcroy was too afraid of the Hag to let his indignation show.

"We asked you to fix the problem of your mongrel get years ago. Instead of solving the problem, you tossed one of them out of this reality and into the very arms of the *Matrarchaí*. I would dismiss you completely were it not that I have Seen the future again and it remains... fluid. There may be hope yet."

"The Brethren's instructions, as I recall, my lady, were to do something about RónánDarragh because you Saw they were going to destroy us," he reminded her, feeling the need to defend his actions so far, actions which had - in no small way - been driven by Jamaspa, acting on behalf of the very same Brethren the Hag claimed to represent. "I did as much as I could to sunder their power within the constraints of the Treaty of *Tír Na nÓg*. I worked tirelessly to remove them, my lady, and then, at the very moment of my triumph, Jamaspa intimated that far from being our ruin, RónánDarragh may be the key to our salvation and you wanted them saved." Marcroy didn't mind taking responsibility for what he'd done. It was the constantly shifting opinion of the Brethren regarding the value of his actions that irked him.

"And although you claim to have Seen them," he added cautiously, not sure of the reaction he would get to telling the Hag she was wrong, "I fear your hopes may be misplaced. The transfer killed them, my lady. Nobody has seen or heard of Rónán or Darragh in years. Jamaspa even sent Ciarán mac Connaught after them and he has never been seen again, either. I do not wish to question the veracity of your Sight, my lady, but one has to wonder -"

"Ciarán is dead," the Hag said. "Or he soon will be. RónánDarragh live. Their spawn are the key to our salvation."

There was clearly no arguing with her. He bowed, hoping she didn't notice his heavy sigh. "What would you have me do, my lady?"

"Find them," the Hag said. "Bring them to me."

He looked up, a little surprised by her request. "Surely you do not intend to kill them yourself?"

"I must speak with them," she explained, which was remarkable in itself. The Brethren were not in the habit of explaining themselves to anyone. "I must make certain they will do what must be done."

"And what is that, my lady?"

"They must destroy the children they spawn. Anything less will spell our ruin."

CHAPTER 21

When Hayley arrived back in her own reality she was freezing. The gossamer gown she wore was ill-suited to the damp, misty dawn in which she found herself. The lightning of the rift faded away to nothing as she wrapped her arms around her body, wondering where she was. There was nothing here to mark this as a magical portal, or to prove it had ever been anything more than an old, worthless ruin other than some ancient, moss-covered stones etched with Faerie symbols nobody in this world could read.

Hayley stepped gingerly over the rough ground and onto the cold - but much easier to walk on - manicured stretch of grass she could spy through the patchy mist. She glanced around, puzzled at first, and then realized she was standing on a golf course.

Why had the odd little man who'd brought her back to this reality left her on a golf course of all places?

Wouldn't it have been easier to drop her home?

The cold was seeping into Hayley's feet. She was barefoot and would be in serious trouble if she didn't find something warm to wear soon. She looked around and began walking down the fairway, hoping the direction she had chosen was taking her toward civilization and not away from it. Although the mist was patchy she could hear the faint sounds of traffic and, after a few moments, she spotted a golf cart and two golfers in the distance. She smiled with relief, even though her teeth were starting to chatter. Riding back to the clubhouse in a cart was a much better idea than traipsing over wet grass on foot. They would have a phone there. From the clubhouse she could call her father and ask him to come pick her up.

Setting out across the fairway at a brisk pace, her heart tightened a little at the pain her family must have suffered, wondering what had happened to her. She must have been away more than a week, although she couldn't be sure what the date was. In the strange world of Ren's alternate reality, time seemed to move at a different pace.

She hoped they hadn't been too worried.

Hayley was certain they would be relieved when she returned, rather than angry with her and Ren for disappearing.

As she hurried across the fairway, Hayley wondered what had become of Ren. She hadn't laid eyes on him the whole time she was in *Tír Na nÓg* with the *Tuatha Dé Danann*. She didn't know where he'd gone. Or what he was doing, although she suspected that whatever he was doing, he was doing it with the Faerie Elimyer's daughter, Trása, because

Hayley hadn't laid eyes on that boyfriend-stealing cow the whole week she was away, either.

As she neared them, the golfers belonging to the cart in the distance resolved into two grey-haired men dressed in warm jackets and those ridiculous tartan plus fours - pants that otherwise sane golfers liked to wear for no logical reason that Hayley had ever been able to fathom. She called out to them as they shouldered their clubs and prepared to head back to their cart. If she didn't catch them before they moved on, who knew how far she'd have to walk to get back to the clubhouse.

They turned at her call, their eyes widening at the sight of a scantily-clad girl appearing out of the mist.

"Hi," she said through chattering teeth as she approached them. "I'm sorry to disturb your game, but I kind of got dumped out here and I need to get to a phone so I can call my dad to come get me."

The men stared at her as if they couldn't believe what they were seeing, and then one of them muttered something under his breath and hurried toward her, unzipping his jacket as he went.

"Jesus Christ, lassie," he said as he slipped off his coat and wrapped it around her shoulders. "Are you okay?" He glanced at his companion and added with a frown, "Do you think we need to call the Gardaí?"

"No! Of course not," she said, before the older man could answer. Ren was in enough trouble without making more for him by getting the police involved. "Really, I'm okay. I just need to get to a phone."

The other man reached into his coat and produced

a small rectangular device and handed it to her. "Here, you can call him on the way back to the club. Who dumped you out here? Why?"

"Long story," she said, accepting the device. Hayley stared at it for a moment, not sure what it was.

"There's no password on it," the man said. He studied her for a moment with an odd expression. "What's your name?"

"Hayley Boyle," she said, and then she smiled helplessly and held the phone out to him. "I'm sorry, I don't know how it works."

The other man, the one who had given his warm tobacco-smelling jacket to her, laughed. "Christ, Mick, a teenage girl who doesn't know how to use an iPhone! I'll be tweeting that when we get back. Come on, let's get you into the cart and back to the clubhouse where it's warm. You must be freezing."

The old man who owned the odd phone didn't laugh. Without a word, he took the phone, pressed the screen a few times with his index finger and then looked at her. "I'll call it for you. What's the number?"

The man dialed the number as she recited it, and then handed the phone to her. She put it to her ear as it began to ring, wondering where he'd got such a cool thing. It must be some kind of prototype. Kiva would want one as soon as she saw it. The phone rang a few times and then a male voice answered

"Hello?"

"Hi Dad, it's me. Can you come get me?"

"Wha- what?" the man mumbled so sleepily she realized the call must have woken him.

"It's Hayley. I'm back. Don't worry, I'm okay. Can you come pick me up? I'm at the ..." she realized she had no idea where she was. She looked at the two golfers for help.

"Castle Golf Club," the man who owned the slick new phone told her. "At the Castle Golf Club," she repeated.

There was silence for a long time and then her father said, "You sick fuck," and the line went dead.

Hayley stared at the phone for a moment, a little stunned by the man's vitriol, then she looked at the man who owned the phone. "Can you check the number you called? I think you must have mixed it up. That wasn't my dad."

The man pressed the screen a few more times and held the display up for Hayley to see. It really was an amazingly cool phone. "Is that the number?"

She read the digits and nodded, frowning. "I'm sorry, can you try again?"

"Sure, but why don't we call him from the cart. You're turning blue. I'm Mick, by the way, Mick Murphy. This is my brother-in-law, Lionel."

Hayley nodded gratefully and climbed into the back seat of the golf cart as Lionel climbed behind the wheel. Mick dialed the number for her again and she waited, hoping this time that her father was fully awake. That was the only reason she could imagine for his reaction to her first call.

This time, the phone was answered after the first ring. "Dad?"

"Look, you psycho little bitch. I don't know how you got this number, or why you're doing this, but it's not funny. Now leave me alone, or I'll call the

Gardaí, have your number traced, and you and your sick friends will be arrested for harassment."

The phone went dead before Hayley could get out another word.

Hayley lowered the phone, her eyes welling up with tears as the cart bumped over the grass and onto the path. I've been gone a bit over a week.

It never occurred to Hayley that her father would do anything other than welcome her home. She never expected him not to believe it was her.

"Is there a problem?" Mick asked.

"He doesn't think it's me."

Mick held out his hand for the phone. "Not surprising, lass, given how long Hayley Boyle's been missing."

Hayley stared at the old man in surprise. "How do you know I've been missing?" She closed her eyes. "Oh god, it's been on the news, hasn't it? Kiva's probably holding daily press conferences. How much trouble is Ren in?"

"Mick's a retired cop," Lionel informed her with a smile, glancing over his shoulder. "The Hayley Boyle case was big news back in his day."

"Back in his day? Back when?" Hayley asked, thinking Lionel looked younger, but he was apparently the more senile of the two. "I haven't been gone that long."

"Hayley Boyle was blind, as I recall," Mick reminded her, turning in his seat to watch her closely.

"I know that," she said. "I'm Hayley Boyle."

"And yet... you seem to see just fine."

"I was cured."

"Convenient," the retired cop said in a tone Hayley didn't much care for. "How old are you supposed to be?"

"Seventeen."

"Yeah ... that's where your story falls down, lass."

Hayley was starting to get angry. First her father didn't believe she was on the phone and now these two old men - complete strangers, both of them - were trying to tell her she wasn't herself.

"I'm not telling a story. I'm Hayley Boyle. Call the Gardaí if you don't believe me. Call my dad. Ask Kerry, my stepmother. My brother, Neil. Ask the great Kiva Kavanaugh. I practically grew up at her place." She leaned back and crossed her arms, looking away from the unsettling scrutiny of the old men in the front seat of the cart. The clubhouse appeared out of the mist in the distance. It wouldn't be long now and she could call a cab and go home and confront her father in person.

Then he'd know she wasn't some prank caller looking for a bit of a lark.

"Be interesting to see what they have to say," Mick Murphy said, although Hayley still refused to look at him, "because if she was still alive, Hayley Boyle would be twenty-seven years old by now."

That got her attention. "You're kidding me? What are you talking about? I've been gone a frigging week!"

"Hayley Boyle disappeared ten years ago, as I'm sure you know. It's been all over the news again, now that her family are about to have her declared legally dead. Not sure what your game is, my girl, but you are most definitely not Hayley Boyle, and you're not going to win any friends around here trying to pretend you are."

The man's words made no sense. "Twenty-seven? That's ridiculous. I know who I am. I'm not playing any games. I..."

She didn't bother finishing because the retired cop was no longer looking at her; he was making another call. This time he was talking to someone in the Gardaí, she guessed, because he was talking about bringing her in.

Let them, Hayley decided as Lionel bounced the cart toward the clubhouse. I don't know what's going on here, but Dad will know me as soon as he sees me. Jesus, Ren, what sort of a mess have you got me into this time? I should know better than to listen to you.

But she had listened to him. That's how she got her sight back...

And then another thought occurred to Hayley. If her own father didn't even believe she was his daughter, perhaps it might be prudent to keep the news about having her sight healed by magic in another reality, populated by Faerie, to herself.

CHAPTER 22

"I hate the idea of destiny, but I have a bad feeling circumstances are conspiring against me," Ren announced, taking a seat on the long bench by the table where Pete and Logan were eating their dinner. The table was tucked into the dark corner of a small, cosy pub in the bustling village of Draffaugh, several hundred miles from *Tír Na nÓg*. There was a stone circle on the edge of town so it was easy enough to get to, and being on a major trade route meant there were enough strangers coming and going in the town that their presence attracted little or no attention. It helped that the local gossips believed the great sorcerers who aided and advised their beloved Empress were wizened old Asian men. Pete and Logan, and occasionally Ren, came here when they needed to feel like ordinary humans for a while, and because nobody had the faintest idea who they were they were invariably left in peace.

For a cop and a journalist, the news they were

magically gifted part-*sídhe* princes was something they still had trouble coming to terms with at times, even with a decade to get used to the idea. Even with everything Pete had seen and done since Delphine knocked him and Logan out with *Brionglóid Gorm* and brought them through the rift at the top of the Sears Tower in Chicago, he still struggled some days, certain he wasn't tripping through alternate realities as much as, well, just tripping.

Ren took a swig of his ale and grimaced. He didn't really like the flavor, but the wine here tasted even worse, like sewage effluent. And nobody in their right mind would touch the water they served in these low-tech realities; the ale at least had the advantage of being alcoholic and therefore far less likely to infect them with something dire, although it was probably wreaking havoc on their brain cells while it numbed their taste buds on the way down.

The pub was crowded with merchants, here for the monthly wool market, which gave their discussion a certain amount of privacy as the ambient noise level precluded anybody from listening in. The raucous group in the opposite corner struck up another bawdy song celebrating what seemed to be the youngest of them losing his virginity. Pete glanced around as the harried serving girl unloaded their meals onto the table and hurried off to tend her other customers, then raised his wooden tankard in Ren's general direction. *"Sláinte!"*

"To destiny!" Ren responded, with a distinct lack of enthusiasm, which Pete thought odd because it had been Ren's idea for them to slip away from *Tír Na nÓg* and its attendant dramas for a "boy's night out" here in Draffaugh and he had brought up the whole topic of destiny in the first place.

"You're troubled about Isleen, I take it?" Pete asked, as he began to tuck into a juicy, roast lamb shank. The food in this pub was great. Pity they'd not seen the need to invent forks in this reality. Even though chopsticks were the utensil of choice in the more civilised establishments, down here among the peasants, hands were considered good enough. Eating everything with his knife and his fingers was something Pete had become used to over time, but of all the things he missed about the reality they'd left behind, civilised tableware was in the top ten.

"What makes you think I'm troubled about Isleen?"

Pete was never quite sure what Ren was thinking or, for that matter, what he was doing. He couldn't avoid the feeling that Ren had his own agenda, and while it might run parallel to Pete and Logan's ambition to discover why Delphine had raised them in a reality without magic when they so obviously originated from one that was steeped in it, Ren still wasn't after quite the same thing.

"You seem upset."

"Upset?" Ren shook his head. "Pissed off, actually. And not at Isleen. At myself for not seeing this coming."

"How could anybody see it coming?"

"I should have known. There's probably something tucked away in Delphine's memories about it."

Logan laughed at the very idea. He'd ordered the stew and was slurping it up with relish. "Seriously? You think Delphine planted some secret ability to break the bonds in her mind and you couldn't see it?"

"Maybe."

"You don't allow for the possibility that Isleen's just a curious young woman with lots of power and a sister who's been missing for seven years who she misses desperately and that she'll not turn to the dark side just because?" Logan asked.

"The *Matrarchaí* bred her for the dark side," Ren pointed out. He pushed his own bowl of stew away, as if he'd lost his appetite. "I was a fool for thinking we could circumvent the inevitable."

"They're not breeding Undivided twins for the dark side," Pete corrected. He sucked the last of the tender lamb from the shank and took a mouthful of ale. *What does it say about me that I'm actually starting to like this stuff?* "They're breeding sociopaths."

Logan smiled, breaking a chunk off a crusty loaf to soak up the gravy in his stew. "Can't let the science go, can you, little brother? Ten years we've been here. Ten years where we haven't aged a day, can wield magic with a wave of our hands - or a bit of origami. You're sleeping with a frigging Merlin, for god's sake and yet you're still clinging to the notion of a scientific explanation for everything."

Pete shook his head. "Not everything, just what the *Matrarchaí* are up to. It's what Empress and Emperor twins are, you know - sociopaths. No empathy. No conscience. That's what they're breeding them for. Anything less won't cut the mustard."

"Can't commit genocide, I suppose," Ren said, "if you're going to agonise over it afterwards. Or - even more inconveniently - beforehand."

"How do the *Matrarchaí* even know what a sociopath is?" Logan scoffed, not convinced.

"I imagine they don't have a clue," Pete said with a shrug. "Not to start with, at any rate. They might now, given they seem to be headquartered in our reality. But you don't need a degree in criminal psychology to spot a sociopath. One in twenty-five people - at least was the statistic they were throwing about when I was doing my Masters."

Funny how we all still refer to it as "our reality". Or that it matters a rat's arse, any longer, that I have a Masters degree in anything.

Ren looked thoughtful, not nearly as skeptical of his theory as Logan. "Do you really think the *Matrarchaí* go rift running across realities just so they can fiddle with the Undivided bloodlines to get the most powerful and sociopathic twins they can breed?"

"And then what?" Logan asked. "When they find a set that happens to be the one in twenty-five... what? Jackpot?"

"Pretty much," Pete agreed. "I figure they get as much *sídhe* blood into the mix as they can safely conceal first. It's why they murder any babies with even a sniff of *sídhe* characteristics - to hide what they're up to. So much as a hint of a pointy ear or a cat-slit pupil and they're culled."

Ren nodded. "It's true. They breed Undivided

twins to be as powerful as possible and still look human. That way the *sídhe* are none the wiser."

Pete nodded in agreement. "Sociopathy is a uniquely human trait. You need a human mother with the right credentials in the mix if you hope to score with the next generation so you can start your next killing spree."

"Why a mother?" Logan asked. "Why not a father?"

"Mothers are easier to trace, easier to control. The matrilineal line is much cleaner, and this is an organizastion run predominantly by women."

"Fair enough," Logan said with a shrug. "So why were we preserved for the breeding pool and not given a whole reality full of *sídhe* to eradicate?"

"We have a conscience."

"Are you sure about that?" Ren asked, so darkly, it made Pete wonder if there was more to the question than a simple reassurance.

"Still, what's the point?" Logan said before Pete could answer Ren's question. "The *Matrarchaí* can't seriously expect to rid every reality of the *sídhe*."

"They appear to be giving it a damn good try."

"And why keep breeding psycho twins? Why not just find a few that work and have them leap from reality to reality to do what needs to be done? I mean, their way is nuts."

"There's an infinite number of realities," Ren reminded Logan. "I suspect a few that work won't cut the mustard."

"But how would you know if you've scored a win? You can't tell a psychopath until they've grown up and turned into a killer. And you'd need two of them to make it work if they're using twins. The chances of that are infinitesimal."

"Actually, one sociopath and another twin who's easily led would probably suffice," Pete said, after taking a swig of ale to wash down his lamb. He wiped his greasy hands on his trousers - something he would never have dreamed of doing ten years ago - and pushed away his empty plate, adding, "A description I wouldn't hesitate to apply to Teagan and Isleen, by the way."

Ren was silent for a moment, swirling the ale around in his wooden tankard before he looked at Pete and asked, "Do you really think only one of the twins needs to be a sociopath for them to qualify as Emperor twins?"

"Why?" Logan asked with a laugh. "You afraid Darragh's a psychopath? Is that why you're not in any hurry to find him and bring him home?"

Ren didn't even crack a smile, which bothered Pete for no reason he could readily put a finger on. "Maybe it's me. Maybe I'm the evil twin."

Okay ... where did that come from?

"Let me ask you a question," Pete said, wondering if fear of being as evil as those they were trying to defeat was the reason for Ren's increasingly dark demeanour lately. "Suppose you leave home to go on a yearlong trip around the world. You've been planning it for ages and it's cost you a fortune. Just as they announce your first flight, you realize you accidentally locked the cat inside the house with no food or water. There's nobody you can call to let her out, so you either miss your flight and your dream trip, or hope the cat will be okay and go on the trip anyway? What do you do?"

Ren didn't hesitate. "I'd miss the flight."

"There," Logan said, "you're not a sociopath." He emptied his tankard with a swallow and grinned at Ren. "Why don't you get the next round to celebrate?"

Pete shook his head, ignoring Logan. "Actually, it doesn't prove he's not a sociopath. The question is why would he miss the flight?"

Again, Ren didn't hesitate to answer; although it was obvious he couldn't see the point of the question. "The poor cat would starve to death or dehydrate and die of thirst, or both. Nobody could leave an animal trapped like that and enjoy a holiday. That's a horrible way to die."

"And that, my friend, is empathy," Pete explained, leaning back against the wall behind him. "A sociopath might miss the flight too, but he'd be missing it because he didn't want the place stinking of dead cat when he got back. He may even do it because he wanted to be seen doing the right thing. A smart psycho knows doing something selfless is a great way to hide the fact that you couldn't give a flying fuck if the cat died or not. You, however, said "poor cat". You said "horrible way to die". You empathise with another living creature. Ergo, you are not a sociopath." He finished his ale and added with a smile, "Now, Logan, on the other hand..."

Logan laughed and elbowed him. Hard. His brother had taken to this strange life so much more easily than Pete had. He'd been awed to discover he was a part, if not mostly, Faerie. He even seemed not to miss their former lives that much - perhaps because instead of a steady stream of model-slash-actresses to date, he found himself with multiple realities full of stunning Faerie women to keep him company with no inhibitions to speak of. Pete was enchanted with his new life too, and he tried very hard not to wonder too much about what would happen between him and Nika if he ever found his way home, but he missed matching knives and forks, internal plumbing, hot showers and - however mistaken he had been about it - knowing who he was.

Ren's brow furrowed as he thought on Pete's explanation.

What's he getting up to on those trips he keeps making into other realities to gather intelligence, Pete wondered, to make him worry he's a psychopath?

"That would explain why the *Matrarchaí* is willing to go to such lengths," Ren said, nodding, "to nurture the ones they do find to maturity."

"I think they're pretty good at spotting them," Pete agreed. "I think that's why Delphine took Logan and me out of a magical world and into a depleted one. We weren't the right stuff, but she didn't want to lose our line. Take us to a world without magic, let us lead normal lives, get married, have kids ... she keeps the bloodline, but doesn't have to worry about us turning on her someday with magic. Creeps me out when I think how often she used to nag us about grandchildren."

"That's ridiculous, Pete," Logan said. "How could Delphine know we weren't going to cut it in the psycho-genocidal-megalomaniac stakes? We were babies when she took us from our real mother. Toddlers at best, or we'd remember something of our lives before Dublin." He turned to Ren then, as an idea occurred to him that seemed so obvious, Pete was wondering why they hadn't thought of it either. "Why can't we unearth the reason she stole us, in the memories you shared with Delphine?"

Ren shrugged. "Maybe she didn't know."

"That's bullshit," Pete said, watching Ren closely, unable to tell if he was lying. "Of course she knew. She raised us like her own kids."

"What can I say?" Ren replied apologetically. "Other than a vague memory of your real mother defying her, there's nothing specific about you two I've been able to uncover. All her memories of you seem to be of your lives *after* she took you, not before."

It was a plausible explanation, Pete supposed, but that didn't make it true.

"She had the power to erase your early memories and replace them with others," Ren reminded them, directing his comments to Pete. He'd explained this before, more than once, but Pete wasn't buying it.

"You think that's why Delphine shared the *Comhroinn* with Teagan and Isleen when they were younger?" he asked, watching Ren closely.

The young man nodded. "I think she didn't plan to unlock the information until they were old enough to appreciate what she was giving them, and therefore why she wanted to get rid of Wakiko. Like your mother must have been planning to do, their mother was trying to teach them some values. I don't know how much of being a sociopath is nature and how much is nurture, but I'm pretty sure it's better for the cause if your Angels of Death aren't struggling with the notion of right and wrong."

"So what does that make Isleen?" Logan asked.

"Confused, I'd say," Pete said, impressed by the skilful way Ren had turned the conversation away from how much of Delphine's memories he was holding back. "Only time will tell if she's the raw material the *Matrarchaí* are looking for," he added, realizing there was no point in confronting Ren head on about this.

"So, if either one of the girls has a conscience, eventually she'll come home?" Logan asked, intrigued enough with the subject not to have noticed how expertly he'd been steered away from the real issue. "*That's* your solution to what we should do about the powerful magician who has just run off to join her sister and our enemies so she can blab everything she knows about us? I feel so much better now." He shoved his empty tankard across the rough-hewn table to Ren. "I'd drink to it, too, if the person supposed to be shouting the next round would get a move on."

"At this moment in time," Ren said, ignoring Logan's unsubtle hint, "there is no point in agonising over what Isleen may or may not be up to. She'll be looking for Teagan and the *Matrarchaí* but they're not that easy to find. The knowledge she's unlocked is more than a decade old. She won't find much in the realms she'll visit, to lead her to their bosom."

Ren seemed very sure of that, which worried Pete a little.

"Isleen is a distraction, anyway. We have

something more important to do." Ren reached into his vest and pulled out the ruby they'd taken from Abbán and placed it on the table between them.

Pete stared at it for a moment and then smiled as he realized why Ren had asked to meet with them here, and not back in *Tír Na nÓg* where Trása would want to be involved in the discussion. "It's time to go home?"

Ren nodded. "Let's go get Darragh."

What's brought this on? He's been making excuses to avoid going back for a decade.

"You don't want to tell Trása about this?"

"Last time she was in our realm, Trása, among other things, got me framed for murder, Logan," Ren reminded them. "Her latest effort has landed us with a merman and the inimitable Plunkett O'Bannon. I'm not giving her any more opportunities to help. Besides, we three are the only ones who can move about in that realm with ease."

"So... you're just going to waltz into our reality, grab Darragh and leave?"

"Sort of."

Pete shook his head. "Is that your plan? Sort of?"

Ren shrugged. "It's a bit more detailed than that, but essentially, yes, that's the plan."

"Do tell," Logan asked with mock enthusiasm and a pointed look at his empty tankard.

"I'll need help when we get back, both to find Darragh and to get him out. I was thinking of taking Plunkett so we've got someone who can acquire things we need there without suspicion."

"You want to take a *Leipreachán*?" Pete asked, rolling his eyes. "To our reality?"

"Trása survived in there for six months thanks to a *Leipreachán*," Ren reminded him.

"Fair point, but I would like to point out that she's not going to be happy about being excluded from something as big as this." That was something of an understatement given the trouble she'd gone to in order to procure Marcroy's gem and Plunkett O'Bannon in the first place. "Are you expecting us to come back with you?"

Ren hesitated, as if he wasn't sure what their reaction would be to his answer. Over in the corner, another two young men were signing another lewd song to a melody that sounded disturbingly like the "Londonderry Air".

"That's entirely up to you, I suppose. If you think you can go back to your old lives after what you've seen and done here for the past decade... I can't stop you."

"I take you're not planning to stay in that reality long?" Logan asked.

Ren shook his head. "I don't belong there. I never did."

His answer didn't surprise Pete. What did surprise him was his own reaction to Ren's suggestion they go home. All this time he'd thought it was a no-brainer. If he had the chance to get back to his own world he'd jump at it. Now, confronted with the opportunity, he wasn't nearly so sure.

"I need to let Nika know I'll be gone for a while," Pete said, wondering what her reaction would be to his destination.

Ren removed the problem for him. "Absolutely not," he said, shaking his head. "The first thing she'll do is tell Trása."

He was right about that much. "I'm not going to lie to her, Ren."

"I'm not asking you to. She simply doesn't need to know. I, on the other hand, need to know if you two are going to make this a one-way trip."

"Why?" Logan asked.

"Because I need someone to stay in Darragh's reality to open the rift when we come back," Ren said.

Ren had thought this through, Pete realized. He hadn't come up with this plan in the last few hours.

"Why not just open the rift from here?" he asked, deciding to put aside his own conflicting emotions about returning home for the time being. He could examine them - and what he was going to do about Nika - later when he had time to reflect, somewhere quieter than this rowdy tavern.

"Because this jewel has only ever opened a rift between Marcroy's reality and ours," Ren reminded him. "And from Marcroy's reality to this one. There's no way to go directly to the reality we think of as home from here."

"I thought you wanted to keep a low profile," Pete said. "Isn't stepping into your reality to use it as a waystation just asking for trouble?"

"Can't be helped, I'm afraid. The only talisman capable of opening a direct link between our reality and this one was the crystal wand Delphine used to get here and that broke the day I killed her. We'll be able to come back here from there, because we know this one. But, as I said, to get there we'll be using Marcroy's jewel, which opens a rift to this world and to the reality we think of as home, but only via the reality it came from. Hence the question I have for you two... do you want to do this, and when we get back to our reality, are you planning to stay there?"

Neither Pete nor Logan answered immediately.

Pete wasn't sure what to say. *Is it possible to go back?* Even with the prospect of decent cutlery, did he *want* to go back? He glanced at his brother. *Did Logan?* The life they'd had in that reality was based on a lie, but it hadn't been a bad life...

"I don't want to go back," Logan announced with hardly any hesitation, surprising Pete. "Not to stay."

"Really?" Pete asked. "You sound very certain of that."

Logan nodded. "It all seems so trite and insignificant now. Compared to this place, anyway."

"You had a career, Logan, a life there."

"Here I have magic," his brother said. "That's pretty hard to top."

Logan had a point, but Pete was still surprised by how easy the decision had been for him. *Why am I having trouble with the decision to stay or go? I have a life here, a beautiful woman who loves me...*

Ren seemed to accept Logan's decision without surprise. He fixed his expectant gaze on Pete.

"What about you?"

"To be honest, I haven't decided," he said.

"Does Nika know that?" Logan asked pointedly.

Pete didn't answer him.

"Will you at least help me bring Darragh and Sorcha home before you make up your mind? You can stay behind when we close the rift, if that's what you really want."

Pete nodded. It seemed a fair compromise and he genuinely didn't know what he might eventually decide. "What about Trása? Are you sure you don't want to involve her in this?"

"I'm working on the same principle she's so fond of," Ren said. "It's better to ask for forgiveness than permission."

"Fair enough," Logan chuckled. "I'll stay and mind the door. You and Pete can go back and do the hero thing."

Pete was still surprised at how quickly Logan volunteered to stay behind. "Are you sure?"

Logan shrugged. "You're itching to get back, Pete, for no reason I can imagine. But I like it here. You go. Save Darragh from whatever terrible fate has befallen him in our reality as the coddled only child of a major movie star. " He smiled and turned to Ren. "Have you considered that your brother might not want to come back with you?"

"Trust me, he wants out," Ren said, with such utter certainty that Pete knew there was something else going on.

"How do you know that?" he asked. Ren hesitated, glanced around, and then stood up. He unlaced the ties at his waist and pushed his trousers down a short way. His abdomen was wrapped in a crude bandage and there was a little blood seeping through, which was very strange because Ren had the power to heal himself with a thought. Pete grimaced as Ren pulled the ragged end out and slowly unwound the bloody bandage. Once it was off, he moved his hand so they could see the wound.

Pete and Logan both gasped. Carved into his flesh in painstaking letters in were the words, *get me out.*

CHAPTER 23

"Please, can I just call my dad?" Hayley wasn't feeling well. She wasn't physically ill, but there was a knot forming in her stomach; a sense of something terribly wrong and being stuck here in the Gardaí station was only making it worse.

It felt like she'd been here for hours. They'd loaned her some clothes that didn't fit very well and offered her a greasy breakfast from McDonalds, but they wouldn't let her call anyone and they'd fingerprinted her like a common criminal.

It was mid-morning now, and nothing much had changed. She was still stuck here. Nobody would call her father. And nobody believed her when she claimed she didn't know where she'd been, only that she'd woken up on the golf course and was able to see. It was a stupid story. Hayley could hear how ridiculous it sounded every time she repeated it. And she could tell they knew she was lying.

What they couldn't understand was why.

The woman on the other side of the desk looked up from her computer. She was a brusque woman in her fifties, Hayley guessed, and pretty high up the chain of command in the Gardaí because she had her own office. The name on the door said Superintendent Brendá Duggan.

Hayley didn't know why someone so important was taking her statement, or even why she needed to make one. She just wanted to phone her dad so he could take her home.

"We still have some details to sort out yet," Duggan said. "There are a few... inconsistencies in your statement."

"Like what?"

Duggan glared at her over the rim of her glasses. "Let's start with the fact you're claiming to be Hayley Boyle."

Oh God, we're back to that again.

"It's the truth." They'd been denying who she was all morning.

You can't be Hayley Boyle.

She's blind.

She's a grown woman.

Hayley felt as if she'd been sent back to the wrong world, but there was nobody she could explain that to, because if she tried, she'd never get out of here. "Please, I just want to go home."

"All in good time," the superintendent said. "We'll get your fingerprints back soon enough. Then we'll know who you really are, where home actually is and we can be rid of this Hayley Boyle nonsense. Whatever your name, I'm guessing you'll be in the system. What brought this on? A foster home you didn't like? Or did you think this way you'll get to meet a movie star?" The superintendent smiled and adopted a much more sympathetic tone. "I can help you if you're in trouble, lass, but not if you keep lying to me."

Hayley wanted to scream with frustration. "I'm not lying to anyone!"

It didn't seem to matter how many times she said it. Surely her photo was around here somewhere? After all, she'd been missing for days. She pulled up the sleeves of her borrowed shirt and crossed her arms belligerently. "I am Hayley Boyle."

"Really?" Brendá Duggan leaned back in her chair. "If that's true, where have you been all this time, Hayley Boyle?"

Hayley opened her mouth and then clammed it shut, unable to bring herself to say "In *Tír Na nÓg* with the Faeries". *I'll sound like a lunatic if I say that.*

Duggan smiled at her obvious reluctance to answer. "There ... you see, that's my problem. Right there. That bit where you open your mouth to speak and nothing comes out."

Hayley shook her head. "I'd like to tell you where I've been, I truly would, but you wouldn't believe me."

"Try me," the superintendent said. "I've been doing this job a long time, my girl. I've pretty much heard it all."

A knock on the door saved Hayley from having to prove her wrong on that point. "Come."

"A moment, ma'am?" the clean-cut young man at the door asked. He was another one of her detectives, she supposed. Or some sort of clerk. He wasn't wearing a uniform so it was hard to say. He was holding a manila folder, but he didn't offer it to his boss.

Brendá let out a sigh and pushed herself up. She walked to the door and pulled it closed until there was a sliver left open for her to keep an eye on her guest. Hayley glanced around the office wondering where the Gardaí got the money for expensive flat-screen computers. Kiva had been talking of buying one for Ren before the accident, but even she had balked at the cost. Every desk in this place had one, and everybody she'd seen using them also seemed to have one of those neat little cell phones.

Hayley watched the superintendent and the detective talk. Eventually, the young man showed the superintendent the file and spoke to her in a low but urgent voice. Duggan turned and glanced at Hayley thoughtfully for a few seconds and then ordered the detective to do something Hayley couldn't quite catch. Then she opened the door and came back into the room.

"So... we have your prints back," the superintendent said, as she resumed her seat, placing the manila folder unopened on the desk. She studied Hayley for a long time before she took a deep breath and said, "According to your fingerprints, you are Hayley Boyle."

Relief flooded through Hayley, although why they hadn't just taken her word for it hours ago and let her call her father, she couldn't figure out. "So can I please go home now?"

"I have someone calling your dad as we speak, sweetie. Can I get you anything?"

Hayley shook her head. With confirmation of her identity, funny how she'd gone from *What are you playing at, you horrible delinquent?* to *Can I get you anything, sweetie?* "I just want to go home."

"I'm sure you do," Duggan said, "but we need to get you checked over first."

"Checked over? Why?"

"You've been missing quite a while, Hayley. It's routine procedure when someone is kidnapped to give them a thorough medical and given the miraculous return of your eyesight, it's doubly important. I've arranged to have your parents meet us at the hospital."

"Fine," Hayley said, jumping to her feet, glad this would soon be over and she could get back to her real life - the life she had before Ren met Trása, before she was wiped out by Murray Symes's car. Before she lost her sight.

Before she spent a week in *Tír Na nÓg* with the Faeries. "Let's go, then."

Brendá Duggan didn't get up immediately. She was watching Hayley like she was some sort of alien creature just unearthed from under a rock in the back garden. It was quite unnerving.

"Do you know the date, Hayley?"

The question was alarmingly similar to the ludicrous suggestion the retired cop and his brother-in-law were making on the golf course about her disappearing ten years ago. She'd not seen anything with the date on it, since she got to the Balbriggan Gardaí Station on Drogheda Road, to confirm or dispel that alarming notion.

"I don't know. I'm not even sure what day it is. It's September something, isn't it? I've kind of lost track of the exact date."

"It's February, actually."

"No way," Hayley said, shaking her head. "I was gone a week, tops."

"Is that what you really think? "

"Of course it's what I really think."

Was that their problem? She'd been gone for months? That would explain a few things about the odd looks and their attitude. She couldn't image how it could be. She could have sworn she'd been in *Tír Na nÓg* little more than a week. "Are we going to the hospital, or what?"

Brendá nodded and rose to her feet. "Sure we are. Ever ridden in a squad car?"

"No."

"Well, perhaps, if we ask nicely," she said, coming around the desk to open the door for Hayley, "I can get the driver to turn the siren on for you."

"I'm not a child."

"No, you're most definitely not," Brendá agreed. "Shall we?"

Hayley followed the superintendent out into the hall, past several glass-walled offices where the occupants stopped and stared at her as she passed, leaning across to say something to their workmates, undoubtedly about her.

They're wondering what happened to me, she realized. *They think Ren abducted me and that I've been raped or something. God, they're not going to give me an internal examination, are they, to see if they can prove that?*

Hayley had seen enough police TV shows to figure it must be a fairly routine test on all kidnap victims.

But I wasn't kidnapped. I went willingly. And nobody hurt me.

Quite the opposite. *I had a ball and they gave me my sight back.* Her protests remained silent ones, however. She followed Brendá and kept her gaze fixed on the back of the superintendent's tweed jacket, certain she knew what the owners of all those curious eyes were thinking, resigned to the fact that she could say nothing to correct them.

It didn't matter, anyway. She'd be home soon and then she could put this craziness behind her.

CHAPTER 24

Twelve years ago, a good two years before Delphine stepped through the rift into this reality with Logan and Pete, bound and unconscious - intending to dispose of them now that one of them had fathered a child - the *Matrarchaí* doyen had signed a lease on a building in London, one not even built yet. Designed by Italian architect Rienzo Piano, when completed it would be the European Union's tallest building. Piano's vision was for a new concept for the twenty-first century: a "vertical city" in the heart of a great metropolis, and even before the foundations were dug, people were calling it the Shard.

The elongated glass pyramid, built over a train station in a less than salubrious neighbourhood near the Thames on London Bridge Street, would tower over London. Construction had been scheduled to start in 2009 and with 87 floors, it was funded by the insanely wealthy royal family of Qatar, making it almost immune from whatever economic turmoil might befall the world in the time it took to complete. Delphine was well pleased with her arrangements. The *Matrarchaí* planned to use it as their European headquarters.

Although they had had an office in New York, in the now-destroyed World Trade Centre, and a backup stone circle located at the top of the Sears Tower in Chicago, as well as another circle in Asia's tallest building in Taipei, they had hankered for one closer to Delphine's base in Dublin. The Shard was ideal and Delphine had secured the very top floors while the building was still nothing but blueprints and a grand idea, even prevailing upon the architect to mark the floors she was leasing as "plant rooms". There were 44 lifts in the Shard; nobody would question why, out of the 87 floors of the building, only 72 were habitable.

Ren knew this because he'd taken Delphine's memories from her as she died. He also knew the reason she'd gone to such trouble and expense: the Shard's upper floors pierced the Enchanted Sphere, that thin layer of magic which accumulated at around 280 metres above sea level on depleted worlds, like a wisp of fog rising off a damp moor. The Shard would comfortably pierce the layer, making it possible to open rifts in this depleted realm. The *Matrarchaí* could use this reality without any magic to speak of as their headquarters, while they planned their assault on the magical realms still populated by Faerie.

There will be no stumbling about on golf courses in the dark and getting shot at on this trip, Ren thought determinedly. They had originally had no choice but to arrive at the same stone circle in Dublin, but now that they knew of the Enchanted Sphere and had Delphine's memories of how to access it, they could use the Shard. There was no need to rely on someone to open a rift for them from the other side. That was assuming, of course, they could leave the same way they arrived. If they couldn't get back to London to leave through the Shard, they would have to use one of the countless stone circles that dotted the other reality. That required someone to open it from the other side.

Ren was hoping that wouldn't be necessary. All they had to do was collect Darragh and Sorcha, make their way to back to London (which is where the *Leipreachán* came into the planning) and return home through the stone circle built into the Shard. Chances were good they wouldn't have to confront the *Matrarchaí*, because the building wasn't due to be opened to the public for another year and the magical stones that would enable the portal between realities to be opened were built into the walls and the floor.

Ren hadn't given Pete and Logan much time to think about this trip. On the surface the Doherty twins appeared to have adjusted quite well to their new circumstances, but Ren suspected that given half a chance Pete certainly, and possibly Logan, despite his stating otherwise, would be very tempted to try to regain their old lives.

That wasn't possible, Ren knew from experience, but he wasn't sure Pete had quite come to grips with it yet.

It didn't surprise him Logan had elected to stay behind and open the rift for them. He'd adapted a lot quicker than his twin brother.

Ren wasn't sure he even needed Logan - assuming the Shard performed as expected, Ren should be able to open a rift himself with Marcroy's jewel provided the stone circle was intact and pierced the Enchanted Sphere. He couldn't be sure, however, that he could get back to the Shard once he'd located Darragh ... or that when he took the jewel out of the Enchanted Sphere, the magic wouldn't leach from it, making it impossible to get home. Even searching Delphine's memories hadn't helped there. In some things, she was extremely knowledgeable. In others, it seemed she either didn't know, or the knowledge was buried behind a trigger Ren couldn't find and therefore out of his reach.

That's why he still wanted a backup. Logan knew how to open a rift and he would be the one to guard their escape route. Ren wasn't going to go and rescue his brother, just to get stranded there himself. He closed his eyes for a moment, hoping to quell the surge of Delphine's other memories threatening to overwhelm him. It was hard, sometimes, to shut them off. She had been such a powerful creature. Carrying her life around inside his head was more akin to being smothered by her knowledge, rather than enlightened by it.

"Well, ye be needing me after all, then?"

He opened his eyes to find the *Leipreachán*, Plunkett O'Bannon standing at his knee, hands on his hips, looking mightily displeased. Ren was never sure if Plunkett was pissed-off because he had been brought to this reality against his will, that an alarming number of humans appeared to know his real name, or if he was just being a *Leipreachán* and cranky was the status quo.

"Hello, Plunkett."

The *Leipreachán* glanced around, taking in the stone circle lit by the rising moon and Logan standing by the sentinel stone holding Marcroy's precious rift-opening jewel. Pete and Ren were dressed in clothes that clearly didn't belong in this realm.

"Ye be going rift running."

"You're coming with us," Ren told him, wondering if it was the best idea he'd had all day or the worst. Trása had taken Plunkett with her when she went looking for him. Plunkett had kept them well supplied with the essentials of modern life and a roof over their heads in that reality, mostly by robbing drunks of their cash and credit cards. Ren wasn't planning to be in his old realm for long enough for hotels to be necessary, but having access to a lesser-*sídhe* who could still wane in and out of places at will was worth more than all the stolen credit cards in the realm put together.

Being *Tuatha Dé Danann*, rather than a lesser *sídhe*, Ren's ability to wane would be lost once they reached the other realm. He needed far more ambient magic to perform the feat and it simply didn't exist outside of the Enchanted Sphere in that other reality, and even at that level, it was doubtful.

"And where did ye think to be goin'?"

"The reality we came from. We're going to get Darragh and Sorcha."

Plunkett perked up considerably. "I see," the *Leipreachán* said rubbing his hands together. "And ye need my special skills, I suppose?"

"Always," Ren said. He glanced at Logan and Pete. "You two sure about this?"

Ren wasn't asking about the advisability of taking a *Leipreachán* with them. They both nodded as another *Leipreachán* waned into the circle. The newcomer - dressed from head to toe like a short, fat ninja - studied them for a moment and then crossed his arms across his portly belly and glared at them with vast disapproval. "Oh, so you be leavin' without me, then."

Plunkett turned to stare at Toyoda, crossing his arms in the same manner. "It be nothin' to concern ye, laddie."

Ren found the animosity between the two *Leipreachán* quite fascinating. They were, essentially, the same being, just different versions of each other. And yet each seemed to resent the other mightily. In the brief time they'd had together, the *Leipreachán* hadn't formed any sort of bond; they'd decided they loathed each other.

Is that what happens, Ren wondered fleetingly, *when you get to truly see yourself through someone else's eyes?*

"Lady Trása be mentioning nothing about this." Ren glanced at Pete and Logan and knew they were thinking the same thing he was... that the first thing Toyoda would do after they left, now he'd discovered them, was report back to Trása and tell her where they'd gone.

Trása would be furious when she discovered Ren had gone to rescue Darragh without her. But he had a plan to disarm her rage and Toyoda's appearance was a part of it.

"He's not going to come with us, too, is he?" Pete asked, before Ren could say anything.

"Are you sure that's a good idea?" Logan asked, assuming that's why Toyoda was here.

"How much trouble can one *Leipreachán* cause in a world without magic, anyway?" Pete said, glancing at Ren.

"Wouldn't it mean taking him through Darragh's realm," Logan asked his brother. "I thought they had pretty strong feelings about bringing *eileféin* through rifts."

Although he had his back to him, Ren could tell from the tone of his voice that Pete was rolling his eyes. "Christ, Logan... we have Marcroy Tarth's stolen jewel, we've kidnapped one of his mermen and already brought Plunkett through to meet his *eileféin* in this realm. Are we really going to start agonising over breaking the rules now?" He frowned then, and glanced around. "Speaking of our kidnapped merman, what happened to him?"

"He's swimming in the Pool of Tranquillity," Ren told him with a rare flicker of a smile. "He's so drunk on the magic there, I don't think he even remembers he's in the wrong realm."

It was Nika who'd come up with the inspired solution of letting Abbán loose in the enchanted pool. Although there was an equivalent place in the realm he came from, in Abbán's realm the Pool of Tranquillity was reserved for the highest echelon of the *Tuatha Dé Danann*, mostly because the magic in the water was so intense, it intoxicated to the point of being dangerous to lesser beings. On his brief visit back to *Tír Na nÓg* to tell Trása he was returning to Chucho - a handy lie that should keep her from seeking him out until he returned home with Darragh - Ren had gone down to the pool to take a peek at the blissfully unaware merman splashing about in the magical water, wondering if they'd ever be able to get him out of it.

Abbán was no longer a problem. At least, not until Marcroy missed him and realized his jewel was gone along with the merman.

"Which just leaves the knee-high ninja," Pete said, looking pointedly at Toyoda.

"He's not coming with us," Ren explained. "I have another job for him."

The little *Leipreachán*'s chest puffed out a little. "What ye be wanting of me, then, me lord?"

Ren turned to face the *Leipreachán*, squatting with his back to Logan and Pete. "You have a safe place for all your treasures?" he asked in a low voice.

"Why ye be wanting to know that?" Toyoda asked.

Leipreachán were very tetchy when it came to their treasures. Ren had never heard of one ever sharing the location of his hoard and knew the *Leipreachán* would fight like a cornered rat if he thought his hiding place had been compromised. He reached into his pocket and took out the large enchanted amethyst. Toyoda's eyes widened at the sight of it.

"This jewel is very precious to me," Ren explained in a low voice. "I am entrusting you with it. You must keep it safe until I return. On pain of death."

Toyoda stared at the jewel in Ren's palm and said nothing.

"Repeat what I said."

Toyoda's eyes never left the gem. "This jewel be very precious to ye. Ye be entrusting it to me. I must be keeping it safe until ye return. On pain of death."

Ren placed the jewel in Toyoda's hand. "This is the most important thing you've ever been asked to do, Toyoda. Do you understand that?"

He nodded, closing his hand over the jewel.

"Don't let me down." He rose to his feet and turned to look at the others. "I suppose we should get go-"

"Shit, where did Toyoda go?" Logan cut in. There was no sign of the little ninja-*Leipreachán*. He'd waned himself away the moment Ren turned his back.

"We have to go," Ren said. "Now."

Pete nodded in agreement. "How long until he's told Trása everything?"

"Before we can close the rift behind us if we don't get a move on," Logan suggested, offering Marcroy's jewel to Ren. "You want to do the honors?"

Ren nodded. He knew Toyoda was headed to his hoard and not to betray him to Trása, but Pete and Logan didn't need to know that. "Stand back."

He opened his palm and, taking a deep breath, he closed his eyes and opened himself to the magic, letting it flow through him. The jewel felt like an extension of his arm, a part of him that was so natural, so right, that before he realized what he was doing lightning was surrounding him and the rift began to open.

He opened his eyes a few moments later to discover the open rift. Darkened trees and a light mist were waiting for them on the other side.

Never before had he opened a rift so easily; so intuitively.

And then he realized why.

The jewel had opened a doorway into Marcroy Tarth's world. His father's realm. His brother's realm.

From there they could find their way to the reality where Darragh was stranded.

But the realm on the other side of that lightning-framed rift was the reality where Ren was born.

For however brief a moment, he would be home.

CHAPTER 25

"What date is it?"

Hayley only asked the question to make conversation. She'd been waiting in this hospital room for the better part of an hour as they poked, jabbed and prodded her, took blood for testing and asked her a whole raft of absurd questions that didn't seem to make any sense.

There was still no sign of her father, which was decidedly suspicious. Brendá had said he was on his way, but that was ages ago.

"February tenth, 2012," Brendá Duggan added, watching her closely.

"2012?" Hayley decided she'd misheard.

"Yes."

It can't be. I was gone a week... "Are you sure?"

Brendá's lips turned up in the briefest of smiles. "Yes, I'm sure."

"I was only gone a week."

"So you keep insisting. Where's your cousin, then? He disappeared the same time as you. Has he only been gone a week, too?"

"How should I know where Ren is? I haven't seen him since..." She trailed off as she realized she was stepping into dangerous territory again. Hayley knew, without a shadow of a doubt, that any mention of Faeries or magical portals would have her on Murray Symes's couch before she could finish the sentence, probably medicated and certainly treated like a madwoman It worried her a little that nobody had seen Ren since Trása pushed her through the portal, but it was also possible the Faeries had helped him, too, so she wasn't overly-concerned. Even if she'd been worried sick about him, there was no way she could tell this hard-nosed, pragmatic cop about it.

"Since when?"

"Since the night he came for me at St Christopher's."

"Ah... yes... back when you were blind."

Oh Christ, how am I going to explain that away? "He told me he knew people who could help me get my sight back."

"Did he say who?"

She shook her head.

"But you went with him anyway."

"No. I went with his friend, Trása. I never saw Ren after that. I heard him, though, later on, when the police were chasing us, but I never actually... you know... saw him. I was still blind."

"Where did you go?"

"I can't remember. "

"And yet you have your sight back. How did that happen?"

"I'm not sure," she lied. "Maybe I hit my head again in all the excitement."

"Do you know where you were being held, all this time you were gone?"

"No." Hayley knew the superintendent wasn't buying a word of her denials. Not that she blamed her. The story reeked. Pity there was no way to tell the truth and not get locked up as complete nut job.

Before she could answer, there was a knock on the door. Hayley sat up a little straighter, her pulse racing. Maybe her dad was here. Maybe he could explain what was going on. But the door opened and a stranger walked in. He was a handsome man with caramel-colored skin. Wearing a sympathetic expression and a suit, he looked like a doctor. The man nodded to Brendá and then smiled at Hayley.

"Hello, Hayley," he said in a soft lilting brogue that belied his Asian features. "My name is Annad Semaj."

"Where's my dad?"

"He'll be here soon."

"Dr Semaj works for the Gardaí as a consultant," Brendá explained. "He's going to stay and talk to you, while I find out what's keeping your father. Is that okay?"

Hayley shrugged. What was one more doctor? "I suppose."

"I'll see you later then," Brendá said, and fled the room so quickly Hayley was certain this changing of the guard was prearranged.

She folded her arms crossly. "What sort of doctor are you?"

"I'm a psychologist."

"So... not a real doctor then." He smiled and sat himself down on the plastic chair opposite the narrow hospital bed. "I have a PhD. Three of them, actually, so I am a real doctor. You could call me Doctor Doctor Doctor Semaj."

Hayley didn't think that was the least bit amusing. "That's stupid."

"Call me Annad, then."

"I don't care what your name is. Why won't they let me see my father?"

"Because they're confused." He smiled again. It made him seem very likeable, which was irritating because Hayley was determined not to like him. Or trust him. He worked for the Gardaí. He was not her friend. He might even be here to make her confess to something that would get Ren into even more trouble. "The Gardaí don't like to be confused."

"Is that why they sent you in here to interrogate me?"

"Of course it is. And for the record, I did warn them you would see right through this rather transparent ploy."

"But you're still here."

He smiled and shrugged a little. "What can I say? It's my job. I have a mortgage."

Despite herself, Hayley liked that he wasn't trying to win her over with false promises or pretending he was here for any other reason than to extract the truth from her. "What are you supposed to ask me?"

"Let's start with where you've been for the past ten years."

Hayley shook her head. "I haven't been anywhere. It's only been a week."

"You have no memory of the past decade?" Annad asked. He seemed fascinated by the idea, rather than convinced she was lying, which was a nice change. But still...

"From my point of view, a decade ago I was six."

"That's amazing. So you have no memory of anything that's happened in the past decade?"

"Like what?"

"The war in Afghanistan? The war in Iraq? The London subway bombings? Saddam Hussein? The arrival of the iPhone? The iPad?" He looked at her quizzically, apparently stunned by her ignorance. "Not even Kanye dissing Taylor Swift at the VMA's?"

"Who is Taylor Swift?"

The doctor seemed quite intrigued by her ignorance. "What is the last bit of news you remember?"

Hayley shrugged. It was hard to say. She wasn't one to pay much attention to current affairs, even before she'd lost her sight. "I don't know... oh... hang on, something happened in New York to those buildings. Some planes flew into them."

"Nine eleven."

"Was that the date? You have a good memory if it happened ten years ago."

"Everybody knows the date," Annad said, not taking his eyes off her for an instant. "It's become synonymous with what happened that day. Do you remember anything else?"

"No. Where is Ren?"

"You don't know?"

She shook her head. "I haven't seen him since... well, since we left St Christopher's."

"By we, you mean you and Ren?"

"No. It was Trása and me. Will my dad be much longer?"

"I really couldn't say. Why do you suppose you can't remember the past few years?"

"You tell me," she snapped. "You're the one with three PhDs."

That seemed to amuse him. "Okay, then ... here's my theory... I think you do know. But I think what you've been through is so traumatic you've blocked it out. Do you recall your sight being restored?"

Hayley remembered it clearly, but telling a police psychologist a Faerie slapped her on the forehead to magically restore her sight so she could then help him dig a bullet out of a *Tuatha Dé Danann* prince's chest with his bare hands wasn't going help her ambition to get home today.

"It just came back." Even to her own ears it sounded like she was lying.

Annad gave no indication of whether or not he believed her. "Do you recall anything at all?"

Hayley shook her head, as she realized Annad had given her the out she needed. "Nothing. You're probably right. Whatever happened to me, I've blocked it out because it was too traumatic."

He smiled, as if he could tell she was clutching at anything that sounded plausible, just to be rid of him. "We'll have to see what we can do to help you recall it, then."

"What if I don't want to recall it?"

"I think, in the long term, you'll do better if you can confront what's happened to you and deal with it."

"Whatever," Hayley said, looking away. She had a bad feeling this man could see straight through her lies. He wasn't like Murray Symes, the expensive celebrity shrink Kiva had sent Ren to. This guy seemed far more intuitive. Far more sympathetic.

Far more dangerous to someone trying to conceal the truth.

It was probably the reason he worked for the Gardaí.

Annad seemed content with her story for the time being, however. He stood up, still smiling, and asked, "Would you like to see your father?"

"He's here?" Hayley's heart began to race. She jumped off the bed in anticipation. Any minute now, this nightmare would be over. Her father would make it right.

Annad reached over and knocked on the door. Bastards. They must have been waiting outside this whole time, because with that apparently prearranged signal, the door opened and her father, Patrick Boyle, her stepmother, Kerry, and a young man she didn't recognize stepped into the small hospital room.

There was a moment of stunned silence as they stared at one another. And then Hayley burst into tears.

They weren't tears of happiness.

Her tears were tears of shock. Tears of distress, perhaps even a little anger. It wasn't just that Kerry looked so worn-down and wrinkled, or that her father was grey-haired and quite a few pounds heavier than he had been a week ago.

What upset her was the tall young man standing behind them. He was over six foot, slim, athletic and horribly familiar. He seemed to be in his early twenties, and looked just as stunned to see her, as she was to see him.

When Hayley left a little over a week ago, he'd been an annoying twelve-year-old child.

But her brother Neil was now a grown man and the reality of her circumstances hit Hayley with the force of a sledgehammer.

Whatever had happened in that magical place Ren had sent her to, the cost of restoring her sight was ten years of her life.

Her knees gave way, but it was Annad Semaj, the Gardaí psychologist who caught her and helped her sit on the bed. Her father, her stepmother and her brother did nothing. They just stood there, staring at her like she was an alien creature dragged up from the depths of the oceans and laid out on the wharf for passers-by to gawk at.

Hayley sobbed inconsolably, her head on the rough tweed shoulder of the shrink she'd met only a few moments ago, while her family did nothing.

As Annad held her and let her cry, Hayley realized her life was never going to go back to the way it was before.

Her family were strangers to her, her friends would have grown and moved on... *I hate you Ren, and if I ever find you again I am going to destroy your life as comprehensively as you have destroyed mine.*

CHAPTER 26

The Warden had called Darragh in to let him know a court date had been set for the hearing to declare Hayley Boyle dead. He'd suggested - as both Eunice Ravenel and Annad Semaj had previously - that Darragh could expedite the process and ease her family's pain by taking responsibility for his crime by telling them what happened to her.

Darragh declined the offer and was sent back to his cell.

Two days later, he was called back to the Warden's office, but it wasn't the Warden who wanted to see him this time. There was a Gardaí superintendent named Brendá Duggan waiting for him in the Warden's office and the news she had for Darragh left him breathless.

Hayley Boyle had returned, unharmed and sighted.

Darragh could barely contain his excitement. Surely Rónán was responsible. Surely this meant his brother was on his way.

At the very least, Darragh figured they'd have to release him now the girl he was convicted of kidnapping had returned, alive and well, and could explain that he'd had nothing to do with her disappearance.

He said as much to the Gardaí superintendent who shook her head, surprised he would consider such a thing possible. "This does not absolve you of your crimes, Darragh," she said, glancing at the Warden who seemed almost amused by the suggestion that he should be freed in light of this new development.

Darragh was confused. "But surely, now you know I had nothing to do with her kidnapping ... that she was, in fact, not kidnapped, but left of her own volition... I should be allowed to go free."

"Hayley Boyle can't remember what happened to her," Superintendent Duggan informed him. "In fact, she has no memory of her kidnapping. She claims she was only gone a week. Sorry, but far from absolving you of any responsibility, you may well be responsible for ruining the poor girl's life."

Darragh frowned. "Hayley believes she's only been gone from this realm a week?"

"So she claims," Duggan said, watching him closely.

"And her sight is restored?"

"Yes."

"Then she has been in *Tír Na nÓg*."

"Do you really think so?" the superintendent asked. The Warden just rolled his eyes. "Time is different in *Tír Na nÓg*," Darragh explained, shaking his head. Rónán should not have taken

Hayley there. It was a dangerous place for someone with no magical ability. "What a human perceives as a few days in *Tír Na nÓg* can easily be years in the mundane world. Sorcha spent what she thought was five or six months in *Tír Na nÓg* and emerged to find fifty years had passed on the outside."

The Warden and the Gardaí superintendent said nothing for a time, just stared at him as if he was speaking a foreign language. Perhaps he was. These people had no experience, no context, for the things about which he spoke.

"That's your statement then?" Superintendent Duggan asked after a moment. "That you had nothing to do with her abduction because she was actually kidnapped by Faeries and kept in *Tír Na nÓg* these past ten years."

"I never said she was kidnapped by Faeries," Darragh corrected, taking exception to the superintendent's tone. "I said she has been to *Tír Na nÓg*. I suspect she remembers everything that happened to her, but knows that if she speaks of it she would be met with the same ridicule with which you have just greeted my suggestion and she is pleading ignorance of these events for that very reason."

"I notice you're quite happy to speak of it, though," the Warden pointed out.

"I am not from this realm, sir, and expect to be returning to my own realm soon. I do not fear the censure of you or your people because I know your ignorance of the wider universe leaves you with no other choice."

"How considerate of you," the Warden said, picking up the phone on his desk. He pressed a button and spoke into the receiver, his eyes never leaving Darragh. "Mister Aquitania is ready to go back to his cell," he told whoever picked up the call.

The Warden hung up the phone. "Exactly what do you mean when you claim to be returning to your own realm soon. You're not planning to harm yourself again, are you?"

Darragh composed his face into a neutral mien. He was treading on very dangerous ground here. "Of course not," he said. "I merely maintain what I have always claimed, sir - that one day people from my own reality will come for me." Darragh knew it made him sound crazy, but he couldn't afford to be thought of as a danger to himself or others. Most of the prisoners in this place were a little insane, either because they had been sentenced here in the first place, or as a consequence of being incarcerated in this harsh environment. The Warden knew it and usually didn't make a fuss about his prisoners' beliefs - however outlandish -provided they didn't disrupt the daily operations of his facility. It was a different matter entirely when there were sharp implements and self-harm involved.

The office door opened and a prison officer stepped into the room, ready to escort Darragh back to his cell. The Warden studied his prisoner for a moment longer, his expression thoughtful, and then spoke to the officer. "Take him down to medical first," he ordered. "I want a full examination."

"I am not feeling unwell," Darragh said, knowing a medical examination would cause him nothing but trouble. "I would prefer to return to my cell."

"I'm sure you would," the Warden agreed, "which is why I'm going to get you checked out first. I want to know if you're cutting again." Then he added to the guard: "So much as a shaving nick and I want to know about it."

There was no point in objecting further and if Darragh protested too much, all he would do is raise the Warden's suspicion even more. Besides, there was a slim chance the doctor would only examine his limbs for evidence of self-harming. He might get away with it yet.

His fate was pretty much sealed if the doctor noticed the words "get me out" carved across his abdomen.

Why haven't you healed the wound yet, Rónán? Darragh asked his missing brother silently as the officer took him by the arm. *Are you back in this realm? Is that why Hayley has surfaced again after all this time? What possessed you to leave her in Tír Na nÓg for so long? Where are you?*

The door closed on the Warden and the superintendent, leaving Darragh to shuffle in his shackles along the corridor, beside the officer escorting him to medical, wondering how his plans could have gone awry so quickly.

There would be no trip to court now that Hayley was not to be declared dead and him charged with her murder. No chance to take advantage of the lesser security of the courthouse cells. No chance for an easy escape.

No easy way for his brother to get to him.

Rónán couldn't step foot in this place without being recognized and arrested.

As they moved ever closer to the medical wing, Darragh felt himself teetering on the edge of despair.

He'd had enough of this realm and he was so close to being done with it...

But if they discovered the words he'd carved into his belly, he'd be put in isolation. Probably medicated so heavily he wouldn't be able to think straight and then Rónán wouldn't find it hard to rescue his brother.

He would find it almost impossible.

CHAPTER 27

The view from the top of the Shard was spectacular. Pete stared out over the lights of London and found it strange that he felt the need to pinch himself to see if it was real.

Once, this had been his reality. His only reality. Now he was here, looking out over the London skyline and wondering if he was dreaming.

"Wow."

"Spectacular, isn't it?"

"Windows must be tinted well, or you'd be able to see the lightning when the rift opens." He glanced at Logan and smiled. "Thought you were going to stay in the other realm?"

"Doesn't mean I can't do a bit of sightseeing before we close the door." Logan looked over his shoulder at the darkened stone circle visible through the lightning-edged rift. Ren was standing on the other side with Plunkett, as if he was suddenly hesitant about stepping through. "Thought he'd be the first one through."

"It's the first time he's been back to his own realm in a decade," Pete reminded his brother. "He's probably wondering what he's getting himself into this time."

"We're all feeling that, and we don't have time for him to be wondering anything," Logan pointed out. "If Marcroy gets wind of this little excursion through his reality, we'll have a great deal more than a pissed-off merman to deal with."

Logan was right. But, for them, there was no direct way here from the ninja realm - which is what they jokingly called the place they'd been living these past ten years. They had had no choice but to travel to this realm using Marcroy's jewel and through Marcroy's reality.

Only someone born in that ninja realm could find it again *without* the aid of a talisman, so knowing how to get there wasn't enough. One still needed something magical to open the rift... Teagan or Isleen, if they ever got hold of such a talisman, could find their way home whenever they wanted. With the aid of the magically-infused paper from the ninja realm, and the right folding, Isleen had been able to run off in pursuit of her long-lost sister.

Ren could have returned to his own reality anytime these past ten years, had they not known that to do so would probably result in his death, and soon after, his brother's; and almost certainly, if he was discovered, Trása would also be found and brought back to serve out her life as a cursed barn owl for defying Marcroy Tarth.

But to get to this particular technological realm that loomed so large in all their lives, was not simple. To find it they'd needed someone from this realm, or a talisman that had been here before. Not one of them was native to this reality, despite their thinking of it as home. For the same reason, they couldn't return to the ninja reality directly, either.

Although they had a supply of *kozo* paper to open the rift to return, the fatal weakness of *ori mahou* was its transient nature. Hard talismans, like Marcroy's jewel, Delphine's crystal wand, and even Nika's hideous mummified baby's foot, could retain the location of a reality and allow the user to return there by using it. The process of folding the *ori mahou* shape from the fragile *kozo* paper destroyed the memory. *Trust the Japanese*, Logan had remarked with wry smile when they realized the limitations of the system, *to be the only magicians to invent a system with disposable talismans*.

The plan for this trip was for Logan to close the rift once they were through and open it again at sunset. He would return to the ninja reality and await their call if their plans changed, once he and Ren had retrieved Darragh and Sorcha. Contacting him would be easy enough. They could scry out Logan from here in the Enchanted Sphere of the Shard - where such a task should be relatively easy - and have him ready to open a rift from Marcroy's reality to the ninja reality as soon as they stepped through from this one if need be.

Opening a rift from the Shard would be simple, as it comfortably pierced the Enchanted Sphere. It was Ren's home realm, which meant he didn't need anything other than his own senses to find it. There was a magical stone circle built into the walls - at least Pete assumed it was built into the walls because there was no visible sign of the circle on this otherwise empty floor. They had also brought a supply of precious *kozo* paper with them to open the rift, and a bowl of clear rainwater from their realm so they could dial up Logan on the puddle phone and ask him to open the rift.

What, Pete thought to himself with more than a slight touch of irony, *could possibly go wrong?*

Ren stepped through the rift, holding Plunkett's hand, probably to stop the *Leipreachán* having second thoughts about aiding them. "You'd better get back," he said to Logan. "We'll call when we're ready to come back through."

"Are you certain about this?"

Ren nodded and glanced at Pete. There had been a number of discussions in the past few hours about how they were going to do this, not the least of which was how they were going to find Darragh and Sorcha in the first place. Ren was convinced it would take little more than a call to Kiva Kavanaugh's house to get Darragh on a plane to London with Sorcha. With luck, they shouldn't have to venture too far from the Shard at all.

"We'll be fine," Ren said.

Logan nodded, glanced at Pete who gave him a look that said more than he could ever put into words, and then held out his hand. Ren - with some reluctance, Pete thought - handed over Marcroy's jewel.

"Don't lose it," Pete said.

"Oh, okay," Logan replied. "Good advice. Would never have thought of that on my own."

"Stay near water," Ren added, not even cracking a smile at the exchange between Pete and his brother. "We can't afford to hang around in Marcroy's reality on the way back. We need you waiting for us."

"Gee, I'm so glad you two are here to explain things to me," Logan said, stepping back through the rift. "I can see now why you need Plunkett."

With that, the rift closed, although Pete wasn't sure if Logan had closed it to be dramatic or Ren had done it to cut him off.

Either way, for the time being, Ren and Pete were alone here in the reality they'd once believed was the only reality, with only an irritated *Leipreachán* for company.

Pete's eyes were left with an afterimage of the lightning. He blinked a couple of times and allowed his eyes to adjust to the darkness. Plunkett waddled over to the glass wall and looked out over the city.

"It be unsettlin' still feelin' the magic with so much technology down there."

"That's because we're in the Enchanted Sphere," Pete told him, marvelling a little at his own words. Of all the things he'd imagined he'd say if he ever found his way back to this reality, explaining the presence of magic in the Enchanted Sphere to a *Leipreachán* wasn't among them. "There won't be any magic once we get down to street level."

"I hope the lifts are working," Ren said coming to stand beside them. Pete couldn't tell if he was excited or terrified by this foray into a world they had worked so hard to put behind them.

"You hankering for a ride?"

"Not especially. I was just wondering what it would be like to climb eighty-odd flights of stairs on the way back."

Pete's thighs burned just at the thought of it. "Point taken. Shall we find out?"

"Where we be going first?" Plunkett asked. Whatever Ren had said to the *Leipreachán* on the other side of the rift appeared to have done the trick. He seemed... cooperative.

"We need to find out if Kiva's still living in the same house," Ren said. "From there, we should be able to track Darragh down."

"How we be doing that?" Plunkett asked. "We be in London, not Dublin."

"Same way I used to find out where she was and what she was up to when I lived with her," Ren said. "The tabloids."

It wasn't as easy as they'd hoped to come and go through the Shard. There was no power to the elevators on the first four floors they tried. On the fifth floor down from the stone circle, they opened the fire escape door and walked into a room that obviously had power. There were banks upon banks of lights trained on what looked to Pete like the largest and most extensive hydroponic marijuana growing operation he'd ever seen - and he'd seen some impressive installations in his time with the Gardaí.

"Crap," Ren said, looking around in awe. "What is this place?"

"The bank," Pete suggested, as he walked to the nearest bench to see the seedlings beginning to poke through the growing medium in their hydroponic tubes. The sound of water being pumped through the troughs filled the air, which was humid and moist and completely unexpected this high off the ground.

"What do you mean?"

"The *Matrarchaí* has to get their money from somewhere. What do you think keeps the Mafia cashed up? That's what drove organized crime to drugs, you know. Ready cash."

"You think the *Matrarchaí* is funding itself by growing dope?"

Pete leaned a little closer to the seedlings and shook his head. "I'd say yes, but this isn't pot."

"What is it then?"

"They look like *kozo* trees."

"*Kozo* trees can't survive here," Ren said. "Not in this realm. There's no magic to sustain them."

"There is here in the Enchanted Sphere."

"What's the point of that?"

"I don't know. Let's find someone from the *Matrarchaí* and ask them."

"Very funny. Maybe they're using them to help sustain the Enchanted Sphere."

"These poor little buggers don't look like they could sustain much of anything," Pete said. "They're too small."

Ren looked around the room, shaking his head. "There're thousands of them, though."

"Which makes it interesting, but a mystery to be solved some other time. Try the lift."

The power was - thankfully - connected to the elevators from the hydroponics floor down, and as the sun rose over London, the building began to fill with workmen. Some were working on the Shangri-La Hotel that would occupy a good portion of the building between the thirty-fourth and the fiftieth floors, others on fit-outs of the offices, restaurants and shops that would occupy the rest of the building. Although there was nothing special marking the floor where the stone circle was concealed, there was nothing else marked as special, either. As they stepped into the elevator, however, Pete noticed the initials ORM written on tape and stuck on the several of the upper floors.

"The *Matrarchaí* are planning to move in soon, I'd say," he noted, as the doors closed. Plunkett waned out of the elevator as soon as it started to move. He didn't like elevators.

"How do you know that?" Ren asked.

Pete pointed to the tape and the handwritten initials. "Well, besides the *kozo* farm, look at this. ORM. That's the modeling agency Delphine used to run as a cover for the *Matrarchaí*."

Although he had Delphine's memories, Ren seemed to have little interest in her activities in this realm that didn't directly impact on her plans to eradicate the Faerie. There was too much information in his head, Pete supposed; too many other-people's memories. Sometimes, it really was just easier to ask.

For himself, Pete found the idea that he was back home more than a little surreal. Alarming even. Oddly, he discovered had no desire to look up old friends, not even to enquire after his cousin Kelly or his grandmother. He knew now that neither of those women were related to him. They were *Matrarchaí*, just like Delphine and apparently most of the models who'd worked for her. It had been a truly inspired cover for an organizastion whose main purpose seemed to be the blending of bloodlines designed to produce twins dedicated to the genocide of the Faerie. All those gorgeous girls coming and going. In one day and out the next.

Nobody suspected a damned thing.

But the mention of ORM must have sparked an odd random memory in Ren's mind and, curiously, the memory apparently belonged to him, not the other people he carried around which Pete privately thought made him more than a little unstable. "I think that's the modeling agency Kiva was with before she got her big break as an actress."

"There's a shock." It would make sense that Kiva, who'd adopted a child thrown into this reality from another, was somehow connected to the *Matrarchaí*. There were no coincidences in their worlds. Everything was connected and although Pete disdained the notion of fate, there seemed to be something more than random chance governing the series of events that had brought them to this place, at this time.

"Are you okay?"

Pete nodded, and forced himself to focus on the problem at hand. The life he'd had in this world was lost to him. He couldn't get it back, even if he wanted it. "I'm fine. Its just feels a bit weird being back here. Almost as if it was meant to be."

Ren nodded in agreement. "I know what you mean. I worry sometimes, that we're just puppets ... even though we think we're fighting them, the *Matrarchaí* are secretly pulling our strings."

"There's a cheery thought," Pete said, wondering why Ren sounded so bleak. He thought he'd be a little cheerful, at least, at the idea of being reunited with his brother.

The elevator doors opened into organized chaos. They'd not taken the elevator all the way to the ground floor; they were still thirty-five floors up. They needed a reason to be coming and going in this building, which was still a construction site even if it was just the finishing touches.

They needed to find something less obvious to wear. Ren and Pete were both wearing the clothes they'd entered the ninja realm in, over a decade ago. At least Pete was. Ren had matured into a man in that time. His clothes no longer fitted so he was dressed in the jeans, polo shirt and sports jacket Logan had been wearing when Delphine knocked him and Pete out cold with *Brionglóid Gorm* and carried them through the rift with the intention of murdering them. Tiffany had been killed in the same fracas that had seen Ren kill Delphine, and Pete realized he hadn't spared her a thought in years. For a fleeting moment, he wondered if Logan thought of her very often, or wondered about his unborn child who had died with her that day.

"Hey!"

Pete realized Ren had been talking to him. He hadn't heard a thing. "What?"

"Over there." Ren was pointing at a set of hooks across what was soon to be a foyer to a temporary wall that held a number of fluorescent yellow, high-visibility vests with hard hats hanging over them. There were signs everywhere warning that this was a hardhat area and the few figures they could see in the distance were dressed in a similar fashion. Pete nodded and they headed for the hooks. A few moments later they were dressed like every other workman in the building and able to move about with a little more freedom.

Pete straightened his fluorescent yellow hat and turned to Ren. "Ready to do this?"

"Can you feel it?"

"Feel what?"

"There's no magic on this level. We're out of the Enchanted Sphere."

Pete could feel the lack of magic, now Ren pointed it out, and it shocked him to realize how much he missed it. He didn't have time to say so, though. The elevator chimed as the door opened and another couple of workmen emerged talking to each other. They nodded to Ren and Pete as they walked toward the far side of the floor, but didn't challenge them.

First test passed with flying colours, Pete thought, pulling his hat down over his eyes. He hurried into the elevator before the doors closed again with Ren on his heels and pushed the button tape-marked Lobby, same as the one that had identified the ORM Agency and the various other tenants moving into the building.

"You ready for this?" he asked Ren as the elevator began to descend.

Ren shook his head. "No."

"Me neither," Pete admitted as they began to descend. "Not even a little bit."

CHAPTER 28

"They've gone?" Trása asked. "What do you mean, they've gone?"

Toyoda shuffled his feet uncomfortably, as if he wanted to be somewhere else. "That's all I can be telling ye, m'lady," he said. "Lord Renkavana, Lord Logan and Lord Pete took the merman's jewel and went through the rift. They be taking that pesky *Leipreachán*, Plunkett O'Bannon with them, I be relieved to report. I now be on a mission for Renkavana that be mighty important. I be thinking, however, that ye be interested in knowing they be gone, before I be on me way."

"Interested doesn't even begin to cover it," Nika said, glaring at the *Leipreachán*. "Why did you let them leave?"

"It's not his fault," Trása said, walking to the edge of the bower to look down over the tree-filled twilight expanse of *Tír Na nÓg*. She crossed her arms across her body, suddenly chilled for no reason she could explain. "Toyoda couldn't stop Rónán doing anything he wanted. Or Pete and Logan, either, for that matter. Did you know Pete was planning to go rift running with Rónán?"

"He said they were going for a 'boy's night out' - whatever that means - to that pub in Draffaugh they seem to like so much." She turned on the *Leipreachán*. "Did they say anything to you about where they were going?"

"It's obvious where they're going," Trása said before the *Leipreachán* could answer. "They've taken Marcroy's jewel. They're going to get Darragh."

"Just like that?" Nika snorted with derision. "No planning. No preparation?"

"I wouldn't say that," Trása said. "I suspect Rónán's been planning this for ten years."

"You're taking the news very well," Nika remarked. Trása smiled and turned back to face the tall Briton. "I've nobody to blame but myself, Nika. I sent Pete and Logan to my realm. I enticed Abbán here with the jewel that made access to the realm where Darragh is stranded possible. I can hardly be annoyed they're now doing exactly what I wanted them to do."

"Without you?" Nika asked pointedly.

That was the rub. That was what hurt. Rónán had gone back for Darragh and hadn't asked for her help. Hadn't even told her he was going. *When did he decide to go back and launch this daring rescue? Before he made love to me? After? During?*

"He doesn't need me," she explained, as much to ease her own hurt as to reassure the Merlin. "He grew up in that realm. So did Pete and Logan. They know more about it than I ever will."

Nika looked unconvinced and more than a little annoyed. Pete, Trása guessed, was going to have some explaining to do when he got back. The Merlin turned her aggravation on Toyoda. "What else did Lord Rónán say? You said he gave you a mission. What mission?"

"That be none of ye concern, Missy Merlin. That be between me and Lord Renkavana."

The Merlin advanced on the *Leipreachán* with a threatening glare. "Insolent worm. Do I have to invoke your true name?"

Toyoda glared at her defiantly. "Ye not be knowing it, Merlin. Ye just pretending ye do. And I not be telling ye anythin'. This be the most important thing Renkavana ever be asking me to do, on pain of death."

"Why you -"

"Enough, Nika. Leave him be." Trása normally appreciated the Merlin's desire to watch out for her interests, but they didn't have time for her to get into an argument with a *Leipreachán*. Trása didn't doubt for a moment that Rónán had given Toyoda a task of apparently great import. The *Leipreachán* would have wanted to go through the rift with him - a dangerous risk given they would have to traverse the realm where his *eiléfein*, Plunkett O'Bannon, originated from. Although they only needed to be in that realm long enough to open another rift, if they were caught there with two versions of the same creature, there would be dire consequences.

Nika glared at the *Leipreachán* a moment longer and then turned to Trása. "Are we going to follow them?"

"We can't," she said, although that was not strictly true. Trása could open a rift to her own world using *ori mahou* whenever she wanted. She might be able to catch up to them before they crossed into the other realm. She'd turn back into an owl the moment she stepped through, but it was tempting. Very tempting.

Her thought was interrupted by the sudden appearance of Echo. The pixie was in a panic, flapping her wings so fast they were a buzzing blur. "Trouble! Trouble! Trouble!"

"What?" Trása asked, trying to follow the movement of the panicked pixie who was flitting about so quickly, she couldn't get a fix on her at all. "Slow down, Echo! What trouble!"

"Merman gone! Merman gone! Merman gone!" she shrieked as she skittered about Trása's head like a terrified wasp.

Nika muttered a curse under her breath. "I'll go and find where he wandered off to," she offered. "He'll be staggering drunk from the pool, no doubt. He can't have gone too far."

The pixie buzzed about in a frenzy. "Merman be gone with Stiofán! Merman be gone with Stiofán! Merman be gone with Stiofán!"

"Stiofán?" Trása asked in surprise. She hadn't seen the refugee *Tuatha Dé Danann* lord since her encounter on the stairs when he was complaining about his accommodation. "Why would Abbán go with Stiofán?"

"To cause trouble," Nika suggested. "Why else?"

"Cause trouble," Echo agreed. "Cause trouble! Cause trouble!"

"Do you know where they went?" she asked the pixie, although she wasn't hopeful of getting a useful answer. Pixies didn't view the world the same way as other *Youkai*. Her frame of reference was likely to be so skewed it was useless.

"They follow the face in the water," she babbled, her erratic buzzing giving Trása a headache. "Face in the water. Face in the water."

"Face in the water?" Nika repeated, shaking her head. "Gods above and below, you can't count on a pixie to make sense of anything, not even when... *an Bhantiarna?* Is something wrong?"

All the blood had drained from Trása's face. "If Echo saw a face in the water, then Abbán was scrying someone. Or someone scried him out."

"Who would know he was here?"

"Scrying doesn't need anybody to know where he is precisely," Trása explained, remembering that in the Merlin's reality, scrying was a lost art. "Just knowing who you want to contact, a small body of water. And magic."

"And your merman cousin was immersed in the most magical water in the realm," the Merlin reminded her unnecessarily. "This is bad, yes? I am so sorry, an Bhantiarna... I didn't realize..."

"It might not be so bad. It depends on who he was scrying." Trása didn't add that there was only one person Abbán would probably attempt to scry out. She almost didn't want to admit it herself. "I guess..."

She didn't finish the sentence. At that moment both Toyoda and Echo blinked out of existence as a song began to drift up from the lower levels of the bower. The song was sweet and clear and totally unnecessary, not the least of which because she had only ever heard the song in her realm. It was a song a greeting. A song of welcome reserved for someone of great importance. It was the song they sang when Orlagh descended from her lofty heights to mingle with her subjects.

It was the song they sang to greet royalty.

"Shit," Trása said, hurrying to the edge. She looked down but couldn't see the ground from here. The song increased in volume, the sweet music so joyous, so exultant, that it made her feel sick.

"What's happening?" Nika asked, as she hurried to Trása's side.

"We have a visitor," she replied with absolute certainty.

The music rose up in volume, as if it was moving toward them.

"Who?" Nika asked. Trása could see she was worried, but she couldn't bring herself to speak the name, even though she knew, with every fibre of her being, who approached them on this wave of glorious song. "Who is it?"

Trása didn't answer. She turned toward the bower stairs as the music reached its crescendo. A few moments later, surrounded by a horde of blissful *Youkai*, the reason for the song emerged.

Stiofán came first, followed by Abbán, whose spindly land legs were trembling from the climb up the countless bower steps to this lofty perch. Behind them came a familiar figure, one she loved and feared with almost equal measure. He stepped onto the bower, glanced around and then smiled at her so warmly it made Trása's blood run cold.

"Ah, so there you are, my precious," Marcroy Tarth said, his words laden with equal measures of warm greetings and dire undertones. He was dressed in a pretentious flowing cloak, white thigh boots over white trousers and a gossamer shirt designed to enhance his spectacular physique.

No wonder the Youkai *had greeted him like a king*, Trása thought irreverently. *The only thing missing from his outfit is a crown.*

"We've so missed you back in the realm where you belong, little bird." He glanced around at the once-abandoned kingdom of *Tír Na nÓg* that she had filled with refugees from other realities and then fixed his terrifying gaze on her. It was impossible to judge his mood. "And look at you... not a bird... a queen."

"Not for long," Stiofán announced behind him, with a smug smile as he eyed off what he undoubtedly believed would be his new quarters.

Trása couldn't speak, partly from fear, partly from simply not knowing what to say.

Marcroy stepped forward and studied her for a moment longer and then smiled knowingly. "I see. The curse is not broken, is it? Just suspended for a while. That explains, I suppose, your reluctance to return home."

Trása bent one knee and lowered her head. "Greetings, uncle."

With the gentlest of fingers, Marcroy put his finger under her chin and raised her head, making her stand. He tilted her face so she was staring into his dark, cat-slit eyes. "Where are they, little bird?"

"Pardon?"

"Where are they, Trása?" Marcroy repeated, his finger still under her chin, more threatening than if he had been standing over her with an axe. "And do not lie to me, because I will know if you lie and I can make you speak the truth. Believe me, if you force my hand, it will not be pleasant."

"Where is who?" she asked, a little confused. He couldn't mean Abbán. Maybe he wanted to know what had happened to the original *Tuatha Dé Danann* who'd once occupied this place.

"RónánDarragh," he said. "Where are RónánDarragh?"

Trása's heart skipped a beat. *How does he even know they are alive?*

Abbán, of course. But that had only been a few hours ago, surely? *Has Rónán been seen crossing Marcroy's realm?*

It didn't make a scrap of sense, and she had no time dwell on it. Hesitation would make her look deceitful.

"I have no idea where they are, uncle," she said. "I honestly haven't a clue." Fortunately, she wasn't lying. She *didn't* have a clue where Rónán was and she hadn't laid eyes on Darragh in a decade.

Marcroy studied her closely for a time, his cat-slit eyes boring into her, looking into the very depths of her soul to ascertain the veracity of her words.

Finally, after a protracted, terrifying silence, Marcroy nodded, and then he removed his finger from her chin. "Very well, then," he said, placing his hands on her shoulders in a gesture that seemed more threat than affection. "Then let us discuss, little bird, what they have been doing in this realm and when you expect to see them next."

CHAPTER 29

"Did you ever see Men in Black?"

Ren looked up from his newspaper to stare at Pete, wondering at the seemingly random question. "Are you kidding me? My foster mother was Kiva Kavanaugh. She took me to the premiere in LA. Why?"

"Don't you remember? That's how they figured what the aliens were up to on Earth. Checking the tabloids. It just struck me that we're doing the same thing. I don't know if I should laugh or seek professional help. Any luck?"

Ren shook his head. They had every English tabloid they could lay their hands on scattered about the table of the small café they'd found to eat breakfast, but there was no mention of Kiva in any of them. Their hearty breakfast came courtesy of one Quentin P Smith who had not only lost his wallet to a *Leipreachán* but had been kind enough to write his PIN on the back of his card so he wouldn't forget it. They'd paid for breakfast and then Pete made Ren go outside and toss the card into a garbage bin awaiting collection. Once Mr Quentin P Smith got around to realizing his wallet was missing and he reported it, either to the police or the credit card company, Pete warned, the credit card company could track their movements. One transaction was unfortunate, two was a pattern, three a criminal trend. Better to let Quentin P Smith and American Express think he'd just got his facts wrong about when he'd last used his card before he lost it, than give the police a reason to start investigating a theft.

"Nothing so far," Ren told him, turning another page.

"What are the chances she's retired?"

"About the same as the chance that you're going to denounce all your worldly goods and run off to join a nunnery."

Pete smiled and turned to the next page of the paper he was checking. "That would be a... hang on... here's something. It's not about Kiva, though," he said, folding the paper in half so he could read it more easily.

"What is it?"

"The headline is 'Hearing Cancelled for Star's Missing Teen'." He smoothed out the page in the *News of the World*, folded it over and began to read aloud. *"The Dublin hearing to declare Hayley Boyle, stepdaughter of actress Kiva Kavanaugh's cousin and housekeeper, Kerry Boyle, legally dead was unexpectedly withdrawn by her family yesterday."* Pete looked up and glanced around to see if they could be overheard but the nearest tables were empty and the café owner was busy somewhere out back. He turned back to the paper and continued reading in a low voice. *"Lawyer Eunice Ravenel, acting on behalf of the family, offered no reason for the withdrawal of the application."*

"What else does it say?" Ren asked, reached for the paper.

Pete slapped his hand away. "Stop interrupting me, and I'll tell you," he said, and then continued to read. *"Hayley disappeared nearly ten years ago in an incident involving Kiva Kavanaugh's adopted son, Ren, who disappeared at the same time. Ren's previously unknown identical twin, Darragh Aquitania, is currently serving a life sentence for his involvement in the kidnapping. It was expected that following the issue of a legal death certificate, Aquitania would be formally charged with Hayley's murder. Neither the Boyle family nor Kiva Kavanaugh could be reached for comment. Kavanaugh's manager, Jon Van Heusen, issued a brief statement asking that the family's privacy be respected at this difficult time. He also confirmed that Kiva Kavanaugh would be attending as a presenter at the BAFTA's in London on Sunday night."* He looked up at Ren. "That's tomorrow. That means she's probably here. In London."

Ren wasn't really listening. All he'd heard was, *"Darragh Aquitania, is currently serving a life sentence..."* Everything after that was a blur.

"Where will they be holding Darragh?"

"I don't know."

"You used to be a cop, Pete. Of course you know."

Pete shrugged. He seemed reluctant to answer. "Okay. If he was convicted of kidnapping, then there's a good chance he's in Portlaoise."

"Fuck."

"You couldn't have known, Ren."

The guilt pressing down on Ren at that moment was so crushing he could barely breathe. He stood up and ran outside, needing air in his lungs more than anything. His ears were ringing. His whole head was buzzing. Darragh hadn't been living it up with Kiva. He hadn't taken over Ren's room and spent his formative years being feted as a celebrity in the best ski resorts in Europe. He hadn't been to a single premiere. He hadn't slipped into his brother's life like some twisted, romanticised version of *The Parent Trap.* He'd been in prison. Not just any prison. Portlaoise. One of the hardest prisons in Europe.

Ren headed blindly down the street. He had no idea where he was going. He couldn't really see, anyway, because his eyes were blurred with angry tears. The worst of it was that he was mostly angry with himself. All those hollow reassurances to himself... his justifications to Trása... the excuses he'd made to Pete and Logan.

All meaningless. Every one of them was a pathetic delusion. Darragh had been doing hard time and the one person who might have been able to do something to spare him from it, had spent the last ten years trying to kid himself that he was doing the right thing because his nightmares had stopped.

"Ren! Look out!"

Pete's cry forced Ren to pay attention to his surroundings. He stepped back from the kerb just in time. The car he had almost collided with flew past in a blur, the driver leaning angrily on his horn.

Pete grabbed Ren by the arm and pulled him back. "Not getting yourself killed would be rather useful right now, don't you think?"

Ren shook his head, unable to care about his own life right at that moment. Why did he deserve to be free while Darragh was in prison for his brother's crimes? "Trása's right, Pete. I should have come back for him before now."

"In light of this development, she probably was right, but stepping in front of a speeding car is not the way to apologize for doubting her word. Let's get back to the Shard. We can talk about it there."

"We have to get Darragh out of there."

Pete was staring at him with concern. "Also another good reason to look before you cross the road."

Ren took a deep breath. Pete was right. He needed to be thinking straight if he was going to make this right. "Okay. Let's go back. We need to work out what we're going to do next."

"Are you okay?"

"Not by a long shot," Ren told him. "And I won't be okay until we get Darragh out of there."

"How long are you planning to beat yourself up over this?" Pete asked sometime later as they emerged into the cavernous empty floor of the Shard where the stone circle was concealed.

"The truth?" Ren asked, walking across to the window. He didn't see the view. He didn't care about it. "The rest of my life, probably."

"Fine, then you don't need to do it now."

Although he was loathe to admit it, Pete was right. Wallowing in acrimonious self-pity wasn't going to get Darragh out of anything. But it wasn't easy to let it go. "Why didn't he tell me what had happened to him?"

"Probably hurt less to do the time," Pete suggested, "given an explanation involved carving himself up with a shiv."

Ren didn't think that was even remotely amusing. "I should have come back sooner."

"You needed Marcroy's jewel." Ren paced the empty floor as they talked, wishing he knew what to do to make this right. Everything else he'd been aiming to do, even confronting the *Matrarchaí*, seemed so meaningless, so trivial. "Trása managed to get her hands on Marcroy's jewel about ten minutes after she decided she wanted it." He shook his head, overwhelmed by the enormity of his mistake. "Christ, Pete, what have I done?"

"Nothing yet, but -"

"How do we bust him out?"

"Whoa there!" Pete cautioned. "Nobody busts anybody out of Portlaoise. That place houses some of Europe's worst criminals. It's guarded by a full army detachment. And they're not there for decoration. Those guys have assault rifles and they're not afraid to use them."

"What if we go over the walls?" he asked, thinking of the escape movies he'd seen as a kid where that worked a treat. "Couldn't we hire a helicopter?"

"Sure, we could hire a helicopter. But it won't help." He smiled, as if he knew where Ren got the idea. "They've seen the same shitty movies you have, Ren. There's an air exclusion zone over the prison and they have anti-aircraft machine guns to prevent an aerial escape by helicopter. And that's before you get to the razor wire, the ludicrously high walls, the cameras, the movement sensors and the few acres of tank traps surrounding the place just to make it interesting."

"The newspaper says he's serving life, Pete."

"*Life*. Something he still has. Trying to bust your brother out of Portlaoise would change that, quick smart." Pete walked to the window to stand beside him and stare over the London skyline, adding, "And let's not forget what will happen if you or I - who have both been missing for a decade - suddenly show up on a CCTV monitor at Portlaoise. You think that will go unnoticed?"

"How do we get him out, then?"

"Magic might help," Pete said. "Trust me, nothing else I can think of right now will do it."

Magic. The one thing he couldn't access in this world, except for the Enchanted Sphere. "That's not very helpful."

"Don't shoot the messenger. I'm just telling you how it is." He looked at Ren thoughtfully. "Do you think they withdrew the case to declare Hayley dead because she's back?"

"I suppose."

"Pity."

"*Pity?* You want Darragh charged with another crime he didn't commit?" Pete shook his head. "I was just thinking. If he'd been charged with another crime, they'd move him to the cells at the court in Dublin for the hearing. He'd be much easier to snatch from there."

"Well, that's not going to happen now, is it?" Ren said, finding it hard to form a coherent thought, so devastating was the news about his brother. "Is there another way to get him moved somewhere else? Somewhere higher?"

"Higher?" Pete asked. "Why higher?"

"If he was in the Enchanted Sphere, I could just wane into his cell, grab him and wane out again."

Pete smiled at the thought. "That'd be an escape report I'd like to read."

"Ye could wane him out of there if ye could hold the magic," Plunkett suggested, materialising out of thin air with an armful of wallets and a large pink tote bag. He'd been busy.

"Hold the magic how?" Pete asked, trying to imagine anybody being able to hold something as insubstantial as magic.

"I dinna say I knew how ye could hold the magic," Plunkett said, dropping his loot on the floor. "Just that it be useful if ye could. Are ye planning to get a television in here?"

"What?"

"I'd be interested in seein' if they still be having The Simpsons on."

Pete stared at the *Leipreachán* for a moment and then turned to Ren, shaking his head. "You know, I can deal with the magic, the alternate realities, even learning I'm a frigging Faerie, but I will never, ever, get used to the idea of a *Leipreachán* who's a fan of The Simpsons."

"Marcroy's jewel holds magic," Ren said, paying little attention to what Pete was saying.

"Marcroy's jewel is in the ninja realm with Logan," Pete reminded him.

"That's not what I meant," Ren said, stopping his pacing as the idea formed almost as he spoke of it. "Delphine had a crystal wand. Marcroy uses a ruby. Plenty of realities use crystals to open rifts because they hold magic."

"Rubies be best," Plunkett informed them, as he sat down on the floor and began to rifle through his haul for shiny things.

"Fine," Pete said to the *Leipreachán*, more than a little sarcastically. "Why don't you hold up a jewellery store for us, knock off a handful of rubies, soak them in magic somewhere and then Ren can swallow them. That should charge him up enough for a trip in and out of Portlaoise."

Ren nodded, wondering how Pete had known what he was thinking. Maybe it was because in another reality, Pete might have been him

"That might work."

"I was joking, Ren."

"Still might work," he said, thoughtfully. "You'd have to saturate the jewels in magic, but the Pool of Tranquillity probably has the juice to do that. And they'd have to be small enough to swallow. How long do you think I'd have before they worked their way out the other end?"

"Christ, I don't even want to think about it. Are you serious?"

"Deadly," Ren said, almost overwhelmed with relief at the notion that he might be able to do something to redress the wrong he'd done his brother. "How long before Logan opens the rift again?"

"Sunset," Pete told him. "We have about eight hours."

"That should be enough time."

"Enough time for what?"

"To get a handful of rubies," Ren said, certain he knew exactly where to find what he needed, even if the cost was almost more than he was willing to pay.

CHAPTER 30

It was no mean feat to sneak into a hotel where a celebrity was staying, particularly when an event as star-studded as the BAFTA's were in town, and the Savoy, as usual, had plenty of guests to protect. It was almost impossible to get a room, but Ren managed it by ringing reservations on one of Plunkett's stolen cell phones and claiming to be the personal assistant of the Sultan of Brunei, who would be very put out if he couldn't get a room for one of his wives who had decided, at the last minute, to go shopping in London.

Ren had no intention of staying in the hotel. But one couldn't get past the lobby in most hotels, without a guest key.

If he was going to pay Kiva a visit, he needed to see her in her room. In private.

There was a great deal Ren wanted to ask Kiva. Some of Delphine's memories involved his foster mother. Not many of them. In the grand scheme of things, Ren gathered Kiva hadn't been important enough to Delphine to be anything more that a dim and distant memory. She'd not been with the agency long, and there wasn't enough in her memories that Ren could dredge up to find out if it was coincidence or design that landed him in Kiva's trailer after Patrick Boyle dragged him from the water as a three-year old.

He intended to ask Kiva about that when he saw her, although he said nothing to Pete about it, certain the former cop would try to prevent him from going anywhere near the hotel if he thought Kiva was there. Ren had assured him that on the day before any major awards show, Kiva would be at rehearsals, dress fittings and appointments with her stylist. Truth was, Kiva usually went into a minor meltdown the day before any live appearance, locked herself in her room, and binged on ice cream and alcohol in almost equal measure while she tried to control her stage fright, and her fear that her stylist was going to pour her into something hideous and she would be the laughing stock of the fashionista. It would be worse if she was appearing as a presenter; Kiva hated performing live. Even a walk down a moderately long red carpet was enough to bring on a panic attack. She preferred movie sets where there were no crowds and one could always do another take.

Ren took Plunkett with him, borrowing the idea from Trása who had shamelessly lied her way onto planes, into hotels, and gods alone knew what else, when she was here searching for him a decade ago, by making the most of the fact that a *Leipreachán* could channel what little magic there was in this world, outside of the Enchanted Sphere, to glamour unsuspecting humans. Thanks to Plunkett, Trása had flown into Dublin on a fat, middle-aged Italian man's passport.

Ren figured Plunkett should be able to take care of a hotel receptionist without too much trouble if he could handle an Irish Customs official.

He'd found a long box in the dumpster outside the Shard and covered it with wrapping paper he'd purchased with another stolen card. After coaxing the *Leipreachán* inside - although given he'd been forced to invoke Plunkett's true name to get him in the box, "coaxing" wasn't really an accurate description - Ren walked into the hotel lobby carrying his present, with a stolen baseball cap pulled down to shade his face.

The young woman behind the counter didn't waste a smile on him. He looked like a deliveryman, not a guest in a hotel as expensive and exclusive as the Savoy.

"Who is that for?" she asked, indicating the box as Ren approached.

"Her Royal Highness Pengiran Anak Puteri," Ren said. He'd looked for the name on Google at an Internet café on the way here, just to be certain. In a place like the Savoy, they probably knew the name of every one of the Sultan of Brunei's wives, past and present. "It's a present from the sultan for his wife. I have to collect her key and check her room is ready. She'll be here in about an hour."

"She hasn't checked in yet. I can't give you her key."

"Are you sure?" Ren asked, putting the box on the counter. "It's an awesome present. Have a look."

He opened the lid of the box. Despite her feigned disinterest, the receptionist glanced inside. Plunkett had made himself seem a stuffed toy, his eyes glassy beads shining straight up into the unwitting young woman's eyes.

"I'll need the key to access the same floor Kiva Kavanaugh is staying on," Ren told her in a low voice, as she stared at Plunkett. He could feel the faint magic of the *Leipreachán's* glamour and wished he had the ability to draw on so little and do something useful with it.

"Of course," she said, not taking her eyes from the *Leipreachán* doll.

"Do it now," he told her. "Quickly. And say nothing about this to anybody."

"Okay," she said with a nod.

The receptionist turned to the computer, tapped away at the keyboard for a moment and then handed Ren a plastic, credit-card sized key. "Ms Kavanaugh is on the fifth floor," she said, proof the glamour was doing its job. Kiva never booked into a hotel under her own name, and the Savoy staff would never, in the normal course of events, reveal that someone so famous was a guest. "Enjoy your stay."

Ren took the key. "Why don't you go on a break?" he suggested. "You must be exhausted after all that work."

She looked at him blankly and then nodded. "I am. Thank you."

As the young woman turned and headed toward the back of the reception area, Ren closed the box, ignoring Plunkett's grunt of complaint, and headed for the elevators. He glanced around the fabulous newly-renovated, art deco lobby, but nobody was paying him any attention. He pressed the button to call the elevator and waited an interminable time - although in truth it was probably only a minute or two - before a discreet chime announced its arrival and the door opened. He stepped inside, slotted the card in the panel and pressed the button for the fifth floor. He didn't need to ask the room number. Kiva would be in the Royal Suite. It was her favourite and easier to book than the suites at some of the better known hotels. It was encouraging to think she hadn't changed her routine at all.

That meant she wasn't expecting trouble, which was good for Ren. He wanted to take her by surprise.

It was time to get some answers.

Plunkett made short work of the lock to the Royal Suite. Ren let himself in, placed the box just inside the front door, and entered the suite, overcome by the unfamiliarity of the place. He'd been gone a long time, and although he knew they'd revamped the hotel quite a bit since he was here last, the differences made him a little uncertain.

"Jon? Is that you?"

Ren froze. He had only a moment to be gone from here, before there was no turning back and for a fleeting moment he wondered if that wouldn't be for the best. There were a lot of old wounds to open here, and he may not like the answers he sought.

"Did you get my ice cream?" Kiva called from down the hall. Her voice grew louder as she neared him. "I know I could order it from room service, but I don't want some underpaid busboy selling my room service orders to -"

Kiva stopped and stared at him. For a moment, neither of them spoke. Ren had time to notice how well Kiva had aged. She must be well into her forties now, but she looked thirty. Was that the result of a good surgeon or was she like him? Did she have enough *sidhe* blood in her to delay aging? She was wearing a bathrobe and slippers, and her hair was all over the place, as if she'd just woken. Perhaps she'd taken something to help her sleep.

What is it about your perfect life that has always made it so hard for you to sleep?

"Oh, my God!"

"Please don't scream."

"I... Of course not..." She looked around uncertainly. Ren was sure she was looking for the nearest phone, but there wasn't one here in the hall.

"Or try to call the police." Kiva shook her head, studying him in the dim light of the hall. She seemed surprised to see him, but not alarmed.

"I... I never thought I'd see you again, Ren."

"I never thought there'd be a need," he replied, thinking: *What a strange conversation. Of all the things we could be saying to each other, why are we standing here trading banalities?*

"Hayley's back too," Kiva said, after an awkward silence.

"Do you know where we've been?" That was the crux of the matter, really. Was Kiva a part of this or just an unwitting pawn?

Ever so slowly, Kiva nodded. "I think so."

"Then we have a great deal to talk about," Ren said.

"I can't have children," Kiva told him, as she began her explanation.

They had moved into the sumptuous sitting room of the Savoy's Royal Suite. Ren declined her offer to send out for room service, suspecting she might use the opportunity to call for help. Although she seemed unafraid, and was civil enough, Ren didn't know if Kiva had some sort of emergency plan in the event her errant, adopted son ever turned up again. It wouldn't surprise him if she did. Kiva was good at protecting herself.

"That's the fastest way to end a career with the *Matrarchaí*, you know," she said, straightening the folds of her robe, perhaps because it was easier than looking him in the eye. She sat on the edge of the sofa as if she was about to take flight. "To be barren is... well, let's just say, my career prospects were severely limited, until you came along."

No denials, no pleading ignorance... Ren was almost as surprised by Kiva's lack of histrionics as he was by her honesty.

"Did you know Amergin was going to throw me through the rift?"

Kiva shook her head. "No. Of all the strange things surrounding your arrival, that was the strangest. You just appeared. It really was just luck, Ren, hard as that is to swallow. It started out a normal day on set. Patrick was in the water, doubling for me, and suddenly there you were. Everyone was stunned when he surfaced with a two year old in his arms."

"Actually, I was three."

"And quite blue with cold and fright... it was a bitter, awful day."

"Darragh believes Patrick Boyle is Amergin's *eiléfein*."

"He's probably right," she said with a shrug. "No matter how random things seem, most events are connected somehow."

"If it was Patrick who found me, how did you become involved? And I mean what really happened, not what you're always telling the tabloids."

She smiled faintly at that, but didn't try to stall. "I'd just found out I was infertile - did you know that's one of the reasons the *Matrarchaí* like this reality? We have very advanced fertility science here compared to a lot of other realities. It wouldn't surprise me to learn the *Matrarchaí* funds research into IVF."

"Why?" Ren asked, although he knew he shouldn't let the conversation wander off the point. Delphine's memories could have the same knowledge as Kiva, but it was something he'd never gone looking for, and he certainly didn't have the time to search her memories now. Better to let Kiva tell him what she knew. It was quicker that way.

"It takes a long time to select and breed the next generation of Undivided, particularly when you're working in secret. Many precious years have been wasted on potential mothers, only to discover they couldn't bear children until it was too late."

"So they ditched you because you couldn't have kids."

Kiva nodded. "In a sense," she agreed. "I wasn't cut completely adrift. They found me an agent and helped launch my acting career. The agreement was, of course, that I would always be there if I was needed. In return, I could stay in this reality and lead a normal life." She smiled at him. "I know what you're going to say, Ren. The life we led was anything but normal... still, it was a vast improvement on the life I left behind."

"So I was the price you paid for your fabulous career?"

Kiva's smile faded. "I did love you, Ren."

Interesting that she said *did*. Past tense. He let the remark slide. "What did they ask you to do?"

"To adopt you," she replied, with a shrug. "And it was no mean feat, let me tell you. Patrick was quite determined to adopt you himself."

"Why didn't he?"

"He was planning to. Until his wife died."

Ren sat back in his chair, frowning. "I thought Patrick was already a widower when he found me. He met Kerry on set when she was working for you, didn't he?"

"Yes, but only because the *Matrarchaí* sent her to keep an eye on you. Patrick was quite enchanted with the babe he'd rescued from the deep with the strange tattoo on his palm, you see, and so was Charlotte, his wife. As a good Catholic married couple with a child of the same age, they had a far better chance of getting the adoption approved than a single woman like me. Especially back then."

It took a moment for Ren to realize what she was telling him. "Oh, my God. The *Matrarchaí* killed Hayley's real mother."

Kiva didn't agree with him, but she didn't deny it, either. "Let's just say Charlotte's sudden and tragic demise was... convenient."

It was becoming quite brutally clear. "So Charlotte dies, Patrick abandons any hope of adopting the child he rescued -"

"And the selfless, wealthy actress he was doubling for steps up to help out by adopting the poor baby and offering him a position on her staff so that he stays connected to the child he saved."

"What was in it for you?" There must have been something, he figured. Kiva was far from a selfless creature.

"The *Matrarchaí* promised me it would benefit my career if I took you in, and they didn't just mean the good publicity. After I adopted you, I started being offered roles I'd never dreamed would come my way. I suppose you could say I owe my success to you. The *Matrarchaí* is nothing if not good for their promises."

"Is Kerry actually your cousin?"

"Perhaps," she said. "In another reality, she might be."

"Was she ordered to marry Patrick?"

"Good lord, no," Kiva said, smiling. "She did it because she actually loved him, Ren, or at least she liked him well enough. And poor little Hayley was - tragically - in need of a mother."

Ren wasn't sure he believed that. "Wasn't she good enough breeding stock to produce her own kids?"

Kiva was beginning to relax a little. She sat back on the sofa and crossed her legs, no longer perched like a frightened bird. "Actually, that's surprisingly close to the truth. She'd birthed two or three stillborns in her own reality, I believe, and couldn't have any more children without risking her life. So yes, I suppose you could say she wasn't good enough stock for the *Matrarchaí*."

"Why bring her here?"

"The story told to me was that Kerry came to this realm because her husband in her own reality was considered a good bloodline, and with her multiple stillbirths, they risked losing his seed. She had to 'die' there, so he could be free to marry again. I don't know much about where she came from. We never spoke of it really, but it had, I gather, an absurdly strict moral code and he was something of a brute, by all accounts. She was more than happy to be rid of him. Particularly when his replacement was a man as gentle and kind as Patrick Boyle."

That was a bit rich - the *Matrarchaí* concerned about morals. "Why didn't they just kill her off like they did Hayley's mother?"

"Kerry is one of us, Ren. We don't kill our own."

"Just anybody who gets in your way?" Kiva had the good sense not to rise to that. For once, she remained silent and let Ren ask his questions. "Is Neil adopted, too?"

"No. He was a happy accident," Kiva said. "After the trouble she'd had in her own reality, nobody was more stunned that Kerry when she discovered she was pregnant, although it wasn't an easy pregnancy. In a less vigilant reality, Neil would have been another stillbirth, I suppose."

"Why didn't someone save her babies in the other reality with magic?"

"Magic is only good when you know what it is you're healing, Ren. A well-trained obstetrician, regular ultrasounds and a foetal heart rate monitor are their own forms of magic."

"I'm surprised they left Kerry with you all this time, particularly once she proved fertile." That seemed to be the only thing the *Matrarchaí* cared about, although Ren was sure there was something else, something more, and it was starting to dawn on him that Kiva may be too far down the chain of command to know what it was. Even Delphine might prove to be nothing more than a loyal lieutenant, rather than the general Ren had always assumed her to be.

"There wasn't much else they could do. By then I was too high profile for someone so close to me to disappear without question and, to be honest, Kerry still had some purpose to the *Matrarchaí*."

"What purpose?"

"Well, for one thing, you grew up with someone far wiser and more sensible than me to watch over you, and not once has Patrick questioned Charlotte's death. Besides, we were both loyal sisters of the *Matrarchaí*. They had no need to silence either of us."

"Do you know how insane that sounds?"

She shrugged. "It probably is. But we are mere cogs in the wheel of a vast insane machine, Ren. It was never our job to question the whys and wherefores of what our betters had planned for us."

"Did you never question what they were doing?" That seemed the most remarkable thing of all.

"Most of the girls the *Matrarchaí* recruits, are just glad to be rescued from a life of drudgery, endless painful childbirths and early deaths," she explained, "often at the hands of a senseless brute more interested in his horses than his wife. Step out into the wider universe before you judge us, Ren. You might be surprised by what you find."

Ren had no intention of tell Kiva just how much of the wider universe he'd seen.

"Did you know I was Undivided?"

She nodded. "The tattoo gave it away. I contacted the *Matrarchaí* as soon as I saw your hand. Things moved very quickly after that."

"Why didn't you say something to me, when I was growing up?"

That seemed to amuse her. "Would you have believed me if I had tried to tell you that you came from another reality? You thought I was loopy, as it was. And it's not as if I could prove it."

"You sent me to a shrink, Kiva. You let me think I was going mad. You stood there and said nothing when that jerk, Murray Symes, suggested I needed medicating for my self-harm issues."

"What was I going to say, Ren?"

Ren took a deep breath. He'd thought the pain was long behind him. "What was the plan for my future, then? Wait until I was grown and have me father a plentiful supply of brats on a long line of supermodels provided by the *Matrarchaí*'s modeling agency, all to preserve my precious bloodline?"

Kiva studied him with a puzzled expression. "How do you know the agency?"

"Long story," he said. "Is that what they had planned?"

"I really don't know, Ren."

He believed her. If what she'd told him was true, Kiva would have had no reason to be privy to the inner workings of the *Matrarchaí*. "What happened to Delphine's modeling agency after she disappeared?"

"I couldn't say. I don't have much to do with ORM any longer. It's still going, as far as I know. I could ask Eunice. She probably knows."

Eunice Ravenel. The lawyer always arriving in the nick of time to get him out of trouble. The lawyer representing the Boyles in their suit to have Hayley declared legally dead. She was *Matrarchaí*. Naturally.

"Have you seen Darragh?"

"Your brother?" She shook her head sadly. "I wanted to, Ren. I really did. But they wouldn't let me. It would have been front-page news if I'd had any contact with him. I've seen pictures of him, though. You're very alike."

"We're identical twins."

"Yes, well, that would explain it. Why are you here, Ren? Do you need money? I could arrange for Eunice to transfer some funds to you."

That made Ren smile. "Really, Kiva. You'll arrange to have your *Matrarchaí* lawyer wire me some money. Are you serious?"

She didn't seem bothered by him calling her out on her blatant attempt to hand him over to her superiors. "What do you want then?"

It was Ren's turn to shrug. He wasn't sure what to say. He just had to be careful she didn't realize he was stalling. "Some sort of closure, I suppose. Some reason for having my life ruined."

"It wasn't the *Matrarchaí* who ruined your life, Ren. That was done by whoever threw you through a rift in the first place."

"Fair enough. What else can you tell me about the *Matrarchaí*?"

"I've told you everything I know."

"Not quite," he said. "Who's running the show these days?"

"What do you mean?"

"Delphine's been dead for ten years. Someone is in charge now. Who is it?"

Kiva was silent for a moment and then she shrugged, as if it didn't matter what she told him. That was a warning in itself.

"Her name is Marie-Claire," Kiva said. "She's Delphine's *eileféin*, I think. I really don't know her well. I've only met her once."

Ren rose to his feet, hoping Plunkett had done what they came here to do. He didn't want to visit again. He certainly didn't want to engage Kiva any more than he had to. His feelings for this woman who'd raised him were complex and unsettling. He wanted out of here so he wouldn't have to deal with them.

"I should be going," he said, as she also rose to her feet. "You need to be getting ready for BAFTA's."

"You know about that?"

"Why do you sound surprised? Didn't your publicist send out a press release?"

She nodded and plunged her hands into the pockets of her bathrobe. "I never meant you any harm, Ren. You believe that, don't you?"

"Yes," he said, a little surprised to discover he meant it. He doubted Kiva bothered about someone other than herself long enough to waste the effort planning to hurt them.

"Then can I offer you a piece of advice?"

"This ought to be good."

"The *Matrarchaí* will come for you, Ren. You're special. More special than they ever suspected. You've even managed to lose the tattoo, I see, and that makes you beyond special. It makes you unique. If you've found another realm to hide in, and they don't know where you are, return there now, and don't ever leave it again. It's the only way you will ever be free of them."

It was possibly the best advice she'd ever given him. Pity he had no intention of following it. "How long after I leave will you contact them and tell them you've seen me?"

"I'll have to call them as soon as you go."

Ren nodded. He'd suspected as much. Fortunately, Plunkett could short out the phones just by touching them, along with remote controls and almost anything else that had a battery in it somewhere. He wasn't sure how much time that would buy them, but nobody would be calling in or out of the Savoy for a while.

"Well, tell them I said 'fuck you'," he told her pleasantly.

Kiva smiled at that. "I might word it somewhat differently, but I will pass on your sentiment."

Ren suddenly found himself at a loss for words. "I guess this is goodbye, then."

"I suppose a hug is completely out of the question?"

Completely, Ren thought, surprised she'd suggested it. "We were never that close, Kiva. Don't pretend we were."

"Don't hate me, Ren."

"I don't care enough about you to hate you, Kiva," he said.

"That's harsh," she said, her eyes welling with tears.

He was certain she was acting. Nobody could squeeze out a single poignant tear quite like Kiva Kavanaugh. "Explain that to Hayley," he replied, "when you tell her what the *Matrarchai* did to her mother."

Ren didn't wait for her to answer. He'd spent more time here than he meant to. Plunkett should have made off with the ruby necklace and shorted out the phones ages ago. He needed to leave. He needed to get back to the Shard and be gone from this world before Kiva could warn the *Matrarchaí* that he was back.

Kiva didn't try to follow him out of the hotel room. She probably reached for the phone as soon as he was out of sight, anxious to call her masters and report she'd seen him.

It didn't matter anyway. He found out what he came to learn. Kiva was *Matrarchaí*. So was Kerry Boyle.

What mattered now was that their time here was critical. Even with the phones shorted out, the *Matrarchaí* would know soon enough that he was in London. He needed to get back to the ninja reality, soak the rubies Plunkett had stolen in the Pool of Tranquillity and get back to Dublin to rescue Darragh before it dawned on the *Matrarchaí* that the easiest way to be rid of him was to murder his brother. And he didn't doubt for a moment that the *Matrarchaí*'s long arm reached all the way into Portlaoise Prison.

CHAPTER 31

It was impossible to see the ground from so high up, but Pete couldn't help but try. The sun was sinking rapidly in the west and any moment now the wall would start crackling with lightning and the rift would open.

Pete found himself anxious to step through. Even given its magic and its ninja-*Leipreachán*, its arrogant Faerie lords, psychically-linked twins, pixies and mermen, and gorgeous women who wielded magic and wore mummified body parts around their necks, somehow the other reality made more sense than this one. Although they'd returned to this reality in a different city, even allowing for the obvious differences between London and Dublin, the world Pete had left behind no longer existed.

It wasn't really a surprise to learn he no longer belonged here. He'd had a sneaking suspicion that would be the case. He knew enough about the psychology of the human mind to know that his new reality had become the norm a long time ago, and however much he might pine for the good old days, given what he knew now, given what he could do, what he had seen, he could never go back.

It was good to know that for certain. Interesting, too, that Logan had worked out the same thing with not nearly as much agonised soul-searching, which was probably why he hadn't felt the same need to prove what he felt to be the truth by coming here.

"It be a crazy place, this realm!"

Pete almost jumped out of his skin at the sudden exclamation. Plunkett had appeared behind him without warning, clutching a ruby-encrusted necklace in one hand and a slice of half chewed bacon in the other.

"What is that?"

"It be the rubies the Lord Rónán be after. I stole them for him, just like he asked."

"I meant that," he said, pointing at the bacon.

"That be me dinner."

"Where did you get it?"

"At the hotel where the actress be staying. People be leavin' trays out in the halls with treats on them."

Pete rolled his eyes. "They're not treats left out for *Leipreachán*," he explained. "They're leftovers from guest's room service."

"It be all the same to me," Plunkett replied testily.

"Where's Ren?"

"I don't be knowing that. When I left him he be talking to the actress."

Oh Christ, Pete thought, that's all we need. "She was there? In the hotel?"

"Aye. We had a grand plan, too. Lord Rónán be keeping her distracted while I open the safe and be appropriatin' the rubies." He held the necklace up for Pete to see. "It be a pretty little trinket, don't ye think?" He handed the necklace to Pete, far more interested in the bacon he'd found than Kiva Kavanaugh's priceless ruby and diamond necklace.

Pretty didn't begin to describe it. It was spectacular. If Ren's rather peculiar plan to soak the rubies in magic and then swallow them was going to work, he certainly had plenty to choose from. But the necklace and the desperate ploy to rescue his brother was the least of their problems right now. Ren had promised Pete that Kiva wouldn't be in her hotel. Pete had only agreed to let him go to the Savoy alone because he claimed there was no chance he would run into his adopted mother.

Bastard probably knew she'd be there.

"When did he leave?"

"He not be goin' yet, when I be leavin'," the *Leipreachán* told him. "He still be talking to the actress."

"He saw her then? Spoke to her?"

"Aye. Quite deep and meanin'ful a conversation it be too, if ye get what I mean."

"I'm going to kill him."

"Why?" Plunkett asked, rather startled by Pete's angry declaration. "Have ye been recruited by the *Matrarchaí* while we be gone?"

"I'm going to kill him for lying to me," Pete explained, wondering why he was bothering to explain anything to a *Leipreachán*. He glanced at the rapidly sinking sun. "We're supposed to call Logan at sunset."

Before the *Leipreachán* could answer, the fire escape door banged open across the hall. Pete breathed a sigh of relief and turned to watch Ren exit the stairs at a run. "Get Logan on the puddle phone!" he shouted as he ran. "We need to get out of here."

"What the hell have you done?"

Ren reached him and kept running, straight across the echoing hall to the bowl of pure rainwater they'd brought from the other realm so they could scry out Logan with as little effort as possible. Here in the Enchanted Sphere, the water would not have leeched magic into the barren world around it; it was probably still as magically charged as when they brought it through the rift.

"I spoke to Kiva."

"You said she wouldn't be there."

Ren squatted down in front of the bowl. "I was wrong."

"You mean you lied."

"It doesn't matter, Pete. The *Matrarchaí* are probably already on their way."

"Why? What did you tell her? Did you tell her where we came through? And why? Or maybe you thought it might be a bright idea to tell her she where could find the rest of us?" It occurred to him then that Ren had just admitted Kiva was *Matrarchaí*. Having discovered his own mother was a key member of that menacing organisation, he felt a fleeting moment of sympathy for Ren.

Only a fleeting moment, though.

Kiva had not, apparently, tried to kill him. Not the way that Delphine had been planning to kill her sons.

"They'll be able to work out where we are easily enough," Ren pointed out kneeling down so he could stare directly into the water. "There aren't too many stone circles in downtown London we could have come through."

"You're a fucking idiot, Ren."

"Bite me," Ren replied without rancour, and then closed his eyes, drawing on the magic of the Enchanted Sphere and the water, to enable him to contact Logan.

For a long while, nothing happened, which Pete found a little odd. Logan was expecting their call. He should have been waiting on the other side to open the rift and bring them home. He certainly should have answered the moment he realised someone was trying to scry him out. Perhaps he just wasn't near any water, although how that was possible, given he should have been waiting on a damp cliff top overlooking the ocean, Pete couldn't imagine.

A few moments later, without any answer from Logan to Ren's puddle phone call, the hairs stood up on Pete's forearms, which was just before the embedded stone circle hidden behind the walls began to crackle with red lightning.

With the rift opening, Ren abandoned his attempt to scry out Logan. He stood up and took several steps back, shielding his eyes against the lightning. Logan must have decided not to wait for their call, but to open the rift the moment he felt someone trying to scry him out... assuming, rightly enough, that they were ready to come through. A good thing too, given Ren was worried he had the *Matrarchaí* on his heels.

"He not be wastin' time, ye brother," Plunkett remarked as he stepped back behind Pete. "I be guessin' that ye'll no longer be needing me services after this?"

"We'll see," Ren said, with a non-committal shrug. He turned to Pete. "Do you have the necklace?"

Pete nodded, pulled it out of his pocket and tossed it to Ren, who barely gave it a glance before he shoved into his jacket. "If she doesn't set the *Matrarchaí* onto us, at the very least, Kiva's going to call every cop in London when she realises this is missing."

Pete frowned. "You and I are going to have a long talk about this when we get home."

Ren flashed him a quick grin - a glimpse of a younger, less serious Ren that Pete had not seen a sign of for a very long time - and said, "Yes, Dad."

"I meant it," he said. "You're a fucking idiot."

Ren didn't bother to answer, although he seemed amused by Pete's irritation, rather than bothered by it. They waited in silence for the rift to resolve itself and a few moments later were looking through the lightning at Logan on the other side, framed by the setting sun behind him. Plunkett was through the rift and had vanished with his half-chewed bacon before either Ren or Pete could stop him. Not that it mattered. They knew his true name. They could call him back anytime they wanted.

Pete stepped through the rift with Ren close on his heels. As soon as Ren was through, the rift collapsed, in anticipation - Pete assumed - of opening the next rift back to the ninja realm, where Nika waited for him, and where Ren planned to soak the rubies in his pocket in the intoxicating waters of the Pool of Tranquillity.

It was only then that Pete realised there was something wrong with Logan. He was standing rigidly in front of the closed rift and made no attempt to open another. Pete stared at him for a moment and then realised he had the same frozen stance Abbán had been forced into when Nika bound him with her magic to bring him through the rift.

He didn't get a chance to do anything - not warn Ren it was an ambush, or do anything to help his brother before Pete found himself similarly bound. Out of the corner of his eye, he noticed Ren had been trapped too. He fell to his knees as the invisible magical bindings threw him off balance. A moment later a figure stepped out from behind Logan. He was *Tuatha Dé Danann*, complete with billowing white cloak, thigh boots, white trousers and a gossamer shirt surely meant to entrance any mere human he happened across.

By the look on Ren's face, he knew who their captor was. Pete guessed it a moment later. They were, after all, standing in his realm.

"So," the *Tuatha Dé Danann* prince announced, his gaze fixed on Ren as if Logan and Pete didn't even exist, "the Undivided returns divided."

Ren was still standing, but his mouth must have been covered by the bindings because he could only make a stifled sound that Pete couldn't understand. He turned his eyes to check on Logan, who was frozen in place, unable to do anything more than roll his eyes to let Pete know he was okay.

Jesus, how did Marcroy find us so quickly? They'd been gone about ten hours at most and wouldn't have spent more than a few minutes in this realm. Had Logan stayed here, instead of returning to the ninja realm to wait, as they'd planned? Is that how Marcroy found them?

"And you have come alone," Marcroy added with a sigh, looking disappointed. "Pity."

Marcroy glanced at Pete then and shook his head. His cat-slit eyes were disconcerting. He reminded Pete of Stiofán, that arrogant *sídhe* lord who liked to give Trása so much trouble. "These two, I suspect, are your *eileféin*," he added with a frown. "They cannot stay in this realm."

Pete had heard Trása talk of the punishment awaiting anybody in her realm who deliberately brought a person's *eileféin* through a rift, but she never mentioned the specific details. Pete had always privately considered it a bit of a bluff because, by definition, if you were crossing realities then another one of you probably existed in the world you were visiting somewhere, and you were, simply by being a rift runner, breaking the rules.

Faerie logic, however, seemed to be a fluid thing that often made allowances for the circumstances. A *Tuatha Dé Danann* couldn't break their own rules, Pete had observed, but they were fairly creative at bending them around any obstacles that appeared in their way.

Without any further discussion Marcroy opened his hand to reveal the large ruby they had so recently stolen from Abbán and brought to the ninja realm.

Shit, Pete thought. *Abbán must have scried him out from the Pool of Tranquillity and told him where he was.* The merman hadn't been as drunk on the pool's magic as they thought.

Too late now to do anything about it, he realised, as another rift opened behind him, the air crackling with magic and red lightning. As soon as the rift was stable Marcroy turned to Pete and Logan, opened his arms wide and lifted them off the ground. With a short, sharp, flick of his wrists, he tossed the brothers through the rift to the reality beyond.

As they landed hard on the stony ground beyond the lightning, their magical bonds dissolved in the magic-less air around them. They rolled to a stop against the tall, moss-covered standing stones as the rift closed behind them, cutting them off from Ren and Marcroy.

Bruised, and more than a little stunned by how quickly everything had happened, Pete climbed painfully to his feet, wondering where he was.

Logan did the same, shaking his head. "Where are we?"

He looked around at the ancient stones, worn away to almost nothing, the low bushes shaded by tall trees. The sun had set so it was hard to tell what was beyond the tress, but there was a smell in the air that was hauntingly familiar and in the distance he could hear something he knew all too well.

"Listen," he told Logan. His brother cocked his head for a moment and then turned to Pete.

"Traffic," he said, recognising the sound immediately.

"And no magic," Pete added, breathing in air that seemed barren and dead for the lack of it.

"We're home," Logan concluded, sounding more than a little surprised. "The bastard threw us back into realm you just came from."

CHAPTER 32

Although he would have died before admitting it, at first glance Marcroy was rather pleased with the way his sons had turned out. He still wasn't quite reconciled to the notion that he had sired a couple of half-human brats, but if he had to lay claim to any mongrel get, then as mongrels went, they had grown into handsome young men with more than a touch of their *Tuatha Dé Danann* father's looks and presence.

And more than their fair share of his power, too, Marcroy guessed, as he debated the advisability of releasing Rónán before he delivered him to the Hag. Rónán radiated power as he struggled against the bonds in which Marcroy had contained him, almost to the point where the *Tuatha Dé Danann* lord debated strengthening them for fear the young man would break through. That should not have been possible. Rónán, for all that he looked entirely human, had the strength of a pure *sídhe* prince, something that Marcroy would not have believed possible had he not been confronted with the evidence in person.

But then, RónánDarragh should never have survived the transfer of their Undivided power to BrocCairbre, in the first place. Whatever it was about these young men - whether it was their paternity or some unimaginable forces of Destiny at work, Rónán and his brother Darragh were special and Marcroy was beginning to understand why the Hag was having visions about them.

Not prepared to risk releasing him completely, Marcroy loosened the binding around his mouth, so that Rónán could speak.

"You look like your brother."

"Imagine that," Rónán replied with almost as much disdainful scorn as Marcroy himself could muster when he chose. "What do you want from me?"

Marcroy stared at the young man for a moment, trying figure out what it was about him that he found so disturbing, and then it came to him. "You are not afraid."

"What's to be afraid of?" Rónán asked. "If you were going to kill me, you'd have done it as I was coming through the rift. Better yet, instead of throwing me through a rift when I was a toddler, you could have killed me back then and rid yourself of the problem that is me and my brother, twenty-five odd years ago."

"Do you know who I am?"

"Don't you mean to ask if I know what you are... Dad?" He spat out the word like it had a foul taste.

Gods above and below, am I the only one who didn't know about these boys?

"Who told you I am your father?"

"The *Matrarchaí*. Who told you?"

This was getting him nowhere. Marcroy had expected shock, even a little awe from his son at discovering his lofty parentage, not disrespect. He certainly hadn't expected either of the boys to know who had fathered them. That moment should have been his to reveal, in a time and place of his choosing. One would have thought that on learning of their royal parentage, they might have sought him out, availed themselves of his wisdom and largesse - that he would have vehemently denied owning any mongrel get and refused to have anything to do with either of them before the Hag had ordered it so, was really beside the point. RónánDarragh should be much more impressed by who had given them life.

"The Brethren wish to speak with you," Marcroy said, deciding nothing further was to be gained by engaging this brash young pup in conversation. "I have taken it upon myself to deliver you to them. But I need both of you. Where is your brother?"

"Somewhere you'll never find him."

"The Hag demands to see him."

"Bully for her."

Marcroy found himself at a loss for words, and at a loss about what to do next. Darragh was, he suspected, back in the reality Rónán had just appeared from - a barren, magic-less desert that Marcroy could not enter without dying. He could send Rónán back for Darragh, but it was certain he would never lay eyes on either of them again if he let Rónán loose in a realm where he could not follow.

But he'd been ordered to bring both boys to the Hag. Marcroy was not sure what her reaction would be to him turning up with just one of them.

Better that though, he reasoned, *than trying to explain how I had one in my grasp and let him get away.*

"You will not be so defiant when confronted by the Hag," Marcroy warned.

"The Hag can kiss my ass," Rónán replied with such a complete lack of respect for the Brethren it left Marcroy gasping.

"It is not possible you could be the fruit of my loins," he said, shaking his head. "No child of mine would be so... so... ill-mannered."

"Really?" Rónán asked in mock disbelief. "And here I was thinking I was a just regular chip off the old block. Where's this old hag who wants to see me, anyway?"

"This old hag?" Marcroy found himself having trouble keeping up.

"The old girl who wants to talk to me. When does she get here?"

"One is summoned by the Hag, you impudent mongrel. One does not summon her."

"Then let's go, Dad. This 'impudent' mongrel's in a bit of a hurry, so if we could get this done with."

"The Hag does not care about your plans."

Even though Rónán could only move his eyes and his mouth, he still managed to convey a level of disdain that even Marcroy would have struggled to achieve. "I beg to differ," Rónán said. "I'll bet your shiny Faerie kingdom that she is very interested in my plans, and that is exactly why she wants to see me."

Much as he might want to, Marcroy couldn't argue with his son's logic. The Hag was obviously deeply invested in what this man and his brother had in mind. She was having visions about it.

And she was impatient. It was more than likely she already knew Rónán was here. The lesser *sídhe* would not hesitate to report back to the Hag... she had no doubt set them to watching him. Prevaricating might anger her. Marcroy did not want to anger the Hag.

"I will take you to her," he said, stepping closer, quite appalled at the prospect of embracing Rónán in order to transport him to the Hag.

"No need for that," a voice croaked behind him.

Marcroy jumped with fright and spun around to discover the Hag standing behind him leaning on a gnarly staff, wearing a ragged cloak. Her eyes were cloudy and, with her appearance the mist began to gather on the cliff top, cutting off the wind and replacing the darkness with an eerie white light that seemed to be emanating from everywhere and nowhere. The sounds of the night faded into nothing, all sound muffled by the white fog.

"My lady," Marcroy said, dropping to one knee. Rónán, of course, bound in place by the magical bonds in which he was wrapped, could do nothing.

"You may go, Marcroy," the Hag informed him unceremoniously. "I will call for you when I need you again." She waved her arm. Marcroy found himself standing on the hills overlooking Temair, surrounded by a small flock of shaggy, black-faced sheep.

The sheep looked up from their grazing for a moment, perhaps wondering at the sudden appearance of this *Tuatha Dé Danann* interloper, and then went back to contentedly chewing the grass.

Marcroy could do nothing but quietly fume at the Hag's exclusion of him from what he suspected was a pivotal moment in all their lives, perhaps significant in their very history. And then he realized there was something that required his attention.

If he couldn't do anything about RónánDarragh, he could certainly do something about his errant niece, Trása.

CHAPTER 33

The Hag released the bonds on Ren a few moments after Marcroy disappeared. By then the mist had completely enveloped them, cutting off the outside world. He couldn't even make out the standing stones on the edge of the stone circle. The world was silent and the only two people in it were himself and the Hag.

He turned to find the haggard, wizened old woman gone, a much taller, younger and more attractive blonde woman standing in her place. Were it not for the ragged cloak and the gnarly staff, he would never have known it was the same creature. She looked familiar, but Ren couldn't quite place who he reminded him of.

"What did Marcroy do with Pete and Logan?"

"Who are Pete and Logan?"

He didn't know if she was pretending ignorance, or if she really didn't know what had happened to them. Ren wondered if Marcroy had tossed them back into the other realm. Not that he had time to worry about them now. He had the Hag to deal with first.

"Is that your true form," Ren asked, rotating his shoulders to loosen them after the stiffness of Marcroy's magical bindings, "or do you think I'll respond better to a familiar face - even if it's one I despise?"

The Hag laughed softly and took a step closer. "Would you be surprised if I said both?"

Ren shook his head. "After what I've seen these past ten years, nothing surprises me."

"You are far too young to be so jaded," she said, as she leaned on her staff with both hands and studied him. "I see much of Marcroy in you."

"Hey... if you're going to insult me..."

She chuckled again. "You have just enough human in you to counter it, I am relieved to note." She continued to study him for a long moment, then added, "And you know more than I anticipated. That is good. It means there is less I must explain."

"Why the need to explain anything?" Ren asked as he glanced around. There was no way out of here, he guessed, until the Hag decided to let him go. No harm in looking, though.

"Because I See the things you See."

Ren was tempted to answer with something glib about them both having eyes, so of course they saw the same things, but he knew that wasn't what she was talking about.

"I *See* nothing," he told her. "Not anymore."

"You have found a way to bury the truth of your Sight," the Hag said, "but you have not changed the universe enough to stop it happening."

"You don't know that," Ren accused. He didn't want to hear this. She was wrong. She had to be wrong.

"I do know it," the Hag replied, "and no matter how much you wish to deny it, you know it too. You have the true Sight, Rónán of the Undivided, and what you See must come to pass for the good of life in this realm and every other."

"Oh," Ren said, rolling his eyes at her simplistic view of the world. "No pressure then."

"Why do you fight the truth of your visions?"

"Because they suck," he said, unable to think of a more succinct way of expressing what he felt about his nightmares.

"You don't wish to kill the children in your dream," the Hag said, nodding in understanding. "And yet you have killed how many others in your quest to prevent your dream from coming true?"

"I only killed Empress Twins," he reminded her. "Adults. And most of them were actively engaged in killing your people, sometimes just for fun. I needed to know what they knew. Besides, what do you care? They worked for the *Matrarchaí*."

"We are your people, too," she said. "You may look human, Rónán, but that is the hand of the *Matrarchaí*. You are more *sídhe* than not. More one of us, than you'd like."

"What do you want from me?"

"I want you to do what you have Seen."

"I am not going to kill my brother's children. At least, I'm assuming they're Darragh's kids. Not that it matters if they're mine or his... I'm not murdering any babies to keep you happy."

The Hag sat herself down on a log that appeared from somewhere. Ren hadn't seen it arrive or noticed her doing anything to summon it. "The children in your vision are your brother's children, born of the *Matrarchaí* vessel, Brydie Ni'Seanan."

Ren said nothing, did nothing - he hoped - to betray the fact that he knew exactly where Brydie was, and while she remained trapped in the enchanted amethyst he had hidden with Toyoda in the ninja reality, no dream about murdering anybody's babies need ever come to pass.

"When the time comes," the Hag predicted, "you will not stay your hand."

"And you know that because you've had a vision, I suppose."

She nodded. "You will not need persuading."

"You know nothing of the kind."

"I know the children of that union are damned. They are the pinnacle of two thousand years of careful breeding by the *Matrarchaí* across bloodlines, across realities. Those children, when they are born, will be neither human nor *sídhe*."

"They look pretty human to me."

"Only because you have not, in your dream, seen what they are or can do."

"And what if they're not the monsters you think they are?" he asked, becoming impatient with her calm confidence that he was destined to murder a couple of innocent children and apparently not lose any sleep over the right of it. "And who cares anyway? There are an infinite number of realities, aren't there? Can't you cede a few of them to the *Matrarchaí* and let them be?"

"The *Matrarchaí* are not interested in a truce."

"And I'm not interested in killing my brother's kids to make you happy."

"It does not make me happy to tell you the children in your vision must die."

"Yeah... right... It's breaking your heart. I can tell."

The Hag stared at him for a moment, shaking her head. "If it meant condemning a few realities, we would surrender them readily. We are not greedy creatures, Rónán, nor particularly territorial. It is not in the nature of the *sídhe* to do what the *Matrarchaí* have done. The *sídhe* are an integral part of reality. Humans - and the *Matrarchaí* in particular - are trying to remake reality to suit themselves."

"By making babies you don't like?"

"Those babies have the power to force Partition." The Hag stared at him for a moment. "You have the stolen memories of many *Matrarchaí*. Search their thoughts and tell me - what does Partition mean to them?"

The word sparked a rush of jumbled thoughts and memories in Ren's mind all belonging to other people.

"The mission," Ren said, a little puzzled. As usual, unless someone triggered a word like that, it stayed buried. "Mostly they're just thinking about how important the 'mission' is, not *what* it is exactly."

"This mission they speak of is one several thousand years in the making." The Hag shook her head in wonder. "I can barely conceive of the notion that one could scheme so far ahead. We *sídhe* are doing well if we can plan our next meal."

"So what do they want to do? Break their reality away from the others?"

"In a word, yes."

"So let them. You'd be well rid of them, from what I've seen of the *Matrarchaí*."

"And you would be right. Except for one tiny but pertinent detail that makes that option... inadvisable."

"What's that?"

"If they achieve Partition, all the realities connected to theirs will be sucked into the implosion." She shifted on the log, as if it was not a very comfortable place to sit. "It's why the *Matrarchaí* are trying to eradicate the *sídhe* from as many realms touching theirs as possible. Realities filled with magic and no *sídhe* to put up a defense against the implosion will help replenish their denuded reality during the partition."

"And then you'll be rid of them," Ren pointed out. "Given the damage is already done in a lot of cases, isn't it time to just cut your losses?"

"That's a very human way of thinking. And it would, perhaps, be the sensible course, except for that one tiny thing I mentioned."

"Which is?"

"All other realities will cease to exist."

"What?"

She waited a moment for her words to sink in, before adding, "The *Matrarchaí* intend to start again. To reset the cosmos. If they don't replenish the magic in the core reality in the process, there will be no more magic in their future."

Ren shook his head at the scope - and the absurdity - of such a plan. "That's insane."

"Without question."

"No... I mean, even if you could convince yourself it's a good idea, why pick my reality? It's fucked. They've polluted it. There's a bloody great hole in the ozone layer. Global warming is cooking the planet."

"Your world is just one of billions in that reality, Rónán. That one life form has made one planet uninhabitable with their technology, does not alter the special nature of the reality in which it resides."

"What's so special about it?"

"It is the first, and therefore the only one which can be sundered completely from the others. The damage to the world you speak of only makes the matter more urgent. The *Matrarchaí* need to Partition the reality while the planet is still habitable. With magic, they can reverse the environmental damage."

Ren could barely grasp what she was suggesting. "But... aren't there an infinite number of realities?"

"So there are."

"And you're saying the *Matrarchaí* is going to try to narrow that down to one?"

"Not to *a* one. To *the* one." She frowned, creasing her brow, and for a moment Ren got a glimpse of the old woman she'd been when she first arrived. "At which point the splintering process will start over and soon there will again be an infinite number of realities - but they will be realities filled with magic the *Matrarchaí* can call upon at will and they will be empty of all Faerie. We will cease to exist."

Ren said nothing. He was having trouble processing the scope of such a catastrophe. The Hag seemed to understand his difficulty. She rose to her feet and approached him, placing a hand on his shoulder, as if to comfort him. "So you see, Rónán of the Undivided, the cost of two small lives starts to gain some perspective, when the lives saved by their death cannot - quite literally - be counted."

"You're making this up."

"Why would I bother?" the Hag asked. She seemed amused by the suggestion. "Do you think we would concern ourselves with the affairs of humans, or even the *Matrarchaí* from another reality, if it were anything less than our very existence at stake?"

Ren had known enough *Tuatha Dé Danann* to know she spoke the truth. They were not schemers by nature. It took too much effort. Too much focus.

"Maybe it doesn't have to go down the way you See it," he said, as he shook off her hand, refusing to accept his destiny was so set in place he had no choice in the matter. "If those children are never born -"

"But they will be," the Hag said. "No matter how hard you try, or how clever you think you've been, Rónán, Destiny is a sly and cunning manipulator. He will always win. You can do nothing but embrace your part in his plan and find a way to live with what he has marked you for."

"I don't believe that."

"Whether you believe it or not, does not alter the truth of it."

He stared at her, wishing she'd stayed in the form of the wizened old crone, which would have made her much easier to dislike. "I can't do it."

"You will find the courage when the time comes."

Ren shook his head. "I won't. Because I am not going to do it."

His refusal didn't seem to faze her at all. "Believe what you will, Rónán . Time and circumstances will force your hand. In the meantime, I will help you however I can."

He found that hard to believe. "Even if what I want to do directly flies in the face of what you have in mind for me?"

"Everything you do is driving you down the path Destiny wants you to travel, Rónán. Any help I give you will merely serve to expedite the inevitable."

So you think. "Then help me rescue my brother."

"I cannot enter a magic-less realm, Rónán, not even for the Undivided destined to save us."

He reached into his pocket and pulled out Kiva's ruby necklace. "I need to charge these up with magic."

The Hag seemed a little puzzled by his request. "What good will that do you?"

"I'm going to swallow them, once they're charged. It should juice me up enough to be able to wane in and out of the prison where Darragh is trapped in the other realm."

"And how do you intend to do this 'charge them up' thing?" she asked, still looking confused.

"I thought soaking them in the Pool of Tranquillity would do the trick."

The Hag took the necklace from him and held it up to examine it. Her fingers were long and elegant and unmarked by the liver spots that marred her skin when she was in the crone form. "They are jewels, Rónán, not sponges. They will not absorb magic the way you imagine." She lowered the necklace and looked up at him. "To infuse this many rubies with the sort of magic you require - to produce such a feat in a world without magic - would take the combined power of the Brethren."

And there you have it, Ren thought. *The escape clause.* What was it Pete was fond of saying? *Typical Faerie - can't break a promise, but they can always find a loophole.*

"Figured there'd be a catch," he said, shaking his head, impressed it took her less than a heartbeat to find a way around helping him.

Not that it mattered. He wasn't expecting help. Ren didn't believe her about the pool, anyway. He'd swum in it. He'd seen its affect on anything capable of wielding magic. He reached for the necklace, determined to follow through with his plan to soak the jewels in the Pool of Tranquillity.

But before he could get a hand to it, the Hag vanished with the necklace, leaving Ren stranded in the center of a thick impenetrable mist with no way out and no way of saving anybody, least of all himself.

CHAPTER 34

One of Marcroy's greatest failings, Trása knew, was his tendency to underestimate humans. He liked them; his fascination for their women was legendary - even though he would swear he wasn't the least bit tempted by them if pressed on the subject - and he would not countenance the notion that anybody other than he should represent Orlagh in her dealings with humans and their affairs.

And yet he scorned most *sídhe*-human mongrels and ignored any humans he didn't feel worthy of his attention, to the point of not even noticing they were there.

In that, Marcroy was not alone. Most *Tuatha Dé Danann* princes had a similar opinion of humans and Trása found herself being very grateful for their arrogance. It meant that although she was trapped in the bower and forbidden to leave, Nika, the young human Merlin, who Marcroy and Stiofán barely acknowledged, could come and go from *Tír Na nÓg* as she pleased.

The news Nika brought, however, was not good. There was no sign of Ren, no sign of Pete or Logan, and Marcroy had put Stiofán in charge before stepping back through the rift with a promise that he would be back shortly to take care of the punishment his errant niece had coming to her.

Stiofán, the *Tuatha Dé Danann* refugee Trása had saved from certain death, proved to be an ungrateful wretch, turning on her so fast it made her head spin. He was relishing is new role as king of the Faerie and was being so obnoxious about it, Trása wanted to push him off the edge of the high platform outside her bower, just to see how many bones he could break on the way down.

Most of her lesser *Youkai* friends - even the little pixie, Echo - had gone into hiding, in awe of the *Tuatha Dé Danann* prince who had stepped into their realm. Trása's only company, other than Nika, was Toyoda, who sat in the corner rocking back and forth muttering about his special mission for Renkavana. He was so annoyingly insistent on fulfilling his mission, Trása was forced to invoke his true name, just to make him stay put. She didn't press him on the details though. Rónán had apparently also invoked his true name to extract a promise of secrecy from the *Leipreachán* and he became very distressed if she tried to force the issue.

Nika ignored the *Leipreachán* and placed the basket of ordinary human food she'd brought from the mundane world on the floor of the bower. She squatted down, her back to the entrance, blocking Stiofán's view inside. Not that he was paying any attention to Trása or her human servant. He was busy rearranging *Tír Na nÓg* to his liking, holding court outside with his *Tuatha Dé Danann* friends, reallocating the accommodation in the upper levels to those refugees of higher station than the pixies, sprites, *Leipreachán* and other lesser *Youkai* Trása had favored.

"I wasn't able to scry anybody out," Nika said in a low voice as she took a plump, ripe peach from the basket for Trása and began to peel it with her small, bone-handled knife.

Trása chewed thoughtfully on her bottom lip. "They must still be in the other realm without magic, looking for Darragh."

"Suppose they're trapped in that realm?" Nika asked, glancing over her shoulder to be certain Stiofán's attention was elsewhere.

"They have Marcroy's jewel," Trása reminded the Merlin, unwilling to entertain the idea Rónán and Darragh were both lost to her forever. "Besides, Rónán has Delphine's memories. He knows where the *Matrarchaí* have their stone circles located in the Enchanted Sphere. They'll be back."

"Which is exactly what Marcroy is counting on," Nika hissed, a little impatiently. Trása was fairly sure Nika was concerned for Pete rather than Rónán, but as their fates were so closely intertwined, it didn't really matter who she cared about the most.

"What can we do?" Trása asked. "I promised Marcroy I wouldn't leave. I promised him I wouldn't try to warn Rónán he was coming for him, either."

"You promised him, my lady," Nika pointed out. "I didn't promise that arrogant, ill-mannered, self-important Faerie a damned thing."

Trása smiled. Nika didn't like to be ignored. She certainly didn't like to be dismissed like a common serving wench, which was all the notice Marcroy had paid her since he arrived. Nika was a powerful magician in her own right. At the very least she deserved some respect for that.

"And how are you going to get me out of the promises I've made, Nika?" she asked, appreciating the effort, but not certain there was anything useful the young Merlin could do other than rail against the unfairness of it all.

Nika handed her the peach. "I thought I'd borrow an idea from an old children's story from my realm."

"What story is that?" she asked, biting into the fruit. It was juicy and crisp and tasted faintly of something other than peaches. Trása was intrigued. Nika rarely spoke about her realm. So many lives had been lost there to the *Matrarchaí*, most of the time she didn't want to talk about it.

"We have a legend about a young princess with an evil stepmother. The stepmother hated her stepdaughter so much, she tried to kill her with a poisoned apple."

Trása smiled at the odd notion. "Charming. Are the children in your realm particularly enchanted by tales of infanticide and evil stepmothers?"

"The poison doesn't kill the little princess," Nika explained, quite seriously. "It just sends her into a death-like sleep."

"And then she gets buried alive, I suppose. You must have some seriously disturbed children in your realm, Nika."

The Merlin shook her head, watching Trása eat the odd-tasting peach with an unnerving intensity. "She is awoken by her true love's kiss." "That's ridiculous."

"Of course it is," Nika agreed, "but then, I only borrowed part of the tale."

Trása blinked, her vision blurring a little. "Whish part?" she asked, alarmed to find herself slurring the words. "The kish?"

"The death-like sleep part," Nika explained softly. "I think you should lie down now."

"Why?"

"Otherwise you might fall down, my lady."

Trása's head was starting to spin. "Nika.... What... what have you... done?"

"Nothing but keep a promise, my lady," the Merlin said softly, still sitting with her back to the door, blocking the view into the bower. "You saved my life. Don't you recall what I told you when you saved me and the *sídhe* I was trying to protect? I swore, if the chance ever arose, I would save your life in return."

"By poishoning me?" Trása was having trouble keeping her eyes open. Whatever drug Nika had used in the peach, it was alarmingly effective. "How... doesh that work?"

Nika glanced over her shoulder briefly, to make certain they were still free to talk without being overheard. "Stiofán is a fool, my lady. He doesn't care what happens to you. With Marcroy gone, if he believes you are dead, he will not object to me removing your smelly, mongrel corpse from his lofty new home. When we are gone from here, I will take you back to the mundane world and open a rift from there to your home realm. I have been there now, so I can find it again. After we arrive, you can show me the way to Pete's realm. Once we find *that* realm, we will locate Pete, Logan and Rónán and then we will collect Darragh and your friend, Sorcha. We will then all come back here and take care of these uppity *Tuatha Dé Danann* lords who think they can take over our home."

Nika's explanation was so long, Trása had to fight to stay awake to hear the end of it. The bower was spinning now and the branch beneath her was moving up and down so violently she felt like a small boat being tossed around a stormy sea. She struggled to hang on to consciousness, shaking her head, which just made everything worse. "It won't work. In my realm... I'm curshed... I'll turn back... into an owl..."

"I thought of that," Nika said, reaching for the disgusting woad-marked, mummified baby's foot talisman the Merlin used to open rifts. She leaned forward and slipped it over Trása's neck. "You'll be a bird, but you'll still be you," Nika said, taking her by the shoulders and lowering her to the furs that made up the bower's sleeping area. "You can use my talisman when you wake. You can open the rift with it, even in avian form."

"I..." Trása couldn't remember the rest of what she wanted to say. She simply couldn't fight it any longer and the furs were so soft and didn't seem to be moving about as much as everything else. "I... I... don't..."

Trása didn't have the strength to finish a sentence she lacked the energy to form in the first place. Somewhere in the distance, as if she were listening through a waterfall, she thought she heard Nika calling for help, yelling something about someone dying, but Trása couldn't focus on one thing long enough to be sure.

In the end, she gave up trying to figure it out, snuggled into the warm furs and surrendered to the darkness, thinking if it was her that was doing the dying, as deaths went, it really wasn't so bad after all.

CHAPTER 35

Haley cried a lot the first few days she was home. Sometimes she cried for her lost life, sometimes she cried for the family she didn't know any longer, and sometimes she cried for no reason she could explain.

And sometimes she didn't know why she was crying and it just seemed the only thing she could do.

It wasn't that anybody was being cruel and unkind. It wasn't that they didn't try to understand. Far from it. Everyone was going out of their way to be considerate. But no matter how they tried, nobody could explain why her life had advanced by a week, while the lives of everyone else had moved on by ten years.

She'd been gone no time at all in her mind. In the house she'd grown up in, her room was now Neil's study. He wasn't an annoying pre-teen brat, any longer. He was studying physics at university, working on his master's dissertation on some obscure topic Hayley couldn't even comprehend.

He'd left a few days after her return - relieved to be going, she suspected - for a trip to Geneva and the Large Hadron Collider.

There was no Large Hadron Collider in the world Hayley had left a week ago.

Her father kept avoiding her. He kept finding things that needed to be done at Kiva's house. Her car - no longer a Bentley, but something called a Lexus Hybrid these days - seemed to need an inordinate amount of work. Kerry took a few days off work, but her normally stoic and supportive stepmother couldn't even bring herself to look Hayley in the eye.

They told her to take her time. They told her there was no rush getting back into her old life.

It would have been good advice, too, if she had an old life to go back to.

In between crying fits, she watched TV, astonished and alarmed by the world she'd returned to. Europe was teetering on the edge of economic ruin, America had an African American president and everybody, it seemed - even Kerry and her father - owned an iPhone. There was a war going on in Afghanistan. There had been another war in Iraq. And no matter where she looked, somebody named Kardashian (famous for no reason Hayley could determine) was on the cover of every magazine that had once featured actresses like Kiva.

Hayley splashed cold water on her face, hoping to wash away the evidence of her tears, although she was home alone and nobody was here to witness this latest crying fit. Kerry had gone back to work at Kiva's house today. The actress had returned from the BAFTA's and would be expecting Kerry and Patrick to be at her beck and call, regardless of what might be happening in their personal lives.

Staring into the mirror, Hayley felt like she was looking at a stranger. The girl looking back at her was still seventeen. Still looking forward to her school formal. Still waiting for Ren to notice she was a girl. Still wondering what she wanted to be when she grew up.

Only she *was* grown-up. In the blink of an eye Hayley was twenty-seven. Legally she was an adult. And nobody knew what to do with her.

The distant chiming of the doorbell forced Hayley to abandon her depressing questions about what she was supposed to do with her life now it had been turned inside out. She didn't know who'd be at the door during the day and wasn't sure she wanted to answer it anyway. It might be another reporter trying to get an interview.

She pushed off the basin and reluctantly headed down the stairs as the doorbell rang again. Whoever it was out there had very little patience. Before she was at the bottom of the stairs it rang a third time, and then a voice called out. "Hayley? Are you in there? Let me in, pet, before some nosey paparazzo happens by!"

Hayley reached the front door and jerked it open in shock. "Kiva?"

Ren's mother glanced left and right and then pushed past Hayley to come inside, quickly closing the door behind her. She leaned on it and smiled as she took off her dramatic dark glasses and unwound the Hermes scarf covering her perfectly-arranged blonde hair. "There. I think I actually managed to make it here unseen."

"How did you get here?"

"I drove myself." She frowned at Hayley's expression. "I can drive, you know, Hayley."

"Then why hire my dad as your chauffeur?"

"I find the time travelling to and from the set a good time to study scripts," she said. "One can't read a script and drive. Are you alone?"

Hayley nodded warily, still trying to imagine why Kiva would come here on her own to see her. "Neil left for Geneva yesterday. Mom and Dad are at your place. Working."

"Good, then we can talk. Do you have anything to drink?"

"It's nine-thirty in the morning, Kiva."

"I wasn't thinking of me, pet," Kiva told her as she pushed off the door. "I rather think you're the one who's going to need the drink when you hear what I have to tell you."

"Kerry doesn't know I'm here," Kiva said, as she accepted the cup of instant coffee Hayley made for her. There was an espresso machine on the bench, but Hayley had no idea how to operate it. It was new, along with kitchen cupboards, the decor and the car out in the driveway. When did anyone in this house care that much about coffee, anyway? "I'd rather you didn't mention it to her."

"Why not?"

"Because I'm going to tell you things Kerry would rather you didn't know."

Hayley was intrigued, but she was also acutely aware of who she was talking to. Kiva was the queen of all drama queens. She was probably here to pitch the idea of turning Hayley's life into a movie or something - starring Kiva Kavanaugh, of course.

"What doesn't Kerry want me to know?"

"That we know where you've been, for one thing."

"Of course you do."

Even Kiva couldn't miss her skepticism. "All right, I admit I don't know *specifically* where you've been, but I'm pretty sure I know what happened to you."

"Really? Do tell."

"You been to another reality," Kiva said, in a matter-of-fact tone. "And they healed your sight with magic."

Hayley stared at Kiva for a long moment, not sure if the actress knew the truth or was just indulging in a coincidental flight of fancy.

"Is that what you think?"

"It's what I know," Kiva said.

"And how do you know it?"

"Ren told me."

Hayley didn't have an answer for that. "He came to me," Kiva explained, "in my hotel room in London."

"You're seeing the dead now?"

Kiva shook her head. "He was real, Hayley. As real as you or I."

The idea that Ren was somewhere close by, even if it was London, filled Hayley with a mixture of turbulent emotions, ranging from hope to anger. Ren had got her into this mess and he might be able to get her out of it, but he was apparently flitting about the world, dropping in on his mother for a visit in London, quite content to let his best friend rot here in Dublin with her life falling apart.

"Ren told you that, did he? That I've been to another reality?"

It occurred to Hayley that Kiva might be here to set her up. Had her father engaged the eminent Murray Symes to get to the root of her memory loss? And had Kiva been sent here to pretend they were friends so Hayley would confide her psychosis to her? Was there an ambulance parked down the street with a psych team and a straightjacket, waiting for Kiva's signal? Was Kiva wearing a wire?

Dear God, have I completely lost my mind?

"It's where Ren's been all this time."

"He told you that, too, did he?"

Kiva took a sip of her coffee and then a deep breath, as if she was forcing herself to remain calm. "Have you ever heard of Darragh?"

Hayley nodded slowly, aware she was treading on dangerous ground here, if she didn't want to admit the truth - even if Kiva seemed to have guessed it anyway. "He's Ren's brother, isn't he?"

"Ren's identical twin," Kiva said with a nod. "He's in prison, by the way, for kidnapping you and for ordering some accountant killed."

"I didn't know that."

"After you and Ren disappeared, Darragh came to my house pretending to be Ren."

"How long did he manage to fool you for?"

"Longer than he should have. Not as long as he imagines. Not that I wasn't ready and willing to be fooled. I so desperately wanted him to be Ren. I so desperately wanted Ren to be doing what the Gardaí claimed - keeping watch for some sleazy drug lord while he sold a trunk-load of cocaine. I wanted him to be a normal, troublesome teenager."

"You wanted Ren to be dealing drugs?"

"I wanted him to be doing anything, but what I feared he was actually doing."

"Which was?"

"Discovering who he really was." Kiva was a good actress, even a great one at times, so Hayley knew she should be wary of her, but there was a ring of truth about her story.

"Did you turn him in? Is that why Darragh is in prison?"

"I turned him in, Hayley, but not to the Gardaí. I called the people who brought me to this reality. I told them he was here and that they should come get him, and then nine-eleven happened and the whole world turned pear-shaped. By the time my people got here, Darragh was in jail and his fate was out of our hands."

Hayley waited for Kiva to elaborate. She had no idea what nine-eleven meant.

It took Kiva a moment to realize she'd lost Hayley somewhere along the way. "I'm sorry... you wouldn't know. There was a terrorist attack on the World Trade Centre in New York just after you disappeared. It killed thousands of people. It was appalling, almost beyond description. The world really hasn't been the same since."

"What do you mean: 'the people who brought me to this reality?' Hayley desperately wanted to believe Kiva knew something about what had happened to her, but she'd witnessed Kiva join several different religions as she was growing up. Kiva once announced she was Cleopatra in a past life. It didn't seem possible that the same woman could know anything about what Hayley had been through, or that if she did know about it, that she could be such a ditz.

"I come from a different reality to this one. I was brought here when I was not much older than you."

"By who?"

"An organizastion called the *Matrarchaí*. My mother belonged to them and signed me up as soon as she gave birth to a girl. Once I got older and it was obvious I was going to be pretty, I was marked for bearing children. Turns out I can't. Your father rescued Ren while I was waiting to learn my fate. I'd been in this realm for a fair while by then. I had a life and an identity they'd carefully constructed for me and I wanted to stay. And I really did want to be an actress. Adopting Ren meant I could stay and follow my dreams."

Hayley didn't know what to say.

"They use magic in the realm I come from too, Hayley," she said, as if she understood Hayley's astonishment. "When the Gardaí interviewed Darragh after you and Ren disappeared, he was quite open about coming from another reality. He swore that's where they'd sent you to have your eyesight healed. Everyone thought he was mad."

"Except you."

She nodded. "Kerry knew the truth too, but what were we supposed to do? Tell the Gardaí Darragh was right? That you probably were in another reality having your sight healed by magic? They'd have locked us up alongside Darragh."

"Kerry knows about this?" Kiva shrugged. "She and dad were trying to have me declared dead."

"You'd been gone ten years, pet. We figured you liked it where you were and decided to stay, just as I decided to stay in this reality. It was your father, not Kerry, who wanted the matter settled. He doesn't know about any of this... well nothing but what Darragh may have told him. He was just doing what one does a decade after one's child has been kidnapped and never seen again."

"Why hasn't Kerry said anything to me if she knows the truth?"

Kiva took another sip of the coffee and grimaced. Hayley figured it must be cold by now. "That gets us back to what I said earlier, I suppose ... she doesn't want me telling you any of this. Kerry has tried very hard to put her previous life behind her, Hayley. She doesn't want to go back to it. She doesn't want anything to do with it. Telling you the truth means opening up a lot of old wounds she thought healed over long ago."

"You don't seem to have that problem."

That made Kiva smile. "I'm not the pragmatist your stepmother is, pet. I know it's probably best to pretend ignorance. I know I should probably try to convince you that you've imagined it all. Or that you've just lost your memory for the past decade. But that won't alter what's happened to you, Hayley. Even worse, once word gets out to the press that you've reappeared, you'll become a freak show. Being an object of public scrutiny is not a life I would thrust upon my worst enemy. If I'd known when I was younger what I know now about the high price of fame, I sometimes wonder if I wouldn't have chosen differently, myself."

Hayley thought that highly unlikely. Kiva loved being famous. "What am I supposed to do?"

"That's why I'm here, darling. To ask if you want me to petition the *Matrarchaí* to send you back."

"Send me back to what?" Hayley asked, angry she would even suggest such a thing. "I was gone a week, Kiva. I don't have a fabulous new life in another reality like you do, waiting for my return. I was gone a few days, and then they kicked me out and sent me home."

Kiva pursed her lips thoughtfully. "I thought Ren sent you to Darragh's friends to be healed."

"Some friends! I was met by a handsome Faerie prince, spirited away to *Tír Na nÓg*, dumped on his sister, tolerated until they got bored having me there and then sent home by a merman. I don't want to go back to that reality. I hate the Faerie." It took until that moment for Hayley to realize hate was exactly what she was feeling. That's what her tears were for. Not for her lost life, not for her missing years, but her betrayal by the Faerie who never warned her of the dangers of accepting their hospitality.

"Well then, darling, you'll fit right in with the *Matrarchaí*. Did you want me to arrange a meeting for you?"

Hayley was about to say yes, when another thought occurred to her. "Why is Ren back?"

"What do you mean?"

"You said you spoke to Ren in London. But he's been gone as long as I have. Why is he back now?"

She shrugged. "He didn't say, but if I had to guess, I'd say he's come looking for Darragh. I've always thought it strange he left him here in prison for so long."

"Then he'll have to come here. To Dublin."

"I suppose. Are you expecting him to look you up?"

Why would he? Hayley thought. *He abandoned me to the Faerie and hasn't tried to find me in ten years.*

"I guess not."

"Shall I talk to the *Matrarchaí* for you then?"

Hayley couldn't decide, partly because she still didn't completely trust Kiva, and partly because she wasn't sure she wanted anything to do with any organizastion that dealt with magic and realities full of Faerie.

Magic and realities full of Faerie had brought her nothing but pain, so far.

"I don't know, Kiva."

"I understand," Kiva said, with a sympathetic nod. "I really do." She opened her purse and pulled out a card, sliding it across the kitchen table. "If you change your mind, give them a call."

Hayley looked at the elegant silver card and frowned. "This is for a modeling agency."

"I know. Tell them I told you to call. Ask for Mother. She'll understand."

Kiva closed her purse and rose to her feet. She smiled down at Hayley. "I know you think I'm a bit of a fruit-loop, Hayley. I probably am and you were always such a smart girl. I may not be as clever as you, but I was given a chance at a different life and I was smart enough to grab it. Don't let the same chance slip away, just because it's me that's bringing you the opportunity." She shouldered her purse and glanced at her watch. "God, is that the time? I'm supposed to be meeting Jon and Eunice for lunch. Be a pet and don't mention our little chat to Kerry, will you?"

"If you want."

"And don't fret about Ren," she added, mistaking Hayley's silence for something it wasn't. "He'll be okay. He has powerful magic and I think he's learned a thing or two about how to use it these past few years."

"Will he come back through the same rift, do you think?"

"I suppose. It's easier than finding new rifts, I believe. Not that I ever had the ability to open a rift. Why?"

"Just wondering."

Kiva slipped on her large sunglasses and began to cover her hair with the scarf. "Well, don't wonder too long. And put that card somewhere safe."

"I will."

Hayley saw her to the door, closing it carefully after Kiva kissed her on the cheek and slipped outside, looking about dramatically before she ran to her Lexus and climbed inside.

As the car backed out of the drive, Hayley leaned on the closed front door for a moment, and then glanced down at the card Kiva had given her, before slipping it into the pocket of her jeans. She wasn't interested in Kiva's modeling agency. She had other plans.

Ren was coming for Darragh. Kiva said he would probably come through the same rift, which meant that sooner or later, Ren had to appear at the ruined stone circle in the rough at the Castle Golf Club, and when he stepped through the rift she would be waiting for him.

CHAPTER 36

"Now what?" Pete asked as he looked about, wondering where they were. He had a sneaking suspicion he knew the location, and it would make sense if it turned out to be the place he thought it was. Marcroy had tossed them through a rift with very little forethought. Logically, he would send them to a location to which he'd previously opened a rift.

"We wait, I suppose," Logan suggested, brushing dried twigs from his shirt.

"For what, exactly?"

"The rift to open again?"

"There's a well thought out plan."

"I'm serious, Pete. Ren has to come back for Darragh. Count on it. We just need to be here when it happens. Unless of course, you want to stay in this reality."

Pete shook his head. That decision was long made. And Logan's logic didn't really work for Pete.

"Ren just got ambushed by Marcroy Tarth. He could be dead by now."

His brother shook his head. "Marcroy doesn't want to kill him. He needs him to save the world, or something."

"When did he tell you that?"

"When he ambushed me coming back through the rift into our realm."

Pete smiled. "Our realm? You mean the ninja reality? I thought this was our realm?"

Logan thought on that for a moment and then shrugged. "I guess we've moved way beyond that now."

"Ironic, don't you think, that after a decade of searching, we arrive at this momentous conclusion a few minutes after we get dumped here with no way back."

"We have a way back," Logan reminded him. "If worst comes to worst, we just need to get to one of the *Matrarchai*'s stone circles in the Enchanted Sphere."

"Not without a talisman to open a rift. Should we try scrying Trása or Nika out on the puddle phone?"

Logan shook his head. "Echo told me Marcroy was holding Trása prisoner. She didn't know what had happened to Nika. And we don't have anything magical to fire up the puddle phone with in any case."

"Christ... you mean we're left with waiting for Ren?"

"Looks like." Logan glanced about and frowned. "We're at the golf club, aren't we?"

"I think so."

"Not a very good place to wait."

"And no guarantee Ren will come back through this rift anyway," Pete agreed. "How do we find him when he gets here?"

"We don't. We need to be where he's going to be when he comes back." Logan rubbed his forearms with his hands to ward off the cold. The wind had picked up. Although they were reasonably sheltered here, it was not going to be a fun place to spend the night. "Fancy yourself a seer, little brother? We're going to need one to work that out."

"Portlaoise Prison."

"What?"

"Darragh is an inmate in Portlaoise Prison."

Logan nodded, and began to look about for somewhere to sit. "Off you go then. I'll be waiting here when you get back."

"Very funny."

"If Darragh is in Portlaoise Prison, Pete, I am not going anywhere near the place. It's full of cameras, for one thing, and you and I have been disappeared for a decade. And I sure as hell am not going to do anything to get myself inside as an inmate on the off chance Ren might turn up to rescue me someday."

"Fair enough, but that's where Ren will have to go to get Darragh."

Logan didn't seem all that impressed. "How?"

Pete wasn't sure if he should share Ren's idea with Logan. Without a *Leipreachán* around to agree with him, it sounded more than a little insane. "He had some harebrained scheme underway to wane in and out of there using rubies soaked in magic."

"Oh... what could go possibly wrong with a plan like that? "

"I know it sounds crazy, but it might be his best chance. And ours, if we want to get out of here."

Logan sighed. "Sadly, I have to agree. But if we can't go near the prison ourselves, we need someone who can get in to see Darragh for us. Any suggestions as to who this Angel of Mercy might be?"

It was a very good question. Given their own doubtful history, everybody associated with their previous lives - their grandmother, their cousin, Kelly, and any of their other "uncles" or "aunts" - was suspect. All those people *had* to be part of the *Matrarchaí* to have been part of the deception that was their life before they left this reality. Any friendships they had had before the disappearance were long forgotten, too.

"What if we try Ren's cousin, Hayley?" Logan suggested after a few moments. "She's back in this realm and she's a friend of Ren's."

"I suspect making contact with her will bring down more trouble than it's worth," Pete said. "If Hayley has been gone as long as we have, she'll be getting a lot of attention right now - the sort of attention we don't want to attract."

"Any old work colleagues you can think of? Anybody I contact will report our reappearance in a heartbeat, if only to grab the lead story on the six o'clock news, so they're not much use. Pity your mates are all cops. I doubt they're going to help us bust someone out of Portlaoise."

Maybe not all of them would, Pete thought, as a name occurred to him. *Perhaps a bit of patient-doctor confidentiality might protect us.*

"Annad Semaj," Pete said.

Logan frowned. "Isn't he a police shrink, or something?"

Pete nodded. "I think he's about to acquire two new patients."

His brother smiled as he realized the reason for what Pete was suggesting. "Which means he can't turn us in. That's so clever I could have thought of it myself."

"You didn't, though."

"I like to let you have the glory now and then, little brother. Do you think Ren will be okay with Marcroy?"

"Unless Marcroy's killed him already."

"That would be a shame. He kind of grows on you after a while." Logan walked to the edge of the circle. It was too dark to see much across the fairway, but the traffic noise had not let up since they arrived.

"So does fungus," Pete pointed out, pushing past Logan to pick his way through the rough to the fairway. Enough of this hanging about talking. They had a name and even if their plan was nothing more than a vague idea, it was something. He was cold, hungry and bruised from his abrupt arrival here, and they were on a tight schedule. He didn't know what Marcroy wanted of Ren, but he didn't doubt for a moment that Ren would be coming for Darragh soon. If they wanted to get back to the other reality -

if he was ever going to see Nika again - they needed to be there when he arrived.

Their only alternative was Logan's suggestion that they find a way into one of the *Matrarchaí's* high-rise stone circles in the Enchanted Sphere, and even that escape route was no good to them without some sort of magical talisman to open the rift and the knowledge of how to open it. As the *Matrarchaí* tended not to leave such things lying about, that meant doing this the hard way.

It seemed to Pete that, lately, the hard way was the only way they ever did things.

They used one of the credit cards Plunkett had stolen to get a cab to Annad's house. The cab driver looked up the good doctor's address on his iPhone and then drove them to his neat little suburban house using GPS. Pete tried not to be impressed. Technology hadn't taken a giant leap forward in their absence - both cell phones and GPS's had existed in the world he left behind - so much as a giant embrace by everyone. It seemed every person was connected to something digital. Everywhere he looked, every time he saw people, some of them standing, often walking, head down, thumbs tapping away, so focused on the device in their hands they didn't seem to notice the world around them.

There were lights on in Annad's house when they arrived, but only one car parked in the drive. As the cab pulled away, it occurred to Pete that he didn't know if Annad was married and if he was, his wife might be home, which could complicate matters. Too late to worry about that now, he supposed.

"Let me do the talking," he told Logan as they walked up the neat path to the front door.

Logan was looking around to see if anybody was watching them. The neighbourhood seemed quiet. At this hour most law-abiding people would be eating supper, taking in the late news or getting ready for bed.

"Okay."

"I mean it."

"I heard you."

They reached the door. Pete hesitated for a fraction of a second and then lifted the brass knocker and rapped three times. The sound echoed through the silent neighbourhood, prompting a dog a few doors down to start barking. Moments later they heard footsteps in the hall and the door opened.

Annad had greyed a little at the temples, Pete noted, but he hadn't changed much. He looked at Pete and Logan for a moment and then, as if a light had come on in his head, his eyes widened. "Oh, my God."

"Can we come in, Annad?"

"Oh, my God."

"Yeah, you said that, already," Logan said, pushing the door open. He shoved Annad back, grabbed Pete by the sleeve, dragged him inside and slammed the door.

"Logan! I said I would do the talking!"

"Which leaves me to do the shoving. Is there anybody else here?"

Annad shook his head, his eyes wide with shock. "Anybody expected home?"

He shook his head again. "My wife was called into the hospital for an emergency caesar. She won't be back for hours. I have two kids, but they're at boarding school."

Pete pushed Logan away from the doctor. He was no threat to them and Logan was just making things worse. "Your wife is a doctor?"

Annad nodded. "An obstetrician. What are you doing here, Pete? Where have you been?"

"Long story. This is my brother, Logan."

"I gathered as much. What's going on?"

"You got any decent whiskey?"

"Of course."

"Then why don't you pour us a drink, old friend, and we'll tell you all about it."

CHAPTER 37

It shouldn't be so easy to take a life.

Ren pondered that thought as he approached the cradle rocking gently in the center of the room. He was overcome by a sense of having been here before, and yet it was different somehow. The room was no longer warm or candlelit. It was dark and the walls were glistening in the moonlight seeping through a sliver in the closed curtains.

There was no sign of the nurse. Ren wondered if she'd run away or if her fate had been the same as everyone else who'd approached this nightmare.

He reached the cradle and stopped to study it for a moment. The oak cradle was carved with elaborate Celtic knotwork and inlaid with softly glowing mother-of-pearl, just as it always was, but the mother-of-pearl was splattered with something that smelled like fresh blood.

Ren glanced down at the blade he carried and wondered if it would be enough. The airgead sídhe *caught the light in odd places, illuminating the engraving on the blade. He hefted the razor-sharp weapon in his hand. Faerie silver was useless in battle, but for this task, no other would suffice.*

The twins slept peacefully - he'd not have been able to approach otherwise - curled together like soft, deadly petals, the one on the left sucking her thumb, the other making soft suckling motions with her mouth, unconsciously mirroring her sister. The girls were sated and content, blissfully ignorant of their approaching death.

If they had been awake, would they recognize the danger that hovered over them? Ren wondered.

Maybe they would. Whatever made these children what they were, must give them some inkling of approaching danger.

They couldn't just exist to destroy. Could they?

They looked so innocent. So human.

"Are you sure you can do this?"

He glanced over his shoulder. Darragh stood in the shadows by the door.

"It has to be done, Darragh. I don't have a choice."

Darragh took a step further into the room. Ren saw himself reflected in his twin's eyes. Darragh's face was filled with doubt and anguish.

"I still think they're innocent," Darragh said.

"How can you say that? You saw what they did."

"They didn't know. Didn't understand..."

"They are death, Darragh. The death of billions upon billions more."

Darragh shook his head. "I can't believe..." He didn't finish the sentence. Or couldn't.

Ren didn't respond, turning back to stare down at the twin girls he had come to murder.

Darragh took another step closer. "I won't let you do it. You don't have to do it. You're not a tool of the Matrarchaí. *Neither of us are. We don't have to do her bidding."*

"Even if she's right?"

"She's dead. What difference does it make?"

"I will end this."

"I won't let you."

"How will you stop me?" he asked as he raised the blade. One of the girls was stirring - they were too alike to tell which was which. She opened her eyes to stare up at him, her face framed by soft dark curls, her expression disturbingly alert and aware for one so young. Her eyes were strange ... blue with no pupil and no whites at all. Just a pool of blue terror that had already killed once and would kill again and again until they'd achieved their goal. Her sister remained asleep, still peacefully sucking her thumb. Which will be harder? he wondered. Killing the one who is asleep and ignorant of her fate, or the one staring up at me with that sleepy, contented smile?

Am I strong enough to fight her off if she tries to stop me?

"I'll kill you if I have to, Rónán, to stop this."

Ren stared down at the twins, dismissing the empty threat. "Even if you could get across this room before the deed was done, Darragh, you can't kill me without killing yourself, which would achieve precisely what I am here to prevent."

He moved the blade a little, repositioning his grip. The bedside light danced across its engraved surface, mesmerising the baby. He was happy to entertain her with the pretty lights for a few moments. Better she remain distracted. Once the babies realized why he was here...

There was a drawn-out silence, as he played the light across the blade. Behind him, Darragh remained motionless. There was no point in him trying to attack. They were two sides of the same coin. Neither man could so much as form the intent to attack without the other knowing about it.

The girls would be dead before anybody could reach the cradle to stop him.

"There must be another way." There was note of defeat in the statement, a glimmer of acceptance.

"I wouldn't be here if there was," Ren replied, still staring down at the baby he was destined to kill. "You know that," he added, glancing over his shoulder. "You're just not willing to accept the truth of it yet."

Darragh held out his hand, as if he expected the blade to be handed over; and for this night to be forgotten, somehow. Put behind them like a foolish disagreement they'd been wise enough to settle like men. "They're just babies."

"They are Partition and all the destruction that goes with it."

"But they're innocents... Dammit... they're your own flesh and blood!"

"Tell that to Brydie. And all the others."

Darragh had no answer for that. Perhaps he realized now, why the walls were glistening. Ren gripped the blade tighter and turned back to the cradle, steeling his resolve with a conscious act of will. It didn't matter who they were. It's what they were. That was the important thing.

It was the reason they had to die.

"They are abominations, bred to cause chaos and strife."

"Maybe we can save them."

"I see the future, Darragh. So do you. And I dare you to deny the future you see isn't just as filled with chaos and strife because of what these children are, as the future I perceive."

Silence greeted his question, as he knew it would. They had both seen the future, just as the Hag had seen it. They had seen the destruction, the pain, the devastation.

Turning back to the babies, Ren reached into the cradle with his left hand to pull back the blankets covering the children. The twin who was awake grabbed his finger. Her frightening blue eyes smiling up at him, she squeezed it gently. Behind him, his brother watched, too appalled to allow this, too afraid to stop it.

"Help me or leave," Ren said, feeling Darragh's accusing eyes boring into his back. "Just don't stand there feigning disgust, as if you had no part in bringing us to this pass."

"Perhaps the future we see isn't ours."

"Are you kidding me? Look around you, Darragh. These walls are dripping with blood." Ren was a little amazed that he felt so calm. It was as if all the anguish, all the guilt, all the fear and remorse, all the normal human emotions a man

should be battling at a time like this were a burden being carried by someone else, leaving him free to act, unhindered by doubt.

If that wasn't a sign of the rightness of this deed, he couldn't think of anything else that might be.

He extracted his finger from the soft, determined grip of the baby girl, her skin so soft and warm, her gaze so trusting and serene, it was heartbreaking.

But not heartbreaking enough to stay his hand. He raised the blade, transfixed by the dangerous blue on blue eyes staring up at him. And then he brought it down sharply, slicing through the swaddling and her fragile ribs into her tiny heart without remorse or regret...

He was quick and, he hoped, merciful, but the link between the sisters was quicker.

Before he could extract the blade from one tiny heart and plunge it into another, her twin sister jerked with pain and she began to scream...

Ren jerked awake to find the Hag kneeling over him. He was sweating and shaking. The Dream was back with a vengeance - more real than it had ever been before.

She was in the guise of the crone again. Ren sat up and looked around. He was still in the stone circle, surrounded by the impenetrable mist.

"It came again, yes?"

"What?" He was still shaken to the core by how real the nightmare had been. More real than this strange place with its odd mist and old woman who could change into a beautiful young woman at will.

"The vision. You Saw the future."

Ren shook his head. He wasn't sure if he was denying the dream or the truth of it.

"It was different this time."

"The nearer to the event, the more it will resolve."

"It used to happen in this realm, all caves and candles and firepits. The dream I just had... there were electric lights and central heating. I think it was in my old realm."

"Situations can alter," the Hag said, helping him to his feet. "Your destiny does not."

Ren shook his head again. "You don't understand... it's not possible anything like that could happen there." He shook off her help and put his head between his hands, as if he could drive out the lingering memory by applying enough pressure to his skull. "Jesus, why am I even having that frigging dream?" He turned on her, then, eyeing her with deep suspicion. "Did you do something to me? Something to Darragh? I haven't had that nightmare in years."

"Something has changed. As I warned you it would. You cannot stop this."

"It was so frigging real..."

"The closer your destiny gets, the sharper the vision, the more accurate the dream."

"I'm not your puppet," he said, still shaking his head to deny her and dislodge the memory of his nightmare. "You can't make me kill those kids."

"I won't have to," she assured him. "And that's what really frightens you, Rónán of the Undivided. That you are not being forced to do anything. Even in your vision, you are doing what is right of your own free will."

She was terrifyingly close to the truth, Ren realized. It appalled him that he could contemplate murdering his brother's children, but it horrified him even more that - in his dream, at least - he seemed so convinced it had to be done.

Maybe I go mad. Maybe that's why the Hag is here. To drive me mad.

"It's not free will if it's destiny," Ren pointed out.

"And if it's destiny and you have no choice in the matter, then you have no need to feel guilty about it either," she replied, with infuriating calm. "I have a gift for you."

"What?"

"A gift. You need the power to wane in a magic-less world to free your brother. My Sight tells me you must do this thing to fulfill your destiny, so I prevailed upon the Brethren to help."

"Help how?" He didn't like the sound of that. He knew what the Brethren wanted which made anything they did to help suspect. She untied a small leather pouch from her belt and handed it to him. With some trepidation, Ren opened it and tipped the contents into his palm. The rubies once set into Kiva's necklace tumbled out, infused with so much magic they were glowing.

"They will start to lose their magic the moment you step through the rift," the Hag told him, "but as you intended to swallow them, your body should protect them for a time and slow the loss. However long it takes the jewels to pass through your physical body, we estimate you only have about three hours to find your brother and get him out before the magic is no longer concentrated enough to enable waning. If you intend to wane yourself from one place to another, you will be able to do it a few times, but if you take another person with you it will drain their power completely, so you can only do that once and you must be very certain of the place you are waning to. Transporting another person is dangerous enough in a realm filled with magic. It is a risk beyond reckoning in a realm as depleted as the one you intend to try it in. After that the rubies will be depleted. You will have to find a stone circle and open a rift the usual way if you wish to return to this realm or any other."

"We don't have Marcroy's jewel any longer."

"You won't need it," the Hag said. "My Sight tells me you will find another way out of that realm."

She waved her arm and the mist began to clear, revealing the stone circle and a surprisingly bright day. Ren didn't know how long he'd been trapped in the Hag's mist, but the sun had risen and he was hungry. Thirsty, too, and as he looked down at the glowing jewels in his palm, he realized he was going to have to find something to drink in order to swallow rubies.

The Hag seemed to have thought of that. As the mist cleared, he noticed a basket on the ground beside her, filled with cheese, cold meats and a skin of wine.

Ren began to wonder if he should refuse to rescue Darragh at all; the Hag - and presumably the Brethren - seemed far too encouraging for it to end well. As if she knew what he was thinking, she smiled and morphed back into the hauntingly familiar young woman she had been last night. "You still do not understand, do you?"

"I don't understand why you're helping me."

"I am helping you, because I have seen that I must. I have role to play in this. And some responsibility, too, perhaps. Either way, I can no more deny my destiny than you can yours."

"That's okay for you, lady. Your destiny apparently involves delivering a picnic basket."

"You will see what you need to know before the time comes, Rónán," she promised with a smile. "You only fear it now because you do not know the truth."

"So why don't you tell me the truth and save us both some grief?" The Hag shook her head. "Even if I told you, Rónán, you would not believe me. You must learn some things for yourself for the lesson to have any value."

She leaned forward then, and kissed him on the cheek. "I am glad to have met you, Rónán of the Undivided. I will cherish the memory of you."

"Have you Seen that, too?" he asked, more than a little annoyed with her vague answers. "Are you so sure we'll never meet again?" She nodded. "By the time you have fulfilled your destiny, only one of us will be alive."

"Which one of us is going to die?" Ren asked. But the Hag vanished, leaving him alone in the stone circle with his handful of enchanted rubies and without giving him so much as a hint of the answer.

CHAPTER 38

All the time she'd been blind, Hayley wanted nothing more than to see her family again. Now that she could, she found it almost unbearable. Every time she looked at her father's grey hair, or the crow's feet that creased the corners of her stepmother's eyes, it drove home the tragedy of her return.

As for her little brother... Neil didn't bear thinking about. It seemed like only a few weeks ago that she and Ren had taken him shopping for new shoes at the mall with instructions not to buy him anything with Hobbits on them. Now he was an adult. Studying physics of all things.

He was, effectively, older than she was.

Hayley was relieved when he apologetically left for Geneva. She didn't know what to say to Neil. Or how to look at him without wanting to burst into to tears. She had a suspicion he felt the same.

For several days after Kiva's visit, Hayley kept the business card the actress had given her in her pocket. She would touch it whenever things started to pile up on her; imagine herself calling the number and explaining to the mysterious Mother who she was and what had happened to her. The agency would send someone, she fantasised, and they would make the world right again somehow...

But she never actually called them. She watched her stepmother Kerry with new eyes, however.

Never had Hayley thought to question Kerry on her family history. Perhaps she'd almost reached an age when she might have grown curious about it, but fate intervened and left her blinded and then sent her to another reality so she'd never had the chance, or even the urge, to question anything about her stepmother's life before she married Hayley's father. Hayley had always been told that Kiva and Kerry were cousins. Kerry worked for Kiva because when you're a celebrity, family are often the only people you can trust. Her stepmother had met Hayley's father on set when she was working for Kiva, just after Hayley's mother, Charlotte, died and just before Patrick found Ren in the loch. Hayley had heard the story so many times as a child, it simply had to be real.

Now she knew the truth - assuming Kiva was telling the truth - she looked at her stepmother with a far more critical eye and began to see things she'd never noticed in the past.

There really was no familial resemblance between Kerry and Kiva. And their relationship was far more one of equals than employer and employee, even taking family ties into consideration. Now she thought of it, Hayley could recall any number of times Kiva allowed herself to be overruled by Kerry. Hayley assumed it was just Kiva not wanting to be bothered with details, preferring to defer to her older cousin's wisdom. It made more sense really, to know that in the strange organizastion to which they both belonged, Kerry had seniority and Kiva deferred to her out of respect, rather than laziness.

Hayley had taken to walking a lot since her return. Sometimes it was just around the block, other times she walked for miles, not really caring where she ended up. A couple of nights after Kiva's visit, she had to call her father to come get her - she had her very own iPhone now - because she was utterly lost. There were maps on the phone they told her, but she hadn't figured out how to use half the apps Neil had loaded for her before he left. But walking got her out of the house and gave her a chance to think. Not that her thoughts were very pleasant companions. They were full of dark fantasies about how she would get even with Ren for ruining her life. How she would call the number on the card Kiva gave her and join the *Matrarchaí*, travelling through realities and taking her vengeance on every version of Ren Kavanaugh she get her hands on.

And sometimes she just wanted to go back to *Tír Na nÓg* and listen to the beautiful music, be one of the beautiful people, have no cares in the world and pretend this reality didn't even exist.

It was this impulse that drove her back to the Castle Golf Club and the stone circle where she'd emerged from the other reality. She'd been back a few times now, taking a cab to the course and climbing over the brick fence on Woodside Drive when there were no cars going by. She would cross the course on foot, hiding in the rough if any golfers happened by, until she reached the stone circle and then she would wait...

Hayley wasn't sure what she was waiting for.

The chances were good nobody would ever come through the rift again. But Hayley couldn't stay away, just in case. Ren was back in this reality and probably looking for Darragh. *Will he come through here or are there other stone circles he could use, scattered over the world?* She supposed there were. Ireland and England were dotted with them, and there were thousands of circles in Europe.

Why would he come through this one?

Hayley shivered, and not just because of the bitter wind. It was dark already, even though it was still only early evening. She'd left a note for Kerry and her father, saying she was catching up with friends. They'd be pleased. That was what a normal girl would do. That showed she wanted to get on with her life.

Hayley figured that "I'm meeting with old friends' would prove to Kerry that she knew nothing about alternate realities or the *Matrarchaí*, suspected nothing about them and believed the story that she was suffering from amnesia, which was why she couldn't remember a single damn moment of the past ten years.

Nobody seemed to want to address the fact that she hadn't aged a day. That was just good genes, she'd heard somebody remark at the Gardaí station.

Lucky me.

Hayley zipped her jacket up to the top. It was new. It still smelt like the store. All her clothes were new. Everything she'd owned before she stepped through the rift was gone. Given away to charity, they told her. Her dad had kept a few keepsakes. There were photos of her scattered about the house, and some of the trophies she'd won playing soccer and basketball. There were a few books she'd owned. A certificate she'd been awarded at school for being a good citizen. And the medal made of cardboard colored with a yellow crayon that she'd won in a spelling competition when she was in the first grade.

It was quite terrifying, really, to see how little of her was left. Another few years and she would have been completely forgotten.

Another gust of chilly wind rustled the trees surrounding the old stone circle, There was no point hanging about here. She knew that. It just made her feel worse. Just intensified her anger.

What had that Gardaí doctor said to her? *You'll do better if you can confront what's happened to you and deal with it.*

"I'd love to confront it," she said aloud to the darkness. "Where are you, Ren?"

In response to her challenge the stone circle began to crackle with lightning. Hayley looked about her in a panic and then dived into the bushes outside the circle to save herself from being fried by the lightning. Her pulse racing, she crouched down behind the tallest of the stones, which was barely large enough to offer concealment, and waited for the rift to resolve into an opening between worlds, before she peeked over the top to see who was coming through the rift.

She expected Ren. Her heart was galloping at the thought of seeing him again; at the thought of a chance to even the score. Here was her chance make him take back what he'd done or take her back so she wouldn't be left with this awkward half-life she seemed to have in this reality, where nobody knew what to do with her, and the only person who understood what she'd been through was a ditzy, self-obsessed actress whose word was doubtful at the best of times.

It was dark inside the rift and the angle she was watching from at the side of the circle didn't enable her to see through to the other side. For a fleeting moment, Hayley contemplated jumping up and taking a running dive through the rift, letting fate take her where it would.

She never got the chance.

Almost as soon as the rift stabilized, a woman came through, followed by a screeching owl who dropped like a stone as soon as it appeared. The bird landed heavily on the stones and was replaced almost instantly by another woman, naked and shivering, who immediately began to vomit violently. On their heels was a creature who seemed to be a very short fat ninja and following him came an insect-like creature that flitted about almost too quickly to see, which Hayley thought must be a pixie. She'd seen a few of them in *Tír Na nÓg*. She never expected to see one in this realm.

As soon as they were through, the woman wearing the long cloak clutched at something tied around the neck of the naked woman who had so recently been a bird. Ignoring the vomiting, she turned and closed the rift with a wave of her other hand, while muttering something under her breath that Hayley couldn't make out.

The little pixie seemed distraught. She couldn't ignore the vomiting woman, even if the human woman could. "Is she dying? Is she dying? Is she dying?" she kept asking, flapping about in a panic.

"Echo! Stop that!" the woman in the cloak ordered. "She'll be fine. Go find Pete!"

"Go find Pete! Go find Pete! Go find Pete!" the little pixie chanted and then winked out of existence.

With the pixie taken care of, the woman turned and seemed to notice the little ninja for the first time. "What are you messing about with there?"

"Nothing!" he said, hiding his hand behind his back.

It's a *Leipreachán*, Hayley realized, but she wasn't sure if the women, the pixie and the *Leipreachán* were from the reality she'd come back from. There were plenty of pixies, but no ninja-*Leipreachán* there that she had seen.

"Then come here," the woman ordered impatiently. "We need your help."

"What do ye be expecting me to do?"

"We need money," the naked vomiting girl gasped. "I need clothes. Go steal us some cash."

"As ye wish," the *Leipreachán* said, turning away. He stared down at something in his hand, clearly not wanting to risk his treasure in this unknown realm. He looked about for a moment and then stashed whatever it was at the base of one of the worn-down standing stones not far from where Hayley was hiding. After kicking some dirt and leaves over his hidden treasure he vanished right before Hayley's eyes. The woman wearing clothes didn't seem the least bit surprised. She removed her cloak and wrapped it around the trembling shoulders of the other woman.

"How are you feeling?"

"Like death. Gods... what did you give me, Nika?"

"It doesn't matter. You survived and we are out of our enemy's reach. Echo will find Pete. We'll be safe soon."

The younger woman nodded and looked about, as if seeing the world for the first time. Hayley ducked down behind the stone.

"We're at the golf club, aren't we?" she heard the woman with the long blonde hair who'd been vomiting say.

"I don't know. What is a golf club?"

"I'll explain later." The young woman sounded recovered somewhat and had obviously been here before if she knew where she was. Hayley desperately wanted to look up and see if she recognized anybody, but she was too afraid of being caught. The time for stepping forward was as they arrived. She would just appear to be spying on them, if she revealed herself now.

"We should head for the clubhouse. I'm pretty sure we can find somewhere to hunker down until we locate the others."

"But you have no clothes on," the older one said.

There was a smile in the younger woman's voice as she replied, "Worked the last time I was here, Nika."

Hayley stayed hidden as they moved away, pushing through the undergrowth toward the clubhouse and civilization. Still no wiser about the identity of the women, she waited until she could no longer hear them and then scrambled over to the stone where the *Leipreachán* had stashed whatever it was he was hiding.

If these women didn't know Ren, they at least knew how to come and go through this realm as they pleased. Whatever the *Leipreachán* had stashed behind the stones, he would want to come back for it. There was a good chance, she'd be able to barter for its return, either for information or, if it came to it, passage through the rift to another realm.

It wasn't hard to find. The *Leipreachán* hadn't hidden it very well at all, perhaps relying on the remoteness of this place to keep it safe. When she unearthed the treasure, she gasped. It proved to be a beautiful, polished amethyst the size of a pigeon egg. She dusted off the leaves and rubbed the dirt from its surface on the leg of her jeans. As she did, it seemed the color drained from the jewel.

And then she looked up to discover a very startled young woman in a long linen gown staring at her with a look of utter astonishment on her face.

"*Danú!*" the young woman breathed, looking about in wonder. "*Tá mé saor!*"

I am *free*, Hayley automatically translated. Hayley didn't know what to say. She stared down at the jewel and then at the girl who had just appeared in front of her and realized what had happened. "Oh my God, you were *trapped* in this thing?"

The girl stared at her, not understanding English. Hayley repeated the question in the Gaelish dialect she'd picked up in the other realm, thanks to the magical intervention of a druid.

The woman in the linen nightgown nodded and replied in the same language. "You have rescued me. I am Brydie Ni'Seanan and I owe you my life."

"Anytime," Hayley said, more than a little bemused. "I'm Hayley. How did you -"

Her question was cut off by Brydie's scream. She doubled over, clutching her belly. Then the girl dropped to her knees, crying out in agony.

"What's wrong?"

"The... the... pain..." Brydie cried, falling onto her side. She had pulled her knees up and crossed her arms over her abdomen, but it didn't seem to be doing a thing to help. She screamed even louder, the sound echoing across the golf course. It was then that Hayley noticed her belly seemed to be growing of its own accord at a speed that defied logic.

And it was tearing her insides apart. This was magic, Hayley knew... or the result of it. This girl had come through a rift from another reality trapped in a jewel.

She needed help, but not the sort of help this world offered.

It took Hayley a split second to make her choice. Calling an ambulance would mean involving the Gardaí and a lot of questions she'd been very careful not to answer. Calling Kerry meant admitting she'd been back here, looking for a way out.

Calling Kiva... well, Kiva was pretty useless in day-to-day life. She'd be no help at all in a crisis. Even she would be the first to admit that.

"Hang on," Hayley said, fishing her phone and the rather battered business card Kiva had given her out of her pocket. Brydie needed someone who knew what was going on. The young woman was sobbing with the pain and a dark red stain had appeared on the linen nightgown from between her legs.

Hayley dialed the number on the card and was relieved when it was picked up on the second ring. "Hello?"

"You don't know me. My name is Hayley Boyle. Kiva Kavanaugh gave me this number. I'm at the Castle Golf Club. I'm with a girl called Brydie who just came through a rift from another reality and she's in trouble. Serious trouble."

"What kind of trouble?" the woman on the other end of the line asked after a long silence. She sounded foreign. French, perhaps. Maybe Belgian.

"I don't know for certain," Hayley said, "but it looks like she's having a baby."

This time there was no hesitation. "You did right to call me, Hayley. Wait there. I will have help to you in a matter of minutes."

The line went dead. Hayley pocketed her phone and knelt down beside Brydie. When she'd emerged from the jewel, Hayley could have sworn Brydie's belly was flat. Now it was swollen and distended as if she was nine-months pregnant.

Brydie was crying with the pain.

"Hang in there, Brydie," she said in Gaelish, unzipping her jacket and slipping it off to cover the distressed young woman and keep her warm. "I called someone. Help is on the way."

"Who... did you... call?"

"The *Matrarchaí*." Brydie shook her head. "No... you shouldn't have."

Before Hayley could defend her decision, she heard the distinctive *whumpa-whumpa-whumpa* of a helicopter approaching.

Wow, that was fast.

She supposed that for an organizastion which could manufacture lives and histories for people like Kerry and Kiva, a medivac helicopter on standby was probably hardly any effort at all.

A few moments later the clearing was lit by a bright light from overhead, and then it moved off them and onto the fairway as the helo landed gently in the open space beyond the rough. It was only a minute or two later before paramedics were swarming around Brydie, lifting her - still screaming - onto a stretcher and rushing her out of the stone circle to the waiting helicopter.

Hayley stood back, feeling quite useless. As they hurried away, an elegantly-dressed woman with dark hair approached her. She wore a grey business suit and had the sleek, confident air of the sort of woman who could produce a helicopter and a team of paramedics in a matter of minutes. She reminded Hayley of Eunice Ravenel, Kiva's lawyer, who was always bailing Ren out of trouble.

"You are Hayley Boyle?" she asked, in that slightly foreign accent.

She nodded. "You may call me Mother," the woman said with a friendly smile, offering Hayley her hand. "You are Kerry's stepdaughter, yes? The one who has been missing all these years?"

Hayley nodded again. This woman seemed to know it all.

Mother seemed very pleased. "Have you ever ridden in a helicopter, Hayley?"

"Once. With Kiva."

"Then let us make it twice," she said, holding out her arm. "We have much to discuss, you and I, young Hayley Boyle. And there are some young friends of mine I think you're very much going to enjoy meeting."

PART FOUR

CHAPTER 39

Teagan was woken by the sound of a helicopter landing on the lawn.

She climbed out of bed and walked to the window, looking down over the vast grounds of the Cambria Castle estate, wondering who was arriving at this hour. Mysterious late-night comings and goings were not uncommon here and they rarely affected her, but Teagan was curious nonetheless.

This arrival seemed to be some sort of medical emergency. Someone on a stretcher was hurried from the helo as the blades slowed to a stop and the floodlights that lit the helo pad shut off. In the last glimmer of their light before they faded completely, she spied Mother emerging from the helo with a girl dressed in jeans and one of those warm, puffy jackets they made in this realm that seemed too light to offer any real warmth and yet were as toasty as a big heavy fur. Teagan had a similar jacket hanging in her closet.

I wonder if this new girl is like me? Wide-eyed, innocent... and gullible.

The promise of Teagan's first meeting with Mother had never really been fulfilled. She had promised to unlock Lady Delphine's memories in her mind.

"All in good time, cherie," she'd said. "First, you have to do something for me."

"What do you want?" Teagan had asked.

"Everything you know about the man who killed my sister," Mother said in a quiet voice that even now, when she thought of it, chilled Teagan to her core. "When I come back you can tell me what you know, and if you're a really good girl I might even let you help me avenge her."

Teagan told them everything she knew and had been waiting for the opportunity, for seven years now, to help Mother avenge her sister and it still hadn't happened.

Mother might want vengeance, but it seemed she was more interested in politics.

The *Matrarchaí*, which had once seemed so mysterious and exciting to Teagan, proved to be somewhat less romantic in practice. They had a mission - *dear gods, she was so sick of hearing about the mission* - and everyone had a part to play.

Teagan had come here believing she was an integral part of that mission. Her reality had been chosen by the *Matrarchaí*, after all. She had been chosen by the *Matrarchaí*. Her father came from a bloodline of Undivided that the *Matrarchaí* had carefully nurtured over centuries. Teagan and Isleen were seven years old when they stood by Delphine's side as she and the *Konketsu* drove the last of the *Tuatha Dé Danann* and the greater *Youkai* from their realm, leaving only the hidden lesser *Youkai* to mop up as they found them. Delphine had rewarded her and her sister with the *Comhroinn*, but fearing they were too young to deal with the information she had shared, she'd blocked it with a promise to return when they were older and remove the barriers.

That never happened, of course. Renkavana arrived with Trása and messed everything up.

Her first few months in this realm had been exciting beyond words. This reality without magic had so many interesting things, such intriguing ways of doing things, that for a long while she didn't miss the magic at all. It was all well and good to be able to light a lamp with a thought or toss an underling across the room with a wave of your arm if they displeased you, but here they could record music and play it back over and over so the beauty of it was never lost. They had television and movie theatres that showed fabulous stories in 3D. They could fly thousands of people from one end of the planet to the other. They had visited the moon.

All this had come at the cost of the magic, of course. Technology and magic could not coexist; or so Teagan had believed before she came here and she'd clung to that belief for a long time after she arrived.

Until she learned of "the mission'.

Until she began to fully appreciate what the mission was planning to achieve.

Her role, she learned from Mother, was to ensure that her reality, along with as many other realities as possible touching this one, was filled with magic not hampered by Faerie who might object - or worse, have the power to stop - the *Matrarchaí* achieving Partition. To a large extent, Delphine achieved that aim in Teagan's realm before she had been killed and Teagan and Isleen had been expected to carry on her work by eradicating the lesser *Youkai*. When the time came, the magic from their world, and the thousands of others like it, would spill into this world and replenish its magic before it was severed from the others, leaving this reality with the best of both worlds - fabulous technology, and magic to boot.

There was a catch, Teagan soon learned, which made the *Matrarchaí*'s mission more urgent, and perhaps explained why Mother was prepared to put aside her dreams of vengeance for the furtherance of the mission. The technology that made this world so special was eating it alive: the climate was warming at an alarming rate as a direct result of the development of all this fabulous gadgetry, and along with the ability to make beautiful music over and over, they'd developed weapons so powerful they could make this planet uninhabitable.

The *Matrarchaí*, who'd been content to let this world muddle along as it would until recently, were starting to worry that if they didn't force Partition soon it would be beyond redemption. The politics here, where they had chosen to make their headquarters, were becoming so volatile they feared the end was just around the corner. Thousands upon thousands of years ago when the *Tuatha Dé Danann* occupied Europe, the *Youkai* were spread out across what was now called Japan, the Dreamtime ruled Gondwanaland, the Pristine Ones watched over China, and the hero twins, Hunahpú and Xbalanqué - the first Undivided of this realm - ruled the Americas in remarkable harmony with Chaac, Kukulkan, and K'iche'... the Mayan god responsible for liaison between the magical realm and the mundane one.

They were gone now, victims of the march of progress in this realm. But the *Matrarchaí* had not forgotten any of them and they had grand plans for this world's redemption, too. There was a void left by the gods. It was partly filled by this world's countless religions where they worshipped imaginary gods, who could never answer their prayers. In a post-Partition reality, the *Matrarchaí* would be the only ones capable of wielding the magic that would flood into this realm.

They would be the gods again.

They would bring peace.

They would bring harmony.

They would end the threat of starvation, poverty... even global warming. So they claimed.

It was only recently that Teagan realized that the process of Partition would devastate this world. Peace, harmony and an end to poverty and starvation would be in no small way achieved by the fact that several billion people would die as it happened.

This realm was rich in resources, she had heard Mother explaining to one of her minions. The problem was with the number of people trying to share them.

That wouldn't be a problem after Partition. There would be many less people and the *Matrarchaí* - every one of them able to use the replenished magic now filling the world - planned to bring order out of the chaos.

The scope of the *Matrarchaí*'s mission was daunting. In addition to their plans to breed a set of twins "special" enough to force Partition, they were cultivating as many *kozo* and washi trees as they could cram into their hydroponics labs. When the realm was filled with magic again, they could sustain it with the magical trees brought here from Teagan's realm - the only reality with the special trees where they had successfully eradicated most of the *Youkai* and could harvest the necessary seeds.

The excitement down on the lawn seemed to be over. The pilot had secured the helo, the patient disappeared into the small but astonishingly well-equipped medical ward on the other side of the building, and Mother disappeared from view with the girl in the jacket.

They might tell Teagan what was going on tomorrow. More than likely they wouldn't. Teagan didn't get told much at all, really.

She wandered back to bed and climbed under the blankets, wondering if it would take her long to fall back to sleep. She'd been having trouble sleeping lately, and when she did fall asleep she dreamed of her twin sister, Isleen.

Where are you, Issy? Teagan wondered, wishing she was allowed into the Enchanted Sphere with

Mother on one of her trips. Perhaps then she could scry her sister out and learn what was happening. *Are you well? Have you met a boy you like better than yourself?*

Like herself, Isleen would be nearly twenty now. Perhaps she was no longer a virgin. Teagan was still a virgin. Mother had yet to approve a match for her and her blood was too precious, so she'd been told, to allow her to waste her eggs on foolish liaisons that might damage her ability to carry the children the *Matrarchaí* needed for their breeding program.

Perhaps Isleen had a baby by now.

Teagan remembered thinking how nice it was to not have a twin around to share her glory when she first came to this realm. Lately she'd been missing her sister more than she thought possible.

When she'd heard of the *Matrarchaí's* mission, she'd thought she was one of the special twins. Mother let her believe it for a time, too, until it became clear she wasn't so special. She was an Empress twin, but there were Empress twins aplenty across all the realms the *Matrarchaí* dabbled in.

The twins Mother wanted, were something more again.

Teagan found herself just another cog in a very large machine and it made her angry.

She liked feeling special.

Back in her home realm, even after Renkavana and Trása arrived, she *had* been special.

I am Undivided. I am an Empress.

Here she was little more than a pampered breeding cow, waiting for the farmer to find the right bull to stand at stud.

Teagan pulled the covers up and turned on her side. That's all I am to the *Matrarchaí*, she thought, tears welling in her eyes. A breeding cow.

It was then that Teagan realized something else.

She didn't want to help the *Matrarchaí* achieve Partition. Mother and her vengeance could rot.

I want to go home.

It was a startling revelation and, for the first time since she was a small child, Teagan cried herself to sleep.

CHAPTER 40

"You'll forgive me for asking the obvious question," Annad said, as he poured a drink for everyone in the living room of his tidy suburban home. The house was not especially grand, but you could tell by the quality of the furniture and the eighteen-year-old whiskey they were served, that Annad and his wife were comfortably well-off. "Where the hell have you been?"

"Off with the Faeries," Logan said with a grin, accepting the glass Annad offered him.

"That's helpful," Annad said, after handing Pete his drink and taking a seat in the armchair by the fireplace.

"Helpful or not, it's true," Pete said, imagining how insane they must sound to a man who made his living diagnosing insanity. He took a sip of the whiskey and closed his eyes, savouring the taste.

There had to be a way they could sneak a couple of bottles of decent whiskey back with them when they left this reality.

"Would you care to elaborate?" Annad was a clever psychologist. And far too experienced to appear judgmental.

"Do you remember Darragh? The kid who turned out to be Ren Kavanaugh's twin? Ren was the actress's kid."

Annad nodded. "I not only remember him, I spoke to him the other day."

"Is he still claiming he comes from another reality?"

"I think Darragh has learned the foolishness of stating his belief out loud," Annad said. "I am not convinced he still doesn't believe it's true."

"He believes it's true, because it is true," Logan said, leaning forward with his empty glass. "Any chance of a refill?"

Annad pointed to the bottle on the sideboard. "Be my guest."

"We must sound completely mad," Pete said, resisting the temptation to gulp his drink down like Logan had.

"No," Annad said, "you *sound* quite sane. What you're saying sounds mad, though."

"How can we prove it to you?" Logan asked. He'd poured himself nearly half a glass of Annad's very expensive Kilbeggan single malt.

"Short of taking me to another reality with you and showing it to me in person, I'm not sure you can."

"Ah, that's going to be a problem," Pete admitted. "You see, we're kind of stuck here at the moment."

Annad smiled. "Really? How convenient."

"I know what it sounds like -" Pete began.

"Given your own qualifications, Pete, I'm quite sure you do. I'm interested that you both appear to believe this remarkable tale, which makes me wonder: are you sharing this delusion or playing a prank on me?"

"Annad, do you really think the first thing I would do on reappearing after being missing for a decade is come around here to play a practical joke on you?" He swallowed the last of his whiskey and stood up. Best to get another before Annad decided to call the Gardaí, throw them out or Logan drank it all. "Now that *would* be insane."

"No crazier than what you're expecting me to believe," the psychologist replied, watching them both closely.

"Why were you visiting Darragh?" Logan asked, as he filled Pete's glass with an equally generous dose of Annad's whiskey. "Are you treating him for something?"

"I'm not at liberty to say."

"Unless you're working for the prison service now, he's not your patient," Logan said. "They have plenty of their own psychologists on staff."

"Is it because Hayley came back?" Pete asked. He suspected the only way they were going to secure Annad's assistance was by proving they knew things they could not have knowledge of by normal means. Perhaps then, even if they couldn't convince him of the truth of their tale about alternate realities, they could at least convince him there was more than meets the eye to it.

Annad paused for a moment, and then nodded. "It's been in the papers so it won't hurt to discuss that, but yes, that's one of the reasons. Hayley's family were about to have her declared dead when she miraculously reappeared claiming to have been gone only a week."

"You've spoken to her?" Pete asked.

Annad nodded. "I spoke to her the day she turned up out of the blue, right at the same place where she was last seen."

Pete and Logan shared a knowing look before Pete turned to Annad. "And she thinks she's only been missing a week? What does she look like?"

"What do you mean?"

"I mean she's been gone ten years. Does Hayley Boyle look seventeen or twenty-seven?"

Annad swirled the whiskey around in his glass before he answered. "In truth? I'd have to say she still looks and acts seventeen."

"There," Logan said, "you have your proof!"

"What I have is a young woman who has aged remarkably well, with amnesia, probably brought on by PTSD."

Logan grinned at the psychologist. "I like our explanation better."

"I'm sure you do."

"How's Darragh doing?"

"He has his ups and downs."

Annad was hedging, which meant even if he wasn't treating Darragh directly, he still considered him enough of a patient that he wasn't about to discuss him. Perhaps, if the psychologist could be persuaded they knew things they couldn't possibly otherwise know, he might be a little more forthcoming.

It was urgent they find a way to secure his aid. The only way they were going to find Ren and get out of this reality was to be there when he turned up looking for his brother.

"Has he been self-harming again?" Pete asked, playing a hunch. He remembered Ren telling him about the reaction to injuries he'd received as a child. He guessed the reaction to Darragh and Ren's most recent communication would have attracted much the same unwanted attention.

"Why do you ask?"

"Is that why you're seeing him?" Logan asked, jumping to the same conclusion as Pete. "Because he carved 'get me out' across his belly?"

Pete saw the surprise flicker across Annad's normally serene face before he could hide it and knew he was on the right track.

"Do you know why he did it?" Pete asked, not taking his eyes of Annad.

"I have a feeling you're going to tell me," he replied, still refusing to confirm or deny anything.

"Darragh was sending his brother Ren a message. He's had enough, and he wants out."

"Hardly a brilliant or insightful diagnosis," Annad said, "given the words *get me out* featured heavily in his handiwork."

"Aha!" Logan exclaimed. "You have seen the message."

Annad refused to comment on that.

Pete smiled. He could pretend to know nothing, but it was obvious he knew plenty, a bonus really, because Pete had been hoping merely that Annad might be able to get them in to see Darragh, not that he might already have unrestricted access to him. "Aren't you going to ask how we know what he did?"

"I'm almost afraid to."

Logan spoke up before Pete had a chance. "Ren and Darragh can make injuries appear on each other using *airgead sídhe*."

That made Annad smile faintly. "Faerie silver. Really?"

"Its equivalent in this reality is titanium," Pete told him, not smiling at all.

Annad's amusement faded. "Titanium?"

"Don't know why," Pete said with a shrug, "but it seems to have similar properties."

Annad paused, took a deep breath and then swallowed the remainder of his whiskey in a gulp. "A few days ago," he said, "Darragh prevailed upon me to send him a Remington Titanium 700 electric razor."

"And the next thing you know he's carving messages into his belly."

Annad nodded. "It makes sense, now. If Darragh believes the only way to contact his twin is with titanium... I mean, he could have carved the same message into his skin with any number of sharp implements before now if it was merely the injury he thought initiated the contact."

"It's not just that he believes titanium will connect him with his brother, Annad," Pete tried to explain. "It's true. We saw the message written on Ren."

Annad was suddenly very still. "You've seen Ren Kavanaugh recently?"

"We've both seen 'get me out' carved backward across his belly," Logan told him.

"How long has he been in contact with his brother?"

"He hasn't. We weren't here, Annad. We were in a pub in a town that doesn't even exist in this reality."

"This reality?" Annad asked, his composure rattled for the first time since Pete had known him. "You too, Pete? Christ, is this alternate reality delusion contagious?"

"It's not a delusion."

"Of course not," Annad said, a little impatiently. "There are alternate realities and magic, and Faeries that keep popping in and out of this world, just to frustrate me."

"I wish there was a way to prove what we're telling you is true," Pete said, not unsympathetic to Annad's frustration.

"Show me," Annad said. "Open a door to one of these other realities. Do some real magic. Show me a real Faerie."

Pete opened his mouth to offer an another hollow reassurance which he knew would sound fake, even to him, when out of nowhere, Echo, Trása's annoying pet pixie popped into existence buzzing about in front of his face. She zipped frantically about the room in a panic, screeching, "Trása's in trouble! Trása's in trouble! Trása's in trouble!"

Annad leapt out of his chair. "What the hell?"

Now that's what I call timing, Pete thought as he ducked to avoid Echo smacking into his head.

Logan was on his feet, trying to catch the pixie. He finally caught her in his cupped hands and shushed her gently, while Annad stared at them like they were mad.

Pete smiled. Whatever reason Echo had for being in this realm - and it was likely to be trouble if what she was chanting was even remotely true - she could not have found a better time to appear out of thin air.

Logan, Echo carefully trapped between is palms, walked to over to where Annad was standing, his eyes as wide as saucers. "It's a pixie. Want to say hello?"

"This is some sort of joke..."

"You wanted proof, Annad," Pete said. The look on Annad's face was something to behold. "Show him, Logan."

His brother opened his hands a fraction and peered inside. "Are you going to be good?"

"I'll be good. I'll be good. I'll be good," Echo responded in her tiny, high-pitched voice.

Ever so gently, Logan removed his right hand and opened his fingers to reveal the little pixie standing on his palm. She smiled up at Pete when she saw him and then spied Annad and immediately took off and began buzzing around the room again in a frenzy, squealing, "Humans! Look out! Humans! Look out! Humans! Look out!"

Logan shrugged and looked at Pete apologetically. "I tried." He turned to the pixie. "Echo! Cut it out! Come here and stop that flapping about!"

"Is that really...?" Annad mumbled, as - wide-eyed and bewildered - he watched Logan trying to bring Echo to heel. "It is actually...?" Despite the fact there was a pixie whizzing around his living room, Annad apparently couldn't bring himself to finish the sentence.

Pete nodded. "In the flesh. Annoying little critters they are, as a rule. You don't have any left that are indigenous to this reality."

"Then where did...?" Annad took a deep breath. "It didn't come from here, did it? It came from ... somewhere else."

"Take a deep breath and say the words," Pete suggested. "It gets easier after a while."

Annad shook his head. "I doubt that. What is it... she... doing here?"

"That's a very good question," Logan said, still trying to calm Echo down enough to make sense. She had stopped buzzing around the room and was clinging to the top of the curtain pelmet, glaring at Annad like he was a gargoyle. "I'm sure Echo is going to tell us why she's here. Aren't you, little one? Come on... there's nothing to be afraid of." Logan glanced over his shoulder and smiled at Annad. "They're very friendly, normally."

"Kill the bad human! Kill the bad human! Kill the bad human!"

"Obviously," Annad remarked, still staring at the pixie like he was hallucinating.

"He's not a bad human," Logan coaxed, "He's one of the good ones. Now come down here and talk to me. What's the matter with Trása?"

"Nika killed her! Brought her back. Nika killed her! Brought her back. Nika killed her! Brought her back," Echo chanted from the pelmet, but she seemed to be a tad less frenetic than when she had arrived.

"Is Nika here in this realm?" Pete asked in shock. It wouldn't surprise him to learn Trása had found a way into this reality. She'd spent a lot of time here in the past. But Nika... what the hell was she doing here?

Logan must have read his mind. He looked over his shoulder at Pete, his brow furrowed with concern. "She must have gotten away from Marcroy and come here."

"Nika's here, too."

His brother grinned at the very idea. "Oh, that's going to be fine holiday fun for all."

"What's he talking about?" Annad asked. They were having a conversation he couldn't follow and he was still trying to get his head around the whole idea of pixies. "Who is Nika?"

"The pixie has come here with some friends of ours," Pete explained. He looked up at Echo. "Are they okay?"

"Nika's fine. Nika's fine. Trása's turning inside out. Nika's fine. Nika's fine. Trása's turning inside out. Nika's fine. Nika's fine. Trása's turning inside out."

Pete looked to Logan for a translation but he just shrugged. He had no idea what she was babbling about either.

"We should tell them to come here," Logan suggested.

Pete turned to Annad. "Would that be okay?"

Annad shrugged, shaking his head in complete bafflement. "Why not? Fairies, pixies, strange women... I'm sure Stella will understand."

Stella, Pete realized, must be Annad's wife. He didn't want to think about what they were going to say to her when she got home.

"Echo, I need you to take a message to Trása and Nika," Pete said, stepping between the window and Annad so she couldn't fixate on him quite so obsessively.

"She won't remember a message," Logan warned.

He was right. Pixies had abysmal memories. "Can she carry a note?"

Logan nodded. "A very small one."

"It only needs to be an address and a phone number." He looked back at Annad. "Do you have a pen and a bit of paper I could use?"

"What," Annad said, "no magic?"

"Please."

He pointed to the sideboard where the bottle of whiskey stood. "In the drawer."

Pete hurried across the room and opened the drawer to find a clutter of odds and ends, including a number of pens and the remains of a pack of post-it notes. He scrawled the address of Annad's house on the note, asked him for his phone number and wrote that down, too, then folded the note and handed it to Logan, who seemed to be having some success with handling Echo and her mercurial moods.

Logan held the folded note toward the pixie. "If you take this to Trása, I'll give you a treat."

"Treat? Treat?" Echo asked, suddenly attentive. "What kind of treat? What kind of treat?"

"Take this note to Trása and Nika, first. No treats until I know they've got the note."

Almost before he'd finished speaking, Echo dived toward his hand, snatched the folded post-it note from his outstretched fingers and vanished.

Logan turned to Annad. "Do you have any Christmas decorations left?"

"Why?" Annad asked. "Are we expecting Santa Claus next?"

"Echo likes tinsel. It'll keep her happy when she gets back."

"By all means, we must keep the pixie happy."

"Annad! What's going on?" They turned to find a woman in her early forties standing in the doorway. Her dark hair was pulled back in a ponytail, and she wore a warm, puffy, down jacket over a set of dark blue scrubs. This, Pete guessed, was Stella Semaj.

"Stella!"

"It's almost three in the morning. Don't you have to work tomorrow?"

"Ah..." Annad said, behaving exactly like a man caught doing something he shouldn't have been doing. "This is Pete... and his brother, Logan. They're... they're old friends of mine from university."

"Hello," she said as she eyed them curiously. "Identical twins, aren't you? I don't remember Annad being friends with identical twins."

"That's because he didn't want us meeting you, Stella," Logan said, as smooth as he ever was when dazzling a woman with his charm. "He knew we'd fight you for him."

411

She smiled, not immune to Logan's winning smile, but not falling for it, either. "That's sweet of you, but neither of you look old enough to have been at university with Annad."

"We were freshmen," Pete explained, not realizing until now that their *Tuatha Dé Danann* heritage meant they'd not aged since they'd left this realm. "Was it a boy or a girl?"

"Excuse me?"

"You're an obstetrician, aren't you? Annad said you were called out to an emergency. I was just wondering how it went. Was it a boy or a girl?"

"Girls," Stella said. "Plural. It was twins."

"I didn't know you had any patients with twins due," Annad said, obviously glad for the change of subject that had, for the moment, taken the focus off him.

"Wasn't my patient," Stella said. "Will you boys be leaving soon?" she added, looking pointedly at the clock on the wall.

"Annad kindly offered us a bed for the night," Pete said, before she could ever so politely kick them out. He'd just given Nika this address. They couldn't leave now.

"Well, that was nice of him, wasn't it?" she said, throwing her husband a look that spoke of a brewing "discussion' to come when they didn't have guests. "Then he can make up the kid's bedrooms for you. You know where the sheets are, don't you, dear?"

"We'll be no trouble, Doctor Semaj," Logan promised. "Actually, I'm Doctor Delaney," she said. "I kept my maiden name after we married." She glared at Annad and said, "I think I'm beginning to realize why." With that, Stella turned on her heel and left.

They waited until they heard her footsteps on the stairs and the door closing upstairs before they dared utter another word.

"Sorry if we got you into trouble," Pete said.

Annad shrugged. "She's not really mad. She just doesn't like surprises."

"That could be awkward," Logan said.

"Why?" Pete asked.

"If she doesn't like surprises, what's she going to do when a half-*beansídhe*, a Merlin and a pixie turn up for breakfast?"

CHAPTER 41

Ciarán stood in the center of the exercise yard of Portlaoise Prison, looking up at the windows overlooking the yard, trying to figure which one was the room currently occupied by Darragh. It was raining gently and most of the prisoners were standing in small groups, hunkered down inside their jackets. It was cold, but a chance to be outside, even in this soulless place, was not to be scoffed at because of a bit of water falling out of the sky.

He'd not seen Darragh since the Warden sent for him several days ago, and subsequently ordered him to the prison nurse for a checkup and discovered the words "get me out" scrawled across his belly in bloody, four-inch-tall letters.

Since then, Darragh had been confined to the psych ward for self-harming and Ciarán hadn't been allowed to speak to him.

Ciarán was desperately worried about what they might be doing to him up there. They had doctors who could mess with a man's mind in this realm. They fed you drugs that made a man doubt himself; counseled men into believing their own reality was wrong and the reality the prison authorities preferred was the right one.

Ciarán couldn't protect Darragh in there.

He'd done his best to protect him since coming to this realm, but Ciarán wasn't sure if he'd done all he could. Since he'd decided - as they led him from the courtroom after condemning him to life in prison a decade ago - that rather than return to his own reality, he should stay to protect Darragh, things had not really gone to plan. He remembered optimistically believing Rónán would arrive any day to rescue his brother. It was a given, he'd believed back then. All he had to do was wait for the inevitable return of Darragh's brother, who would use his knowledge of this realm to free Darragh, and they would all go home.

I need his knowledge of this world, Ciarán remembered thinking with a naivety he now considered breathtaking.

What a stupid, optimistic and utterly useless plan that turned out to be, Ciarán thought as he stared up at the razor wire encircling the grey, oppressive walls of Portlaoise.

Rónán and Darragh may be strong enough to survive the transfer, Marcroy had warned him, before sending him to this realm to find Darragh and his brother. *If that happens you must bring them home. Protect them both. As you are sworn to do.*

Marcroy had proved to be right about that - Darragh had survived the transfer - but what good had it done any of them? Rónán had not been seen in a decade. The coward had probably hunkered down somewhere, safe and sound, and left his brother to rot.

And Darragh *was* rotting here, Ciarán feared. They both were. He couldn't shake the guilt he felt at Darragh's most recent confinement in the psych ward, either.

It's my fault he did this.

Ciarán had goaded Darragh the other night, when he learned he had the means to contact his brother. He'd been so anxious to be gone from this place, he'd ignored Darragh's warning about the cost. *"It's liable to have me back in that psych ward I mentioned, if they notice what I'm doing,"* he'd told him, but Ciarán was too excited by the prospect of escaping this place to really pay attention to what he was saying. *"I learned my lesson the last time. I'm not fond of tranquilizers, straightjackets, large doses of antidepressants or padded cells."*

"Then do it," Ciarán had foolishly ordered. He wished he'd understood what he was asking. He realized now what Darragh meant by tranquilizers and padded cells.

Ciarán's culpability over that conversation was eating him up and now they wouldn't let him see Darragh. The Warden had even questioned the advisability of allowing Ciarán and Darragh to share a cell any longer. He was suggesting Ciarán should have known what Darragh was doing and either stopped him or reported him.

Gods alone knew what the Warden would do if he realized Ciarán had suggested it.

Ignoring the gentle rain, Ciarán scanned the windows again, no more enlightened than when he had started this quest to locate Darragh's room. He just felt worse each time, because he blamed himself for him being there.

It is time to accept the truth, Ciarán told himself sternly. Rónán was never coming for them. *If he cared anything for his brother, he'd have been back to this realm a decade ago and brought Darragh home.*

It wasn't going to happen. It seemed Rónán was not made of the same stuff as his twin, despite them being identical.

Ciarán glanced at the gate and noticed Officer Connors was on duty this morning, staying back out of the wet even though he was swaddled in his service-issue raincoat. Maybe it would be better to talk to one of the guards. Some, like Connors, were more gossipy than others. Assuming they knew anything about Darragh, or his treatment, of course. Or how long the doctors were planning to hold him in isolation.

Ciarán turned back to his futile window-guessing quest... Just in time to see Darragh appear in the courtyard not ten feet from where he was standing.

The young man looked around furtively, and Ciarán realized it wasn't Darragh at all. It was – finally - his twin brother, Rónán.

It took a moment or two for the significance of his sudden arrival to sink in. A few of the prisoners had noticed Rónán. One of them was scratching his head, staring at the young man as if he'd just appeared out of thin air - unable to comprehend that that was exactly what had happened - thinking, as Ciarán had at first, that it was Darragh.

After waiting for so long, after counting the days they'd been stuck in this realm, Ciarán had thought he knew exactly how he would respond to Rónán. He was wrong. He was too stunned for a moment to react at all, and then he realized that if Rónán had somehow magically found a way in here, then he probably had a way out.

They needed to get to Darragh.

And they needed to do it before anybody realized what was going on.

Rónán was dressed in jeans and a sports coat, which made him stand out among the raincoated prisoners who'd noticed the new arrival, but couldn't conceive of how this newcomer suddenly appeared in their midst.

As casually as he could manage without breaking into a run and drawing any undue attention to Rónán, Ciarán covered the short distance between them, grabbed Rónán by the arm and turned him around to face him.

"I am Ciarán mac Connacht," he said in a low voice in the language of his own realm, figuring that was the quickest way to establish his credentials with Rónán, a young man he'd only briefly met, years ago, when they first located him and brought him home. Three weeks of weapons training in a hidden *raith* was not likely to be remembered, and Rónán certainly wouldn't be expecting to find anybody else from his realm here in this godforsaken place.

Rónán stared at him for a moment, dealing with his own shock and surprise at finding Ciarán here, but he recovered quickly. "Where is Darragh?"

"The psych ward."

"Can you take me to him?"

"Or die trying," Ciarán promised, looking around. Men were starting to look and point at Rónán. They assumed he was Darragh, naturally enough, but his appearance in street clothes, without warning, in the middle of the exercise yard was unusual enough to raise comment. "We need to get out of here. Some of these men saw you wane in. The only thing keeping them quiet is that they don't believe what they just saw."

"You believe it."

"Not entirely," Ciaran admitted. "Come with me."

Rónán followed him to the gate that led back into the building. As they approached, it occurred to Ciarán that there were a lot of locked doors between here and the psych ward. "Did you bring a weapon?"

Rónán shook his head. "Other than magic, no."

"How is that possible?"

"It's a long story. Suffice to say it has a time limit. We need to find Darragh soon, or we'll all be stuck here." Ciarán stopped walking, and pulled Rónán to a stop beside him to prevent him moving any closer.

"If they realize you're not Darragh," he said in a low, urgent voice, "they'll go into lockdown. If that happens, you'll not get near your brother. Understand?"

Rónán nodded.

"Then follow me, keep your head down, and don't say anything. The guards here all know Darragh on sight. If they realize you're not him ..."

"I get it, Ciarán," Rónán said, a little impatiently. "Can we go? We don't have much time."

Ciarán nodded and resumed walking toward the door where, fortunately, the garrulous and friendly Officer Connors was on duty.

"Hey, Mac," the prison officer said with a smile as they approached. "Had enough of this shite weather?" He squinted through the rain to study Rónán for a moment. "Darragh... didn't realize they'd let you out of the loony bin."

"Before he was ready for it, I guess," Ciarán explained. "He's really not doing well, Officer Connors. Can I take him back to see the nurse?"

Connors glanced over his shoulder. He wasn't allowed to leave his post. But he didn't want a patient fresh out of the psych ward going off on his watch, either.

"Take him through to the next checkpoint," Connors ordered, opening the gate to let them out of the yard. "I'll phone through and tell Mr Fyffe I said it was okay."

"Thanks." Ciarán took Rónán by the arm. As ordered, he was keeping his head down, and looking suitably miserable. Ciarán led him through the gate, and then turned and walked into the main building, out of the rain, not letting go of him until they were out of sight of the yard gate, and not yet in sight of the next checkpoint.

As soon as he was sure they were unobserved, he stopped and jerked Rónán around to face him.

"Why have you taken so long to get here?" he demanded. "Do you know how long we've been trapped in this realm?"

"Yes, and I'm terribly sorry," Rónán said, rather insincerely, Ciarán thought. "But truly, Ciarán, you can bawl me out about it later. We need to find Darragh while there's still a chance I can wane him out of here. This magic isn't going to last much longer."

"How much longer?"

"A couple more hours at best."

"How are you doing it?"

"I swallowed about thirty rubies the Brethren supercharged with magic."

Ciarán stared at him, not sure what surprised him most: the method Rónán had found for bringing his magical powers into this world, or that the Brethren had helped him do it.

"You're mad."

"I'm mad? What are *you* doing here?"

"I am protecting your brother. Waiting for you to come for us. Walk casually. There are cameras here. They will get suspicious if we run."

"I get that," Rónán said as he fell into step beside Ciarán. "What I don't get is how you ended up in here."

"My first thought was to join the prison service as a guard," Ciarán explained as they walked along the linoleum corridor, hoping that if Connors had phoned ahead to the next checkpoint, nobody would bother to call the medical center to check if Darragh had actually been discharged. "An option I discarded when I realized how much documentation I would have to produce to even get through the initial recruitment process."

"I can see how that..." Rónán stopped for a moment as if he was having trouble speaking, and then he finished his sentence: "might be a problem."

"Are you okay?"

"At the moment. What did you do to get in here?"

"I was at a loss to find a way to protect your brother until fate smiled on me a few days after he was sentenced - for your crimes, I might point out. I chanced upon a television program that gave me the idea. In truth, I was idly flicking through the channels trying to frame my explanation to Marcroy about how the Undivided twins the *sídhe* so desperately needed, to save them from the Matrarchai, had survived the power transfer as the Brethren had hoped. Unfortunately, I had no idea where one of the twins was, no way of protecting the other, and at anytime one of these saviors might be knifed in the ribs by some tattooed hoodlum wanting to make the young man his bitch. The words *Prison Break* caught my eye."

"Excuse me?"

"The television program that gave me the idea. It was called *Prison Break*."

Rónán looked appalled. "Tell me you didn't try to break him out of here based on an idea you got off a TV show?"

Ciarán shook his head and glanced up at the cameras. There were no alarms being raised, nothing out of the ordinary. So far they were getting away with their ruse of Rónán being Darragh on his way back to medical.

Ciarán kept walking at the same pace he normally did. Not so fast it looked threatening. Not so slow it seemed suspicious. "The protagonist in the program robbed a bank to get himself sent to the same prison as his brother so he could help him escape," he explained, as if he and Darragh were simply chatting about the weather. Someone would be watching their progress from the control room. It was important they seem to be doing nothing out of the ordinary. "I decided I could do the same." He cast a scowl at Rónán, adding, "Unfortunately, I foolishly believed there would be no need for me to help Darragh escape as you would come for your brother any day - of that we were *both* certain."

"There is a reason it has taken so long, you know." Rónán didn't seem very apologetic for all that he was claiming he was sorry.

"And I'm sure you think it's a grand one. Now stop talking. We're coming up on the next checkpoint. I'm not sure how many more gates we can pretend you're Darragh, by the way. Eventually, we may have to use either some of your magic or find a weapon."

"Let's just see how far we get," Rónán said. He seemed quite pale.

Ciarán led him up the wide hall toward the gate.

Much to his relief, the same story he used on Connors worked at the next two gates they had to pass through. Ciarán supposed it was easier for the guards to believe that Darragh had been returned to the general population and they hadn't been informed, than consider the idea that his identical twin had just appeared in the courtyard by magic and was working his way through the prison to locate his brother. None of the prison officers had objected to him returning to the medical ward - prisoners were allowed to seek medical attention whenever they wanted - but Ciarán kept waiting for one of them to tell him he couldn't go any further with Darragh.

Their luck held, however, and the officers continued to let them through. Perhaps they were short-staffed, today. Even the best run prisons had slip-ups.

Whatever the reason, they were within sight of the medical ward, and Darragh, before someone tried to stop them.

They were always going to run into trouble when they reached the medical center. Darragh was confined here, and they certainly knew he was tucked up safely in his cell.

Although the guard let them through, the nurse on duty took one look at Rónán and hit the alarm.

The air was suddenly filled with the sound of sirens, and the clang of doors throughout the prison automatically slamming shut and locking. The guard on the gate came charging in, baton in hand. Before Ciarán could react Rónán raised his arm and the guard flew backward across the room, slamming into the bars with a bone-crunching thud, and then falling to the floor in an unconscious heap. Ciarán ran to him to arm himself with the baton - the officers didn't carry firearms against exactly this situation - although it wouldn't be long, he knew, before the soldiers got here.

There was no fear of the prisoners taking them down. They were armed with automatic weapons.

A baton wasn't going to be much use against gunfire.

"Where is my brother, Darragh?" Rónán demanded of the nurse who was looking at him with wide-eyed terror.

The nurse had been trained well. She was an older woman, probably nearing retirement. She was frightened, but she wasn't going to sacrifice her life for one, inconsequential prisoner. "Third door on the left. The keys are in my pocket."

"Give them to me." She fished out a set of keys and tossed them to Rónán. "Who else is in here at the moment?"

"Two other prisoners locked in their cells. The doctor's on his morning break."

Ciarán turned to Rónán. "Don't just stand there, man! Go! Get your brother!"

Rónán hurried down the hall, sorting through the keys. Ciarán turned toward the bars and the corridor leading to the medical center. They would know this was the seat of the trouble. There were cameras everywhere in this place and even if they couldn't figure out how Rónán had taken out the guard, they would have seen him flying across the room and hitting the bars.

"You'll never get of here," the nurse told him, as he surveyed the rest of the room, looking for some sort of defensible position.

There was a camera in the corner, watching their every move.

"Give me your sweater," he ordered, pointing to the cardigan draped over the back of her chair.

She tossed it to him without asking why. He threw it at the camera where it caught by one sleeve, blocking the view of the control room. He could already hear the footsteps pounding down the hall. It wouldn't be long now.

Rónán returned, half dragging, half carrying Darragh, who looked dazed and quite oblivious to what was going on. He'd been heavily medicated, and by the look of him, woken from a deep drug-induced sleep. He was in no state to defend himself against anything.

"You have to get him out of here," Ciarán ordered Rónán. "Now. You can come back for me when he's safe."

Rónán stared at Ciarán for a moment, and then shook his head, his expression grim. "I can't come back. I only have enough juice for one trip."

There were shouts in the corridor now. In a matter of seconds they would be overrun.

It wasn't even a hard decision. This is what Ciarán was born for.

"Then go. And do whatever noble thing destiny has in store for you, Rónán of the Undivided, so that I do not die in vain."

Darragh looked up then, and stared myopically at Ciarán. "Die? Who's going to die?"

"Not you, *leathtiarna*. Not today." He clasped the drugged and semiconscious young man by the shoulder for a moment. "It has been an honor, *leathtiarna.*" Then he looked up at Rónán. "Go. Now." He turned to the nurse. "You'd better get down."

She did as he suggested without hesitating, hiding behind the desk, her hands over her ears as if she knew what was coming.

"I'm sorry..." Rónán began, but at that moment the soldiers appeared. Rónán looked up, saw what was coming for them and, without another word, Darragh slumped in his arms, he winked out of existence, waning both of them to safety.

Ciarán turned to find the soldiers charging toward the bars, weapons drawn, demanding he drop the baton. He didn't. His work was done here. RónánDarragh were safe. He had fulfilled his duty as the Druid guardian of the Undivided.

And he had no intention of spending another day as a prisoner in this dreadful realm.

Ciarán raised the baton and charged at the bars, knowing they would cut him down, hoping they would take him out quickly.

The sound of the gunfire was deafening. Bullets slammed into him like a dozen burning knives being driven by hammers into his chest, one after the other.

Ciarán mac Connacht smiled as he fell, proud that even after all this time in this magic-less realm, in this place without hope or honor, he had found a way to die like a true warrior in battle.

CHAPTER 42

Be very sure of the place you are waning to.

Ren remembered the Hag's warning clearly, and had tried to run through a list of places of which he had sufficient knowledge to be sure of where he was going.

There weren't that many places left.

He'd been gone from this realm a long time, and even when he was here, there were not many safe places he knew intimately enough to be sure that when he willed it, the magic would take him there, without fail.

The place had to be somewhere he was familiar with, somewhere private, and somewhere he'd be able to recover and regroup. The magic-infused jewels Ren had swallowed to give him power, burned like dollops of hot lead in his stomach. He wasn't sure how much longer he could keep them down.

Ren was fairly certain the Hag's optimistic estimate of the jewels providing him with several hours of magic was way off the mark. He'd be lucky to make it through the first hour.

He'd waned into the prison yard almost as soon as he stepped through the rift at the golf club. Ren didn't need to know that location very well. Portlaoise was a high-profile prison because of the population it housed. He'd seen it on the television news plenty of times as a kid, and figured he could visualise the yard well enough to arrive there safely. He'd had no plan beyond that, other than to locate Darragh.

His secret hope was that by arriving mid-morning, Darragh would be in the yard and they could wane out of there together mere moments after Ren arrived. If they were lucky, while the other prisoners were still trying to decide if they'd imagined one of their prison mates' doppelganger appearing and then disappearing out of thin air, they could be long gone. In a perfect world, the guards probably wouldn't even realize Darragh was missing until they did a head count later that morning, which Ren was quite sure they did several times a day.

All his plans had gone pear-shaped, of course, when he waned into the yard and found not Darragh, but Ciarán mac Connaught.

Ren was shocked to find Ciarán there, but not really surprised when he thought about it. For all that Marcroy had sired them, Ciarán was probably the closest thing to a father Darragh had ever known. Ciarán certainly treated Darragh like the son he'd never had.

If Darragh had been stuck here in this realm, it was no surprise Ciarán had found a way to stay with him. A warrior Druid wouldn't have known how to do anything else.

Darragh's grief for Ciarán's loss was something Ren would have to deal with sooner or later. Perhaps he wouldn't tell his brother that when they'd waned out of Portlaoise Prison, Ciarán was preparing to die covering their escape. He would have to tell him the truth eventually, but maybe Darragh hadn't noticed what had happened, so he probably had some time before he had to deal with the inevitable questions and, perhaps, the blame Darragh might put on him. His brother had been semiconscious, after all, when Ren dragged him from the hospital bed where he was tied down with Velcro straps, and so heavily medicated he barely recognized Ren, let alone understood he was being rescued.

Ren forced himself not to dwell on Ciarán's choice. There was nothing he could have done to change the outcome. He hadn't known Ciarán was in Portlaoise. And Ciarán could have chosen to surrender peacefully. Ren would have promised to come back if he had, although Ciarán had probably known any such promise would be a hollow one at best. Ren had risked everything to rescue his brother and that had taken him ten years. The Druid warrior clearly didn't want to wait that long again for his own liberation.

So Ren had taken Darragh and waned to the place he knew best in this entire realm - his old room in Kiva's house.

It was a huge risk, he knew that. Kiva might be back from London. Kerry might be vacuuming the room when he appeared. She might have sold the house to someone else... any number of things could go wrong.

But he knew the location of his room, knew that if they could stay hidden until the house was empty, he could take Kiva's car, or even sneak next door and borrow Jack's car - assuming the old guy was still alive and speaking to him. He could then drive them back to the golf course, where, according to the Hag, he would find a way to leave this world.

He wasn't sure what that meant, but he was hoping it meant Pete or Logan were in this realm and had found a way home. It made sense that Marcroy would have tossed them back into the realm from which they had just appeared; and the one stone circle he was sure they all knew about here in Dublin, was the ruined old circle at the Castle Golf Club. How they were supposed to open a rift from there without magic remained an unanswered question. Maybe the Hag would open it for them from the other side. Remarkably, he hadn't needed any help opening the rift from his realm to this one when he was artificially charged up on magic. He'd been able to will the rift to open with a thought.

That feeling almost made the sickening sensation of all that dead weight in his stomach tolerable.

If there was no sign of Pete or Logan at the golf club, Plan B was to find a way to get Darragh and himself to London so they could use the Matrarchaí's rift in the Shard. It wasn't a very good Plan B, as Plan B's went. It would be a much more difficult proposition to reach the Shard with an escaped convict as a companion and international borders to cross.

Ren lowered Darragh to the floor as soon as they appeared in his old room, as gently as he could manage. Then he staggered to the door to make sure it was locked from the inside before stumbling to the bathroom. He began to retch violently.

For a time Ren forgot all about Darragh, too busy wondering if he was dying. It felt as if his insides were trying to claw their way out of his body via his oesophagus, using grappling hooks and barbed wire to haul themselves out. The first of the rubies landed in the sink in a puddle of vomit, no longer shiny and glowing with magic, but dull and lifeless. He didn't like the look of the blood, but there was more of it to come. He vomited again, hoping nobody could hear him, wondering idly if he should have turned Darragh on his side like they warned you to do with unconscious people in first-aid classes, so they didn't suffocate, before he hurled again and brought up more of the depleted stones.

Again his stomach heaved and the rubies, which had seemed so benign and harmless on the way down, wreaked their revenge on the way back. He wished he'd counted the exact number he'd swallowed. He wouldn't know if they were all out once his stomach settled down - assuming it ever felt normal again.

"You... okay?"

Ren turned his head a little to find Darragh leaning against the door jamb, holding it for support.

He nodded. "I'll be fine."

"What did you do?"

"What I had to," Ren told him, as his gut spasmed violently and he vomited out another half dozen or so rubies into the sink.

Darragh watched him in the mirror for a time as he heaved again, before saying in a carefully neutral voice, "You took a long time to come for me."

Ren closed his eyes for a moment, knowing he had no answer which didn't sound either cowardly or self-serving. Eventually, he looked up and spoke to his brother in the mirror.

"I'm sorry." He couldn't think of anything better to say.

"You had your reasons, I don't doubt."

Darragh was being very understanding. Was he really feeling forgiving, or had the drugs they pumped into him calmed him down to the point of apathy?

"I did."

"When we share the *Comhroinn*, I'm sure I'll understand."

Still feeling like his stomach wasn't done rejecting the indigestible stones he'd swallowed to rescue Darragh, Ren turned to his brother, shaking his head. "There won't be any *Comhroinn*. Not in this realm. Not without magic."

Darragh nodded. "When we get home then."

If we get home...

"How long can we hide here?"

"Overnight if we have to, I hope," Ren assured him. He looked past Darragh into what had once been his old room. It was elegantly decorated now in a peach and cream palette... soulless and with no hint this had ever been the room of a teenage boy. "It looks like Kiva's turned my room into a guest room, but as she hates having house guests, I'm betting nobody will have a reason to come up to this end of the house if we're quiet."

"You'd best stop puking so violently then."

Ren smiled briefly. "Excellent suggestion."

"Can we talk, Rónán, if we can't share our news any other way?" Darragh asked, searching Ren's face for something... perhaps a sign that his brother was going to be honest with him. "Will you tell me what's been going on?"

"Of course. What did you want to know?"

"Let's start with what happened to Ciarán," Darragh said.

CHAPTER 43

"Is this the place?"

Trása looked down at the address scrawled on the post-it note Echo had brought them and nodded. "That's what it says here. Are you okay?"

Nika was pale and more than a little shaken by her cab ride. It had been so long since Trása first stepped into this magic-less world with its automobiles, telephones and television, that she had forgotten what it must be like for someone to experience it for the first time. Even though Nika was a seasoned rift runner, used to seeing realms far different to her own, she had never stepped through to a reality so devoid of magic before, or one so reliant on technology. She seemed uneasy and restless. Trása doubted she'd be truly happy until they were back in a realm where there was true magic to be had for the taking.

She glanced up at the sky, detecting the first glimmering of dawn creeping over the roofs of the neat row of houses where Pete and Logan were apparently hiding. Trása had no idea whose house this was, and it didn't really matter. Echo had found "the boys" and to prove it she'd brought the message they'd sent to come here. The only reasonable conclusion was that this house must be safe and whoever owned it was willing to aid them... and hopefully, not aligned with the *Matrarchaí*. Unless, of course, they'd done what Trása, Ren, Darragh and Sorcha had done when they came here looking for Hayley, and had found some random stranger to take them in.

For a fleeting moment, Trása wondered what had become of Warren. Did his wife ever realize her house had been invaded by visitors from another reality? Did his kids miss the clothes they'd stolen?

It didn't matter. Warren was barely a wisp of a memory. Right now, there were more practical considerations to deal with. "Take care of the cab driver," she ordered Toyoda.

The little *Leipreachán* nodded and waned into the front seat where he appeared on the lap of the rather bemused cabbie and proceeded to convince him he'd never been here, nor expected payment for the rather long cab ride they'd just clocked up.

As they climbed out of the cab, Echo reappeared, flitting about excitedly at the prospect of seeing "the boys" again. Toyoda appeared on the sidewalk as the vehicle pulled away, the driver not even looking back at them.

"Should we have kept the carriage and its driver here?" Nika asked.

Trása glanced at her and smiled. Echo had found her some jeans and a sweater but Nika looked so out of place in the long, dark woollen Merlin's robe she insisted on wearing, even though the realm where she had been Merlin was long gone. "Not really. We can always call another one."

Trása studied the neat house and noted the cars parked in the street in front of all the other neat houses. They all seemed quite new and expensive, even to her untrained eye. "We may not have to worry about it anyway. Pete and Logan might have already found a vehicle to return to the rift."

Nika glanced at the cab disappearing down the deserted, dawn-lit street for a moment and shook her head. "Are you sure? Do Pete and Logan know how to operate such a machine?"

"Of course, they do. It's easy," Trása assured her, smiling at Nika's concern. "Even I can drive."

"Truly?" Nika seemed very impressed.

Trása nodded, not going into the details of her one and only driving stint in a stolen car. Nika did not need to know that it was more good luck than good driving skills which got her and Ren's friend, Hayley, to their destination without killing either herself or any number of innocent bystanders along the way.

"You'd be surprised to learn some of the things I've seen and done when I've been rift running," she said. "Just wait until you see television for the first time. Toyoda, Echo, come here!"

The pixie and the *Leipreachán* did as she ordered, appearing in front of her to receive their orders. Trása marvelled at their obedience. And lamented the loss of her *Youkai* kingdom. Now that Marcroy had found the ninja reality, she was a

Faerie Queen no more. She was back to what she had always been - a troublesome, mongrel, half-*beansídhe* rift-runner desperate to find her place in the world. This one or any other.

Trása forced her attention back to the job at hand. She may not be their queen any longer, but she was responsible for these creatures and it was her job to ensure they remained protected, particularly in this realm full of limited magic and unknown dangers. "I want you two to stay out of sight until I know it's safe."

"Boys asked us to come. Boys asked us to come," Echo insisted zipping about Trása's head so fast it made her dizzy to try and stay focused on the little creature. "We'll be well. We'll be well. We'll be well."

"Let me be the judge of that. Now scat. I'll call you back when I need you."

The *Leipreachán* and the pixie - somewhat to Trása's surprise, did exactly what she asked. They winked out of existence, leaving Trása and Nika alone in the quiet suburban street.

Nika looked up and down the street, frowning. "It is hard to credit this is the world Pete and his brother come from."

"Well, technically, they don't come from this world," Trása reminded her turning to study the house. There was a light on in the front room, but no indication of who might live here. "They just grew up in this realm."

"Do you think they'll want to stay here now they've found their way back?"

Trása turned to Nika, curious about her tone. "Is that what's bothering you? You think now Pete's back in this world he'll want to stay here?"

"This place has many temptations," she said, as if bracing herself for the inevitable. "You said it yourself. This realm has many strange and wonderful contraptions. What if Pete misses them? I would not be surprised if he chose them over ... his other life."

"He won't," Trása assured her friend with a confidence she certainly didn't feel. "Pete loves you."

"He has never expressed that opinion to me."

Really, Trása wanted to ask. *We have to talk about this now?* "Some men don't seem to think it's necessary to tell a woman they love her," Trása said, thinking of Rónán rather than Pete.

"I would not make him choose," Nika said, squaring her shoulders with the stoic determination of somebody who has already lost the fight. "If Pete wants to stay in this realm, I would not try to dissuade him."

"Let's cross that bridge when we come to it," Trása said, thinking the last thing they should be worrying about right now was Nika and Pete's love life. They had to survive the next few days first. "Let me do the talking."

"What?"

"When we get inside. Until we know for certain that Pete and Logan are here and this place is safe for us, let me do the talking."

"It they have harmed Pete in any way, I will turn them into cockroaches and step on them," she said, in a matter-of-fact sort of voice as Trása headed up the neat path to the front door.

Trása glanced over her shoulder at the Merlin. "No magic in this realm, remember?"

"Then I will find another way."

Oh dear, Trása thought, as she lifted the brass knocker and rapped on the door a couple of times. *And I used to think Sorcha being in this realm was a problem.*

Pete opened the door almost as soon as Trása finished knocking. "Get inside, quickly."

She hurried through the front door and into an elegant, carpeted hallway followed by Nika who stepped over the threshold with great trepidation.

"Nika! Thank God you're safe," Pete said when he saw her.

Of course he loves you, you fool, Trása thought. *Anybody can see that.*

Nika wasn't buying it. She bowed her head and then stared coolly at Pete. "My lord."

He looked stunned by her aloof reception. "My lord? What?"

Trása sighed. "She thinks you're going to choose staying in this realm over her. Whose place is this?"

"It belongs to someone I used to work with," Pete told her as he stepped forward and took Nika in his arms. He really wasn't interested in Trása. He only had eyes for the Merlin. "I'm not staying in this realm, Nika. I promise."

"He says that like we have a way out of here," Logan remarked from a door a little further down the hall.

Before Trása could say hello, another man pushed past Logan with a panicked look on his face. "Shhh! You'll wake Stella."

"Who is Stella?"

"Annad's wife," Pete explained, still holding Nika in his arms. She wasn't convinced by his assurances, Trása guessed, because the Merlin was still scowling and holding herself stiffly apart from him, refusing to melt into Pete's embrace the way he obviously expected her to.

"This is Annad?" she asked, turning from Pete and Nika to study the man who'd scolded them for making too much noise. When Pete said this house belonged to someone he used to work with, she'd assumed he meant another cop. This man didn't look like a cop. He was Asian, with a delicious caramel-colored skin, a soft brogue, kind, although worried, dark eyes and the air of a man unused to the trouble that was visiting his house.

"I am," Annad said. "Now, please, can we go back to the kitchen? My wife is asleep right above us. I'd prefer she stayed that way so I don't have to explain even more strange visitors arriving at the crack of dawn."

It seemed a reasonable suggestion. Without another word, they followed Annad through the tastefully furnished living room to the kitchen at the back of the house. He closed the living room door behind him and leaned on it for a moment, before looking around. "Is the fairy here?"

"Pixie," Logan corrected. "And no, she's not here. Where is Echo, by the way?"

"I sent her away with Toyoda until I was sure this place was safe," Trása told him. "What are you doing here?"

"Making my life a misery," Annad remarked, as he pushed off the door. "Would anybody like some tea? I think I need to make some tea."

"Is this where you'll be staying?" Nika asked Pete, looking around the room, probably trying to figure out what the strange appliances were.

"Why do you think I'm staying?" Pete asked, and then turned to Logan. "Why does she think I want to stay in this realm?"

"I have no idea," Logan said, not the least bit interested, Trása guessed, in what Nika was worried about. "What I want to know is what the hell you're both doing here in the first place?"

Trása shrugged. "Marcroy found us. Nika decided we should escape and convinced everyone I was dead, used her talisman to bring us first to my realm and then I opened a rift to here, looking for you. Where is Rónán? Has he found Darragh, yet?"

"We don't know," Logan told her, taking a seat at the table. "Darragh's in prison here, and the last we saw of Ren, Marcroy had him."

Trása stared at Logan, not sure which bit of the devastating news he had just so casually delivered was the one of most concern.

Darragh is in prison.

Marcroy has Rónán.

It was almost too much to take in. "How... how did Marcroy find Rónán?"

"How did he find *you*?" Logan asked.

Trása sat down opposite Logan. "Um... I think Abbán may have contacted him from the Pool of Tranquillity."

"You *think*?" Logan asked with mock surprise. "What happened to asking Ren to wipe Abbán's memory and send him home with some story about how he lost the jewel in a bog?"

"We were still talking about it when Isleen went missing, remember? Things got rather hectic after that. And why is this suddenly my fault, anyway?" she asked. "You're the ones who left without telling anybody. If you were so worried about Abbán, why didn't *you* ask Rónán to do something about him before you went haring off across realities to save Darragh?"

"My lady is right," Nika said. "This is not her fault. What is this?"

Trása glanced up. Nika was staring at a box with a glass door and glowing numbers sitting on the kitchen counter. "It's a microwave," Logan told her. "Leave it alone."

"Do you have a television?" Nika asked Annad who was spooning tea from a small metal caddy into a teapot, concentrating on the task as if he believed that by doing something normal, the abnormal things happening around him would make sense.

"Over there," he said, jerking his head in the direction of the set on the sideboard.

Nika turned to study it for a moment and then looked at Trása. "I do not see what you find so intriguing about this thing, my lady. It does nothing."

Annad glanced at Pete. "Is she serious?"

Pete smiled, walked over to the sideboard, picked up the remote, and pushed the power button. "It's a bit more interesting when it's on." Nika's eyes widened at the sight of the screen coming to life. "This button here changes the picture," he explained. "This one controls the sound. You just point it at the TV and push, okay? Don't turn it up or you'll wake Stella."

Nika nodded, her eyes glued to the set. Without taking her eyes off it, she dragged a chair over, perched herself close to the set and started flicking through the channels forgetting, apparently, all about her fears that Pete was planning to stay here in this realm without her.

With Nika concentrating on the TV, Pete returned to the table and took the seat opposite Logan. Annad brought a tray to the table with the teapot, cups, a jug of milk and sugar bowl. Without asking if they wanted any tea, he began to pour a cup for each of them.

"Is Darragh really in prison in this reality?"

Pete nodded, his expression grim. "He's in Portlaoise. Don't know if you've heard of it, but it's not a very pleasant place."

Trása's heart went out to Darragh. All this time he was in prison. What had they done to him? What had prison done to him?

And Rónán. What must he be feeling? He had been so sure Darragh was living a life of luxury and extravagance in this realm with Kiva. It was how he'd justified leaving him here for so long. He'd clung to that belief so strongly. It was how he slept at night. His nightmares had stopped and he didn't need to feel guilty about it because Darragh was living it up and loving every minute of his time in this reality.

Rónán had been telling himself the same story for years.

"What did Rónán do when he found out?"

"Before or after I stopped him walking in front of a speeding car?"

Trása couldn't find it in herself to be angry at Rónán, certain nothing she could say to him would come close to inflicting the guilt or remorse he must be inflicting on himself since learning of his brother's fate. "After, obviously."

"He went to see Kiva."

"His mother from this realm? Was that wise?"

"Of course not, but that didn't stop him." Pete looked at her like she was just a little bit dim. "This may come as a shock to you, Trása, but Ren frequently doesn't do the *wise* thing. Haven't you noticed?"

She had noticed. But this was probably the dumbest thing he'd done in the past few years - stepping into a realm that had no magic to save his brother without an actual plan notwithstanding. "Where is he now? You said Marcroy has him? How can that be? Marcroy would die the moment he set foot in this realm."

"He ambushed me in your realm," Logan explained. "It had to have been the jewel we used to open the rift, I figure. He must have some way of tracking it... some innate sense of where it is, perhaps. I was at the Drombeg circle in your realm, waiting for the right time to open the rift for Ren and Pete to come back when next thing I know, there's *Tuatha Dé Danann* everywhere, I can't move a muscle, Marcroy's invaded the circle, taken back his jewel and there is no sign of you or any hint about what had become of you back in the ninja realm."

"He put Stiofán in charge."

"Seriously? That guy's a monumental pain in the arse."

"And he's loving every minute of being the new king of *Tír Na nÓg*," Trása said, realizing now why Marcroy had arrived in the ninja realm and then left again so quickly, allowing her and Nika to escape. Marcroy had other fish to fry. He'd been on Rónán's trail the whole time.

She shouldn't have been surprised. *Where are they, little bird?* It was the first thing Marcroy had said to her when he arrived in *Tír Na nÓg* and took her prisoner. *"RónánDarragh. Where are RónánDarragh?*

Trása sighed. It was the story of her life, really. Marcroy hadn't wanted her. He hadn't really cared about her at all, which is why they got away so easily. There was a time when this realization would have burned Trása like acid in the pit of her belly, but now she just accepted it, marvelling at how the more things changed, the more they stayed the same. "Why does he want Ren?"

"He didn't say," Logan told her. "I take it he didn't tell you why?"

"No."

"It can't be for anything good," Pete said. "How long have you been in this realm?"

"A few hours. We came through the circle at the golf club."

"What did you use to open the rift?"

"This," Nika said, holding up the mummified baby's foot talisman she'd brought with her from her own realm without taking her eyes from the TV. She had the remote in the other hand and was changing the channels so quickly it was impossible to fix on any one program for long enough to tell what it was.

Annad paled and turned to Pete. "Dear God, is that..."

"No," Pete lied. "Of course not."

Logan's eyes lit up at the sight of the morbid talisman. "That means we have a way out of here. We can open a rift."

"Not here in Dublin, we can't" Pete reminded him. "We'd have to get to London or one of the other circles the *Matrarchaí* has built in the Enchanted Sphere. That thing won't work at ground level. There's no magic."

"Details," Logan scoffed with a grin. "Point is, we have a way out of here."

Trása stifled a yawn, adding, "Wonderful. Maybe when we leave here we can find somewhere safe enough to sleep. I'm exhausted. We've been up all night and I was dead yesterday. I don't think I'm over that yet, either."

"I know how that feels," Annad remarked sourly. "Are you people planning to sleep at all?"

"I'd love to get some -" Logan began, but Nika cut him off.

"Did you say Darragh was in Portlaoise?"

They all turned to look at her. "Why?"

"There is something about it on the television."

Annad's tea forgotten, they jumped up from the table and clustered around the TV set while Nika tried to work out which button on the remote increased the volume. Logan snatched if from her after a few seconds and pointed it at the TV where a reporter was talking to the camera, standing in the rain outside Portlaoise Prison. As the volume increased, the reporter glanced over her shoulder at the high, razor wire-topped walls, saying, "... are refusing to confirm or deny that an escape or an escape attempt took place here yesterday, although multiple reports of shots being heard coming from the prison have been received by local media outlets. Authorities are only admitting, at this stage, that an incident took place and there was one casualty, a prisoner named ..." She stopped and glanced at the notepad she was holding. "... Ciarán mac Connacht, serving a term for armed robbery."

"That's not possible," Trása said. She couldn't believe it. *Not Ciarán. Not here. Not in this realm.*

"What's not possible?" Pete asked, as the others shushed him so they could hear the rest of the report.

She turned to Pete, shaking her head in bewilderment, and said in a low voice, "Ciarán mac Connacht. That's the name of the Druid warrior who is... was Darragh's guardian and protector in our reality. He's not here in this realm."

"Coincidence?" Pete asked, not quite as ready to accept that there was something odd in the name. "I mean, aren't all realities connected in some way?

Don't the same people keep cropping up in the same places, over and over?"

"Not in a reality that's as diverged from ours as this one. I mean, they do, and Ciarán mac Connacht's *eileféin* is almost certainly in this realm, but he'd have a different name, and wherever he is, Ciarán's *eileféin* is *not* in jail for armed robbery. There is no more honest or honorable man alive in any realm."

"Can you please be quiet?" Annad hissed. They turned to look at him and realized he was on the phone to someone. Logan muted the TV as Trása began looking about for the nearest exit. She didn't know this man. He didn't really act like a friend. Was he calling someone, even now, to tell them what he knew? Was he ringing another one of Pete's old workmates in the Gardaí to tell them...

What? That his house was full of travellers from another reality?

"... no, I just saw it on the news," Annad was saying to whoever was on the other end of the telephone. "Yes... no... of course..."

Trása wanted to snatch the phone from him and find out what he was being told. Pete must have guessed her intentions. He placed a hand on her arm and shook his head when she looked at him.

"... if I hear anything," Annad assured whoever we was talking to. "I've had limited contact with him these past few years. I don't know that he'd try to contact me." He stopped to listen for a moment and then added, "No... no... I don't think it's necessary to send a car here. I'm leaving for work soon, and truly, he probably doesn't even remember my name. Who is the treating psychologist? ... Then he'd be a much more likely prospect if he's going to make contact ... yes ... of course ... if I hear anything at all."

Annad hung up the phone and turned to face his expectant audience.

"Darragh escaped from Portlaoise yesterday morning," he said. "His cellmate, a man named Ciarán mac Connacht was killed covering his escape. The nurse who witnessed the escape claims Darragh walked into the medical unit with mac Connacht, disappeared into the room he should have been confined to, came out with another version of himself and then vanished into thin air. She's being treated for post-traumatic shock. They're not sure they'll ever get the 'real' story out of her." He stared at the four of them for a moment. "Only she didn't imagine it, did she?"

None of them answered him.

It was Pete who broke the silence. "I guess he managed to pull it off."

"So where are they?" Logan asked. "If Ren actually succeeded in waning out of the prison with Darragh, where did he go?"

"Why not send the pixie to find out?" Annad said.

CHAPTER 44

It shouldn't be so easy to take a life.

Darragh pondered that thought as he watched Rónán approach the cradle rocking gently in the center of the room that was somehow different from before. The room was no longer warm or candlelit. It was dark and the walls were glistening in the moonlight seeping through a sliver in the closed curtains.

There was no sign of the nurse. Darragh wondered if she'd run away or if her fate had been the same as everyone else who'd approached this nightmare.

He watched Rónán step up to the cradle and stop to study it for a moment. The oak cradle was carved with elaborate Celtic knotwork, inlaid with softly glowing mother-of-pearl, just is it always was, but even from his vantage here in the shadows, he could see the mother-of-pearl was smeared with something that smelled like fresh blood.

Dear God, is he really going to do this? Am I going to allow it? Am I going to stand back and do nothing while he kills my children?

Rónán glanced down at the blade he carried. Darragh wondered if it would be enough. The airgead sídhe *caught the light in odd places, illuminating the engraving on the blade. He hefted the razor-sharp weapon in his hand. Faerie silver was useless in battle, but for this task, no other would suffice.*

She'd been very clear on that. Before she died.

The twins must be asleep - Rónán would not have been able to approach otherwise. If they had been awake, would they recognize the danger that hovered over them?

Maybe they would. Whatever made my children what they were, must give them some inkling of approaching danger.

They really couldn't just exist to destroy. Could they? They seemed so innocent. So human.

"You can't seriously mean to do this."

Rónán glanced over his shoulder and saw Darragh standing in the shadows by the door.

"It has to be done, Darragh. You know that."

He shook his head and took a step further into the room, filled with doubt and anguish. Rónán's face was calm and resigned to what must be done.

"They are innocent."

"How can you say that? You saw what they did."

"They didn't know. Didn't understand ..."

"They are death, Darragh. The death of billions upon billions more."

He shook his head. "I can't believe ..." He didn't finish the sentence. He couldn't.

Rónán didn't respond, turning back to stare down at the twin girls he had come to murder.

Darragh took another step closer. "I won't let you do it. You don't have to do it. You're not a tool of the Matrarchaí. *Neither of us is. We don't have to do her bidding."*

"Even if she's right?"

"She's dead. What difference does it make now?"

"I will end this."

"I won't let you."

"How will you stop me?" Rónán asked as he raised the blade.

"I'll kill you if I have to, Rónán, to stop this."

Rónán stared down at the twins, dismissing the empty threat. "Even if you could get across this room before the deed was done, Darragh, you can't kill me without killing yourself, which would achieve precisely what I am here to prevent."

He moved the blade a little, repositioning his grip. There was a drawn-out silence as he played the light across the blade. Behind him, Darragh remained motionless. There was no point in him trying to attack. They were two sides of the same coin. Neither man could so much as form the intent to attack without the other knowing about it.

The girls would be dead before anybody could reach the cradle to stop him.

"There must be another way." There was note of defeat in the statement; a glimmer of acceptance.

"I wouldn't be here if there was," Ren replied, still staring down at the baby he was destined to kill. "You know that," he added, glancing over his shoulder. "You're just not willing to accept the truth of it yet."

Darragh held out his hand, as if he expected the blade to be handed over, and for this night to be forgotten, somehow. Put behind them like a foolish disagreement they'd been wise enough to settle like men. "They're just babies ..."

"They are Partition and all the destruction that -"

"Hey, wake up."

Darragh jerked awake to find Rónán standing over him, shaking him by the shoulder. "What? What is it?"

"You were talking in your sleep," Rónán told him softly. "Something about partitioning. I can hear them moving about downstairs. We need to be quiet."

Darragh sat up and glanced around the unfamiliar room, a little unsure of where he was, not entirely certain this wasn't the dream and what he'd just been seeing was reality. Perhaps neither of them was real. Perhaps he was still in his cell in Portlaoise and Rónán waking him from his nightmare was just wishful thinking ...

And then Darragh remembered Rónán coming for him, and Ciarán dying and realized it wasn't a dream. This was Rónán's old room. There were in Kiva Kavanaugh's house.

Rónán had finally come for him.

"What time is it?" Darragh asked.

"Just on dawn," Rónán said, sitting on the bed beside him. "Kiva must have an early call. She's not normally up this early."

"Did you get some sleep?"

Rónán shook his head. "Someone needed to keep watch."

Darragh pushed himself up on his elbows, surprised at how awkward this soft bed with its down comforter felt. He was used to the hard foam mattress of his cell. This luxury made him uncomfortable. "I thought you said we were safe here."

"We are," he said softly, "but not if we're discovered. You're a dangerous escapee, remember."

Darragh didn't want to think about that. In fact, if he never spared Portlaoise another thought as long as he lived, it would suit him just fine.

"How's your head?" Rónán asked. "You were pretty out of it yesterday."

"Better. How are you feeling?"

"None the worse for wear," his brother assured him. "I think all the jewels are out, from one end or the other. Were you having the dream?"

Rónán didn't need to elaborate. Darragh knew what he meant. He nodded. "I haven't had that nightmare in years. It's different now, though."

"Let me guess. Now it's set in this realm, not yours?"

Darragh searched Rónán's face in the gloom. His brother was not betraying any visible emotion. But his question told Darragh a great deal more than the few simple words it took to ask it.

"What do you think has happened to change it?"

"The Hag told me it changes as it gets nearer. The closer it gets the more accurate it gets."

"That's been my experience with the Sight," Darragh agreed, certain he needed to get the full story of how Rónán came to be discussing such matters with the Brethren. "But I don't see how it can be true. I've been in prison for the past decade. I've sired no progeny." He smiled thinly. "Despite the attempts of several inmates to make me their bitch."

Rónán must have lost his sense of humor these last years. He didn't so much as crack a smile. "So is my dream just confused? Are the children yours?"

Rónán shook his head. "I'm pretty sure they're yours. They always are in my nightmares, anyway."

"Then we have nothing to worry about. At least not for a while yet. Even if I meet someone and impregnate her in the next day or two, we have a minimum of nine months to figure out a way to avoid this dreadful thing."

"Sure we have," Rónán said with a smile, but he seemed unconvinced.

"Odd though," Darragh said, "that after all this time the nightmare should come back."

"Yeah ... weird." Rónán stood up and walked to the window. He pulled the curtain back a fraction, revealing the soft post-dawn light outside. The faint sound of tyres on gravel reached them, rapidly fading as the car pulled away from the house. "Looks like Patrick is driving Kiva today. I'm going to risk going downstairs to see if we're alone. Do you know if Jack is still living next door?"

Darragh stared at Rónán for a moment, surprised by the question. It drove home to him how long they had been divided. How little they knew of each other's lives. "Of course, you wouldn't have heard."

Rónán let the curtain fall and turned back to look at him. In the gloom it was hard to make out his expression. "Heard what?"

He tossed back the covers and sat on the edge of the bed. "Jack was gaoled for his part in Hayley Boyle's kidnapping, Rónán. He was in Portlaoise with me."

Despite the dimness, his shock was clearly evident. "Jesus... is he all right?"

"He died about three years ago," Darragh told him. "Had a stroke. Collapsed right in the middle of the exercise yard. Dead before he hit the ground, they say."

Rónán was silent. "That's too bad," he said eventually. "Are you still in touch with Sorcha?"

"She died too, Rónán," he said, his brother's ignorance driving home the vast gulf between their experiences this past decade. "The lack of magic in this realm killed her. Aged her into an old woman in a matter of days."

"I'm sorry," Rónán said after a moment. "I know she was a friend of yours." He turned and headed for the door. He eased it open, apparently satisfied they were now alone in the house and no longer in danger of discovery. And, Darragh guessed, rather anxious to change the subject. "Let's see if we can find you a change of clothes. Kiva's manager keeps a few things in the guest room wardrobe up the hall. They should fit."

"Rónán ..."

"What?"

"I'm sorry about Jack. I know he was your friend. He proved to be a good friend to me, too."

"Not half as sorry as Jack is about it, I imagine," Rónán said, stepping out into the hall. He left the door open for Darragh to follow.

With a sigh, Darragh pushed himself off the bed and headed after Rónán, wishing they could share the *Comhroinn* so they would know what each other had suffered.

And wondering how many more awkward conversations like that were ahead of them until the *Comhroinn* was done.

CHAPTER 45

Brydie opened her eyes and lay in bed for a time, trying to figure out where she was. The last few days were such a blur. The room gave little hint of her location, other than the obvious realization she was no longer in her own reality. The elegant furniture, the expensive fabrics, the glass in the windows so clear it was like it wasn't there at all; the sterile cleanliness of the place and even the flowers artfully arranged in the fabulous porcelain vase on the carved wooden table by the door ... all screamed wealth and, more importantly, that she was no longer in her own realm.

After years trapped inside an amethyst, witnessing the machinations of Álmhath's court and then being stolen by Rónán of the Undivided and kept in his pocket for another seven years -to be brought out anytime he wanted someone to unburden himself to - Brydie figured she had just about seen everything.

She knew now that she had seen nothing, done nothing and that the idea of other realities was something she had never fully appreciated until she found herself in this one.

It wasn't just the curious girl who rubbed the jewel and set her free. That made sense really. Even in her own realm the way to summon a *djinni* was to polish the item in which he was confined. It was wasn't even that she went from wondering if she might be pregnant to giving birth to Darragh's children in a matter of hours. The spell that trapped her in the jewel had unravelled alarmingly, but not unexpectedly, as soon as she was released.

But the flying machine the *Matrarchaí* had sent for her. That was truly something.

As was the fact that she had gone from enchanted prisoner to exhausted mother overnight.

Brydie hadn't seen her babies. The efficient but not very talkative midwives overseeing her care had bustled them away almost as soon as they were born. She didn't remember much about the birth, either, other than she had delivered twins and that the babies had been cut from her womb to save them.

The doctor had explained it to her afterwards. Or at least, she'd tried to. Brydie really wasn't sure what she was saying. She spoke a foreign language to start with, and when she finally switched to a language Brydie could understand, the dialect seemed wrong and many of the words she used were unfamiliar.

In the end, one of the other women translated for her. The babies were in trouble, she'd said.

They'd been trying to fight their way out but she wasn't dilating fast enough for them to escape, and so they had to help them out. Brydie had tried to explain why she wasn't able to birth them naturally. Her babies had been waiting all this time, but her body hadn't known anything about being pregnant. It had no time to prepare. No time to do much of anything.

But they'd given her something for the pain, and then she'd fallen asleep. When she woke her body showed evidence of her recent - and exceedingly brief - pregnancy: she had a dressing just above her pubic bone covering the incision the doctor made to remove her babies, a needle in the back of her hand attached to a tube running clear fluid into her arm from a bag on a stand beside the bed, and a clutter of strange women smiling at her, congratulating her on giving birth to two beautiful baby girls.

Brydie couldn't decide how she felt about being a mother so unexpectedly. She'd not had time to feel the new life growing inside her. She'd not felt her babies kick, or move, or hummed lullabies to them in the womb so they would know the sound of her voice, as she had seen other expectant mothers do.

Her babies seemed to have come from nothing. Perhaps that explained why she felt nothing for them.

Come to us, mama, she imagined them calling to her. *Come to us now.*

The door opened and a woman entered carrying a tray. She smiled when she saw that Brydie was awake and put the tray down on the dresser under the window to then draw back the curtains, flooding the room with bright sunshine. She came to the bed and helped Brydie to sit up, checked the drip, rearranged her pillows and offered to help her out of bed and into the bathroom, speaking a language close enough to her own that she understood almost every word. Brydie declined the offer. Her bladder felt near to bursting, but she had no intention of relieving herself in a bath.

The woman brought Brydie the tray - a large wicker affair with legs that kept the weight off her sore body. She lifted a silver dome to reveal a plate piled with bacon, poached eggs, mushrooms, thick toast and what looked like fried potatoes next to a steaming cup of tea. There was a knife made of silver and another eating implement that looked like a tiny pitchfork, but no spoon. Perhaps they ate everything in this realm with their fingers.

Brydie accepted the food gratefully, though, not caring how she ate it, ravenous now she was awake. This would be the first food she'd eaten in years.

Nothing, she suspected, would ever taste quite so good again.

The midwife saw she was settled and then left the room as another woman came in. This one was tall and elegantly dressed in a grey suit whose tight-fitting skirt finished - scandalously - just above her knees. She smiled at Brydie, closed the door and came to sit at the foot of the bed to watch Brydie eat.

"You are consuming that food like you haven't been fed in a month," the woman remarked with smile.

"It's been far longer for than a month," Brydie told her through a mouthful of delicious bacon and mushrooms. "More like years."

"Did they not feed you, in your realm?"

The seemingly inane question told Brydie a great deal and reminded her sharply of where she was. These people were not random strangers doing her a kindness. This was the *Matrarchaí*. "I was trapped in an enchanted jewel. I never really got hungry until now."

The woman didn't bat an eyelid when Brydie told her about being trapped, accepting the statement as if it was a perfectly normal occurrence. She shouldn't be surprised. It was likely that Delphine had reported back to the *Matrarchaí* about the girl trapped in Anwen's necklace. Years ago, Anwen had told Delphine about her, but Delphine never came back to give Anwen any orders about what to do with her and then Ren had come for her and stolen the amethyst from Anwen's necklace, taking her out of the reach of the *Matrarchaí*. Ren had known where to find her, he told her later in one of their many one-sided conversations, because he'd taken the memory from Delphine when she died.

"Well, we shall have to see about a second helping, won't we? With two lusty babes to feed, you'll need to keep your strength up for when your milk comes in. Do you have a name?"

Odd that they hadn't asked her that before now. Not that there'd been much time, what with her sudden onset of labor. Good to know the babies were fine, although Brydie struggled to feel something for them other than mild relief to learn they had survived.

"My name is Brydie Ni'Seanan," she said.

"My name is Marie-Claire," the woman said, nodding, as if Brydie had simply confirmed something she already suspected. "I come from a realm not dissimilar to the one you hail from." She smiled, adding, "Although I have to say, my arrival here was not nearly so dramatic as yours. I'll see you have help adjusting while you're here."

"And where am I, exactly?"

"Cambria Castle estate near Dublin. *Eblana* you'd call it in your realm, I think."

"I don't mean that. I mean what realm is this?"

"It is... the true reality," Marie-Claire said with a shrug, as if the question puzzled her.

"Does that mean this is Ren's reality?" Brydie asked, wondering if she should be mentioning his name almost at the same time as she realized she didn't owe Ren Kavanaugh anything. "The one where Darragh has been trapped all this time?"

Marie-Claire hesitated for the briefest of moments. "Do you know where Darragh is?"

Brydie shook her head. She was about to say Ren came to this reality looking for him, and then thought better of it. *Why not say something? It's not as if you've ever actually met Ren in person.* "I have no idea were Darragh is. Do *you* know him?" Marie-Claire hadn't asked for any sort of explanation about who Ren or Darragh might be. She obviously knew.

"Only by reputation," Marie-Claire said. "We've not met. What do you know of his brother?"

"Not much," Brydie lied. "I've been kept in the dark these past few years. Literally."

This time Marie-Claire didn't even try to pretend she wasn't surprised. "You have spoken to Ren Kavanaugh recently?"

"Not spoken to him as such," she explained, as she bit into the delicious toast. "I couldn't talk to anybody trapped in that damn jewel, but he talked to me... now and then. Guess I made a good listener, what with not being able to answer back and all."

"And how is it you were trapped inside a jewel in the first place?" Marie-Claire asked. "What did you do to anger one of the *Djinn*?"

"I have no idea," she said with a shrug. "I was on my way to *Sí an Bhrú*, when Marcroy Tarth gave me the jewel. I think the *djinni* was already inside. After Darragh disappeared, Jamaspa - that was the *djinni* - trapped me in the jewel and kept asking me questions about Rónán and Darragh that I couldn't answer, then one day he stopped coming and I never saw him again."

Again, Marie-Claire didn't even blink at the oddity of Brydie's tale. "And how did you end up tucked behind a rock in this realm?"

"Well, let me see." She took a deep breath. "First I was in Darragh's room at *Sí an Bhrú*, and then Colmán stole me from Darragh's room and gave me to Anwen who told Torcán to hide the stone, so he took me to a goldsmith and had the amethyst set into a necklace for Anwen to wear at her wedding, and then Ren stole the jewel from her and took me back to his realm and I was there for ages, and then he was leaving to go to another realm because Darragh asked him to come, so he gave me to a *Leipreachán* to keep the jewel safe, but then Marcroy found the reality and took Trása prisoner, so Nika decided to pretend she was dead and smuggled her out of *Tír Na nÓg* and they came to this realm to find Pete and Logan, which probably means it's the same realm where Ren and Darragh are, too." She shrugged. "I think Toyoda shoved me down behind the rock at the stone circle because Ren made him swear not to lose the jewel while he was away and he was worried Trása might see it and take it from him."

Marie-Claire smiled. "That's quite a tale. And you managed it without taking a breath."

"Haven't needed to breathe much lately either."

"So, the babies you birthed. Darragh of the Undivided is the father?"

"I suppose he must be." Brydie frowned. Marie-Claire seemed to know an awful lot about Darragh. "Are the *Matrarchaí* here the same as the *Matrarchaí* from my realm?"

"You've heard of us?"

"I think my mother belonged to the *Matrarchaí*," Brydie said. "I know Anwen did. And so did Álmhath and Colmán. Ren thinks you're trying to kill the Faerie."

Marie-Claire didn't bat an eyelid at that, which Brydie found very interesting. "And what do you think, my dear?"

Brydie shrugged, interested that Marie-Claire hadn't denied the accusation. "I don't know."

"Are you fond of the *sídhe*?"

She may have been trapped for the past decade with nobody to talk to, but Brydie hadn't lost all her common sense. She could tell a trick question when she saw one. "I just spent years trapped by one of the *sídhe* in a lump of polished crystal, my lady," she said. "What do I owe the *sídhe* of this realm or any other?"

Marie-Claire smiled. "Good answer. Would you like to see your babies?"

Come to us. Come to us.

Brydie knew she should say yes. She knew the right thing to do was pretend some enthusiasm, but she could not bring herself to muster any interest at all. "Perhaps later," she said. "I'm still feeling very tired. They must have given me something to make me sleep after the babies were born. I don't remember much of anything about the past few days."

"Then you should rest," Marie-Claire said, patting Brydie's leg. "I shall send someone in to keep you company and instruct you on the way we do things in this realm. It can be a very daunting place without some guidance." She rose to her feet and smiled down at her. "You may not realize it, but you are very special to us, Brydie Ni'Seanan."

"Why?" Brydie asked, trying to imagine any reason why this woman whom she'd only just met would care about her.

"Because you are the mother of our future," Marie-Claire said, "and for that you will be honored above all others."

Brydie stared up at her, wondering if she was talking metaphorically or literally.

Marie-Claire must have guessed what she was thinking. "You have made Partition possible," she explained.

Brydie couldn't think of a single thing Marie-Claire could have said that would have surprised her more. "Oh... good."

Marie-Claire smiled. "And I am only telling you so you can appreciate what special children you have given us. You should be very proud."

"What about Ren and Darragh? Will you find them?" She wasn't feeling particularly proud. Just tired. And shocked. "Bring them here?"

"Darragh and Rónán? They are of no consequence now. We have their seed. You brought us our future. Have you thought of names?"

"For what?"

"For your daughters."

Brydie shook her head. "Not really."

"Do you mind if I name them?"

"If you like."

Marie-Claire smiled. "Then we shall name them Hope and Calamity. For that is truly what they are."

CHAPTER 46

One of the advantages of people thinking you were twenty-seven, rather than seventeen, is they acted like you were a real grown-up, which meant things that had bugged Hayley a week ago, like curfews and rules about what she could and couldn't watch on television, had miraculously disappeared.

That meant that when she returned to the house after a whole night away, instead of the fight she was expecting over where she'd been all night, nobody said a word. They didn't even wait around for her to get home. There was a note on the fridge from Kerry telling her there were leftovers inside. Her dad would be away until late taking Kiva to the set she was working on. Kerry was going into the city to take care of some errands, and then she was going to Kiva's place, and also wouldn't be back until late.

The house was unnaturally quiet. Hayley showered and changed and checked the leftovers. It proved to be a curry, which seemed a bit rich for breakfast, so she made herself some toast and a cup of tea and then sat down to eat at the kitchen table, all the while trying to make sense out of everything that had happened to her recently.

She was still reeling a little from her encounter with the *Matrarchaí*. They had their headquarters in Cambria Castle on the outskirts of town, although there was nothing about the building that indicated it was anything other than a well-kept historical landmark. Hayley had always thought the place had been converted into an expensive Bed and Breakfast, like lots of other Irish castles had been. Until the helicopter landed on the lawn, she hadn't realized just how extensive their operation was. Or what they were trying to achieve.

She still had no idea what the *Matrarchaí* were doing here in this reality, if indeed, they were doing anything at all. The only thing Hayley knew for certain about the *Matrarchaí* was that they had pulled out all the stops to help the strange girl who had appeared out of a jewel when Hayley rubbed it, and had asked for nothing in return, either of Hayley or the distressed young woman. Everyone she'd met at the castle was polite, if not very informative and, after assuring themselves she was well and not in need of further assistance, they'd let her leave without any strings attached. They had arranged a car to drop Hayley home and asked only one thing of her - she was to report to the *Matrarchaí* immediately if she saw either Ren or his brother in this realm.

Hayley had agreed quite happily to the condition. She thought it highly unlikely she would see either of them ever again, but if she did, she was sufficiently angry at Ren that she didn't care one jot what the *Matrarchaí* had planned for him.

But her encounter with the *Matrarchaí* filled her with more questions than she could find answers for and the one person who might be able to give her a straight answer, rather than the dramatic slant Kiva tended to place on things, was her stepmother, Kerry Boyle.

Kerry knew about the *Matrarchaí*, according to Kiva. She probably came from another reality herself. If anybody could tell Hayley the truth, it was Kerry.

The note said she was running some errands and then going to Kiva's. That was something that hadn't changed. Even before she'd left, barely a day went by when Kerry wasn't at Kiva's house. Her fridge note had said she wasn't planning on being home until late. Kiva would have any number of things Kerry needed to take care of, even if it was just preparing her evening meal and leaving it in the oven for when she got home from work.

With her father waiting around for Kiva on the set, that meant Kerry would be alone in Kiva's house and Hayley might have a chance to question Kerry in private. She needed answers, and she wasn't in the mood to wait around for Kerry to decide she was willing to talk to her.

If Kiva was to be believed, that day may never come.

The decision made, Hayley shoved her dishes in the sink, called a cab and ordered the cabbie to take her Kiva's house. The car dropped her at the gate and the driver took every last bit of cash she had in payment. Hayley still hadn't got her head around using Euros, but she didn't want to argue with the cabbie, so she handed over the exorbitant fare and then turned to face the wrought iron gates and high brick wall of Kiva's house. There were no paparazzi waiting outside, a sure sign Kiva wasn't home. They were probably parked near wherever she was filming for the day. Or perhaps they didn't follow her around anymore. Kiva wasn't on the cover of magazines as much as she used to be, Hayley had noticed, and she'd been able to drive herself to visit Hayley without being spotted. Maybe Kiva's star had dimmed over this past decade.

Maybe she'd been replaced by younger, fresher faces.

The gates were closed, as usual, and it was only as the cab was pulling away that Hayley realized she didn't have any way to open them. She'd had her own remote before the accident - every member of the family had one - but she'd not seen it since she was run over. Hayley looked around in surprise... it had happened in almost this exact spot.

There was no evidence on the street, of course, of the accident. Murray Symes had run her down over a decade ago. There were no bloodstains on the bitumen, no skid marks on the road. The trees lining the street were taller now and there was no sign this had ever been the place where someone's life had had been changed forever by the thoughtless act of an impatient man in a silver BMW.

She turned back and stared at the buzzer by the gate, debating whether or not to ring it. If Kerry was back from her shopping trip, she'd answer it and let her in, Hayley didn't doubt that for a second. But it would also give her stepmother advance warning that Hayley was on the way to see her. She didn't want Kerry to have time to get her story straight or be prepared for whatever Hayley might ask her. She wanted the truth and was damn sure she didn't want Kerry to have time to think up any convenient lies.

Fortunately, she knew another way into Kiva's house. There was a gate connecting Jack's property with Kiva's. Although it wasn't Jack's house any longer. He'd died in prison, her father told her when they were filling her in on what had happened while she was away. He'd had his parole revoked for his involvement in her kidnapping, they told her. Hayley didn't know whether to feel guilty about that or not. Jack had not done anything wrong. Not really. But if he had helped Ren send her to another reality, then he was instrumental in the mess in which she now found herself.

That made it hard to feel sorry for him, even if dying in prison seemed a bit excessive in the way of punishments for his part in her predicament.

The house next door had a new front fence and a children's swing set in the front garden, but the gate was unlocked. Hayley slipped into the shadow of the trees bordering the properties and made her way along the fence until she came to the overgrown gate, only to find it padlocked.

Cursing, she kicked the gate in frustration. The boards broke away with the force of her kick. Curious, Hayley knelt down on the loamy ground and discovered that although the gate was secure, the new neighbours had built up a layer of mulch under the trees which over time had rotted the wooden gate away at the base.

A few more kicks and there was a hole large enough for her to wriggle through. Hayley removed her jacket, balled it up and shoved it through ahead of her and then wriggled, commando style, under the gate on her belly. The ground was damp and she was covered in wet leaves by the time she got through, but she brushed them off, put her jacket back on, and figured that if she kept it zipped up she didn't look any the worse for wear.

Hayley glanced at the gate and realized there was no way to conceal her point of entry, and then she realized there was really no need for concealment. Once she had her conversation with Kerry, a mere broken gate and hole under the fence would be minor considerations.

She walked across the lawn to the terrace and then stopped when she saw a movement through the kitchen window. Although it had only been a shadow, it was too tall to be Kerry. Maybe Kiva had houseguests. Maybe her manager, Jon, was staying over, as he sometimes did when he was visiting from Los Angeles.

Hayley swore under her breath. There going to be no grand confrontation about alternate realities if Kiva's manager was lolling about the house.

She crouched down and moved closer to the window, this time taking care not to be seen. If Jon were in the house, she would make her way back through the hole under the gate and confront Kerry some other time. Then again, best to find out who was in the house, first, before she decided to leave. She was out of money and if Kerry wasn't here, perhaps Jon would loan her some cash to get a cab.

Very slowly, so as not to attract attention, Hayley rose to peek over the windowsill. She could hear voices, male voices, which meant Jon might be meeting with someone or taking one of his endless calls on the speaker phone.

When she finally managed to raise her eyes over the lip of the sill, she discovered Jon wasn't alone. There were two men inside, although they seemed too young for either one of them to be Kiva's manager. She watched for a while, wondering at the identities of the men. They had their backs to her. Whoever they were, they were making themselves at home in Kiva's kitchen as they talked in low voices, so Hayley couldn't make out their words.

And then one of them turned and she saw herself staring at a hauntingly familiar - yet older - face. She gasped as the other man turned to answer the first and realized he and the first man were identical.

Hayley dropped below the level of the sill, unable to breathe.

Ren is here. Ren and his brother, Darragh.

Only time for them had not stopped. They were grown men.

And they were hiding in Kiva's house.

Did she know? Had she invited them here? *Isn't Darragh supposed to be in jail?*

Hayley's heart was racing. She didn't know what to do. She'd promised Marie-Claire she would call her if she saw Ren or Darragh.

But wouldn't that mean betraying them? What did it matter anyway? She didn't owe Darragh anything and Ren had ruined her life.

But he was here, and while the *Matrarchaí* people seemed nice enough, they were strangers.

Besides, Ren knew the way through the rifts between realities. If she betrayed him to the *Matrarchaí*, how would she have him redress the wrong he'd done when he sent her through a rift to the *Tuatha Dé Danann*?

But still...

Hayley reached into her jacket for her phone and turned it on. The last number she'd dialed was the *Matrarchaí*. The digits sat there in the recent-calls screen, taunting her. With a single call they could be here.

Would they make Ren pay? *Do I really want to make him pay?*

Whatever she did, Hayley realized she needed to talk to him. She needed to know what had happened to her. Why he had left her there and never come back for her. Why he'd ruined her life. Hayley glanced down at the phone. It all came down to that, really.

Fuck you, Ren Kavanaugh. You ruined my life.

CHAPTER 47

"Annad? A word?"

Pete glanced up from watching the escape drama unfold on the television news to find Annad's wife standing at the door to the kitchen looking mightily displeased that her houseguests had doubled in number while she was asleep.

The psychologist spared Pete a pained look as he stood up from the sofa and went to speak to his wife.

"She doesn't look happy," Trása remarked.

"She'll get over it. How are you feeling?"

Trása shrugged. "Better now I've had something to eat."

Trása had spent quite some time earlier this morning in the bathroom throwing up, a reaction, she claimed, to the potion Nika had tricked her into drinking to fake her death so they could escape *Tír Na nÓg* in the ninja reality. She still looked a little pale, even though she claimed to be feeling better.

"Well, say something if you start to feel ill again," he ordered as they turned back to the news. They had been watching for most of the morning, but had learned little more than they'd known when Nika first stumbled across the bulletin. There had been an incident in Portlaoise, a prisoner named Ciarán mac Connaught was dead, and someone - who they knew to be Darragh, thanks to Annad's contacts - may or may not have escaped. "We don't need any heroics, right now."

"I will," she promised.

Annad had made several calls to ascertain what he could about the events of the previous day, although he had to be careful. If he seemed overly interested by making too many calls, he risked awkward questions about what his interest in the case was.

They now knew Darragh was out of the prison, and the only possible explanation was that Ren had managed to wane in and out with his brother. Now they had to find them.

And then there was Annad's wife to deal with.

She'd been up late, delivering twin girls by the sound of it, so it was mid-morning before Stella appeared again. When she realized her two guests had turned into four - thank God she hadn't seen Echo or Toyoda yet - she took Annad aside to discuss it with him.

They were gone for quite some time.

When Annad returned to the kitchen, Stella was with him and appeared to be in a less belligerent mood. He introduced Trása and Nika as friends of Pete and Logan. She eyed the two young women curiously for a time, before offering to make tea. Pete didn't know what Annad had said to his wife, but for the time being, she seemed to accept this unwelcome invasion of her home, albeit begrudgingly.

"Your husband tells us you are a midwife," Nika said, as Stella poured the boiling water over a teabag in a mug with "*World's Greatest Dad*" printed on it.

"A midwife?" Stella asked, glancing at her husband with a raised eyebrow. She squeezed the teabag with more force than was absolutely necessary and tossed it into the sink.

"Stella is an obstetrician," Pete corrected. Winning Stella over was not going to be accomplished by belittling her years of hard work to become a specialist in her field.

"What does that mean?"

"I'm a doctor. I specialise in caring for women during pregnancy, childbirth and the recovery period afterwards," Stella explained, leaning on the bench to sip her tea.

"How is that different to a midwife?"

Stella looked at her husband. "Is she for real?"

"Nika's trying to be funny," Pete explained, shooting Trása a warning look. Nika wouldn't understand the danger here, but Trása would. "She's not trying to offend you, Stella. She's just not very good at it."

Fortunately, Trása realized how awkward this was about to get. She turned to Annad with a cheery smile. "Would it be all right if we watched the news on the TV in the front room, Dr Semaj?"

"Be my guest," Annad said, looking a little too relieved. As Trása all but dragged Nika out of the kitchen, he glanced around with a frown. "Where's Logan?"

"He went for a walk," Pete lied. Actually, Logan was out in the backyard trying to summon the pixie and the *Leipreachán* to see if they'd had any luck locating Ren or Darragh. He didn't want to imagine what Stella's reaction would be if he mentioned that.

"Will you be heading into the hospital later?" Annad asked his wife.

"Are you trying to get rid of me, dear?" she asked with a small smile. "Have you got even more friends I've never met on their way over?"

"No... it's just you said you delivered twins last night. You usually check on your patients."

Stella shook her head. "The mother isn't one of my patients. I was covering for Anthony." She took a sip of her tea. "I think I need to rethink my practice demographic. All I see are boring, nice, middle-class couples with mortgages. Anthony gets helicopters sent for him."

Annad's eyes widened in shock. "You never said they sent a helicopter for you."

"I did the caesarean in a private clinic better equipped than most major public hospitals. Maybe if you'd come to bed last night at a reasonable time, I might have told you."

"Are there many private clinics in Dublin?" Pete asked. He didn't really care one way or another, but even though she was being civil, Stella obviously still mad at her husband, and by extension

480

him and his friends. Long experience with interrogating angry people had taught Pete the easiest way to get people to calm down was to encourage them to talk about themselves and feign interest in their answers long enough to disarm their rage.

"A few," Stella said with a shrug. "I thought I knew all of them, actually. This one was in Cambria Castle. I'd never heard of it until last night."

"I thought that was a hotel now," Annad said.

"Well, if it's a hotel, they must have an interesting clientele. You should have seen this place. There was *nothing* they didn't have in there. They even had a POC ultrasound unit. I've been trying to get the hospital to invest in one of those for months."

Pete had no idea what that was, but Stella was warming to her topic and her anger seemed to be fading as she spoke of something she was obviously very passionate about.

"POC ultrasound? What does that do?" he asked as the phone rang again.

Annad hurried off to answer it before his wife could pick it up, leaving Pete to learn more about delivering babies that he ever cared to know.

"POC is an acronym for Point of Care. Essentially, a POC ultrasound unit lets you guide the needle when you're administering an epidural, so you know precisely where you're injecting the anesthetic."

"Sounds useful," he said, acutely aware that he hadn't stepped foot in this technology-filled realm for a decade and had no idea what innovation or inventions were now part of daily life.

Stella was nobody's fool. She could tell he was humouring her. "You've never been in a delivery room, have you?"

He smiled. "Does it show?"

"I've never met a man whose wife wasn't screaming or about to start crowning who gave a pig's fart about obstetric equipment."

"I can appreciate that."

"So why do you care?"

I don't, was Pete's instinctive answer, but he was able to stifle the urge to say it. "Well, if I ever have kids..."

"You won't be having kids," Stella pointed out, as she took another sip of her tea. "Your wife... your significant other, or whatever the hell they'll be calling it next, will be doing all the hard work. You just get to stand around trying to look supportive, which, in my experience, is something most men aren't very good at faking."

He was never going to win this argument, so he smiled and threw his hands up in surrender. "Point taken."

"Here's something else you might be interested in knowing," she said, looking like someone ready to deliver a lecture. "More often than not, it's the father who asks about pain relief in the delivery room before the mother does. Why is that, do you think?"

Logan saved Pete from having to answer such a loaded question. He burst into the kitchen and then stopped abruptly when he realized Stella was there. "'Morning Doctor D," he said. "Good sleep-in?"

"Yes, thank you."

"Ah... Pete... got a minute?"

"Gladly," Pete said, smiling apologetically at Stella. "Will you excuse me?"

She shrugged, clearly not caring one way or the other.

Pete followed Logan outside to the back garden. There was a paved area next to the house with a large stainless-steel barbeque and an outdoor setting. Beyond that was a well-kept lawn bordered by flowerbeds filled with Easter lilies, amaryllis, roses, chrysanthemums and wildflowers. It surprised Pete a little. He never pegged Annad for the gardening or barbequing sort.

"What's up?" he asked, as soon as the back door closed and they were out of Stella's hearing.

"Toyoda's back," Logan said. "And you're not going to believe what he's got to tell us."

Toyoda was waiting for them with Echo, who was flitting about like an angry bee. Just from the way Toyoda was standing, Pete knew something was wrong.

"You found them." It wasn't a question.

"Aye," Toyoda said, "I be doin' as ye asked."

"Did you speak to Ren? Did you tell him where we are? Is he okay? What about Darragh?"

"Slow down, Pete," Logan advised. "You need to hear all of this."

"The pixie be finding them first," Toyoda said, wringing his hands like a worried old woman. "I be havin' something to check on at first. While I be... doing the checking... she appears out of nowhere, squawking, *Undivided gone with the evil ones, Undivided gone with the evil ones.*"

As soon as he uttered the words, the pixie began to chant frantically, "Undivided are gone with the evil ones. Undivided are gone with the evil ones," as she flitted around their heads in a panic.

"What's she on about?" Pete asked Logan, shooing her away from his face.

Logan didn't answer, letting Toyoda tell the story. "I be following Echo to the place where Renkavana and his brother be."

"You found them?"

Toyoda nodded. "They be in a big house, Lord Pete. A huge house. A mansion. A -"

"Okay, I get the picture, what happened when you found them? Did you talk to them?"

The *Leipreachán* shook his head. "There be no opportunity. The *Matrarchaí* be getting to them first. They be bound and gagged and pushed into one of those carriages with the growling monster inside."

"The *what*?"

"He means a car," Logan explained. "He thinks the engine is a growling monster."

"But why do you think it's the *Matrarchaí*? I mean... how would they know where to find them? Are you sure it wasn't the Gardaí? Men in uniforms?

Flashing blue lights?" That the Gardaí had tracked down the escapee from Portlaoise made more sense than the idea the *Matrarchaí* had located Ren and Darragh, particularly given the effort the authorities would be expending to find a dangerous escaped prisoner.

"I be seeing Delphine," Toyoda announced. "That's how I be knowing it be the *Matrarchaí*."

Pete stared at Logan. "Delphine is dead. We burned her body."

"Alternate realities, Pete," Logan reminded him. "It might not be our Delphine."

"They not be calling her that," Toyoda said. "They be calling her Mother. But she be the same Delphine who killed the *Youkai* in our realm. And she be the one driving off in the monster carriage with Renkavana and his brother."

"Did you follow them?" Pete asked, still trying to digest the information that the *eiléféin* of the woman he'd grown up loving like a mother - right up until she tossed him and his brother through a rift with plans to murder them - was here in this realm and that they'd have to confront her.

There was no question in Pete's mind that there would be a confrontation. If the *Matrarchaí* had Ren and Darragh, what else could they do?

Toyoda nodded. "Aye. They be taking them to this place." The little *Leipreachán* fished a crumpled piece of paper from one of his many pockets. "It be a likeness of the building I be finding while I be lookin' around. I not be knowin' exactly where it be, though. Do ye think ye can find it? Do ye know where this place be?"

Pete took the paper from Toyoda and smoothed it out. It turned out to be a glossy, three-fold brochure. The kind they have racks of in airports and train stations. He stared at it for a moment and then closed his eyes, wondering at the bizarre coincidences that plagued them in this reality and if they really *were* coincidences or this was fate dealing them a hand they had no choice but to play.

"Show me," Logan said.

Pete handed him the brochure and smiled down at the *Leipreachán*. "You did good, Toyoda. We can definitely find them from that."

Logan studied the brochure. "Cambria Castle," he said. "For the best in fine dining, elegant luxury, private fishing and hunting. They've taken them to a *resort*?"

"You don't know the half of it," Pete said. Logan hadn't been in the kitchen just now, so he hadn't heard the discussion with Stella about the private clinic where she'd delivered two baby girls last night.

"If that be all ye needin' me for, can I be leavin' now?" Toyoda asked. "I still need to be checkin' up on the thing I be looking for."

"Knock yourself out," Pete told him distractedly. The *Leipreachán* winked out of existence, leaving Pete and Logan with Echo who was still buzzing about chanting "Undivided gone with the evil ones. Undivided gone with the evil ones."

"We have to go rescue them, don't we?" Logan asked, as if it was even a question.

Pete nodded. "'Fraid so."

"Any ideas how we even get past the front door, let alone get them out of there with the Gardaí hunting for them, and then back to a rift where we have enough magic to get home?"

"Actually, I do. The front door part, at any rate." He held out his hand. "Echo, come here and shut up for a moment."

The pixie, remarkably, did as he asked and landed on his palm with a soft, "shut up for a moment, shut up for a moment," as if she just couldn't help herself from getting in the last word.

"I need you to be good," he told the pixie sternly. "I need you to meet someone and be nice to them. If I give you a treat, can you do that?"

Logan looked at him with a worried expression. "What are you going to do, Pete?"

"Introduce Echo to the inimitable Dr Stella Delany."

"What the fuck do you want to do that for?"

"Because last night Stella delivered two bouncing baby girls." Pete ever so gently covered his palm with his other hand so Echo couldn't escape. She had the ability to wane herself somewhere else if she thought about it, but pixies weren't over-endowed with intelligence or the wit to formulate an escape plan.

"I know that, but -"

"In a private clinic at Cambria Castle."

Logan was silent for a moment. "Well, that changes things somewhat, doesn't it?"

Pete nodded. "So, let's start our assault on the front door by showing Stella the Faerie we captured at the bottom of her garden."

CHAPTER 48

Teagan knocked on the door of the room in the guest wing where the young woman who'd arrived in the middle of the night by helicopter was resting and waited for permission to enter.

If there was one thing Teagan had learned about being in the *Matrarchaí*, it was that you never, *ever* walked into a room in this place without permission.

A voice called "Enter", so she opened the door and discovered a young woman with long, dark hair lying on a hospital bed. Although the décor here was just as elegant and expensive as the rest of the castle, this wasn't part of the hotel, Teagan knew. In fact, in seven years, she'd never been allowed in this part of the building before.

"Mother sent me to look after you," she announced, as she closed the door. The young woman looked at her blankly. "Mother sent me to look after you," Teagan repeated in Gaelish. She'd been here long enough to speak the language fluently, but she'd had to learn it the hard way. In this realm without magic, there was no opportunity to learn quickly through the *Comhroinn*.

"I'm fine, really," Brydie said.

Mother had told Teagan the girl's name and that she was new to this magic-less realm. She would need help adjusting to life here.

Teagan well remembered how that felt. "Is there anything you want?"

The girl shook her head and then she seemed to change her mind. "Actually, there is something."

"Name it."

"I need to pee so badly," Brydie confessed, "but there is nowhere to go here."

"You have your own bathroom," Teagan pointed out and then she smiled as she realized the problem. "Come on, let me help you up and I'll show you how it works. They're insane in this realm. They using drinking water to flush everything away, but you'll love having hot showers, I can promise you that."

"Thank you."

Brydie was quite sore, apparently. She'd given birth by caesarean and it would be weeks before she would be back to normal. Teagan helped her to the bathroom without tangling herself in the drip line, wheeling the unit as Brydie shuffled slowly alongside. Teagan showed her how everything worked in the bathroom, and then waited in the room with the door open for Brydie to finish. Once she was done, she helped her back to the bed, rearranged the drip and then straightened her blankets for her.

"Thank you so much," Brydie said with a sigh.

Poor girl, I wonder how long she's been holding on? "That's okay."

"My name is Brydie."

"I know," she said taking a seat at the foot of the bed. "They told me. My name is Teagan. Mother says I'm to show you how to get by in this world." She smiled. "It takes some getting used to."

"I'm still getting used to daylight," Brydie said with a sigh. "Everything seems different when you're not looking at it through an amethyst wall."

Teagan had no idea what Brydie was talking about and decided not to inquire. That was something else she'd learned here. Uninvited curiosity was frowned upon. If the *Matrarchaí* thought you needed to know something, they would tell you, otherwise it was none of your business.

"Oh, and I can take you to see your babies, if you feel up to the walk. Apparently it's supposed to be good for you to start moving about."

"Maybe later," Brydie said.

Teagan was surprised by that. She thought the new mother would be champing at the bit to see her babies. She'd expected to have to hold Brydie back, but the young woman seemed disinterested. Maybe she was suffering post-partum depression. Or perhaps it was pain. They'd cut the babies out of her, after all.

"Do you live here?" Brydie asked.

"In this place? Or in this realm?" Clearly this girl came from somewhere other than this world, so Teagan figured she was safe asking that.

"Are you not from this realm?"

"I was brought here from another realm about seven years ago."

Brydie studied her for a moment with a thoughtful expression. "And your name is Teagan, you say?"

"Yes... why? Is that a problem?"

Brydie nodded, as if she had worked something out for herself that Teagan wasn't privy to. "I suppose ... makes sense, really. I mean they always thought it was the *Matrarchaí* who took you."

"What are you talking about?"

"You are the Empress Teagan, aren't you? Your sister is Isleen. Your mother is Wakiko."

Teagan stared at her in shock. "How could you possibly know that?"

"I've just come from your realm," Brydie informed her. "Ren told me about you."

It was as if the air had suddenly been sucked out of the room. For a moment, Teagan couldn't breathe. "*You* know Renkavana?"

Brydie nodded and then she shrugged. "Kind of. He talked to me a lot when I was... well, in your realm. Did you ever catch up with Isleen?"

"What do you mean?"

"Didn't you know? Isleen broke through the bonds Ren put on Delphine's memories and went rift running looking for you. I suppose it must have only been a couple of weeks ago, now, but I really have no idea. Time was... different where I've been." She stopped talking and looked at Teagan with concern. "I'm guessing, from the look on your face, that you didn't know any of this."

Teagan shook her head, almost speechless with shock. "They keep promising me they'll go back for her when we're twenty-one."

"Why twenty-one?"

Teagan shrugged. "I don't know. How is she? How's my mother?"

"I couldn't say, Teagan. I'm sorry, but I only know what Ren told me about you and your sister. I never actually saw anyone other than Ren the whole time I was in your realm. Well, eventually I saw the *Leipreachán*. And Trása. And Nika, too, come to think of it, and some of the *Youkai* in *Tír Na nÓg*. But really, that was just toward the end before we came to this realm."

"Trása is in this realm *now*?" Teagan wasn't actually under instructions to report her conversations with Brydie to the *Matrarchaí*, but she had a feeling they'd want to know something like that. "Why did they come here? Are they looking for Isleen? Is she here, too?" That possibility made her almost giddy. Teagan rarely admitted, even to herself, how much she missed her twin. But the thought that Isleen might be stuck in this realm with no chance to use her magic and no way of coping without it ...

That was something else Teagan had figured out over the years. It took her a long time to understand why, when in a magical realm she had the power to flatten buildings if the mood took her, they had kept her here where she could do nothing and learn nothing about her power. Teagan had eventually realized it suited the *Matrarchaí* for people like her to be rendered powerless.

In her own realm, had she stayed there, they would have welcomed her ability and used her to further their ambition to strip as many realities as possible of their *sídhe* populations. But here in this realm, in the very bosom of the *Matrarchaí*, in the place where the true power resided, the *Matrarchaí* kept a very tight leash on potential powerhouses like Teagan. Had the *Matrarchaí* been successful in bringing Isleen through the rift, the same night they stole Teagan from the Edo palace, it might have been different. Twins provided their own innate set of checks and balances. But without Isleen here, with no way of controlling both of them, or knowing what her twin was up to, the *Matrarchaí* never fully trusted Teagan, despite the promises they had made to her the first day they brought her here. By now, of course, she'd realized they had no intention of sharing their innermost secrets with her, just to have her sister turn up someday and entice her away, or worse, entice her to join the *Matrarchaí*'s enemies.

Teagan understood their reasoning, she even sympathised with it. But that didn't alter the fact that she had been denied the chance to become a great sorcerer because her twin sister hadn't made it through the rift with her.

"I'm sorry, Teagan. I don't know where she is," Brydie explained.

"She'd know the way here," Teagan said. "When Mother finally unlocked the memories in my mind, I knew immediately how to get here through a rift. I even knew who to contact when I got here and how to do it. Do you suppose she came here?"

"Surely they would have said something to you if your sister had arrived in this realm?" Brydie said.

Teagan nodded. "Of course they would." She wished she felt as confident of that as she sounded.

Before Brydie could ask anything further, the door opened and a smiling face appeared around the door. "Ah! There you are," the woman said. She was an older woman, with a round face and a warm smile, wearing a nurse's uniform. "Not interrupting anything important, am I?"

"We were just talking," Teagan assured her. "Come in."

"I just came to tell you the babies are ready when you are," the woman announced from the door. "A pair of fine wee babes they are, too. Take your time and don't strain anything. Teagan can show you the way."

Brydie smiled, but it looked quite forced. "Be right there!"

The door closed and Teagan turned, expecting to see Brydie throwing back the covers. But she hadn't moved. In fact, she looked quite pale.

"Are you okay?"

Brydie's eyes welled up with tears. "Can you keep a secret, Teagan?"

"Sure."

"I don't want the babies." She looked panic-stricken but almost relieved to admit such a thing out loud.

Teagan wasn't sure what to say. She was barely twenty, hadn't even thought about having her own children yet, and Brydie looked no older than she was. Far from being shocked by her admission, she was actually quite sympathetic. "I understand, but maybe once you see them..."

Brydie wiped away her tears, and sniffed, as if she was angry at herself for being so emotional. "There's something not right with them, Teagan. I know it."

"Ana just said they were fine."

But Brydie was adamant. "They're not fine. They were caught in an enchanted jewel for ten years and went from nothing to being born in a matter of hours."

"That's magic for you," Teagan said with a shrug.

"But this realm has no magic, Teagan," she reminded her. "So tell me, how can that be?"

Teagan had no answer for that.

"Do you know, they didn't cry."

"What?"

"The babies. When they were born. Neither of them made a sound."

"That might have been because of the drugs they gave you," Teagan suggested, uncomfortable with the whole discussion. What would she know about having babies?

"It wasn't the drugs. There's something not right with them, Teagan."

"Tell you what," she said, "why don't we go and see them? Then we can find out, one way or another."

"Do you believe me?"

Teagan thought about that for a moment before she shrugged. "I don't *disbelieve* you."

"That's a start," Brydie said with a sigh. "Will you come with me?"

"Sure," she said, "I like babies."

"I wish I did," Brydie said.

The nursery was a short way up the hall in a room so well set up, Teagan figured there must be a lot of babies born here. It made sense, she supposed. Babies were the *Matrarchaí*'s stock-in-trade. It shouldn't surprise her to find they were well equipped to cope with a couple of newborns.

"Ah, there you are," the cheerful, tubby nurse overseeing the nursery pronounced as they opened the door. Teagan followed Brydie into the nursery and looked around with interest. It looked like any hospital nursery, with mobiles hanging from the ceiling, nursery rhyme characters painted on the walls and a couple of unoccupied neonatal humidicribs parked in the corner, obviously not needed for Brydie's babies.

The babies were not in the clear plastic cribs hospitals favored, however. In the center of the room was a massive wooden cradle carved with elaborate Celtic knotwork, inlaid with softly glowing mother-of-pearl. Teagan studied the cradle with interest.

"Solid oak, it is," the nurse informed them with a smile. "The wee babes should fit in there together for a while yet."

"It's beautiful," Brydie said, looking a little bemused.

"Aye, it is. That mother-of-pearl was brought up from the very depths of the ocean by the *mara-warra*. It was a gift from a faerie queen centuries ago, according to legend. It's rocked many a generation of twins to sleep since then, I don't doubt."

"I thought we hated Faeries," Teagan said.

"That we do, lassies," the nurse agreed, and then she turned to Brydie, "but it doesn't mean they can't turn out the odd craftsman when it suits them. My name is Ana, by the way. I'll be helping you with the bairns until you're properly on your feet again."

"Er... thank you," Brydie answered.

"Have you given them names yet?"

"Marie-Claire named them. Hope and Calamity."

Ana said nothing for a fraction of a second and then she smiled. "Well, Mother knows what she's about. They're lovely names."

Hope, maybe, Teagan thought. *But Calamity... really?*

"You can come closer," Ana said, as neither Teagan nor Brydie made any attempt to move further into the room. "They won't bite."

Using the wheeled drip stand to support herself, Brydie took a step closer. Teagan couldn't believe how reluctant she was to see her children. Surely she was a little bit curious?

"You'll be able to spend more time with them once the doctor's been to check on your stitches and you get that drip out. She's already rung to say she's on her way, so that should be sometime after dinner. Then we can bring them to you and you can try feeding them yourself. It's important for you to begin the bonding process."

Teagan glanced at Brydie and realized that far from looking forward to having her babies with her, she was terrified by the idea. "I'll stay with you," she offered.

Brydie shot her a grateful look and then turned to stare at the cradle. "It's very... impressive."

"An impressive cradle for some impressive babes," Ana said. She fussed over the cradle a little more, smoothing the mattress out and arranging the blankets, and then she stepped back and allowed them to come closer.

A step behind Brydie, Teagan followed her toward the cradle. She heard Brydie gasp before she saw the babies for herself. Brydie covered her mouth with her hand as Teagan stepped up beside her, wondering at the horrified look on Brydie's face, and then she looked into the cradle and understood why.

The babies weren't human.

There were human-shaped and they looked the size of day-old babies, but they had distinctly pointed Faerie ears, a shock of dark hair and when one of them opened her mouth a little, she spied a mouthful of tiny, pointed teeth.

"What... what are they?" Brydie gasped.

"The future," Ana replied.

"I never gave birth to these... monsters."

"I'd not be saying that in their hearing," Ana warned. "Whatever you might think of the bairns, lass, they are your flesh and blood. You are their mother. You are required to love them."

Brydie shook her head. Tears streamed down her cheeks. "They're not even human."

"Of course they're not. What good would human babies be to us at this juncture?"

Brydie didn't answer. Instead, she turned and struggled to flee the room, dragging the drip stand in her wake. Teagan stared down at the babies for a moment longer and then looked up at Ana, feeling the need to apologize for Brydie's odd behavior.

"She'll come around."

"She'd better," Ana said, rather ominously, and then she turned to attend to something over by the change table near the window.

Tell her to come back. Teagan let out a yelp as the thought filled her mind and she realized it had come from one of the babies. They were both staring up at her with creepy, disconcerting, blue on blue eyes.

"Did you say something, dear?"

Teagan shook her head, transfixed by the babies in the cradle. *Tell our mother to come back.*

Teagan broke away from the glamouring effect of the babies' stare and fled the room almost as fast as Brydie had done, more frightened by those eyes and the tiny voices in her head than by anything she had ever before experienced in her entire life.

CHAPTER 49

Ren woke to the familiar, and unwelcome, *Brionglóid Gorm* headache. For a time he kept his eyes closed, knowing that the pain of forcing them open and facing the light would be intense. But then he heard someone groaning and remembered Darragh, and knew he was going to have to open his eyes eventually, and that without magic, the headache would take a long, long time to fade.

He blinked painfully as he manoeuvred himself into a sitting position - no mean feat with his hands tied behind him - and discovered Darragh was lying opposite him on the floor of an empty room, just coming to. His face was powdered with the telltale blue dust of the *Brionglóid Gorm*. Ren supposed he must look the same.

There were tall, diamond-paned windows on one wall with no curtains. Daylight streamed through the windows onto the polished floorboards, taking the chill off the air. Ren glanced around, trying to determine where they were, but other than high ceilings, cream walls and a boarded-up fireplace, there was nothing in this room that gave him any obvious hint as to where they were being held.

The only thing he knew for certain was that they were still in a realm without magic and that Hayley had betrayed them.

He should have known something was wrong when she appeared in the kitchen window of Kiva's house, waving and smiling. Hayley looked exactly the same as she had when he'd last seen her a decade ago. It made him feel old to realize she was still a child and he was a grown man, a decade full of dark and unwelcome memories creating an unbridgeable gulf between them.

Hayley had let herself in and began chatting away as if there was nothing the least bit odd about Ren - who'd been missing for a decade - and Darragh, the escaped convict, having breakfast in Kiva's kitchen. In hindsight, he realized she wasn't chatting to them... she was babbling. She asked how they were, what they'd been up to, but didn't draw breath long enough for them to get a word in, and kept up the conversation for so long Darragh had thrown him a look that Ren just knew meant: *Seriously... we gave up the last ten years of our lives for* this *girl.*

There had been a reason for Hayley's nervousness. She was stalling. Ren realized that too late. By then the *Matrarchaí* were at the door and someone was blowing *Brionglóid Gorm* in his face and then he woke up here, tied hand and foot, with no idea how he was going to get himself or his brother out of this predicament and back to their own realm.

Not that their own realm was really the place for them, either. In their own realm the Hag was waiting for him to murder a couple of innocent children. Besides, the Druids believed he and Darragh were dead and would likely kill them if they turned up out of the blue, and destroyed everything they believed about magic by still being alive when they should have died ten years ago.

"How's your head?"

Darragh groaned in response, summing up exactly how Ren felt. He managed to get himself upright and looked about the room, frowning. "Any idea where we are?"

Ren shook his head and instantly regretted the movement. "There's no magic. I'm pretty sure we're still in my old realm." He glanced around the room, wishing it would give him some hint as to where they were. "I'm guessing it's the *Matrarchaí.*"

He'd had time to explain some of what he know about the *Matrarchaí* to his brother, but not all of it.

"How did they find us?"

"Kiva told them. Maybe Kerry. Maybe we weren't as clever as we thought we were, hiding in Kiva's house."

Darragh nodded slowly, obviously suffering from a headache similar to Ren's. "I have to admit, I did think hiding out in your mother's place was somewhat... risky."

Ren gave his brother a thin smile. "Nice of you to say risky, when I know you really want to say insane."

"I've learned to be tactful, these past few years. It was something of a survival strategy in prison."

Ren didn't want to think about what Darragh had suffered in prison. Particularly as it was his fault. Better to change the subject. They could talk about what Darragh had had to do to survive some other time. If they survived this latest calamity. "Why didn't they kill us, do you suppose?"

"Do the *Matrarchaí* usually kill people? I thought you said they were only targeting the *sídhe* races."

"We are *sídhe*."

"We are Druid."

"No, actually we're *sídhe*," Ren said, as he realized how much he needed to tell his brother. "Almost pure, believe it or not."

Darragh shook his head with a grimace. "We look nothing like the *sídhe*."

"Selective breeding. That's why the *Matrarchaí* are midwives, you know. They mix the right bloodlines and then they're on hand to smother any babe with a hint of *sídhe* features. Eventually, if you do that for long enough, you get almost pure *sídhe* that look human."

Darragh was not convinced. "But our mother was a Druid. Our father was -"

"Marcroy Tarth."

"Was *who*?"

"Marcroy Tarth. He's our father."

"Did you hit your head when they knocked us out?"

Ren smiled. "Don't worry. It took me a while to get my head around the idea, too."

"But... but... are you *serious*? *Marcroy*? The same Marcroy..."

"The one and only."

Darragh's disbelief might have been comical, had not the pain in Ren's head robbed him almost entirely of his sense of humor.

"Does he know?"

"Oh, yes. But I think he only found out recently and if it's any consolation, he's no happier about it than you are." Ren recalled Marcroy's haughty disdain, adding, "In fact, I think he's quite horrified by the notion. Of course, he doesn't realize we're not half-blood mongrels, we're almost all *sídhe*. Or that our mother, despite looking quite human and belonging to the Druids, was almost as *Tuatha Dé Danann* as he was."

Darragh closed his eyes and leaned his head against the wall. "That's why we can wane. Why we survived the power transfer. We weren't ever really given any power. We had it all along. It was innate."

"So when they branded the new heirs, we didn't lose anything."

"God... it's almost too much to take in. And yet it makes perfect sense. Who else knows what we are?"

"Just about everyone in the ninja reality."

"The *what*?"

Ren smiled a little. It sounded quite ridiculous when he said it out loud. "It's the nickname we gave the reality where we were dumped after the rift collapsed on us. I told you about it last night."

"You never mentioned anything about ninjas."

Ren shrugged. "Don't know how it happened exactly, but the Japanese pretty much rule the world in that realm. The *Leipreachán* have taken to dressing like ninjas, hence -"

"Ninja reality," Darragh finished for him. "I think I'd like to visit this ninja reality of yours, Rónán."

"We'd be there right now except for, well, the whole abduction thing."

"There is much you should have told me, I suspect," Darragh said, as if he knew Ren didn't know where to begin.

"More than you'll ever know."

"Give me the highlights, then," Darragh suggested. "We can fill in the details later."

Ren nodded, wondering if he could summarise things any better than trying to explain it in full. "Okay... how about this. The *Matrarchaí* have been plundering all the realities they can get control of. They decimate the *sídhe*, destroy their homes, make it impossible for them to stay. Sometimes they do it by deception, occasionally they do it with an all-out war. What they're aiming for, are worlds full of magic and no *sídhe*."

"I'm not sure which question bothers me the most," Darragh admitted. "Why the *Matrarchaí* are doing this, or how you know so much about it. Do you know what they hope to achieve by ridding these realms of *sídhe*? It seems a bit extreme if all they want is not to share magic."

"The Hag has a theory about that."

Darragh sighed. "God, even if I could think straight from this headache, I can't imagine any reality where the Hag sits down for a chat with one of the Undivided."

Before Ren could answer that, the door opened. They turned to find a middle-aged woman with a pleasant face and what looked like a couple of dinner suits on coat hangers draped over her arm. She smiled at them, acting as if there was nothing out of the ordinary about two men bound hand and foot sitting on the floor of this large, empty room.

"Ah," she said, "you're awake. Do you want something for your headache? I imagine you both feel like you've been hit by a truck."

"Thanks," Darragh said, "but I'm not sure I'd trust anything the *Matrarchaí* served up in the guise of a headache cure."

"Suit yourself," she said, walking over the mantel and the empty fireplace. She hung the two suits on the edge of it and turned to look at them. "I am going to untie you now. I realize your first instinct will be to try to overwhelm me and escape, so I have been asked to give you a message."

"By whom?" Ren asked. Clearly this was not the woman in charge, just one of her minions, if she was being asked to deliver messages.

"You'll find that out at dinner," she said.

"What's the message?" Darragh asked.

"I've been asked to remind you that all of Europe is on the lookout for you, the dangerous escaped prisoner who looks just like your brother, so neither of you is safe beyond these walls and we will do nothing to discourage your apprehension by the authorities of this realm if you choose to leave. You might decide escape is still worth the risk, so let us make the decision easier for you. If either of you attempts to escape, commit any act of violence, or do anything other than exactly what you are told to do, we will order Kiva Kavanaugh, Kerry and Patrick Boyle and your young friend, Hayley Boyle, killed within the hour." The woman smiled pleasantly. "How's that for an incentive to behave?"

Darragh glanced at Ren and then back at the woman. There really wasn't much to say. "I give you our word as the Undivided that we will behave."

"You've no need to give me your word, dear," she said, removing a small knife from the pocket of her cardigan. "Just trust that ours is exactly what we say it is. Oh, one other thing. We dress for dinner here."

"Seriously? You want us to wear those?" Ren asked.

"There is nothing wrong with being civilised," the woman said.

"That's not civilised. It's ridiculous and anachronistic."

"Be sure to tell Mother that when you meet her at dinner," the woman replied, in a tone that spoke much of what she thought the reaction would be if they mentioned it. She approached Darragh first and sliced through the cable ties holding his feet together, then asked him to lean forward and sliced through the bindings around his wrists. She did the same for Ren and headed for the door as he rubbed the circulation back into his hands.

"Someone will be along presently to escort you to dinner," she said, before closing the door behind her. A moment later they heard the key turning in the lock.

Ren looked at Darragh and smiled dourly. "We have to dress in a tux for dinner. Do you suppose the mysterious Mother will be waiting for us, stroking a fluffy white cat?"

Darragh smiled. "One can only hope."

"Do you think they're going to kill us?"

"No. But I might know the reason we're being dressed up for dinner like a couple of prize fools, and why they haven't killed us yet."

Ren climbed to his feet and rotated his shoulders to loosen them. The headache was starting to fade - thank God - and he was feeling a little more like himself, something he hadn't felt since swallowing those wretched rubies. Outside, the sun was beginning to set. He glanced out the window, but could glean nothing of their location other than an expanse of carefully manicured gardens. "You mean there's another reason other than a perverse need to act like a villain out of an Austin Powers movie?"

He held out his hand to Darragh and helped him to his feet.

"One of us is going to sire the children in our nightmare. The children the Hag spoke of," Darragh reminded him. "Don't know about you, but I haven't really had an opportunity to sire anything these past few years."

"What's your point?"

"I think we're still alive, because we haven't done the job yet. I'll wager dinner involves a bevy of selected beauties designated the right bloodline to bear the *Matrarchai*'s version of twin saviors."

"Could be," Ren agreed, hoping that was the case. The only potential mother of Darragh's children was safely locked away inside a jewel in another realm, but he'd not mentioned Brydie and didn't intend to. Unless he was forced to share the *Comhroinn* with his brother, he planned to keep her predicament to himself. The resurgence of the prophetic dreams he kept having - and which Darragh was obviously having too - must be something to do with being back in this realm. It had to be. "Or Mother, whoever she is, has just seen too many movies."

"Either way, we'll know soon enough," Darragh said.

CHAPTER 50

The voices wouldn't leave Brydie alone. They called to her. They beckoned and cajoled by turn, one minute filled with sweetness and light, the next with horror and darkness.

She lay in bed, the covers pulled over her head, trying to block them out.

She knew who the voices belonged to. She knew what they wanted. And they terrified her.

Come back, the voices beckoned. *We need you. Come back.*

Brydie couldn't understand how they could be calling her. They were barely a day old. And yet the voices of Hope and Calamity filled her head, making her wish she had died in childbirth.

As if not being able to block out their voices was enough, every time she closed her eyes she saw them. The stark blue-on-blue eyes. The pointed Faerie ears, the shock of dark hair and those mouths full of tiny, pointed teeth.

Brydie didn't know if the babies were deformed because of the long time they'd spent unrealised in the womb, trapped by a *djinni* spell along with her for years, or because Darragh's seed was corrupt. In the end, it didn't matter. The babies weren't babies. They were monsters. And they knew what she was thinking.

She tried to explain it to the nurses who came to tend her, but they hadn't seen the babies. They weren't appalled by what she'd seen. They weren't repulsed. They weren't even frightened.

I should be frightened, Brydie knew. *I should be terrified.* And so should everyone else here. *Don't they understand the danger?*

Don't be frightened of us, mama. We love you.

Brydie screamed and buried her face into the soft pillow, pulling the edges up about her ears.

Teagan had stayed with her for most of the day, but couldn't understand what was upsetting the young woman so much. She was sitting beside Brydie on the bed and reached out with a comforting hand to pat her on the shoulder, as if that small gesture could in some way mitigate the enormity of Brydie's distress. "It'll be okay, Brydie."

"Can't you hear them?" Brydie asked, sitting up so sharply she was afraid the stab of pain across her lower abdomen meant she'd burst her stitches.

"I think they're sleeping."

"I don't mean that," Brydie snapped. "Can't you hear them in your head? Aren't they calling to you?"

"It's probably your hormones," Teagan suggested. "I hear they do crazy things to new mothers."

Brydie didn't even know what hormones were. But she knew patronising condescension when she heard it. "Get out."

"What?"

"You heard me, get out."

"Mother told me I had to stay with you."

Mother loves us. Mother knows how special we are.

"I don't care. I want to sleep," Brydie said, trying hard to ignore the voices. She realized that seeming hysterical was only going to make Teagan watch her closer. She forced a smile. "I'm tired, Teagan. Really, I just want to sleep."

Sleep with us. We love you. Come to us. We want you here with us.

Teagan seemed undecided, probably conflicted over her orders to watch Brydie and Brydie's demand that she leave.

"Maybe I should talk to Mother myself," Brydie suggested, guessing it would take something as important as fetching Mother to get Teagan out of here. "Would you get her for me."

Don't talk to Mother. Come to us. We want you.

"I don't know, Brydie. It's getting late and Mother doesn't like to be disturbed when she's at dinner. Particularly when she has guests."

Come now. Come to us now.

Don't worry, my darlings. I'm coming soon, Brydie told her daughters, not even sure they would hear or understand her. *As soon as I get rid of Teagan.*

But they did hear her. Almost as soon as she'd formed the thought, Teagan rose to her feet and announced in a voice devoid of emotion. "I will fetch Mother for you."

Without waiting for Brydie to respond, Teagan turned and headed for the door.

There. She is gone now. Come to us, mama. We're hungry.

Brydie shuddered as she realized Hope and Calamity must have made Teagan leave. *Gods, can they control everyone? What about me? Can they make me do things too?*

We would never hurt you, mama. We love you.

Brydie closed her eyes and made herself think of nothing but being a good mother. That's what they wanted, after all. Their mother. With her eyes squeezed tightly shut, she waited until Teagan's footsteps faded down the hall outside and then threw back the covers.

"I'm coming, my darlings," she whispered, hoping the thought was filling her head as she picked up one of the large fluffy pillows she'd been resting on. *I'm coming to take care of you.*

With a grimace, Brydie pulled the needle from the back of her hand and let it drop to the floor. The vein on her hand began to drip blood, but she didn't try to stem the flow. She didn't have time. Hope and Calamity were calling to her. She had to take care of them.

I'm coming to take care of you.

She kept repeating the phrase in her head as she headed down the wide hall toward the nursery.

I'm coming to take care of you.

Brydie smiled at Ana when she opened the door. The nurse was dozing in the rocking chair by the window. It was almost dark outside. The nursery was lit by a small nightlight on the side table next to Ana's chair.

The nurse opened her eyes and stared myopically at Brydie for a moment, and then she smiled. "You've come to visit with the bairns then?"

Brydie nodded. "Can I have a few moments with them? Alone?"

I'm coming to take care of you.

Ana pushed herself out the chair, nodding. "Of course. I'll go fetch a cuppa. They're asleep at the moment, but once they wake, I can help you with feeding them."

They weren't asleep, Brydie knew. *They're waiting for me.*

I'm coming to take care of you.

The nurse left the room without commenting on the pillow Brydie carried. She didn't notice the blood dripping from Brydie's hand or question what had happened to the drip stand, just smiled at Brydie as she closed the door behind her.

Brydie turned toward the cradle. *I'm coming to take care of you.*

She approached the cradle rocking gently in the center of the room. When she reached it, she stopped to study it for a moment.

I'm coming to take care of you.

Brydie glanced down at the pillow she carried and wondered if it would be enough. It was stained with blood from her hand, which seemed fitting somehow. The twins appeared to be sleeping peacefully, curled together like soft, deadly petals, the one on the left sucking her thumb, the other making soft suckling motions with her mouth, unconsciously mirroring her sister. The girls seemed unaware of the thoughts Brydie's incessant mental chanting was concealing.

I'm coming to take care of you.

They seemed blissfully ignorant of their approaching death. Brydie found that quite odd. *Whatever made these children what they are, does it not give them some inkling of approaching danger?*

They looked so innocent. With their eyes closed, their teeth not showing and their heads covered by knitted bonnets to keep them warm, they even looked human.

One of girls was stirring - they were too alike to tell which was which. She opened her eyes to stare up at Brydie, her expression disturbingly alert and aware for one so young.

I'm coming to take care of you.

Her strange eyes saw right into Brydie. Her sister remained asleep, still peacefully sucking her thumb.

I'm coming to take care of you.

Which will be harder? Brydie wondered. Killing the one who is asleep and ignorant of her fate, or the one staring up at me?

Am I strong enough to fight them off if they try to stop me?

Brydie changed her grip on the pillow and smiled down at the waking twin. *I'm coming to take care of you. I'm coming to take care of you,* she chanted in her mind, not sure what they would do if they realized her intentions.

The baby smiled up at Brydie, revealing the horrifying row of sharp, needle-like teeth.

I'm coming to take care of you, Brydie thought, steeling her resolve.

It didn't matter who they were. It's *what* they were. That was the important thing.

Mama's here, the voice in her head rejoiced. *She's coming to take care of us.*

Brydie didn't hear the door opening behind her, or the gasp of horror as she was discovered. She was smiling down at her daughter, who stared at her with a gaze so trusting and serene, it was heartbreaking.

So aware and malevolent, it was terrifying.

But not heartbreaking nor terrifying enough, to stay her hand.

Brydie raised the pillow she was holding, transfixed by the dangerous blue-on-blue eyes staring up at her. And then she brought it down sharply, holding the pillow firmly over the babies' heads without remorse or regret. She was quick and, she hoped, merciful, but the link between the sisters was quicker.

"Brydie," she dimly heard Teagan cry behind her. "What are doing?"

Mama? What are you doing?

The babies began to thrash about, starved of oxygen. The light on the side table began to flicker.

I promised I'd take care of you, my darlings, and I will.

But they were quicker than Brydie, quicker than Teagan, and far more ruthless than the mother who wanted them to die. Before Teagan's cries for help could be heard, Brydie's head was filled with their panicked screams, and then a pressure filled her whole body. She fought the screams. She fought the mental begging for mercy, determined to be rid of these monsters.

The monsters responded in kind.

I promised I'd take care of you.

It was Brydie's last thought as the pressure inside her exploded. She vaguely heard Teagan's horrified screams as she rushed to remove the pillow from the babies, and then a feeling of deep regret was the last glimmer of thought or emotion Brydie had before she ceased to exist.

With a burst of pure malevolence, Brydie was splattered across the walls of the nursery in a spray of blood and gore. Even her bones were so pulverized by the force of the twin's determination to stop her, there was nothing left of her at all.

CHAPTER 51

The dining room was on the ground floor. A silent acolyte led Ren and Darragh downstairs through what was obviously a renovated castle. There were plenty of them in Ireland, sold off by their impoverished owners whose titles did little to offset the cost of running such hideously expensive buildings. Those that weren't left to rot were bought by corporations and converted into expensive hotels, their once proud halls now hosting the lifeblood of the Republic of Ireland's tourist industry - rich Irish-Americans searching out their roots.

When they arrived, the dining room was empty of any other guests. The long polished table was set for three, Ren noted with some relief. Darragh's suggestion that they were going to be put on show - like some sort of meat auction - proved to be wrong. Of course, it also meant the whole dressing for dinner thing was either a joke, or an alarming indication of the mindset of the mysterious Mother.

Ren had encountered the title before, when he was stealing the memories of the other twins he had killed, but he'd never really understood there was one Mother who seemed to outrank the others. In a matriarchal organizastion like the *Matrarchaí*, it was easy to mistake the title as one that applied to many women. As he'd been dealing with the lower ranks - or at least the ranks a few degrees removed from the high command - it had never occurred to him that one woman might be behind it all.

"No bevy of willing wombs waiting for us," Ren remarked as he walked past the long table to the window.

"Would you think me appalling if I said I was disappointed?"

"Given your accommodation for the past ten years, I can probably understand it," Ren said, peering into the gathering darkness. The bright sunlight of the morning was forgotten. The night was crowding in, made even darker by an angry sky full of lumbering storm clouds, just waiting their opportunity to vent their fury on the earth beneath them.

"You know, the last time ... well, there was this girl... back in our realm before I came here. Álmhath threw her at me at the shindig I hosted in *Sí an Bhrú* the night before they told me they'd found our replacements. We went at it like rabbits for days until I came looking for you. What was her name? Brendá? Brandy?"

"Brydie."

"Yeah, that's it." Darragh closed his eyes, as if he was reliving the moment. He didn't think to question how Ren knew her name. "Brydie. Brydie Ni'Seanan, her name was. I wonder what happened to her? She's probably married to some border lord Álmhath needed to appease by now, with a half dozen noisy brats and looking like an old woman."

"Probably."

Darragh looked across the room at Ren. "Tell me again what the Hag said."

Ren closed his eyes for a moment, trying to recall every word the Hag had told him, glad of the change of subject. He didn't want to talk about Brydie. He didn't think he was that good a liar. "She said the *Matrarchaí* are going to force Partition. That they intend to start over again. To reset the cosmos."

"I suppose that's reason enough for the Brethren to become involved."

Ren shrugged. "She told me she was helping because she'd Seen she must. She also said something about having a role to play. And some responsibility."

Darragh shook his head, still trying to grasp the scale of what the *Matrarchaí* were planning. "But... such a plan is insane. Don't they realize there will be no more magic in their future if they do this? This world is depleted."

"According to the Hag, one life form making one planet uninhabitable through their technology does not alter the special nature of the reality in which it resides. Besides, they have a plan for that, too. It's why they've been breeding Empress and Emperor twins - so they can take over as many realities as they can, get rid of the *sídhe*, but leave the magic intact. Any reality connected to this one will be sucked in, with its magic for the taking, recharging this one."

"And then what? Have you seen this realm... oh, well, of course you have. But I mean... why bother? They've murdered most of the trees here for a start. How will they sustain it, even if a billion realities give up their magic to replenish this one? In a couple of generations they'll have used the magic up and they'll be screwed."

Trees. The word triggered a thought in Ren's mind and a memory. He had stolen so many of them over the years, from the men and women he'd murdered. The information was so vast now, it was rendered all but useless by its sheer volume. Until, like now, a single word or idea triggered a memory and he was able to recall some of the more useful information he'd stolen at the point of an *airgead sídhe* blade.

"*Kozo* trees."

"What?"

"*Kozo* trees. The magical *kozo* trees native to the ninja realm. They fairly drip magic. With them planted here, they could easily sustain the magic without the *sídhe* to interfere by dictating how it could be used."

"Then why not take over that realm? What's so special about this reality?"

"Apparently, it's the first, and therefore the only one which can be sundered from the others."

Darragh grasped what they were up to much faster than Ren had. "At which point the splintering process will start over and soon there'll be an infinite number of realities - but they will be realities filled with magic the *Matrarchaí* can call upon at will and they will be empty of all Faerie. Or at least pure *sídhe*." Darragh fixed his gaze on his brother with a look of dawning comprehension. "My God. That's what you've been doing all this time. Trying to stop them."

Ren nodded, a movement he regretted the moment he did it. "I think our nightmare is a part of it. At least that's what the Hag claims."

That gave Darragh pause. "So the children I sire someday are going to be the *Matrarchaí*'s instruments to force Partition?"

"So the rumour goes."

"Good thing I've been in prison then," he said with a sour smile. "Check this out."

Darragh had been inspecting the room as they talked. Ren tried to make out what he could of their location from the view outside, but like the view from upstairs, other than the gardens there was nothing to give any indication of where they might be, particularly now it was almost completely dark.

He turned and walked to the fireplace where Darragh was standing. On the mantel sat a glass case with a spectacular dagger resting on a red velvet bed.

"Bet you anything you name that blade is *airgead sídhe*."

Ren had to agree. The silver blade was engraved with the language of the *Tuatha Dé Danann* and the hilt was inset with amethyst, garnets and a large sapphire on the pommel. Its value must have been incalculable.

"We use it to test for the psychic link between twins."

They hadn't realized they were no longer alone. Ren and Darragh both turned to find a tall woman dressed in a long, dark-red, off-the-shoulder evening gown standing in the doorway, hand on the latch, smiling at them. It was impossible to guess her age. She could have been anything from twenty-five to fifty - or, given the likelihood of her *sídhe* origins, far older, even than that. Around her neck she wore a necklace almost identical to the one Ren had taken from Kiva. The one he had pulled apart and then swallowed after the Hag had had the rubies infused with magic.

But it wasn't the necklace that made Ren stare at her in shock. Take away the evening gown, the French-tipped nails and the sleek chignon, and he was looking at the Hag in her aspect of a younger woman.

And she, he realized now, shared a disturbing resemblance to the long dead Delphine.

The woman smiled at their shock, although Ren guessed she believed it was from her sudden and unexpected appearance. Unless she'd been listening to their conversation just now, she couldn't know he'd had any dealings with the Hag in his own realm.

What had the old woman said? *"I am helping you, because I have seen that I must. I have a role to play in this. And some responsibility, too, perhaps."*

Some responsibility, indeed, Ren thought, *when it's your* eileféin *who is out to destroy your world.*

"Let me look at you," the woman said. And then she smiled warmly and added something even more shocking than the realization that this woman was just another, perhaps more corrupt - and certainly better dressed - version of the Hag.

"I want to see what sort of men my sons have grown into," she said.

"Sons?" Ren managed after a moment.

Mother looked at him oddly for a moment and then laughed. "Dear God, did you think I meant that literally?"

For a moment there, he *had* thought she meant it literally, but before he could admit to anything so ridiculous, Darragh answered for him. "Of course he didn't," Darragh said. "Our mother was a *beautiful* woman."

She seemed amused. "I see a decade in Portlaoise has sharpened your tongue and stolen your manners, young man."

"Who are you?"

"I am Mother."

"Whose mother?" Ren asked.

"I am the Mother of the *Matrarchaí*."

"You look like the Hag."

Her smile faded as she turned her attention to Ren. "You have met my *eileféin*?"

"Briefly."

"You can't be the Hag's *eileféin*," Darragh said, grimacing as if the idea was made even worse because of his *Brionglóid Gorm* headache. "She is one of the Brethren. She is *sídhe*. This realm has no magic. It would kill her to step into this realm. If you were *sídhe*, it would kill you, too."

"Doesn't that strike you as bizarre?" Mother asked. "Doesn't it seem foolish that a race as powerful as the *sídhe* - a race with the ability to heal with a thought, travel instantaneously through space and time and cross realities at will - would allow themselves to be so vulnerable to something as unstable as atmospheric magic?" When neither of them answered her, she smiled. "I see. Is it that you are ignorant of the true purpose of the *Matrarchaí*, or that you just don't care?"

"Why should we care?" Ren asked. "According to the Hag, your true purpose is to force Partition."

"Because apparently it doesn't bother you that by doing that," Darragh added, "all other realities and every living creature in them will cease to exist."

"So you're not completely ignorant of what Partition means then."

"What do you want of -" Darragh stopped as the lights suddenly dimmed and then, after a second or two came back on again.

Mother glanced up and then smiled. "Don't worry, we have backup generators here."

"Of course you do," Ren said.

She stepped further into the room, closing the door behind her. "You know, to be honest, I'm not entirely sure what to do with you two. You were have supposed to have died a decade ago. It always bothered me that you didn't, but as nothing seemed to happen with you afterwards, I guess I fell into the trap of thinking your continued existence wasn't important. You'd think, after all this time, I'd know better than to assume any such thing."

"Are you going to kill us?" Darragh asked wearily. "Because if you are, could you do it soon, please? I have a splitting headache and, really, I'm not in the least bit interested in listening to you justify the obliteration of trillions for whatever obscure reason you've thought up to rationalise it away in your own head."

Mother's smile had faded. She clearly wasn't used to being dismissed in such a cavalier fashion. Or having her plans trivialised by someone who should probably be begging for his life. "Be careful what you wish for, Darragh of the Undivided. I haven't decided if you will die or not."

"Well, make up your mind soon," Ren said, taking his cue from Darragh. He wasn't sure if Darragh was being clever or he genuinely did want to die, but his attitude was riling Mother and that was probably useful if they wanted to learn things other than what she wanted them to know. "I have a headache, too."

Mother looked at Ren and then at Darragh, and then laughed as if she realized what they were doing. "Ah, the boldness of young men who imagine they're immortal. Do you think I am fooled by your bravado?"

"Don't care to be honest," Ren said with a shrug. "But if you are going to kill us, then please do it soon. I -"

There was a knock on the door before Ren could add anything further. Clearly annoyed by the interruption, she walked to the door, jerked it open and leaned out to speak to whoever was on the other side of the door. After a brief exchange she closed the door again and turned to them with all trace of humor, or interest in them, gone.

"I'm sorry, something has come up that needs my attention. I may be a while. I'll have your dinner sent in. We can talk later."

Without waiting for them to answer, she turned on her heel and left them alone in the dining room.

Ren stared after her for a moment and then looked at Darragh. "How can that woman be the Hag's *eiléféin*?"

"Same way you and I are almost pure *sídhe*, I suppose," Darragh said. "You claim *Matrarchaí* have been manipulating bloodlines for thousands of years. I guess there's your proof. She must have enough human blood in her so she can walk magic-less worlds with impunity. Do you suppose the Hag knows her *eiléféin* is the ringleader of the *Matrarchaí*?"

"She did worry about having some responsibility for this fiasco. What do you suppose happened to make Mother run out of here like that?"

"Who knows?" Darragh said, pulling out one of the carved, tall-backed chairs at the dining table. He sat himself down and put his head in his hands. "I just hope she stays away long enough for us to figure out how to get out of here and home."

Ren walked back to the window. It had started to rain; a gentle fall that was as much mist, as it was actual rain. In the distance, he noticed headlights coming toward the main building up the long driveway, but it was impossible to tell what sort of vehicle it was. At least it didn't seem to have flashing blue lights on the roof. He turned to

Darragh and smiled sourly. "In that case, let's hope she doesn't come back for a very long time."

CHAPTER 52

Annad's wife didn't take the news that Pete and his brother and their friends, had come here from another reality filled with Faerie terribly well, even with a pixie and a *Leipreachán* right in front of them to prove their story.

Stella decided they were mad and told them so. Annad was a criminal psychologist. He was much more considered in his response, but he was still speaking to Pete and Logan like they were sharing a joint delusion, rather than just lying to him, and even though he'd had more time to adjust to the idea, he still didn't seem convinced. If anything, his wife's scepticism had hardened his resolve. Last night, when he'd first met Echo, Pete thought Annad was a believer.

"I'm sure you think you've been to these wonderful places," Annad said carefully. "But -"

"Annad, there is a *Leipreachán* sitting on your kitchen counter. There is a pixie perched on top of your fridge. You've had conversations with both of them. What part of this isn't real enough for you?"

"They're probably some sort of remote-controlled toys," Stella scoffed, staring at Toyoda in utter disbelief. "I mean... a *Leipreachán*? Please! He's dressed like a ninja."

"Don't even try to explain *that* part," Trása sighed, shaking her head. She had Toyoda firmly by the hand to stop him waning out of the kitchen, but even his presence wasn't convincing Stella of anything. "What is it about humans in this realm? Why can't you just accept what Pete's telling you? What you can see with your own eyes, for that matter?"

"Because it's insane," Stella told her bluntly, not nearly as considerate of their mental health as her husband.

Pete turned to Annad. He'd had longer to get used to the idea that Faeries were real. If he could be convinced, maybe that would convince his wife. "Where do you *think* I've been these past ten years, Annad? Didn't anybody do anything when I just vanished?"

"I thought you were in America."

That was unexpected. "Why America?"

"That's what Brendá Duggan told everyone. She said you'd gone to America. She said you resigned."

Pete glanced at Logan in surprise. For some reason, he imagined that he'd be listed as a missing person somewhere. That someone still occasionally glanced through the files and tried to solve the mystery of what had happened to Pete and Logan

Doherty, last seen walking into the Sears Tower in Chicago and never heard from again. "What about Logan? How did they explain away his disappearance?"

"I've no idea where he is supposed to have been," Annad said. "Why would I even bother to ask? Or for that matter, even be aware that he was missing?"

"He's got a point," Logan agreed with a shrug, "although I would have thought someone might have questioned my sudden resignation."

"Why would they?" Stella muttered.

Why would they, indeed?

Annad seemed surprised he'd even asked the question. "Brendá said you'd been offered a chance to do your PhD in the Forensic Psychology program at Yale. I was a bit miffed, actually, that you didn't call me and tell me yourself."

That was clever. And something he hadn't expected, although now he thought about it, Pete supposed he and Logan weren't the first twins brought here to this realm by the *Matrarchaí* to be raised away from the magic they could so effortlessly wield. And they wouldn't be the first human-looking *sídhe* twins to have lived here, leading ordinary lives among ordinary people, and not know a damned thing about what they were while the *Matrarchaí* dabbled with their breeding lines. The *Matrarchaí* must be well practised in "disappearing" people whose agelessness would start to raise questions if they remained in this realm for too long.

That wasn't something he could explain easily to Annad and his wife, though. "Look, whether you think we're nuts or not, Annad, I just need you to believe us long enough for your wife to get us into Cambria Castle."

"Why?" Annad asked, putting his arm around his wife's shoulder in a very protective gesture.

"That doesn't matter. We just need to be there."

Annad was no fool. He figured it out in a few seconds. "You think Darragh is there, don't you? And maybe even Ren." Pete might have been impressed by his quick wit, if he hadn't caught Annad's gaze flickering over to the phone on the wall by the kitchen door. He had to remind himself that Annad, even though he seemed to be a friend, still worked for the Gardaí and they had probably just given away the location of the dangerous fugitive every cop in Europe was looking for.

The psychologist's face softened and he shook his head sadly. "My God, Pete, what happened? You used to be a cop. You were a rising star in the Gardaí. Now you're hiding out here, trying to find a way to aid a couple of deluded criminals who are responsible for at least one death we know of, and probably many more."

"Definitely more than one. Don't forget the girl they kidnapped and killed," Stella reminded him.

"Actually, it turns out she wasn't killed. She came back."

"Really?" Trása asked in surprise. Pete realized that with everything else going on, he hadn't had time to tell Trása and Nika about that.

"When did that happen?" Stella asked.

"A few days ago," Annad told her.

Trása threw her hands up impatiently. "Then why don't you believe us? Surely Hayley told you where she's been."

"She says she doesn't remember."

"Can't blame her for that," Nika said, "given the reaction of people in this realm to the truth."

"This is ridiculous," Stella scoffed. "I don't know what you people are on, or what you slipped into my tea to make me see things, but there is nothing for you at Cambria Castle. It's a private clinic, that's all. There are certainly no escaped prisoners lurking in the halls."

"We're wasting time, Pete," Logan announced impatiently. "Just have Toyoda glamour her and be done with it."

Pete shook his head. "She has to talk us through more than the door," he reminded his brother. "A glamouring won't last more than a few minutes."

"Isn't this place a hotel?" Trása asked, as if she agreed with Logan. "Why don't we just check in?"

"Because we need to get to the clinic part of the castle."

"Why?"

"That be where Renkavana and his brother be," Toyoda announced. "That be where the *Matrarchaí* be taking them."

Everyone was silent for a moment. It was Nika, impatient and practical as always, who broke the tense silence. "Oh, please! You are all acting as if anybody here is surprised to know that our purpose in this realm is to find Ren and Darragh. You," she said, pointing to Annad. "You will wait here with Trása and me. Pete and Logan will go -"

"Absolutely not," Annad announced.

"I wasn't asking."

"But I am telling you," the psychologist informed Nika with quiet confidence. "Under no circumstances are you bringing more trouble to our home."

Nika glared at him for a moment and then she seemed to concede the point. Pete thought he understood. The loss of Nika's home still galled her, even after all these years. Annad was much more perceptive that Pete gave him credit for.

"Very well... in that case you will take Trása and me back to the stone circle where we entered this realm. The midwife will go with Pete and Logan to this castle. They will find Rónán and his brother, and meet us back at the circle."

"What's the point?" Trása asked. "We can't open the rift from this side."

"Actually, we might be able to," Pete said, thinking Nika might be on to something. "Ren's managed to wane in and out of Portlaoise to rescue Darragh. He's packing some powerful magic to do that in this realm. He might still be charged up enough to get us home."

"If he has the power to wane, then why doesn't he just wane out of Cambria Castle?" Logan asked.

"The *Matrarchaí* be using *Brionglóid Gorm* on Renkavana and his brother," Toyoda told them. "They not even be awake when they be taken. And they still be asleep when me and the pixie be seeing them last."

"But when he does wake up, waning out of there is likely to be the first thing Ren does, so if we're going to find him and our way out of here, we need to get to the castle and find our boy before he uses up all the juice for our ticket home." Pete turned to Stella. "Can you ring the clinic and let them know you're coming to do a checkup on the woman who delivered last night?"

"I'll do no such thing," Stella announced, folding her arms across her body. She seemed to be avoiding looking at Toyoda or Echo, as if by acknowledging their presence she'd have to accept the rest of their crazy story was true, also. "And there is nothing you can say or do that will make me take part in this."

There was a moment of tense silence before Nika strode to the kitchen counter and grabbed a framed photo of a boy and a girl dressed in private school uniforms. "I will hunt your children down and kill them if you don't."

Pete stared at her in surprise. He was certain she wasn't capable of doing anything of the kind, but she sounded frighteningly convincing.

And apparently it was enough to convince Stella. The doctor snatched up the framed photo, glowered at Nika for a moment, and then glanced at her husband. She was blaming him for bringing these people - and this threat to their children - into her house. "Fine. I'll call them. I'll take you there. I'll even get you inside. But it won't do you any good. Nobody is harboring any escaped fugitives in the Cambria Castle birthing suite. This is a waste of time, and when the Gardaí catch you, as they inevitably will, you're all going to wind up back in Portlaoise alongside your friends."

CHAPTER 53

At first, Teagan didn't know what had happened to Brydie. One minute she was there, the next she was gone. The incomprehensible truth took a little time to register.

When she did realize what had happened, when she looked down to find herself covered in blood and bits of gore, she bent over and was violently ill, her vomit adding to the stench of fresh blood that made the walls glisten in the moonlight.

Will you be our mother now?

Teagan wiped her mouth and looked up, wondering who had spoken. "What?"

Will you be our mother now?

You won't try to hurt us, will you?

"Oh, my God," Teagan muttered, putting her hands over her ears. *It's the babies. How can it be the babies?*

Teagan turned for the door, but it slammed shut before she could take a step.

Don't leave us. Come back to us. Be our mother. We're hungry.

"How... how can you..." she couldn't finish the sentence. The idea that these babies, barely a day old, were inside her head, that they were...

That they are killers, she realized.

Teagan glanced down at her jeans and realized what the blood was.

Or rather who it had been. She felt her knees go weak and her stomach clenched again, but she fought back the nausea. If they were in her head, did they know what she was thinking?

You'll be good to us, won't you, mama?

I'm not your mama.

Our mama tried to hurt us. You won't try to hurt us, will you?

Teagan wanted to walk to the door. She tried to think about walking, running, even crawling toward the door, but for some reason her legs wouldn't obey her. Tears began to roll down her cheeks. She didn't know if she was rooted to the spot out of fear or because of something the babies were doing to her. She just knew she wanted out of there and that she couldn't move a muscle...

And then the door opened and she cried out with relief as Ana stepped into the room and took in the nightmarish scene before her.

The old nurse frowned but didn't otherwise react. "Where is Brydie?"

Teagan raised her hands, although she wasn't sure why. It was part shrug, part "look around you". She didn't have the words to answer Ana coherently.

The same torpor robbing her of the ability to flee this room seemed to have also paralysed her tongue.

"Are the babies all right?"

"They're... fine..." she managed to squeeze out.

It was hard to know what Ana was thinking. Teagan closed her eyes, trying to block out the horror she had witnessed.

And the knowledge of who had perpetrated it.

Ana loves us.

Maybe Ana could be our mother.

Our mother tried to end us.

Will you try to end us, Teagan?

We're hungry.

Teagan's eyes flew open. It was worse with them closed.

"What happened?"

"I... She..."

"Out with it, girl," Ana snapped.

"Brydie had a pillow... she tried to..."

"Oh dear lord," Ana said pushing past Teagan to get to the cradle. She leaned over it and began to fuss over the babies. The voices quieted a little in Teagan's head as they vented their anger to Ana, telling her about their evil mother who had come in here and tried to suffocate them.

And apparently about how Teagan had tried to intervene.

Teagan found she could move again. She took a cautious step through the blood on the floor, and then another, and another. She was almost to the door before Ana stopped her.

"Teagan!"

She turned slowly, afraid to look, afraid not to.

"You did well."

"I... I didn't know what else to do. She tried..." Teagan pointed to the cradle and shrugged. "They're just babies..."

Babies who can explode people with a thought, a dangerous voice in her head reminded her, but she quashed the traitorous thought ruthlessly. Teagan had seen what these babies would do if they were threatened. Thoughts like that would have her splattered over the walls beside Brydie, if they caught a hint of it.

Fortunately, the twins seemed to be focused on Ana. For the time being, Teagan was safe.

"I want you to fetch Mother for me," Ana said. "She will want to know what's happened."

"Okay."

"She's in the dining room entertaining some guests. Don't let them see you like that. Just ask Mother to come here."

Teagan glanced down and realized she was soaked to the skin.

"Go now, Teagan," Ana ordered. "There's a good girl."

Teagan looked up, still dazed, still not sure if what she thought she'd seen had really happened or if she was having some sort of hyper-real nightmare.

"Will you...?"

"I'll be fine with my girls," Ana assured her. "You run along and fetch Mother."

She nodded and did as Ana ordered because it required no thought and right now, her thoughts might get her killed too, if she allowed them to escape.

Teagan headed downstairs, first at a slow stumbling pace which gradually picked up until by the time she reached the formal downstairs dining room she was running. She couldn't really pinpoint what she was running from: whether it was from the horror she had just witnessed, or the voices she could still hear faintly in her head as they scolded Ana for leaving them alone with someone intent on doing them harm.

It was a very one-sided conversation. Teagan didn't know what Ana was saying to the babies to calm them down. Or indeed if she was calming them at all. Her answers might be antagonising the girls.

If Ana answers the wrong way, will they kill her too, or do they just disintegrate people trying to smother them?

Teagan stopped when she reached the dining room, a little surprised she'd managed to get from the nursery down to the ground floor without running into anybody else. Down the hall to her right was the reception area, where the staff who worked the hotel side of the *Matrarchai's* operation would be getting ready to change shifts, she supposed. Off to her left were the kitchens, but she couldn't smell any enticing aromas of cooking over the stench of the fresh blood in which she was drenched.

Taking a deep breath, Teagan turned and knocked on the thick oak door. She waited a moment, wondering if Ana had been wrong and Mother wasn't here at all.

And then the door opened. Mother was dressed in a gorgeous, long red evening dress and was wearing her ruby necklace. Whoever her guests were, they were obviously important.

"Teagan?"

"Mother ... I ..."

"Dear God, is that blood?" she asked in a low voice.

Teagan nodded. "The babies... Ana said..."

"Are they hurt? Is that their blood?"

She shook her head. "It's Brydie."

"Brydie's blood?"

"No... I mean it's Brydie."

Mother stared at her for a moment before saying anything. When she did speak, she was all business.

Why am I the only one here who thinks this is horrific?

"This is marvellous news."

"Excuse me?"

Mother smiled at her. "Don't you realize what this means?"

She shook her head. "Not really."

"The babies can wield magic in a realm that only has what's left in the Enchanted Sphere. With them, we can finally achieve Partition." When Teagan didn't light up with happiness at the prospect, Mother sighed. "I need to see to my guests. Go to your room. Have a shower. And say nothing to anybody. Do you understand?"

"I understand."

Mother closed the door on her. A few minutes later - presumably after making her excuses to her important guests - she emerged from the dining room, hurrying past Teagan without even noticing that she was still there.

Teagan leaned against the wall, tears welling in her eyes again, although she wasn't sure why she was crying. It might be for Brydie. It might be from fear.

Or her tears might be for hopelessly wishing they'd never taken her from her own realm.

Whatever the reason, she crumpled against the wall and sank to the floor, unable to stop her tears. She pulled her knees up, folded her arms across them and wept for the horror she had just witnessed and the dread realization that with the arrival of Hope and Calamity, her world was probably going to end.

The *Matrarchaí* had their tool to force Partition and it was more than they had even imagined.

Unless Isleen found her way to this realm before Partition, her twin would die when all the realms collapsed in upon each other.

And that was unfortunate, because she and Isleen were Empress Twins. Like Renkavana and his brother they were psychically linked. When one died, the other would soon follow.

Partition for Teagan wasn't going to be something to celebrate.

It would condemn her to death.

CHAPTER 54

"Do you hear that?" Darragh asked as he turned from the window. It was raining outside now - not a gently pleasant rain, but a savage storm that lashed at the windows and streaked the night with lightning. It was more than an hour since Marie-Claire had left them here. Their meal - a remarkably good filet mignon - had been silently delivered and devoured ages ago. Now they were just waiting. Darragh couldn't decide what they were waiting for.

Ren didn't even look up from staring at the knife in the glass case on the mantel. He seemed fascinated by it. He'd been studying the etchings on the blade for the past fifteen minutes like they held the meaning of life. "Hear what?"

"I thought I heard voices."

"Maybe this place is haunted."

"There's no such thing as ghosts."

"Really?" Rónán asked, glancing over his shoulder. "And yet there are all manner of other supernatural creatures. You'd think ghosts would be as real as Faeries."

Darragh smiled. Despite being stranded in this realm, despite being on the run and a prisoner of the *Matrarchaí*, it was good to be reunited with his brother. "The purists among the *Tuatha Dé Danann* claim there is nothing *super*-natural about the *sídhe* at all. They claim the Faerie are the only truly *natural* creatures. Humans, with their base appetites, greed, and voracious need to change the world about them, are the ones that don't belong in the natural world."

"Spoken like a true *Tuatha Dé Danann*," Rónán said. "What do you suppose is keeping Marie-Claire?"

"Who knows? Did you try the windows?"

Rónán nodded. "They're locked. So is the door."

"We could break a window. We're on the ground floor here and those dining chairs look pretty solid."

"They're alarmed." Then he added with a thin smile, "The windows, I mean. Not the chairs."

"We might make it to the road before they catch us," he said. "I'm game if you are."

"And what will we do when we get to the road? Flag down a passing car and tell them we were kidnapped by a bunch of evil women from another reality, who made us dress in tuxedos and forced us to eat filet mignon?"

Darragh smiled. "It's true. Even if it does sound ridiculous."

"It doesn't matter anyway. Even if we get away from here, even if we found someone who believed such a ludicrous story, your face... and mine, by definition, have been plastered over every news channel in Europe for days by now." He turned from the mantel to look at Darragh. "We step foot outside this place, we're done for. Much as it pains me to admit it, the *Matrarchaí* are our best chance of getting out of this realm. They have access to stone circles located in the Enchanted Sphere, they are -"

"Whoa! Back up a bit," Darragh said, wondering if he'd heard right. "The enchanted *what*?"

"The Enchanted Sphere," Rónán explained. "What little magic is left in this realm settles in a band that circles the planet around the height of a hundred-storey building. You can open a rift from there and come and go as you please, although for some reason, they work better in large cities. Something about the life-force a large concentration of people gives off."

Darragh was stunned. He'd never heard of such a thing. "How is it our rift runners know nothing of this Enchanted Sphere?"

"I'm guessing it's because the few who do venture into magic-less realms don't hang about long enough to go visiting ultra high-rise buildings so they can discover it for themselves."

The implications of such a discovery were astounding. Thousands of years of rift-running and no-one Darragh had ever spoken to had mentioned such a thing. It explained so much.

It explained how the *Matrarchaí* had been able to grow so large and so powerful without the *sídhe* knowing anything about them until it was too late. "My God... That's how they did it. It's how they've stayed under the radar for so long. We never heard of the *Matrarchaí* - except as a fairly benign sisterhood of midwives - because they did their plotting out of the reach of the *sídhe*. Why are you smiling like that?"

"You said they'd stayed under the 'radar'. Last time I saw you, you didn't even know what radar was."

"I've learned a lot since I was stranded here," Darragh told him, deciding they might as well have this long overdue discussion. "Much of it I will spend the rest of my life trying to *unlearn*."

"I am sorry," Rónán said, thrusting his hands into his pockets. "I really am. If I'd known ..."

"It's okay, Rónán. I understand."

Rónán shook his head. "I'm not sure you do. Not entirely."

"Explain it to me then."

His brother seemed extraordinarily uncomfortable with the topic of Darragh being stranded in this realm. Every time Darragh broached the subject, Rónán found a way to steer the conversation away from it. Darragh believed Rónán had his reasons. He was prepared to be sympathetic to them. He didn't even blame his twin, confident he would have come for him as soon as he was able. But knowing *why* was important too. He'd put the past decade behind him happily, if he understood Rónán's motives.

But Rónán was still hedging. "I'd rather wait until we can share the *Comhroinn*. Telling you why might not be enough. You need to understand it, too."

"Don't you trust me to understand?"

Rónán hesitated and then shrugged. "I'm not sure. I used to think you'd be fine with it. Then I discovered you were in prison here for the past ten years - and Portlaoise at that - and my grand idea didn't seem such so brilliant any longer."

"Why don't you let me be the judge of what's brilliant and what isn't?"

Rónán looked at him, perhaps debating how much of his reasoning to tell his brother, and then he took a deep breath and said, "How often have you had The Nightmare since you got stuck here?"

The question took Darragh by surprise. He wasn't expecting Rónán's explanation to have anything to do with his nightmares.

"Once or twice," he said. "Not for years though. Not until recently."

"That's because I found a way to stop them."

"So it was a true dream, then?" Darragh didn't need to ask that. Not really. He knew the taste, the feel of a dream that was prophecy, rather than wishful thinking.

Rónán nodded. "The children are yours. The babies. They get younger every time I see them."

"Then we're safe," he reminded his brother. "Is that why you left me in prison? So I would be denied a female who might bear my children?"

"I didn't know you were in prison. And that's the problem. You'd planted your seed before you left our realm."

Darragh frowned. "Who... *Brydie?*"

Brydie... Brydie... Darragh thought he heard someone calling her name. Rónán nodded.

Well... that explains a few things. "That's how you knew her name when I couldn't recall it."

"Yes."

Brydie was our mama. Mama tried to hurt us ... mama tried to hurt her babies.

Darragh shook his head to clear the imaginary voices from it and focused on Rónán. His reasons seemed rather far-fetched, given the timing. "But her children must be half-grown by now. If the babies are getting younger in your dreams, she can't be their mother."

Rónán's expression was bleak. "Brydie was trapped by a *djinni* in a jewel given to her by Marcroy. I found the jewel and I kept it."

Darragh let that sink in for a moment, trying to imagine what it must have been like for Brydie to be trapped like that for a decade or more. "Do you still have it?"

"Yes... and no. I left it with someone before I came here. I was afraid stepping into this realm would break the enchantment, like it did with Trása when Marcroy turned her into a bird."

Papa can protect us... come to us, papa... we love you...

"Did you hear that?"

"Hear what?"

Darragh was certain he was hearing things. He pulled out one of the chairs and sat down, trying to take in what Rónán was telling him. "So all this time..."

"Brydie has been pregnant with your children. The children in the dream."

Come, papa... we need you.... The lights flickered again. That storm was really getting savage out there.

"And Trása? Have you seen her?"

Rónán took a moment to answer, which was odd. "She's been in the ninja reality with me."

There was something in the way Rónán phrased his explanation, something about the way he said "with me" that caused Darragh a momentary surge of jealousy. Although his youthful romance with Trása had ended when they were both still too young and innocent for it to be anything more than a few meaningful looks and stolen kisses, he knew without having to think about it that Trása was now a woman, and if she had spent the last decade with his brother they could only be enemies or lovers. There was no chance of anything in between.

Rónán wasn't speaking of her like she was an enemy.

But the admission made Darragh uneasy. It was the first time he'd caught his brother in a lie. When he'd suggested earlier that Brydie might look like an old woman, be married to a border lord and have half-dozen children by now, Rónán had answered "probably", when he'd known of her fate all along.

Before Darragh could call him out on the lie, however, the lights dimmed again and then flickered back on. He glanced up at the crystal chandelier, waiting to see if the power would cut out completely, but then the light steadied and returned to normal.

Papa... papa...

"Must be the storm," Rónán remarked.

"I suppose." It wasn't what he wanted to say, but the banal reply gave him time to gather his thoughts and push away the absurd voices in his head so he could decide how he should react to this new information. First Rónán had lied about Brydie, and now he'd all but admitted he and Trása were together. A part of Darragh felt betrayed, and more than a little suspicious. Were Rónán's motives for abandoning him in this realm so noble, after all, or had he committed an act of unconscionable cowardice? Did Rónán really want to defy destiny, or had he decided it would be easier to leave his brother to rot so he could have Trása for himself, while holding onto Brydie in her enchanted jewel and ensuring his brother's children could never rise up and force him to face his responsibilities?

Darragh dismissed the thought as absurd, almost as soon as it occurred to him. Whatever had gone on this past decade, the dreams *had* stopped, which meant Rónán had stalled the events leading to that awful, watershed moment for the better part of a decade.

Given they both had the ability to see the future, given the nature and the intensity of their nightmare, given their knowledge of what was to come, Darragh was fairly certain that if their roles were reversed he'd do exactly the same thing.

They were twins, after all, and despite their diverse upbringings more alike than not in so many, many things.

"How is she?"

"Trása?"

"Of course."

Rónán's face softened for a moment, which told Darragh more than any words might about his brother's feelings for her. "She's become the de-facto Queen of the Faerie. The lesser *Youkai* are nuts about her."

Darragh smiled. "She'd like that."

"She never let up demanding I come rescue you," Rónán added. "I ended up having to tell her about the dreams to shut her up."

"I wondered if she was still angry with me for not insisting she be allowed to stay in *Sí an Bhrú* when her father sent her away."

"I think that's long forgiven and forgotten," Rónán assured him.

"Where is she now?"

"I'm not sure, to be honest," he said. "She was in the ninja realm when I left. But Marcroy has got the jewel back that Abbán used to open the rift. I don't know if that means he's been to the ninja realm already, or he's planning to go. Either way, I'd like to get back there before Marcroy finds Trása again and decides to punish her more severely than the last time."

Don't leave, papa, not now ...

"Did you break Marcroy's curse?"

Rónán shook his head.

"Why not?"

"I didn't want her going back to our realm. It was the only way I could ensure she didn't."

Ever the pragmatist, my brother. Darragh had a feeling that of the two of them, Rónán was the one better equipped to do what needed to be done. He seemed easier with making the hard decisions than Darragh would have been. He was certain he would not have been able to resist Trása's demands for as long as Rónán had managed. Perhaps that's why the dream, when they were younger, affected them both equally, but as they'd grown, as circumstances had shaped them, Destiny had made a choice and it became clear who would wield the blade and who would stand by and watch. Darragh couldn't help but be relieved that fate had apparently chosen his brother. "Does she love you?"

Rónán smiled. "Sometimes."

The lights flickered again. *Papa, please come. We love you.*

Darragh put his hands over his ears. "Are you *sure* you don't hear anyone calling?"

"Positive. Are you okay?"

Before Darragh could answer, before he could say he was hearing his daughters calling, his daughters who weren't even born yet, a *Leipreachán* dressed like a portly ninja popped into existence on the table in front of him and threw himself at Darragh, wailing, "Renkavana! I be so glad ye are still alive. Lady Trása be comin' with Lord Pete and Lord Logan, and Lady Nika and -" The *Leipreachán* stopped abruptly as he looked up discovered Rónán standing behind him. He stared for a second or two at Darragh, realized he had the wrong man, squawked with fright and then threw himself at Rónán and began his litany of woes all over again, "Renkavana! I be so glad ye are still alive. Lady Trása be comin' with Lord Pete and Lord Logan -"

"Enough! I heard you the first time."

"Who is this? And what is he babbling about?"

"This is Toyoda Mulrayn," Rónán said, and then he smiled with relief, "and I do believe the cavalry is about to arrive."

"Trása? She's coming here?" Darragh asked, frowning.

Papa, can you hear us ...

But Rónán wasn't worried about that. His smile faded as he looked at the *Leipreachán* and asked, "Toyoda, I gave you something precious to mind. What did you do with it?"

The *Leipreachán* puffed his chest out, as if he was inordinately proud of himself. "I be hiding it good, Renkavana. I really do be hiding it good."

"*Where* did you hide it?"

"At the stone circle."

"The one near *Tír Na nÓg*?"

"No, no, no," the *Leipreachán* assured Rónán with a snort that suggested he'd never do anything so foolish. "I never be leaving it in *our* realm unguarded. I not be that stupid. I be bringin' it here to this realm where no thievin' pixie can make off with it. I be hidin' it so well, even I can't be findin' it meself, but Lady Trása is on the way now, so we be rescuin' ye and ye brother from the evil *Matrarchaí* and then we be findin' ye jewel and be on our way home."

CHAPTER 55

It was dark by the time Pete, Logan, Toyoda, the Merlin, and Stella Delaney arrived at Cambria Castle.

Through pelting rain and the rhythmic, periodic moments of clarity provided by the windscreen wipers, Pete could see the hotel was lit up like it was expecting guests, although the car park was almost empty and there was nothing to indicate that the place housed the expensive and well-equipped antenatal and neonatal facility of which Stella was so envious.

If this had been the 1950s, Pete could well imagine a maternity clinic tucked away in the guise of an exclusive hotel. Somewhere well-heeled, indiscreet young ladies wait out their pregnancies and deliver their bastard children out of the sight of prying, gossipy and judgmental eyes.

But in this day and age, there was no need for such a place, which - if there was a clinic here -

made the likelihood it was a *Matrarchaí* stronghold all the more probable.

Stella drove without saying a word the whole trip, her expression thunderous. Pete didn't doubt she was waiting for her moment. She was hanging out for a chance to turn them in, although they had committed no crime. At the very least, they were planning to help an escaped convict. And it could be argued that Nika threatening to kill Annad and Stella's children if she didn't help them was illegal.

If they actually managed to get out of this realm and back home, Pete was going to have to have a long talk to Nika about that.

Even through the rain, he could tell Cambria Castle was an impressive building. The brochure said it could trace its origins back to Gaelic Irish royalty. He wondered if that meant it had been in the hands of the *Matrarchaí* for the past few hundred years or if they'd acquired it more recently.

As castles went, it wasn't that old. According to the crumpled brochure Toyoda had brought them it was "a spectacular Renaissance masterpiece built in the 16th century". The brochure went on to gush about the romantic gardens and fine antique furnishings, the marvellous woodcarvings, stone statuary, hand-carved panelling and priceless oil paintings, and the opportunity to hunt, fish, play golf, tennis and croquet. It mentioned nothing about a clinic, babies, or that it might be the headquarters of an insidious organizastion bent on eradicating the Faerie.

Stella parked the car outside the front door under the large stone portico. Pete glanced around as he climbed out, and realized that over to their left was a helipad with a Eurocopter BK-117 sitting on it. The pilot - or perhaps he was the aircraft mechanic - was struggling to fasten the tiedown ropes to the fuselage mooring points on the skids and then extend them to the ground mooring anchors on the edge of the pad.

He glanced at Logan across the top of the car and pointed to the helo. "If we need a quick way out of here, do you remember how to fly?"

"Six months doing the traffic report twelve years ago isn't learning to fly, Pete."

"Pity." He opened the driver's door for Stella before she could do it herself. "Allow me, Doctor Delany."

Stella climbed out of the car, scowling at him as he thwarted what was almost certainly her plan to bolt across the lawn, or into the building, calling for help. "They're not going to let you in," she warned.

"You are going to *make* them," he assured her. "Then we'll leave you and your husband alone and you'll never see any of us again."

"I'll see you again," she said confidently, shouldering her medical bag. "If not at your trial, then your sentencing hearing. I'm going to enjoy testifying at that."

"I'm sure you will," he said, refusing to rise to her taunting. "Shall we?"

They followed Stella through heavy, studded oak doors and stepped into a large foyer filled with medieval paraphernalia. There were suits of armor in almost every corner, swords and banners on the walls, a dozen or more coats of arms on display.

The foyer was deserted, except for a grey-haired woman standing near the reception desk who was obviously waiting for them. The lights flickered on and off as they approached her. No doubt the storm outside was messing with the power supply. The woman, who was dressed in a white nurse's uniform, stepped forward and held up her hand to stop them going any further. "Doctor Delany? My name is Ana Vaughn. I'm so sorry to bring you out here on a night like this for no reason."

"That's okay," Stella said. "Nothing is too much trouble for a patient of mine."

"I am sure you are a most dedicated practitioner," Ana agreed with a smile, "but I'm afraid your patient is no longer here."

Stella frowned. It seemed she'd forgotten she was here under protest. Suddenly, she was far more concerned about her patient.

"What do you mean, she's not here? Where is she?"

Ana shrugged. "I couldn't really say. She left earlier today."

"But she's just had a c-section," Stella said. "She's just had an anaesthetic. She's still on a drip. Who discharged her?"

"I really couldn't say," Ana said apologetically. "Why don't I see what I can find out and have the information about her new physician emailed to your office in the morning?"

There was something very suspicious going on here, that much was obvious, even to Stella. Annad's wife - who'd been determined not to have anything to do with their plan to infiltrate the *Matrarchaí* -

seemed to change her mind in the face of this unexpected obstacle to her checking on her patient.

"I wish to speak to Marie-Claire," Stella said.

"She's currently in a meeting."

"Then get her out of it," Stella ordered. "If you don't, I'm going straight to the police to report my patient missing."

And the threat to my children, Pete added silently. *And that the prisoner who escaped Portlaoise the other day is probably here. Slick move, Stella.*

Ana, who had given up even pretending civility, eyed the doctor for a moment, as if trying to gauge how serious she was and then she nodded. "Wait here," she said. "I'll see what I can do."

The nurse turned on her heel and left through the door behind the reception counter. Pete smiled at Stella. "Nice work, doc."

"Shut up, you fool."

"I just meant -"

"I know what you meant, and I don't care. That young woman I delivered yesterday needs medical attention. If they've just let her just walk out of here, they may well have endangered her life. Right now, I'm more concerned about her fate than any harebrained scheme you and your crazy friends have cooked up."

Before he could respond, Logan hissed at him from across the foyer. "Hey! Check this out!"

He studied Stella for a moment, decided she wasn't going anywhere until she'd discovered the fate of her patient and hurried across the foyer to the door Logan had just opened.

The room Logan had discovered was filled with hunting trophies. There were at least three deer heads mounted on the walls, their massive antlers looming over the room, a growling lion over the fireplace, a polar-bearskin rug in front of the deep, leather chesterfields complete with snarling head attached, and a score of other endangered species proudly exhibited in a grotesque display of man's supremacy over the animal kingdom. The lights flickered again, lighting the room with a fierce, almost horror-movie ambience.

Pete stared around for a moment and then shook his head. "That's disgusting."

"Not the animals," Logan said. "That."

Logan was pointing to a cabinet on the other side of the fireplace, where a rack of shotguns was displayed.

Pete looked at his brother. "Are you serious."

"This place is a *Matrarchaí* stronghold, Pete. The *Matrarchaí* kill Faerie. We're Faerie. Damn right, I'm serious."

Logan's logic was impeccable, but there was something about being back in this realm that made Pete reluctant. He'd killed *Matrarchaí* - both men and women - before today. But somehow, in this realm where his job had been to uphold the law, not break it, the idea of shooting his way out of anywhere, even a *Matrarchaí* stronghold, felt wrong.

Just because it felt wrong, didn't mean it was, Pete decided. He nodded and turned back to Stella, wondering what her reaction would be to them arming themselves. She was standing by the reception desk, tapping her fingers impatiently on the counter, but she wasn't reaching for the phone. At least, not yet.

He stepped into the shadows, out of Stella's sight for a moment, as he heard a crash of broken glass coming from the trophy room. Logan breaking into the gun cabinet, he guessed.

"Toyoda!" he hissed softly.

The *Leipreachán* popped up beside him in the shadow of a spectacular, if rather short, suit of silver-chased armor, looking about nervously.

"I don't be liking this place, Lord Pete."

He squatted down until he was eye to eye with the *Leipreachán*. "You and me both, pal. So stay out of sight. But I need you to glamour the doctor so she doesn't try to escape or call for help."

"But what be happenin' if the nurse be comin' back?"

"If she tries to send us away, I want you to glamour her, too. Tell her she's to let us through, okay?"

Toyoda nodded. "Didn't ye want me to be locatin' Renkavana for ye?"

"After we've taken care of Stella and the nurse."

The lights flickered again. Pete glanced up and then looked back at Toyoda who seemed very uneasy.

"There be somethin' very wrong in this place, Lord Pete. I want to be going home."

"So do I," Pete told him, rising to his feet, a little startled to realize how much he wanted out of this realm. "So do I."

CHAPTER 56

Ren stared at Darragh, wondering if his brother was experiencing the same horrified realization, that the enchanted jewel was no longer in a magic realm, as he was.

"He brought the jewel here," Darragh said softly.

"To a world without magic."

"Rónán," Darragh said. "I think we have a problem."

"We'll find it," Ren promised, feeling sick to his stomach. There was, Ren decided, a certain inevitability about Toyoda losing the gem he'd protected so vigilantly. It was a stupid thing to do, in hindsight, entrusting something so valuable to a *Leipreachán*, but maybe he didn't have a choice. Maybe it was like the Hag said - it was Destiny at work. Perhaps that was *how* Destiny worked, waiting in the wings for that one slim chance; that once in a lifetime opportunity. That one stupid decision around which empires would rise or fall -

or realities thrive or perish. "We'll get it back to our realm, Darragh. I promise. *Djinn* enchantments are powerful things. Coming through the rift may not have weakened it yet. But even if the spell is broken, even if she's out and wandering the streets of Dublin, we have months before..." His voice trailed off as he looked at his brother.

Darragh was shaking his head. "It doesn't work like that, Rónán. The curse on Trása broke as soon as she entered this realm. Sorcha withered and died of old age in a week."

"Then we have a week..."

"No. We don't have anytime at all."

"What do you mean?"

"I can hear them, Rónán. In my head. They're calling to me."

Ren felt the blood draining from his face. "Are you sure?"

"Either that. Or I'm going mad."

"How is that possible?"

Darragh shrugged. "Between the *Matrarchaí* fiddling with our bloodlines and a decade seeped in a djinni enchantment, who knows what it's done to Brydie or her babies. All I can tell you is they are born," Darragh said, putting his head in his hands.

"That's impossible," Ren said, wishing he had time to murder the *Leipreachán*. Not that this mess was really Toyoda's fault. Ren should have known better than to entrust something so precious to a creature as unreliable as a *Leipreachán*. Still, they had a *Leipreachán* here and help on the way. If the babies had been born...

Ren was too afraid to finish the thought. "Toyoda! Search this place. See if you can find any babies."

"Did ye be wanting me to steal babies, now, Renkavana?" the *Leipreachán* asked, sounding a little miffed. "I not be the baby stealing kind. That be a pixie thing. Ye should be askin' that pesky Echo, if ye be wanting to steal -"

"Just do it," Ren ordered. "And come back here if you find any."

With an indignant sniff, the *Leipreachán* vanished. Ren turned back to Darragh, hoping to reassure himself as much as his brother. "Toyoda only brought the jewel here a couple of days ago. There's no way -"

"I can hear them, Rónán. They're in my head. They know who I am."

"Do you think they're nearby?"

"I suppose the *Leipreachán* will find out soon enough, but I have no way of knowing. They might be on the other side of the world. They might be in the next room. I don't know. They just keep begging me to come to them. They keep going on about their mama wanting to hurt them. And how they need me to protect them."

"Darragh, even if they were born the moment Brydie stepped through the rift, they'd be a few days' old at best."

"Which makes them calling to me like this pretty frightening, don't you think?"

Ren was thinking the same thing, but before he could say so, the door burst open, and a young woman stumbled through the door as if she'd been shoved through. On her heels was a man carrying a long-barrelled shotgun.

"*Pete*?"

Darragh jumped to his feet, knocking the chair over. Hot on the heels of Pete and the young woman was Logan, also toting a shotgun, but with nowhere near the confidence of his brother.

"Ah... there you are," Pete said, glancing around the room. He fixed his gaze on Darragh for a moment and then seemed to notice what they were wearing, and the remains of their meal that was still on the table. "Glad we're able to save you two from the terrible time you must be having at the hands of the *Matrarchaí*."

"Rónán? Who are these people?

"Are you Darragh? I'm Logan Doherty. This is my brother -"

"Pete Doherty," Darragh said, staring at them in confusion. "I remember you. You arrested me."

"Sorry about that," Pete said with a shrug. "Are you two ready to go? I don't know how long before the glamour wears off and Stella turns on us. I suggest we move before the *Matrarchaí* realize they have company."

"Shotguns?" Darragh asked, shaking his head. "Really? Are you planning to *blast* your way out of here?"

"We didn't know what we'd find," Pete explained. "We stumbled across the weapons searching for you two. Turns out skeet shooting is one of the many activities you can enjoy at Cambria Castle if you're holidaying here."

"Of course," Ren said. He glanced at the young woman who'd probably been on guard outside. She was a pretty young thing, about twenty with long blonde hair, but filthy and her face was streaked with tears. She was crying, but making no attempt to escape or even raise the alarm. "What about her."

The girl looked at him imploringly, tears running down her face. Ren couldn't be certain, but it seemed she was covered in blood. "Take me with you, Renkavana."

"*Excuse* me?"

"Don't you recognize me?" the girl sobbed. "It's me! Teagan!"

Ren stared at her, stunned. Of all the things he hadn't expected, top of the list was to run into Teagan now. Even Pete and Logan bursting in here with shotguns made more sense than that. "What the hell are you doing here?"

"I... It doesn't matter. Please... I just want to go home."

"Where's Isleen?"

"Isn't she with you?"

"Jesus, is that blood on your clothes?" Logan asked.

Teagan looked down at her jeans and then nodded. She was covered in gore, Ren realized. It was on her clothes and matted in her hair and all over her tear-streaked face. "Mother told me to take a shower, but I... please. Just take me with you. I want to get out of this place. I want to go home."

"Whose blood is it?"

"It's Brydie's blood. She... she just... exploded."

"*Brydie?*" Darragh exclaimed. "What the *hell*?"

566

"Who is Brydie?" Pete asked. "And more to the point, why are we standing here chatting about her? Come on... let's go."

Toyoda chose that moment to reappear on the dining room table, knocking over the floral centrepiece as he landed on it. "There be babies, here," he announced, "but they not be like any babies I be seeing before."

"Arrgh!" Darragh cried out, clutching at his head. "God... they won't leave me alone!"

"What's wrong with your brother?" Logan asked, looking at Darragh with concern.

"The babies are in his head," Teagan said. "They get in your head. They make you do things."

In two strides Ren was across the room. He grabbed Teagan by the arms and shook her. "What happened to Brydie?" Ren couldn't believe she was dead. It wasn't possible. Even though he'd never met her, he had his brother's memories of her and she'd been his silent confidante for years now. She wasn't dead. She couldn't be dead.

"I don't know," Teagan sobbed. "She said she wanted to see them, but she took a pillow into the nursery and tried to smother them, and then they were in my head too, and they made me try to stop her, but before I could she just... I swear, Renkavana, it was them. They're evil. Brydie knew it and tried to stop them and they just... disintegrated her."

Ren stared at her, feeling his world unravel. He glanced at the mantel, at the *airgead sídhe* blade, sitting there in its glass case, silently taunting him.

"Let's get out of here," he said, letting Teagan go. "Right now."

"I can't," Darragh groaned, still holding his head between his hands. "God knows I want to, but I... I'm sorry... I have to go..."

Before anyone could stop him, Darragh ran from the room, pushing Pete and Logan out of the way in his haste to be gone.

"He's going to them," Teagan sobbed. "They want him, too."

"*Who* wants him, for fuck's sake?" Logan asked, looking thoroughly confused.

"The babies," she told him.

"What frigging babies?"

Pete shouldered his shotgun and stared at Ren. "You going after him?"

No, Ren wanted to say, *I'm going to leave to him here. I'm not going near those children. I'm not going to let this happen.* But he didn't say it.

The Hag had warned him this moment would come.

Dear God, Brydie had tried to put a pillow over them.

What was it about these children that made their own mother want to smother them?

It shouldn't be so easy to take a life. The thought had haunted Ren since the dreams began when he was a boy. The idea that he could kill so carelessly. He realized now that he wasn't condemning himself. Nor was the thought complete in his dreams.

It shouldn't be so easy for newborn babies to take a life. That's what the full thought was. *Nobody should have that much power. Not so young. Not without any sort of self-restraint. Theirs was a visceral need with no compassion or empathy.*

The *Matrarchaí* were fools for thinking they could ever control such power.

It shouldn't be so easy to take a life.

Ren wished he'd realized sooner what was meant by that thought. Perhaps it would have made the nightmares easier to live with.

He stared at the mantel. At the ceremonial knife the *Matrarchaí* used to test the psychic link between twins. If they cut one with *airgead sídhe* the other would bleed. They would have performed the same test on him and Darragh when they were born. Probably with the same knife.

"I have to go after him. I don't think I have a choice."

With a sense of spine-tingling rightness, Ren walked to the case on the mantel, picked it up and threw it down onto the marble hearth, ignoring the cries of surprise and the demands from Pete and Logan for some sort of explanation as it shattered into a million shards of broken glass. The blade tumbled onto the rug. Ren bent down and picked it up. He studied it for a moment, closing his eyes. He savoured the feel of it, astonished at how exactly he had seen it in his dreams. How familiar it felt.

And how, now that he was holding it, the decision seemed so much clearer.

"Take this," Pete offered, holding out the shotgun. "That letter opener isn't going to do diddly-squat if you run into the one of the *Matrarchaí*'s henchmen."

"This will be enough," Ren assured him and then he turned to Teagan. "Get out of this place. Go with Logan and Pete. They'll see you get back to your own realm somehow."

Ren didn't wait for her to answer, or Logan or Pete to dissuade him. He strode from the dining room, the *airgead sídhe* knife clasped in his hand like a long-lost friend, his footsteps heavy with the realization that Destiny had one hand on his shoulder and the other clenched firmly around his heart.

CHAPTER 57

The castle was oddly deserted. As Ren walked the wide, silent halls in pursuit of his brother, he didn't know if the lack of people was because the *Matrarchaí* had arranged it that way, or if this place never operated as a hotel because it was just a front for their organizastion in this realm, or if the babies had driven everyone away.

The storm continued to lash at the windows outside, the lightning splintering the darkness periodically. The lights in the castle dimmed every now and then, but Ren suspected it wasn't the storm making the lights flicker. There was another power in the air here and he could feel tingling along his forearms and felt the hairs on the back of his neck stand up.

It wasn't magic he could feel. Magic was a joyous, giddy feeling. It was something much darker. It felt heavy. Dense. Evil.

He walked past a woman standing at the reception desk who said nothing – still under the effects of the glamour. He climbed the wide stone stairs slowly, not sure how he knew where he had to go. The massive foyer with its faux-medieval decor was deserted. There was nobody behind the large wooden reception desk, no sign of any staff, no sign of anyone at all. It was both a relief and of concern. Ren didn't know how many people normally occupied this place, but Pete had said it was a hotel. Between staff and guests he would have expected a dozen or so people at least.

But there was no-one.

He gripped the *airgead sídhe* blade a little tighter, as if to remind himself he was holding it. He could have left it behind. Perhaps he should have.

Maybe I won't use it. Maybe I won't have to.

With every breath he took he felt the air thickening and Ren knew he was lying to himself, but it was easier to believe the lie than acknowledge the truth.

Another flight of stairs and through a heavy oak door on the landing, marked *Private*. This was not part of the hotel. This was near the room where he and Darragh had been held when they first arrived here, while they slept off the effects of the *Brionglóid Gorm*. He heard the door snick shut behind him and stared down the wide corridor. There was nobody around. He thought he could hear something in the distance. It sounded like sobbing, but a crack of thunder drowned out any chance he had of figuring exactly where the sound was coming from. The lights flickered again and then they died completely, leaving the hall in darkness, to be lit only by the storm's sporadic lightning and the faint illumination coming from the security lights outside, which must be on a separate grid or perhaps had some sort of battery backup to keep them going.

Maybe they're solar powered, Ren thought, concentrating on the lights because it blocked out any other thoughts, any other doubts. *Perhaps there's a generator. Maybe it'll kick in soon and restore the lights.*

He reached the end of the hall, which branched off in opposite directions. To his right was the hall down which he and Darragh had been led several hours ago to join Marie-Claire for dinner. On his left was another door, marked *Authorised Personnel Only*.

Ren turned left.

He pushed the door open, stepped into the hallway and realized why the rest of the place was deserted. Everybody was here. There must have been thirty people standing in the hall. They weren't all women. Ren had learned long ago that the *Matrarchaí* was a surprisingly equal opportunity organizastion. The hotel staff were here, he guessed, looking at the uniforms - domestics, front desk and bellboys, as well as a number of men and women dressed in nurse's uniforms. They were all standing silently in the hall, staring at him with blank, glazed expressions, blocking his way forward.

From what Ren could make out in the darkness, every one of them had the glassy-eyed expression of the enchanted.

Ren didn't know how that could be. They were not in the Enchanted Sphere here. There was barely enough magic this close to the ground to sustain a

Leipreachán. How could this many people have fallen under a spell?

What happens if I try to move forward, Ren wondered, bending his left hand up behind his back to conceal the knife. He didn't know if these people were enchanted, or whether the babies were watching him through their eyes, but he didn't want to chance it.

He took a step. The glassy-eyed people closed ranks.

"I need to see my nieces," he announced. In his nightmare, he remembered, he was trusted; nobody had considered him a danger.

He had to hope that part of the dream was real.

Not much else was the same.

His nightmare always started when he was in the room with the cradle. There was nothing in his nightmare about navigating his way through a hallway packed with zombified hotel employees.

Do you love us? Are you one of us? Mama tried to hurt us... papa is here now... he'll protect us.

Ren felt rather than heard the voices and he began to understand. They were seductive. They were vulnerable. They made him want to kill anybody who dared threaten his precious nieces.

As he felt himself giving in to the voices, overwhelmed with the urge to devote his entire existence to their service, a voice called out, "Let him through."

The crowd parted to reveal a woman walking toward him. She wore a white coat and a stethoscope around her neck, with her dark hair pulled back into a ponytail.

"He said you'd come."

Ren studied her for a moment, wondering if the doctor was *Matrarchaí* or under the same spell as the others. The same spell he could feel himself being sucked into. "Who said I'd come?"

"Papa," the woman replied. She stared at him unblinkingly.

"And here I am," he told her, not sure how much of what he was saying would make an impression on someone as so thoroughly glamoured as she was.

"Are you here to protect us?" the woman asked. "Or to hurt us?"

That was the burning question. Destiny or defiance.

Maybe I can fight this, he realized. *Maybe I can turn the tables on Destiny. I just need to embrace this. We're family, after all.*

And in the end, if Destiny can't be fought, Ren decided, *whatever I say, whatever I do, will be the right thing.*

"You can go." He turned and raised his voice a little and addressed the others staring at him with blank, soulless eyes. "You can all go."

"We have to protect them," the woman said.

"I'm here now," he said. "I will take care of them. With their papa."

As he spoke, he felt the presence in his mind fading. It was as if they knew he was theirs now, and no longer needed to force their will on him.

The woman closed her eyes for a moment, as if she was listening to someone Ren couldn't hear, and then she opened her eyes and nodded. "You are family."

"Yes. I am family."

"We are so tired."

Ren wondered if he was talking to the woman or if she was voicing the words of the babies who had taken over her mind and the minds of everyone else in the hall.

"Go," Ren said. "They will be best protected if you leave this place."

"But who will watch over us?" The doctor spoke the words, but he realized he wasn't speaking to her. He was talking to *them*.

And they were exhausted. It must be taking a lot out of them to control this many people at once. No wonder, the moment they believed he was committed to them, they withdrew from his mind.

"I will."

It seemed to satisfy the woman, if not the babies. With no obvious signal that Ren could see, the crowd began to move toward the door, staring off into space, their minds still dulled by whatever enchantment the babies had managed to work on them. He stood back against the wall, the knife behind his back, and waited for the hotel staff to leave. There was still no sign of Marie-Claire. Nor of Darragh.

He waited for the last of the shuffling mob to leave, expecting the voices to return, but they stayed silent. A soft thud as something landed on the carpet at his feet caught his attention. Ren looked down, wondering what had caused the sound, and then he picked it up. It was the knife from the glass case downstairs, he realized, unsure of why it was here. The last time he recalled seeing the knife was when Marie-Claire told him it was the blade they used to test the psychic link between the twins they bred.

He studied it curiously, turning the *airgead sídhe* blade this way and that to examine the intricate carvings etched into its surface. With his thumb he felt the tip, wondering how sharp it was.

"Ow!" The blade pierced his flesh. It was just a tiny pinprick, really, but the *airgead sídhe* burned his flesh...

And cleared the fog from his mind.

Ren looked around and realized he was standing in a dark, empty hall and, until a moment ago, had been prepared to devote his life to protecting two babies he'd never laid eyes on... two babies he was destined to kill.

They'd taken him over as easily as the doctor and the rest of the people here. Probably as easily as Marie-Claire. And Darragh.

Mama tried to hurt us... papa is here now... he'll protect us...

There was nothing in Ren's dream about fighting Darragh off.

Nothing else is going according to the dream. Why should that be any different?

Clutching the *airgead sídhe* blade once more, Ren pushed off the wall and began walking down the long corridor until he reached the nursery. The room was lit by a security light outside that filled the room with shadows. Rain lashed at the windows and in the center of the room sat the *mara-warra* cradle he'd seen so often in his dreams.

If my Destiny is so set, Ren wondered, *why do I feel like I have a choice here? Why do I feel like I could just open my mind and let them make me their slave?*

It came to Ren, then, what the Hag had meant when she said she wouldn't have to *make* him kill the babies.

And that's what really frightens you, Rónán of the Undivided... Even in your vision, you are doing what is right of your own free will.

Ren closed his eyes. He took a deep breath and concentrated on the *kuji-in.* The skill he'd mastered, when he was searching for a way home. The skill he'd used more times than he cared to count to block his thoughts and his presence from the *Matrarchaí* and the powerful Empress and Emperor twins he'd killed trying to save as many *sídhe* as he could.

Rin for strength of mind and body. Hei to focus psychic power in order to mask one's presence. Toh to balance the solid and liquid states of the body. Sha to heal oneself or another. Kai for complete control over the body's functions. Jin to focus the mind's telepathic powers. Retsu to harness one's telekinetic powers. Zai to bring harmony by merging with the universe.

And Zen. Enlightenment and understanding.

He'd finally worked that last one out. Ren opened his eyes and stepped into the room, armored now against anything they could throw at him.

Destiny had chosen well, he realized, because there was probably no other living soul in this realm, or any other, so uniquely equipped to do what must be done.

THE DARK DIVIDE

It shouldn't be so easy to take a life.

CHAPTER 58

Rónán approached the cradle that rocked gently in the center of the room. Darragh watched him from the shadows, overcome by a sense of having been here before.

But this was altered. In the dream he remembered seeing everything by moonlight, not the lightning of an angry storm. In the dream, he'd been mildly concerned about what his brother intended to do.

The reality was quite different. The walls were glistening with blood. The air reeked. Marie-Claire stood over the cradle cooing to the babies, so enchanted by them she hadn't noticed him, or his brother, enter the room.

Darragh wanted to help his twin. He knew he should, but he was powerless to fight off the need to protect the monsters he'd spawned.

They needed him. They needed someone to protect them.

You'll protect us, won't you, papa?
Of course I will.

Rónán reached the cradle and stopped to study it for a moment. It was the cradle they both knew so well from their dream - oak, carved with elaborate Celtic knotwork, inlaid with softly glowing mother-of-pearl.

Only now it was smeared with something that smelled like fresh blood.

Marie-Claire looked up, as if she'd only just realized Rónán was there.

"Aren't they beautiful?"

Rónán held the *airgead sídhe* blade behind his back. Darragh wondered if it would be enough.

Enough for what?

Don't you worry about Uncle Rónán, my darlings. He won't hurt you.

The *airgead sídhe* blade caught the light in odd places, illuminating the engraving on the blade.

"They're lovely," Rónán replied. "They look so innocent. Almost human."

Marie-Claire smiled. "You don't seriously mean to hurt them, do you?"

He glanced over his shoulder. Darragh wondered if Rónán knew he was standing in the shadows by the door.

Rónán turned back to Marie-Claire. "It has to be done, Marie-Claire. You know that."

"They are everything we hoped for. More even. They can force Partition. They are the start of our brave new world."

"They're not human."

"They are the next step in human evolution."

"They are a testament to your hypocrisy," Rónán told her. "You want to destroy the Faerie, but you needed to create Faerie monsters to do it. You've deliberately bred the *sídhe* into every set of Undivided that you could for the past two millennia, just so you can be rid of them."

Marie-Claire's smile faded. "You seem remarkably well informed about us, Rónán."

"I make it my business to be well informed about the people who seemed to be bent on destroying my life and everyone in it."

"You are being a touch dramatic, I fear. Still ... perhaps there is a place for you in the new realm. Your brother will be joining us, after all."

"No, he won't."

"I think you'll find he has no choice in the matter. He's a father now. He has responsibilities. Isn't that right, Darragh?"

He should have known better than to believe Marie-Claire was unaware of his presence. Realising there was no point in hiding any longer, Darragh stepped out from the shadows.

What's going on, papa? Why is our uncle angry with Mother? Doesn't she love us?

Rónán turned to look at him for a moment. He didn't seem in the least surprised to find him here, either.

"So," Marie-Claire said, "the vision comes to pass."

She must have the Sight, too, Darragh thought, taking a small step sideways. Nobody seemed to notice, neither Rónán, Marie-Claire, or the twins. *I wonder if the future she sees has a different ending*

to the one Rónán and I have shared all these years.
And if it is different, whose version is going to win in
the end?

It will end how we decide, papa.

Rónán shook his head. He still had his arm and the knife behind his back. Darragh looked away and continued to sidle alongside the cradle toward Marie-Claire. He tried to fill his mind with thoughts of love and affection for his daughters. He forced no hint of his despair or horror to show through, afraid they would see through him if he dwelt on it for too long.

"This is not my dream, Marie-Claire," Rónán was saying. He was keeping her engaged and her attention away from his brother, although whether it was deliberate or by coincidence, Darragh wasn't really sure. "You were never in any vision I ever had."

"You've always been in mine, Rónán. Right up until you die."

"You can't kill me," Rónán reminded her. "If the babies want their father around so they can enjoy your brave new world, I get to live. If I die, he dies, remember."

Marie-Claire didn't seem to have an answer for that so she turned to Darragh. He froze. "Talk to your brother, Darragh. Explain this to him."

"They are innocent," Darragh said to Rónán, just as he was meant to. There was no emotion in his voice. They were just words. Words he always said in his dream.

Do I utter the same words in Marie-Claire's
dream? In Rónán's?

583

Would it be enough to allay their suspicions?

"How can you say that?" Rónán asked, staring at his brother in disgust. "You saw what they did to Brydie."

"They didn't know. Didn't understand... She was trying to smother them."

"And you haven't thought to ask *why*?"

Don't let him hurt us, papa. Is he going to hurt us? We can't tell. We can't tell what he's thinking.

"They are death, Darragh. They've killed once already. They'll kill you and I as soon as they don't need us any more. And if *she* has her way," he added, pointing at Marie-Claire, "they'll be the death of billions upon billions more."

Why is he saying those things about us, papa? Doesn't he love us?

Why can't we tell what he's thinking?

Not now. Let me take care of this. Darragh shook his head. "They won't..." He didn't finish the sentence. *Why* can't *they tell what Rónán's thinking?*

"Partition is not the end," Marie-Claire said. "It is a new beginning."

"There's a few million Faerie out there who might disagree with that," Rónán said.

Marie-Claire reached out a hand to him. "You don't have to do anything you don't want to, Rónán. Your brother won't let you. *They* won't let you do it. You're not a tool of the Hag. Neither of you are. You don't have to do her bidding."

"Even if she's right?"

"What is right?" Marie-Claire asked. "You've seen this moment a thousand times in your dreams, I suspect, and how much of it is what you saw? Right is what *is*. Embrace what Destiny has offered you."

"I am embracing it," Rónán told her. "I will end this."

"I won't let you."

"How will you stop me?" he asked as he raised the blade.

Darragh looked down into the cradle. One of girls was stirring - they were too alike to tell which was which. She opened her eyes to stare up at him, her face framed by soft dark curls, her expression disturbingly alert and aware for one so young. Her eyes were strange... blue with no pupil and no whites at all. Just a pool of blue terror that had already killed once and would kill again and again until they'd achieved their goal.

"I won't stop you," Marie-Claire said, "they will."

The other baby's eyes flew open. Darragh realized what she was doing. She was ordering them to kill Rónán.

No! Wait! If you kill Rónán, you'll kill me too! He barely completed the thought when Marie-Claire's hands flew to her ears and she cried out in agony. Her nose was dripping blood, her tears ducts were leaking blood. She dropped to her knees, screaming something incomprehensible. Darragh watched in horror as they pulverized Marie-Claire from the inside out. He hadn't meant to order the babies to kill Marie-Claire. He'd told them not to kill Rónán.

Apparently, you were either with them or against them, and against was a death sentence.

It took Marie-Claire a few long and agonising minutes to die. Neither Darragh not Rónán moved to aid her. There was nothing they could have done, in any case.

When she finally stopped moving, a bloody, broken heap on the floor at the head of the cradle, Darragh turned to Rónán.

He met his brother's eye and knew, at that moment, what they must do. Funny how all this time, he'd believed that one of them would try to kill the babies and the other would try to prevent it. He realized now it was nothing of the kind. The dream had just been a rehearsal, a chance to perfect their script as he distracted these evil-spawned monsters so his brother - who for some reason could block them from his mind - moved in for the kill.

"I'll kill you if I have to, Rónán, to stop this." He said the words, just as he always did in his dream.

Rónán nodded in understanding and replied exactly the way he was meant to, dismissing the empty threat. "Even if you could get across this room before the deed was done, Darragh, you can't kill me without killing yourself, which would achieve precisely what I am here to prevent."

Rónán moved the blade a little, repositioning his grip. The security lighting from outside caught the blade and danced across its engraved surface, mesmerising the baby. There was a drawn-out silence, as Rónán played the light across the blade. Darragh remained motionless.

"There must be another way." He could hear the note of defeat in his voice; the glimmer of acceptance.

"I wouldn't be here if there was," Rónán replied, still staring down at the baby he was destined to kill. "You know that," he added, looking up at Darragh. "You're just not willing to accept the truth of it yet."

Darragh held out his hand, as if he expected the blade to be handed over, and for this night to be forgotten, somehow. They had to believe he was going to protect them. "They're just babies."

"They are Partition and the destruction that goes with it."

"But they're innocents. Dammit... they're your own flesh and blood!"

"Tell that to Brydie. And all the others." Rónán gripped the blade tighter and turned back to the cradle, steeling his resolve with a conscious act of will. "They are abominations, bred to cause chaos and strife."

"Maybe we can save them."

"Marie-Claire was right, you know. I see the future, Darragh. So do you. And I dare you to deny the future you see isn't just as filled with chaos and strife because of what these children are, as the future I perceive."

Papa ... what does he mean? Is he mad at us? Is he mad at Marie-Claire? We killed Marie-Claire for you. Why can't we tell what's he's thinking?

Darragh didn't argue with him. Whatever Rónán had seen, it wasn't in his head, so Hope and Calamity couldn't see it either. Was Destiny so clever that he had manipulated this event, this moment, to happen in *this* world, away from magic, so Darragh couldn't know what his brother knew and give the game away?

Turning back to the babies, Ren reached into the cradle with his left hand to pull back the blankets covering the children. The twin who was awake grabbed his finger. Her frightening blue eyes smiling up at him, she squeezed it gently. Darragh watched and tried to think of anything else other than what was about to happen, too appalled to allow it, too afraid to stop it.

"Help me or leave," Rónán told him, just as he did in the dream. "Just don't stand there feigning disgust, as if you had no part in bringing us to this pass."

"Perhaps the future we see isn't ours..."

"Are you kidding me? Look around you, Darragh." He raised the blade, transfixed by the dangerous blue on blue eyes staring up at him.

"Get the fuck away from that cradle, Ren."

Darragh and Rónán both looked up to find Pete standing in the door, shotgun at his shoulder. Logan was right behind him.

See papa, he can't hurt us. If you can't stop him, we can.

Darragh didn't know if Pete and Logan had been taken over by the babies as everyone else who came near them seemed to be. Everyone but Rónán, who was somehow able to resist their insidious control. It didn't really matter. Even if they had just arrived in time to see Rónán about to murder a newborn baby, their reaction would probably have been the same.

It must have been only seconds; time slowed down for Darragh. He saw Rónán bring the knife down sharply, slicing through the swaddling and fragile ribs without remorse or regret as the flash from the shotgun blinded him. He called out, throwing himself in front of Rónán so his brother could do what must be done before these monsters realized they were powerful enough to do what the *Matrarchaí* wanted of them.

It wasn't about one or two people dying, Darragh realized, in a moment of clarity that made all the nightmares he'd ever suffered gel into a single perfect purpose. It wasn't about killing. It wasn't about right and wrong. It wasn't even about the Undivided, Faerie or human, good or evil.

It was about stopping the universe being reset back to zero and killing every living thing in the process. Creation was protecting itself. They were just the tools the universe needed to set things to rights.

Darragh's moment of clarity seemed eternal, but it couldn't have been more than a split second. His cry of protest was drowned out by the boom of the shotgun and then it vanished to be replaced by a burning, agonising pain as his chest took the full impact of the shotgun blast at almost point-blank range.

Before Darragh hit the ground, before Rónán could extract the *airgead sídhe* blade from one tiny heart and plunge it into another, he heard an agonised wail and realized it wasn't the babies, it was him.

CHAPTER 59

"Something's wrong."

"Something's wrong. Something's wrong. Something's wrong," Echo repeated in a panic, buzzing around like a trapped insect.

Trása peered out of the window of Annad's car at the entrance to the Castle Golf Club. The gates were closed, the rain was pelting down and there was no sign of Pete and Logan, no sign of Ren or Darragh, and no sign of Stella Delany.

"Nothing's wrong," she assured the psychiatrist. And the pixie.

"They should be here by now."

"You don't know that."

"If anything happens to my wife..."

He didn't finish the sentence, probably because he had nothing to more add. There were few threats a law-abiding Gardaí psychologist could make to a couple of fugitives from another reality that would have much of an impact on them.

"They *are* taking an incredibly long time," Nika pointed out from the back seat.

"They're fine." Trása said it for herself as much as the others.

"We could call them," Annad suggested.

"*Call the, call them, call them,*" Echo urged, although nobody paid her any attention.

"How?" Nika scoffed, as if the idea was ludicrous.

"Cell phone," Trása explained, mentally kicking herself for not thinking of it sooner. Of *course* they should call Stella. To cover her annoyance at herself, she turned to Annad and asked possibly the stupidest question she'd ever uttered. "Do you have your wife's cell phone number?"

Annad gave her a look that said he wasn't even going to bother dignifying her question with so much as a nod.

"Okay, then," Trása snapped. "Call her. Wait!"

She grabbed the phone from Annad, found the favourites list and dialed the number for Stella herself, just in case Annad got any ideas about calling somebody else. Like his workmates in the Gardaí.

Stella answered the phone on the second ring. "Annad?"

"No, it's Trása. What's happening?"

"I... I don't know..." Stella's voice was vague. Uncertain.

"What do you mean, you don't *know*?"

"I mean I don't know!" Stella snapped more forcefully. "Something happened. Something upstairs... there were shots... there're all these people milling about... it's like they were drugged, or something and they're just coming out of it."

"What happened to Pete? To Logan?"

"I have no idea ... I haven't seen them since ... where are *you*? Where is Annad? What have you done to my husband?"

"Nothing," Trása told her. Stella sounded as if she was just emerging from a deep sleep and getting angrier the more awake she became. "Annad is fine. Where are Pete and Logan? Did they find Rónán? Or Darragh?"

"I don't *know*, I said," Stella barked. "Maybe it was them in the helicopter that took off a little while ago... but... you know what... screw you, lady!"

Trása handed the phone back to Annad. "She hung up on me."

"Is she all right?"

"She sounded just fine. And I'll bet you anything you care to name she's calling the Gardaí as we speak."

Annad's eyes widened in fear. "You can't blame her for -"

"Give it a rest," Trása cut in. "We're not going to kill you, your kids, or anybody else for that matter. We just want to go home. She said a helicopter just took off from there a little while ago. Can you hear anything?"

"What's a helicopter?" Nika asked.

"You'll know it when you see it," Trása promised with a smile. Things were looking up if Pete had been able to commandeer a helicopter. That meant no Gardaí and a clear run to the golf course and the stone circle. With luck, he'd found Rónán and Darragh, and hopefully Rónán still had enough magical power left to open a rift and get them out of this dreadful place. Stella had said something about shots, but she didn't say anything about injuries or people dying, so Trása decided to hope for the best. Maybe someone had taken a shot at them as they were leaving?

I didn't know Pete or Logan knew how to fly a helicopter.

Trása glanced up, but the rain, the thunder and the lightning meant she couldn't see or hear a damn thing. Across the street, the golf club's gates were closed, but they were mostly decorative and the brick fence either side of them was low enough to step over. They could probably drive the car straight through the gates if they wanted, but that would cause unwanted attention. They would be much better off on foot.

"Come on," Trása said, putting her hand on the door latch. "We'll meet them at the circle."

"It's pissing down rain out there!"

"It's only water," Nika pointed out, "and you can only get so wet. Don't be such a baby."

"Why don't I just wait here?"

"And miss your chance to see a rift opening to another reality?" Trása asked, guessing Annad wouldn't want to pass up a chance to either see for himself that they were right, or gloat a little when it was proved they were wrong.

Annad still hesitated. "Are you sure my wife is okay?"

"Yes. I'm sure. Now are you coming or does Nika have to knock you unconscious to keep you from betraying our presence in this realm before we leave?"

"I'll come," Annad said, glancing at Nika with a frown.

Trása opened the car door and was hit with a wall of wind-driven icy rain. Echo zipped past her ear and was gone before she could stop her. The others climbed out of the car and together, bent over against the downpour, the three of them ran across the street, stepped over the fence and headed across the car park toward the fairways and the stone circle.

They reached the second fairway just as the first, faint rhythmic thumps of a helicopter's rotor blades beat their way through the air, and Trása picked up her pace.

It is nearly done, she realized with relief, not caring about the icy rain.

Rónán and Darragh were almost home. Together, they could tackle anything Marcroy tried to throw at them. They could break the curse on her. They could take their rightful place as the Undivided of their own realm.

She glanced up and spied the helicopter in the distance.

A few more minutes, she promised herself, determined to believe Rónán would arrive with the power to open the rift. *A few more minutes and we'll be home.*

CHAPTER 60

The helo pilot did an admirable job, all things considered, Pete thought. It wasn't easy - and probably against air safety regulations - to fly through weather like this. To do it with a shotgun pressed to your temple was even more heroic.

He spied Trása, Nika and Annad running across the fairway and signaled to the pilot to put down and then glanced over his shoulder. Logan and Ren in the back were working on Darragh, trying to stop the blood loss long enough to get him to the rift. Logan was doing most of the work. Ren cradled Darragh's head in his lap, talking to his brother intently. It was impossible to hear what he was telling him over the noise of the helo. It was possible that Darragh couldn't hear him either. At Ren's feet was a carryall he'd found at the castle, filled with a grotesque souvenir of their visit to this realm.

When they got through to the other side and once they'd sorted Darragh out, Pete intended to have a long and very serious talk to Ren about the contents of that bag.

"Are you sure you can open a rift?" he shouted to Ren as they began to descend. He'd asked Ren the same question back at the castle, in the chaos that followed Darragh diving in front of a shotgun blast, when Ren demanded they highjack the helo so they could get Darragh to the nearest rift and back to a magical realm before he died. So much had happened in such a short time, there had been little chance for anybody to deal with what had happened. Or what they had done.

Ren looked up and nodded. "Trust me!" he shouted back.

"Yeah," Pete muttered to himself, as he turned back to the pilot, "'cause that's worked out so well, lately."

The pilot, a ginger-haired young man, with pale skin that looked positively ashen at the moment, landed the helo with only a slight bump and then looked at Pete expectantly.

"Shut it down," Pete ordered. "All the way down." He didn't want this guy trying to be a hero and taking off while they were disembarking.

The pilot did as Pete ordered. In the back, Logan unlatched the door and kicked it open. He jumped out and then turned to help Ren unload Darragh as Trása ran up to them with Nika and Annad not far behind.

"Are you going to kill me now?" the pilot asked, in the sudden silence once the engines stopped.

"No. Just..." Pete hesitated. It didn't matter what he told him. The moment they were out of sight, he was going to radio for help. "Give me your cell phone."

The young man reached into his jacket pocket and handed it over with a great deal of reluctance.

"Now cover your ears."

The pilot hastily did what Pete asked when he saw him aiming the shotgun at the radio. Pete let it have both barrels. He wasn't sure if the buckshot was enough to disable it, but it scared the crap out of the pilot and probably bought them a few extra minutes.

"We're going now. You can go for help if you want. We'll be gone before you get back. Have a nice life."

Pete jerked open the door in time to hear Trása demanding to know what had happened. He ran around to the other side of the helo to help with Darragh. Annad and Nika moved to assist without asking.

"What happened?" Trása kept demanding, as they pulled him clear. Darragh cried out with the pain, but they didn't have time to be gentle. If Stella hadn't raised the alarm already, the pilot was going to the moment he thought he was clear. "Who shot him? We have to open the rift! He's dying!"

"The bag!" Ren ordered. "Get the bag!"

Pete didn't have time to warn her what the bag contained. Trása reached into the helo and grabbed it, slinging it over her shoulder and running after them.

They pushed their way through the undergrowth to the stone circle and laid Darragh down on the wet ground. As soon as he'd let go, Ren grabbed the bag from Trása's shoulder and turned to Nika. "Give me your talisman."

"It won't work here," Nika said. "There's no -"

"Just give it to me!"

She did as he asked, reaching under her shirt to pull out the disgusting mummified baby's foot that she always wore. In her realm - or any magical realm for that matter - it had been charged with magic and was capable of opening a rift. Here it was useless.

"If you want Toyoda and the pixie to come back with us, you'd better summon them now," he warned as he unzipped the bag.

Trása leaned forward to see what was inside and then stumbled backward, gasping. "Oh, my God! Is that...?"

Ren plunged the mummified foot into the bag and then extracted it, black and dripping with blood. He stood up and held the dripping talisman aloft, then closed his eyes. Pete felt the atmosphere change. The rain around them stopped, falling away from the stone circle as if it was protected by a translucent dome. He felt magic crackling in the air, making the hairs on his forearms stand on end, but it wasn't magic he was used to. This was thick. Ancient. Sour. And when lightning began to steak around them, it wasn't red, but a sinister shade of purple. Out of the corner of his eye. he saw Toyoda appear. Nika had her hands cupped in such a fashion that he guessed she had Echo safely contained. Darragh lay on the ground, fading fast. Logan was on his knees beside him, hands pressed to his chest to stop the bleeding.

Pete stook a step back, bumping into Annad.

"See," he said, smiling at the awestruck look on the psychologist's face as the rift resolved and the world on the other side - moonlight and peaceful - became visible. "I told you it was real."

"I'm tripping on something, aren't I?"

"Feels like it, doesn't it?"

Annad nodded and then he turned to Pete. "You're not coming back, are you?"

"Not if I can help it."

"Then that's what I'll tell them happened here. I was tripping on something."

"Come on!" Logan yelled at Pete. They were dragging Darragh through to the other side and he could see the rift destabilising around the edges already. Whatever dark force Ren had used to open the rift, it wasn't going to hold for long.

"Thanks for your help, Annad." Pete didn't wait for him to answer. He could see the rift collapsing. He dived headfirst through the portal, landing hard on the stones on the other side, rolling to a stop in time to see Trása morph into an owl, screeching furiously at the indignity of it as she flew away.

Standing on the edge of the circle in what had to be Darragh and Ren's home realm was an old crone, clutching a gnarled staff.

"Only one," she said to Ren, while he bent down to save his brother.

"Turns out *your* vision was wrong," Ren said. He tore open Darragh's ruined shirt and placed his hand on his chest. They all felt the powerful surge of magic as Ren drew the shot from Darragh's wounds and healed his shredded chest. This was not the magic he'd used to open the rift. This was clean. Pure magic. *Sídhe* magic, joyous and untainted by the corruption of the babies, Hope and Calamity.

Thinking of them made Pete glance at the bag that lay on the ground near Ren's feet. Did the Hag - for that was surely who this old biddy was - know what the bag contained?

"I am never wrong," the Hag said, as Darragh struggled to sit up, the only sign of his wounds a torn dress shirt and a thoroughly ruined Armani tuxedo. "There can be only one who survives. Do you understand me, Rónán?"

Ren smiled down at his brother and offered him his hand. He pulled Darragh to his feet and then turned to face the Hag. "I understand."

Pete didn't know what she was talking about, but apparently Darragh did. He grabbed at Ren's arm as his brother stepped forward to confront the old woman. "It is done," he said, "but I want a favor in return."

"If I can grant it," the Hag agreed with a nod.

Ren leaned toward her and spoke for a moment, and then he added in a voice so soft Pete could barely make out his words: "Now make the nightmares go away."

The Hag smiled and morphed into a much younger woman for a moment. She reached out and touched Ren's face with gentle finger. As soon as she did, he dropped like a sack at her feet, his eyes wide and staring and very, very dead.

For a moment, nobody moved, too stunned by what had happened to react. By the time Pete looked up again, the Hag was back in her crone aspect. She raised her staff and pointed it at the carryall.

"You must burn that with him," she ordered.

"You know what's in the bag?" Pete asked. He wasn't sure why he asked it. It was obvious she did. Maybe it was because he couldn't think of anything else to say.

"I do," the Hag said. "Guard it well until it's disposed of."

"We will." It was Nika who answered her. She stepped up beside Pete and slipped her hand into his, squeezing it tightly.

The Hag turned to Darragh then and bowed to him. "Welcome home, *leathtiarna.*"

"Are the Brethren turned assassin, now?" he asked. He was kneeling beside Ren's body in shock.

She shook her head. "It would make things considerably easier for us if we were."

He looked up at her angrily. "Why not just let me die and be done with it?"

"Because that is not how Destiny wanted it."

"What difference does it make? We're Undivided. You've killed me, anyway."

"How long does he have?" Logan asked.

"As long as he's got," the Hag replied, and then she vanished, leaving them alone in the moonlit stone circle with Ren's lifeless body, and no sound but the plaintive wail of a barn owl circling overhead, crying out in pain.

CHAPTER 61

They burned Rónán's body, the carryall and their clothes from the other realm on a pyre overlooking the same loch where Amergin had thrown the baby Rónán through the rift into a world without magic. Trása stood vigil over the flames, remembering her father, wondering what had driven him to do such a terrible thing. She had always thought it a weakness of character on his part, but now she wondered if the Hag was right. Destiny ruled some more than others. Rónán was destined to save them all, what set them on the path leading to that fateful moment her father and Marcroy colluding to separate the Undivided and throw a young child into another realm and let Destiny rule his fate.

She felt, rather than saw, Marcroy arrive behind her as the sun set behind the hill and the flames licked at Rónán's shroud. There was a time when his arrival would have set her pulse racing in fear. Odd that she was no longer afraid of Marcroy. There was no reason not to be; he was still as powerful as he ever was. Still as fickle. Still prone to cursing those who disobeyed or disappointed him.

And just as much a tool of Destiny as the rest of them. It made him seem much less scary. "You managed to get Darragh to break the curse, I see."

"Your son lies dead. You have another son about to die. And that's all you can think of to say?"

"I never really knew Rónán."

"You know Darragh well enough."

Marcroy was silent for a moment before he asked, "Is it true Rónán saved us all?"

"We're standing here talking about it, aren't we?"

He nodded. "It is to be expected, naturally, that any son of mine would be capable of great heroism."

"So you don't mind owning a couple of mongrel *sídhe* now they're heroes."

Marcroy chose not to answer that. He glanced around, as if expecting more mourners. "Where is Darragh? I thought he would be here, farewelling his twin."

"No need for a farewell. He'll be joining him, soon enough."

"And what of your accomplices?"

She glanced at him curiously. "My what? Oh! You met Pete and Logan? And Nika?"

"Their names are irrelevant."

"I'm sure they'd disagree," she said, "but you'll be pleased to know they're leaving your realm as soon as the Brethren have finished with them."

"What do the Brethren want with more mongrel *sídhe*?"

Trása smiled. She was going to enjoy this. "Pete and Logan are Undivided, uncle. Didn't you know that? At least they would have been if they hadn't been taken from their own realm as babies by the *Matrarchaí*. With the loss of Teagan, and therefore Isleen - wherever she was - the ninja realm has lost its Undivided. The Brethren have agreed to brand them with the triskalion so they can go back as Undivided, and continue helping the *Youkai* and *sídhe* refugees who've made that realm their home. Nika will be their Vate."

"And you will be their *Youkai* queen, I suppose?"

Trása tried not to smile too broadly. Marcroy didn't take well to people gloating at him.

He scowled at her. "What spell did you work on the Brethren to allow *that* to happen?"

"I didn't work any spell. Rónán asked a boon of the Hag before she killed him."

Marcroy couldn't do anything about that, but he wasn't going to let her enjoy a single moment of her victory over him. Not if he could help it. "The *Tuatha Dé Danann* refugees in that realm will never stand for you as their monarch, petal."

Trása nodded. "I know. But I thought of that, too. I petitioned the Brethren on their behalf and they have agreed to let the pure *Tuatha Dé Danann* come here to this realm." She glanced at Marcroy's thunderous expression and smiled. "I told the Hag you'd really like the idea. I mean, you and Stiofán were such firm friends so quickly when you came to my new realm, it seemed a shame not to let you enjoy his company all the time."

She was rewarded by an exasperated cry as Marcroy vanished into thin air, too angry at her to even argue about it. Trása turned back to the pyre, wishing Rónán had been here to see it. He didn't know Marcroy that well, but he knew how much Trása had feared him as a child.

"You would have been very proud of me, just now," she told him.

"He can't hear you, Trása, or have you decided there is an afterlife?"

She turned to find Darragh coming up the hill behind her. He looked more the Darragh she remembered from her childhood, but in many other ways, he was unrecognizable. "You just missed Marcroy," she told him.

"No. I waited until he left. He didn't look happy."

Trása smiled. "No, he didn't, did he?"

He climbed the last few steps, panting a little from the exertion.

"How are you feeling?" she asked. It was two days since they had come through the rift and he was still alive. The record, as far as Trása knew, was about a week between one psychically linked twin dying and his other twin dying too. Darragh looked too healthy to only have a few more days to live.

"I'm not about to drop dead at your feet," he assured her. "At least, I don't think so. I assume there'll be some warning. If not, it's been good knowing you, Trása."

"You shouldn't laugh about it."

"Rónán would have. He was much braver than I."

"You're brave, Darragh. You survived ten years in prison in that horrid realm."

"And my brother resisted the temptation to come for me," he said, "knowing the moment he did, our fates would be taken out of our hands. I would not have had the courage to do what he did. Either to wait it out or -"

"Or to kill two babies."

Darragh placed his hand on her shoulder. "Do not judge him harshly, Trása. I know you and he... he did what needed to be done. Our dangerous line is dead so the *Matrarchaí* is rendered powerless. Whatever you think of my brother, remember that."

"I will."

He put his arm around her shoulder, and they stood there watching the fire burn in companionable silence. After a few moments she put her head on Darragh's shoulder and closed her eyes.

Our dangerous line is dead so the Matrarchaí *is rendered powerless*, Darragh had said.

If he thinks his line is dangerous, Trása thought, as they watched the pyre burn down to coals and then ashes, *it's probably best I don't mention that I think I might be pregnant.*

EPILOGUE

Hayley's first day on the job was both exciting and terrifying. It was exciting, because she actually had a job at a time when so many people didn't. There had been something called the GFC while she was away that meant lot of people were out of work. Somehow, despite that, she'd found a job as an office junior. And it wasn't just any old boring office, either. It was a modeling agency.

Kiva had pulled some strings, Hayley was certain. She'd been represented by this agency once, back before she made it as an actress.

Or perhaps it was some sort of reward. Hayley didn't know what had happened to the girl who came through the rift and went straight into labour. She hadn't seen her since she was whisked away to Cambria Castle in a helicopter. Hayley hadn't seen Marie-Claire since then, either.

She wanted to ask after them, but she wasn't sure who she should ask. She'd had no interview for her new position. Just a phone call informing her she had a job with ORM if she wanted it, working in reception, and if she was interested to be at the office first thing Monday, ready to start work.

Perhaps the *Matrarchaí* remembered her phone call. Perhaps they only hired people who knew their secret and they felt could be trusted with the truth about other realities.

Hayley didn't really care. She was twenty-seven, hadn't finished high school, had never had a serious boyfriend and everyone thought she was crazy. Employment of any kind was welcome, although she'd expected to end up talking into a headset all day, asking a steady stream of customers if they wanted fries with their burgers. To have scored a "real" job was more than she could have hoped for. To be working in the only place where they knew she wasn't crazy, was beyond a dream.

She hadn't dared imagine such an opportunity existed.

Hayley pushed open the heavy glass door of the ORM office and walked up to the reception desk, trying not to look too overawed by the glitzy, modern office. There was nobody at the desk when she reached it, just a phone ringing incessantly.

She looked up and down the hall, either side of the desk, but there was nobody there. The phone kept ringing.

Hayley wondered if she should answer it.

"Are you the new girl?"

She turned to find a young woman shouldering her way through the glass door, carrying a tray of coffee in one hand and a cardboard tray full of pastries in the other. Hayley hurried to the door and held it open for her.

"Thanks," the young woman said. "My name is Teagan. You're Kaylee, aren't you?"

"Hayley," she corrected. "Can I help you with anything?"

"Take these," she said, offering her the tray of pastries. "We'll put them in the conference room."

Hayley followed Teagan past the reception desk and the still-ringing phone to the double doors at the end of the hall. She opened them to reveal a long conference table surrounded by twelve, deep leather chairs. Hayley put the tray on the table and turned to Teagan. "Will I be collecting stuff from the bakery in future?"

Teagan let out a short laugh. "Seriously? This is a modeling agency, sweetie. Nobody here eats anything. These are for a special occasion."

"What's the occasion?"

"The new boss is arriving."

"What happened to the old one?" Hayley cringed when she realized how that sounded. "I mean... I thought Marie-Claire... Well, I just wondered..."

"And I'd tell you if I knew," Teagan said, opening the door of the credenza. She pulled out a serving platter, peeled the clingwrap from the top of the cardboard tray and began arranging the pastries on the platter. "All I know, Marie-Claire is gone and someone named Charlotte is coming to take her place."

"Is she...?" Hayley began, but she hesitated, not sure if Teagan knew about the *Matrarchaí*, although working here, she couldn't imagine she didn't know about them.

"Were you going to ask if she's from *here*?"

There was enough emphasis on the word "here" for Hayley to have her question answered. She nodded.

Teagan shrugged. "Maybe. I don't know, and I've learned not to ask."

"Are you...?"

"From here?" Teagan said. "No. But my sister's missing. Without her, I'm just an office girl."

"That seems harsh." Hayley began to help move the pastries onto the platter. Menial and insignificant a task as it was, it made her feel useful.

Teagan didn't seem unduly bothered by her sister's disappearance. "I'm just grateful she's alive somewhere. Maybe she'll turn up, someday."

"But the *Matrarchaí* gave you a job in the meantime."

"They like to keep an eye on their investments," Teagan said. "After we're done here, I'll show you around and organize for you get a computer log-in. Is your mother one of us?"

"My mother's dead. My stepmother is, though... I think. And Kiva Kavanaugh is her cousin."

"Well, that explains what you're doing here."

They both turned to the door at the unexpected comment to find a tall, elegantly suited woman standing in the doorway. She smiled at them and stepped into the conference room like she owned the place. "I always like to see the next generation doing their part."

Hayley didn't know who the woman was, but she seemed very familiar. After a moment, she realized why. This woman was blonde and Marie-Claire had been dark-haired, but the two were almost identical.

Was this Marie-Claire's sister? Or was it just a different version of her from another reality?

Is there another one of me out there somewhere? Is she starting work today, too? Or did none of this ever happen to her? Maybe she's having a perfectly ordinary life.

"Charlotte?" Teagan asked, although she must know who this was, given how much like Marie-Claire she was.

"You're Teagan, yes? And who is this?"

"Hayley Boyle, miss... ma'am."

Charlotte smiled at her awkwardness. "You may call me Mother. What time will the others be here?"

"Everyone is usually on deck by nine," Teagan said.

Charlotte frowned. "Well, that will have to change. We've too much work to do to have people wandering in here mid-morning to start work."

"What work?" Hayley asked, guessing Charlotte wasn't talking about rounding up a posse of models for a runway show.

"Why, Partition of course," she said, looking at Hayley as if she should have known the answer. "We've had something of a setback, but there are seers among us who can see the future. All is not lost."

"Setback?" Teagan asked. "What setback?" She glanced at Hayley with a questioning look, but Hayley didn't know any more about it than Teagan did.

"Nothing you two need to worry yourselves about," Charlotte said, with a wave of her hand, as if that put an end to the subject. "But rest assured, my dears, we are far from done. Somewhere out there the children we need will soon be born.

"Trust me, my dears, in your lifetimes, we will achieve Partition."

THE WORLD OF THE UNDIVIDED AND THE FAERIE

Proper names are in bold type

A Mháistir (a MAW ster) Master.

A Mháistreás (a MAW stress) Mistress.

A Stóirín (ah stor-een) Term of endearment. Roughly translates as "My love".

Aintín (ann-teen) Faerie word for Aunt.

Airgead sídhe (AR-gat Shee) Faerie silver.

Airurundo (air-RU-run-doe) Japanese name for Ireland in the *ori mahou* reality.

Amergin (aw-VEER-een) Vate of All Ireland until his death. Trása's father.

An Bhantiarna (on can-teer-na) Lady.

Aoi (ow-ee) Eldest daughter of the Ikushima clan.

Arigatou gozaimasu (ah-ree-gah-tou Go-zai-mah-su) Thank you very much.

Banphrionsa (ban frinsah) Princess.

Bealtaine (byawltuhnuh) Summer equinox.

Beansídhe (ban-shee) Faerie with long hair and red eyes due to continuous weeping. Their wailing is a warning of a death in the vicinity.

Brendá (BREN daw) Queen of the Celts. Mother of Torcán.

Bríghid (breed) Celtish princess. Niece of Brendá. Cousin of Torcán.

Brionglóid Gorm (bring-load gurm) Roughly translates as "Blue Dreams". Magic powder used by the Druids to induce instant unconsciousness.

Brithem (bree-them) A Druid judge or an arbitrator. They specialise in lexichemy - magic using the spoken word.

Broc (brok) Undivided heir.

Brógán (BRO gawn) Druid healer.

Brydie Ni'Seanan (BRY dee nee SHAR nan) Celtic princess; niece of Álmhath; cousin of Torcán.

Cainte (KIN-cha) Master of magical chants and incantations.

Cairbre (CAR bry eh) Undivided heir.

Chishihero (chee-she-here-oh) Japanese sorceress in charge of the *kozo* plantation in Dublin. Head magician of the Tanabe Clan.

Ch□ch□ (choo-cho) Middle Kingdom. Alternate name in the *ori mahou* reality for Japan.

Ciarán (KEER awn) Ciarán mac Connacht, Warrior Druid.

Cillian (KIL ee an) Half-Faerie/half-human *sídhe*.

Colmán (KUL mawn) Vate of All Eire. Amergin's successor.

Comhroinn (KOH-rinn) Name of the sharing ceremony that transfers knowledge between Druids.

Daiko (dy-ko) Japanese drums.

Daimyo (die-mee-oh) Head of the clan.

Danú (DA nu) The Goddess worshipped by both Faerie and Druid alike.

Daoine sídhe (deena shee) "People of the Mounds". Refers to the Faerie race as a whole. Also known as the Tuatha Dé Danann.

Darragh Aquitanina (DA-ra) Druid prince. One half of the Undivided.

Éamonn (AY mun) Elimyer's latest lover.

Eblana (e-BLAN-uh) Druid name for Dublin.

Eburana (eb-oo-rah-nah) Japanese name for Dublin/Eblana in the *ori mahou* reality.

Eileféin (ella-phane) The alternate reality version of oneself.

Elimyer (ellie-MY-ah) Trása's mother. *Leanan sídhe* who becomes Amergin's muse.

Farawyl (farra-will) Druidess and High Priestess of the Barrows.

Futagono Kizuna (foo-tah-goe-noe-kee-noo-zah) The Undivided.

Gochisosama (go-chee-sosah-mah) Thank you for the meal.

Hai (HI) Yes.

Haramaki (ha-ra-ma-kee) Belly protectors, containing chain mail or articulated plates of iron, made of silk and lined with various materials.

Hayato (hi-AH-toe) Head of the samurai charged with protecting the Tanabe Clan's *kozo* plantation.

Hayley Boyle (Hay-lee Boil) Daughter of Patrick Boyle and his first wife, Charlotte. Stepdaughter of Kerry Boyle.

Higan No Chu-Nichi, (hee-garn-no-choo-nee-chee) Autumn equinox in the *ori mahou* reality.

Iie (i-ee) No.

Ikushima (ick-ISH-oo-mah) One of the clans of *Airurundo*.

Imbolc (im-bolk) Spring equinox.

Isleen (izs-lean) Empress of the *ori mahou* realm.

Itadakimasu (ee-tah-dark-eemar-soo) I gratefully receive.

Jamaspa (j'MAS puh) Djinni. One of the lords of the Djinn.

Jotei (joe-tay) Title used when addressing the Empresses.

Kabuto (kah-boo-toe) Samurai helmet.

Katsugi (ka-tsu-gi) Lightweight drum played while carried by a strap.

Kazusa (kah-zoo-sah) Youngest daughter of the Ikushima clan.

Konketsu (kon-ke-tsu) Humans with Faerie blood able to practise folding magic.

Lá an Dreoilín (lah-ahn-droh-il-een) Also known as Wren Day. The winter solstice. Celebrated on December 26.

Leanan sídhe (lan-awn shee) A Faerie muse of exquisite beauty who offers inspiration, fame and glory to an artist in exchange for his life force.

Leathtiarna (lah teerna) Half-Lord.

Leipreachán (LEP-ra-cawn) One of the lesser fairies.

Liaig (lee-aj) Druid Healer.

Lughnasadh (loon-a-sah) Autumn equinox.

Mahou tsukaino sensei (mah-hoo-tsooo-ky-no-sen-say) Magic master.

Mara-warra (MA ra WOR ra) Sea-people also known as the Walrus People.

Marcroy (MARK-roy) Lord of the Tarth Mound. Elimyer's brother.

Máthair (mahar) Mother.

Merlin (MER-lin) Head Druid in Britain. Second only in power among the Druids to the Vate of All Eire.

Namito (na-mee-toe) Head of the Ikushima clan.

Niamh (neev) Druidess.

Oceanus Britannicus (o-she-AR-nus-bree-TAN-ee-eoos) Roman name of the English Channel.

Ori mahou (oree-mah-hoe) Folding magic.

Orlagh (*OR-la*) Queen of the Faerie.

Ossian (Ocean)

Prionsa (frin-sah) Prince.

Ráth (rar) Ring fort consisting of a circular area enclosed by a timber or stone wall with a ditch on the outside called a cashel.

Ren/Rónán Druid prince. One half of the Undivided.

Rifuto (ree-foo-toe) Rift.

Samhain (sow-en) Winter equinox.

Shàngqıng (shang-ching) The Supreme Pure One - One of the three Chinese Faerie Elders who make up the Brethren.

Shillelagh (shil-LAY-lee) Short, gnarled club usually fashioned from a tree root. Commonly made with a knobbed head, they often serve a secondary purpose as a walking stick.

Shime Daiko (shee-meh dy-ko) Small Japanese drum. Has a short, wide body with thick rawhide on both sides and is tuned by either rope or a bolt system.

Sí an Bhrú (shee-ahn-vroo) Traditional home of the Druids.

Sídhe (shee) Common name for the Faerie race in general.

Si☐illinn a (shool-leen ah) "Walk with us..." Druid ceremonial chant invoking their gods and goddesses.

Sorcha (shore-shah) Druid warrior.

Stiofán (stee-farn) *Tuatha Dé Danann* refugee living in *Tír Na nÓg* in the *ori mahou* realm.

Tàiqıng (tie-ching) The Grand Pure One - One of the three Chinese Faerie Elders who make up the Brethren.

Tanabe (tan-ah-bee) One of the clans of *Airurundo*.

Teagan (tee-g'n) Empress of the *ori mahou* realm.

Tír Na nÓg (tear-na-knowg (with a hard g)) Land of Perpetual Youth. The traditional home of the *Tuatha Dé Danann*.

Torcán (TURK awn) Prince of the Celts. Son of Brendá.

Trása (TRAY-sah) Trása Ni'Amergin. Half-Faerie/half-Druid offspring of Amergin and Elimyer.

Tuatha Dé Danann (tua day dhanna) Commonly known as the Fae.

Faerie or Fairy. Also known as: Children of the Goddess Danú, the True Race, or the *Daoine sídhe*.

Uncail (UN cayl) Faerie word for Uncle.

Vate (VART eh) Druid. Second only in power to the Undivided. Acts as regent when the Undivided are not yet come of age at their ascension to power.

Wagakimi (wa-goh-kee-me) My lord.

Yabangin (ya-bahn-gin) Savage, feral.

Youkai (yo-kigh) Faerie Yukata (yoo-kah-tah) Informal, unlined cotton kimono tied with a narrow sash (obi).

Yùqīng (yoo-ching) The Jade Purity - One of the three Chinese Faerie Elders who make up the Brethren.

ALSO BY JENNIFER FALLON
(JJ FALLON)

Hythrun Chronicles
Wolfblade
Warrior
Warlord
Medalon
Treason Keep
Harshini

Second Sons
Lion of Senet
Eye of the Labyrinth
Lord of the Shadows

Tide Lords
The Immortal Prince
The Gods of Amyrantha
The Palace of Impossible Dreams
The Chaos Crystal

Rift Runners
The Undivided
The Dark Divide
Reunion

ABOUT THE AUTHOR

JJ Fallon has Masters Degree in Research and is a trainer and business consultant with over 20 years experience in designing and delivering courses ranging from basic computer training to advanced project management.

Fallon currently works in IT and spends several weeks each year at Scott Base in Antarctica.